To

WRECKING CHRISTMAS

LIZA JONATHAN

Nice meeting you! Enjoy!

Liza Jonathan

Self-published by the author.

For more information, visit www.lizajonathan.com

First edition, Fall, 2019

ISBN 978-1-951209-03-2

Attention Bookstores & Organizations

This book is available on OverDrive and Ingram Spark, as well as all major retail platforms. You can also order large orders directly from the author at readlizajonathan@gmail.com.

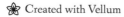 Created with Vellum

Kathryn walked right up to him and poked her finger in the middle of his chest. "I don't want to hear any arguing. You saved our lives, and I'm not leaving you to celebrate the holidays alone in a hotel room. From now on, you're with us. Understand?"

She gazed up at him with her bottomless grey eyes again, eyes that wouldn't let him hide. His breath hitched.

Hunter surely hadn't expected any of this. He hadn't expected to be so drawn to her...to want to be her hero. He swallowed hard. He was too aware of her—her shy smiles, her tempting curves, the way she made him feel when she put her simple trust in him. His whole body hummed in her presence. And that couldn't be good. Stranded or not, he knew he should refuse and put some distance between them.

But who was he kidding? He couldn't say no to her any more than the sun could say no to the sunrise...

CHAPTER 1

KATHRYN WINSLOW WAS knee-deep in a bad dream.

She had to be.

That was the only explanation for this strange, heavy feeling, like she was drowning somehow in the river that separated waking from sleeping. She willed herself to snap out of it, just get up and *move*, but her traitorous body wouldn't obey.

Until a sharp scream shocked her back to consciousness.

"Momma, wake up! Wake *up! Pleeeeease!*"

Wilson...

My boy...

His voice sounded so ragged, so high-pitched and desperate, Kathryn hardly recognized it. Her active, fearless eight-year-old had never been prone to hysterics. What on earth could be making him *wail* like that? Her maternal instincts flared, blaring like an alarm that cleared away the strange, cloying fogginess from her mind.

I have to get to him...

With one last shake of her head, Kathryn forced her eyes open, finally cracking them to slits.

A long moment ticked by before she understood that

she was slumped over the steering wheel of her SUV, her long hair flayed out over her hands.

Dammit, where are we?

Fighting against the pounding pain in her head, she groggily swiped her hair out of her face. She grimaced, shocked at the slippery red mess that came back on her hand. A taste of something thick and coppery lingered in her mouth. *Ah, blood.* The itchy throb of cuts registered, high up on her forehead. Bits of airbag were littered about her. *Broken* airbag. Groaning, she began to sit up.

"Momma! You have to turn off the car," Wilson shrieked. "*Right now!*"

With a fresh burst of adrenalin, she punched away the last of the bag. And what Kathryn saw froze her in terror.

Oh God.

They were dangling over the side of a mountain so steep that it was damn near a ninety-degree angle. Her front wheels tilted down toward a ravine. By all rights, their vehicle should be a twisted heap of metal down at the bottom of it. But her SUV's front wheels, by some cosmic mercy, were tangled in the tops of two young trees, rooted to the sheer slope right below them. The slick, ice-covered branches snapped ominously under the weight of her enormous Chevy Suburban, their spindly trunks the only thing keeping them in place. In a sickening flash, Kathryn realized the grinding, splattering noise she heard was her back tires, still miraculously in contact with the hillside, lurching them one inch closer to certain death with each muddy spin.

Screaming, Kathryn yanked her foot off the gas and desperately fumbled for her keys. The ignition clicked off, and the car shuddered to silence. Her heart thundered in her ears—one beat, two beats, three...

With the car now perfectly still, the terror lodged in her

throat unwound a bit, and she could finally gulp in a breath or two.

We're still alive. Thank you, thank you, thank you, Lord.

Her mind reeled and her chest still heaved with fright. Kathryn knew she had to somehow collect herself before she turned around to face her young son. She took a long, calming breath to try to tamp down her panic. But the icy winter wind blew in great, heaving gusts, and the car teetered precariously back and forth. Bracing herself, she bit down hard on her lip to keep from screaming again.

"I thought you were dead," Wilson sobbed from the seat behind her.

The words hit her with the force of a sharp slap. Taking care not to move too fast or too much, Kathryn gingerly turned her head to look at her son. She was soggy with relief to see him still safely strapped in, unharmed. His sandy-brown curls peeked out around his ever-present Captain America toboggan, and his big blue eyes were wide and wild with fright. Reaching around, she gave his little leg a reassuring squeeze. "I'm here, baby, and I'm banged up, that's all. It looks worse than it is. We're going to get through this, I promise. Keep your seat belt on, and stay *real* still, okay?"

Thankfully, the words seemed to calm her boy. His tears slowed. She pasted on her best brave smile, hoping against hope it might give the child a boost of confidence she surely didn't feel.

"Where's your granddaddy?" Kathryn asked.

Wilson hiccupped and wiped his tears with his coat sleeve. "I think he rolled off the back seat. He had lain down and was sleepin' back there before the crash. I yelled and yelled for him, but he wouldn't answer."

Kathryn looked through her rearview mirror, taking stock. The rest of the car was intact, which was a good sign.

There was no evidence of her father flying through a window, or hitting his head on the glass. *Please Lord, let Daddy only be knocked out and not seriously hurt.* After all, she couldn't go crawling to either one of them, or they'd all fall to their deaths.

Their *deaths*. That single, paralyzing thought focused her mind to a single point. She couldn't let them all die like this. Not after the way Kathryn had found her own momma last year, dead in her bed, shot by her own hand the day after Christmas. Not after the year she'd spent, ferrying Daddy in and out of rehab, coaxing him out of his grief and depression. No. *No, dammit.* They'd clawed their way back from the worst year of their lives. And they were making progress, all of them truly beginning to come to grips and move on. Wasn't that what this Christmas was supposed to be about—healing? Making new traditions?

No matter what, she couldn't lose sight of that. This family wasn't going down without a fight.

Kathryn spooled through her blurry memories of these last desperate minutes, trying to piece together how the crash had happened. The SUV had spun out so fast, she barely remembered the squeal of her brakes and the lurching horror of her tires leaving the pavement. She rubbed her throbbing forehead. Damn defective airbag. They must have jumped the guardrail and jackknifed through the air to be at this ridiculous angle.

Looking down into the chasm that lay below them, she knew she had to somehow gin up her courage. But the cruel irony of this situation wasn't lost on her. All she'd wanted was to have a happy, normal Christmas for the three of them, for once in their lives. She'd planned this trip to the famous Greenbrier Resort, cradled in the shadow of the Allegheny Mountains, to be the kind of luxurious holiday treat that would make them forget. How stupid and naïve that all seemed now. Their lives were hanging by a thread, because of *her*.

"Kathryn?" Daddy groaned from the third row.

Daddy! Oh, thank God! Her heart leaped for joy. "I'm right here!"

"Where are we?" he croaked. Kathryn caught sight of her father's tousled white hair. *Oh, no!* The man had crawled over to look out the side window, and the truck teetered again.

She turned. "Daddy! Stay down! Don't move!"

Shock dawned on his face. "Holy shit!" he hollered, diving back down hard on the floor again. The truck lurched forward, and they all heard the worrisome sound of rocks and dirt under the back tires crumbling away.

Kathryn whipped back around, gripped the steering wheel, and braced herself until the SUV's swaying finally, blessedly, came to a stop. She took a deep, shuddering breath. "Daddy, to answer your question, we're somewhere up past the Jefferson National Forest. Some mountain that starts with a P. Peter something? Or Pots? Oh, I don't know. It's been a long while since I've seen a town. I—I'm not sure whether I got myself turned around or not, and my GPS is broken and—Daddy? Are you okay?"

"Don't worry about me, girl. I'm too hardheaded to die from something like this. I got a big bump on my head and a cut on my arm. But I'll live."

Kathryn's heart warmed at her daddy's bravado. *Okay. Okay, then.* She straightened herself up a bit in her seat. Despite their circumstances, this one bit of good news strengthened her spine. Maybe they could do this, and figure a way...

They were down, but they weren't out, by God. She focused on their limited possibilities.

Kathryn was sure her door would open and she could

5

jump out, maybe even grab onto a tree. The back doors looked fine too. But the swaying would pry the car loose, for sure. It would take all three of them jumping out in perfect unison to make that work. Hell, the motion of Daddy climbing out of the third row would be easily be enough to push them over the edge.

No, she'd have to make a call. Of course, the crash had emptied every single item out of her purse and onto the floor. Looking around, Kathryn finally spotted the edge of her phone just out of her reach, peeking out from underneath the far side of passenger seat, near the door. *Dammit!*

"Daddy, do you know where your cell phone is?" Kathryn called.

"Well yes and no," he called back. "It's in my briefcase. I think it slid underneath my seat. Damn thing's probably mixed in with the luggage now. I could crawl to it."

"No. That's too much movement. Wilson's is in his duffel bag, and it's in the back too. I'll have to get mine off the floor. Nobody make any sudden moves, okay?"

This is going to be a trick, isn't it?

Without unhooking her belt, she slowly, oh-so-carefully began to reach across. Even that small movement set the car swaying dangerously again. Then, with a terrifying crack, one of the trees holding them up snapped in two. Metal scraped and whined as the car lurched forward, *hard*.

She closed her eyes again.

I'm not going to scream. I'm not going to scream.

She tried so hard to be brave, but her heart sank. There would be no phone call. Even that amount of movement was tempting fate.

She met Daddy and Wilson's gaze in her rear view mirror. Long seconds marched by as all three of them realized how bad their situation really was. Nobody dared speak.

Oh dear God, what are we going to do?

The truck was deadly silent—the only sound her own shallow breaths as they formed in icy puffs around her.

"Momma?" Wilson yelped. "Did you hear that?"

"What, baby?"

"That cracking and snapping."

Then, she heard it too—the sound of heavy boots crashing through underbrush behind them, and the hasty unrolling of heavy chains. In an instant, the car lurched as something grabbed onto their back bumper.

And when she looked around, she saw a man looking right back at her, his eyes level with the bottom ledge of her driver's side window. They were the most reassuring brown eyes she'd ever seen.

Dear Lord.

Could it really be possible we're saved?

CHAPTER 2

"I've got you hooked up to a tow truck," the stranger called. "I'm pulling you backward! Stay strapped in until all four wheels are on the ground, all right?"

Kathryn screamed with jubilation, nearly crying again. And Wilson and Daddy cheered right along with her. She gave tow truck guy a thumbs-up to let him know they understood.

We're not going to die. We're not going to die!

Before she could thank this man, or even get a better look at him, he ran off and started the winch. The Suburban lurched steadily back to safety, disentangling from the trees. A few more tugs from its motorized pulley and heavy chains, and it'd be over.

No words could explain the relief now surging through her. She sagged in her seat as the adrenalin in her system gradually ebbed a bit. They were safe, and it was nothing short of a miracle. If their unidentified savior had been ten minutes later, they'd have been gone, surely. The car shuddered as it disengaged from the trees, and the front tires crashed to the dirt. The slam rattled her teeth, and made her obscenely happy, all at once. Finally, they were on solid ground, *together*.

She turned around. "See, Wilson? I told you we were going to get out of this."

The boy beamed back at her. "Whew!"

"Whew too!" Daddy answered, popping up. He crawled up to Wilson's row and high-fived him with his good arm. As the car slowly lurched back up the incline, Daddy removed Wilson's restraints. Kathryn popped her seat belt too.

With a few more turns of the pulley, their savior finally came fully into view. Staying right at her window, he told her over and over that they'd be okay.

Tow truck guy walked with their banged-up truck, both hands on the window and watching them like a hawk on their ascent up the hill. The man seemed surprised that she was up and conscious, smiling with relief when she responded to his questions with coherent nods. With his battered work coat and padded beige overalls, this guy clearly dressed the part of a tow truck driver. But there was something about him that made him look like more than just another hired hand—a set to his shoulders, or an air of authority perhaps. She tried not to stare as she took in his rugged appearance—his stubbled jaw, his close-cropped brown hair, and even the enticing cleft in his chin. This man, whoever he was, was more than a little good-looking.

Wondering what his looks had to do with anything, Kathryn chuckled ruefully under her breath. *I shouldn't have needed him to save us.*

As the chain continued to pull them, the requisite guilt and self-recrimination crept in. Obviously, she should've taken the perfectly safe interstate, instead of the shorter, more scenic route. But she'd wanted to see the snow-capped mountains as she drove. She should've had a better grasp on her directions, but she'd gotten cocky about her map-reading skills. She should've seen the sheet of new ice forming on that hairpin curve, but she'd been too busy enjoying the view and singing Christmas songs with Wilson. Kathryn couldn't do anything more than shake her head, disgusted with her own carelessness. Here she was, thirty-four years old, and she still couldn't manage to get everything right, no matter how hard she tried. Maybe *especially* when she tried.

But there was no time to beat herself up. Not now. They finally reached the relatively level ground on the road's meager shoulder. Tow truck guy popped open her door and held out his hand to help her down. She took it with profound gratitude, emotionally exhausted but ecstatic beyond words to have her feet on terra firma again. Running on shaking, rubbery legs, she flew straight to Wilson and her daddy and exchanged fierce hugs. Her heart felt like it was turning itself inside out, but they were all here. They were all still together.

Wilson patted her hair and frowned. "Momma, your face—it's all bloody!"

"Don't worry, baby. It's only a few scratches. Remember what I told you about how wounds to your head bleed a lot more than other places on your body? I promise you, it's true. I only have a few and they don't seem to be deep. I'll be okay, boo." She patted her son down one more time with a critical eye. "You're sure you didn't get knocked around?"

"Nope," he answered, looking up at her with big, round, earnest eyes. "The seat belt held me nice and tight. I'll never, ever complain again about wearing my seat belt, Momma, no matter how much it pinches up my coat."

Kathryn laughed with relief and pulled her precious, precious boy into another long hug. Looking over Wilson's shoulder, she motioned for her daddy to stop gawking at his injuries and bend his arm up, to keep the bleeding to a minimum. He complied.

Her poor, pitiful Suburban rumbled up onto the shiny metal platform, a loud clanking rattle announcing it was locked securely in place. The flatbed rose back up again into its traveling position. Tow truck guy came around the side, and Kathryn turned to thank their rescuer. But before she had a chance to even introduce herself, the man was on them like white on rice, patting them down, asking them if they were okay, and checking for broken bones. Determining that Wilson was fine, the man sent her boy off to the warmth of the oversized cab on his tow truck.

Daddy had hit his head when he'd fallen, and the metal seat legs had cut a sizeable gash on his forearm from his wrist to his elbow. Blood was everywhere. He'd definitely need stitches. Needing no prompting, the man set Daddy down on the platform steps and began cleaning the wound and unwinding fresh bandages.

Kathryn gratefully watched their rescuer work while she sat waiting on the tow truck platform. Daddy yelped in pain from the stinging antiseptic, and her stomach lurched. She'd never been that queasy over blood, but this wasn't some TV drama, or a demonstration in a medical class. This was personal. And that rewrote every rule, circumventing any chance she had at objectivity. Momma had taught her that lesson, hadn't she?

Another rattling, constricted breath, another stab of anxiety in her chest... Kathryn chuckled bitterly to herself. She'd been in no way prepared for this day. And then, like a wave, it hit her.

They'd almost died.

Died.

Before she could stop herself, a macabre vision of them all hurtling over the mountain played in her brain like the worst horror movie imaginable. The picture was too real, too palpable, this glimpse of what almost and *probably would have happened* to them.

The shaking started then as every kind of raw, unfiltered emotion assaulted her at once—relief, anger, and regret, for starters. Uncontrolled and unbidden, fear came in for the knockout punch, even though she knew, objectively, that the danger had passed. Now she was quivering from head to toe, dammit, and breathing way too fast.

Shock. That was what it was—the physical manifestations of psychological shock. Nothing about that was surprising, really, considering the trauma they'd experienced. Clearly, this was a textbook physiological reaction, merely the brain's natural response to extreme danger. But even though she knew these scary thoughts were clearly attributable to the stress hormones coursing through her body, it didn't make any of it easier. Kathryn may be on solid ground now, but she still could practically taste the horror and helplessness.

Tugging her coat tightly around her, she tried to keep her shivers at bay. But it was no use. She shook so hard, her bones rattled. Thankfully, Wilson was already resting in the cab of the tow truck, and Daddy and their rescuer were occupied with his bandages. No way did she want anyone to see her like this.

Kathryn pushed herself up to standing on the tow truck platform and wobbled over to her wrecked vehicle. Opening the door, she began picking up her scattered possessions. But she was too shaken up, her fingers too quivery for the task. She reached for her wallet but fumbled it, dropping it once, twice.

Finally she flung the effin' thing into her big hobo purse, but the change pouch was open and spilled everything all over.

Argh!

She stopped, balling her unruly hands into fists.

Kathryn leaned her head against the side of the seat, her chest heaving with frustration. And though she promised herself she wouldn't, she cried. *Quietly.* It wasn't about the stupid change, of course. It was about everything—every wrong decision and misplaced good intention that had led her to the side of this road, right here, right now.

Goddammit! She helplessly pounded the seat cushion. Hot, angry tears couldn't wash away her stupidity today. But she allowed herself a few tears anyway. Just a few. Then, marshaling her resources, she finally managed to steady her breaths and force her tears back down.

We're going to be okay. We're going to be okay.

She let this be her mantra, because falling to pieces wouldn't help anyone today. She wouldn't become some useless, sobbing mess. She *wouldn't*.

If you're not strong for them, who will be?

Closing her eyes, Kathryn took several cleansing breaths until she got her heart rate settled. The snow had stopped, but she was shivering worse than ever. She cursed herself for not taking the time to change out of her work clothes before she left. The dress she'd worn for her morning appointments was no match for the elements. She sucked down gulps from a bottle of water tow truck guy had pressed in her hand when she'd exited her SUV. After a few swishes, she finally got all the blood washed out of her mouth and leaned over the side of the truck to spit it onto the ground.

God, her head was *throbbing*. Rooting around on the floorboards, she managed to retrieve the rest of the scattered contents of her purse. Blessedly, she found her last two ibuprofen pills, picked the lint off them, and swallowed them down.

The distractions helped. By the time she plunked herself on the platform and their white knight had turned his attention to her, she'd powered through the worst of her adrenalin spikes. He'd sent Daddy off to keep warm in his truck too, so now it was her turn.

Kathryn watched the man approach from her perch on the freezing metal platform. Eager not to stare, she quickly switched her attention to kicking the mud off her hopelessly impractical stiletto boots. Her gray wool pea coat was short, and the icy metal beneath her legs soaked right through the sweater dress she was wearing.

He must have taken note of her shakes. Turning around, he trotted to the tow truck's cab, pulling out a thick, battered quilt. He gently tucked it around her and closed the distance between them, his amber-brown eyes level with hers. They were the most extraordinary eyes she'd ever seen, tinged dark around the edges with flecks of rich, honeyed gold running throughout them. She had a hard time looking away from his gaze, to be honest. But then a spot of something got in her eye, and she blinked. Kathryn hastily wiped at it with her coat sleeve.

And of course, her sleeve came back bright red. *Great. More blood.* The bleeding hadn't stopped, apparently. Kathryn sighed and shook her head as she surveyed her favorite coat, now ruined.

Tow truck guy looked down at her, pulling her attention away. "Hey," he greeted her, his voice soft and reassuring.

"Hey," Kathryn answered. She couldn't help but smile. Even with his obvious economy of words, she could tell this man had been born and raised around here. Their rescuer had a quintessentially warm, deep voice that sounded deeper for the low way he spoke in his throat—with the lilt of a faint mountain accent that was Southern, but all its own. The man pushed back her hair with a clean rag and quickly set to work scrubbing up her cuts.

His manner was brisk and all business, but Kathryn still found his strong, masculine presence calming. He was younger than she expected—mid-thirties, perhaps. And he was big, too, easily standing six foot three. As he leaned over her, she marveled at how his broad shoulders were nearly twice as wide as her own slender frame. He popped a knee up on a step to lean up and over her a bit, so he could get a better look at where the wounds began and ended in her hair. And that had him right up in her personal space, his hard chest mere inches from her face. A chill zinged up her spine that she suspected had nothing to do with the freezing weather and everything to do with *him*. Somehow, this stranger smelled like the mountains themselves, as if the clean air and the pine trees had somehow gotten mingled up with his ruddy skin. Kathryn breathed in his clean, delicious scent and let the proximity of his body heat warm her.

He was so solid, so masculine, that for one weak moment, Kathryn was struck with the impulse to curl herself against him and let him wrap those strong arms around her. He was...comforting.

Kathryn almost laughed out loud at that. *Of course he's comforting. He saved your life.*

But it was more than that, wasn't it? As if he felt the weight of her gaze on him, tow truck guy shifted a little uncomfortably and continued to work on her cuts. But somehow, his body had twisted a bit closer to her in the process. He was near enough now that she could pick out the hints of the spicy soap he'd used, tangled up with his woodsy musk. She swallowed against her dry throat.

Dear God. You're attracted to him, aren't you?

She breathed deep, inhaling more of his delicious, masculine scent. Mmmmm, she supposed she *was* attracted.

For another weak moment, Kathryn wondered what would it be like to lay down everything she was carrying and lose herself in the arms of a man like him. Damn, he was so strong and real and—

Wait—what am I doing? This wasn't at all like her. Checking this total stranger out was such a small mental indulgence, but a pathetic, ridiculous grasp at avoidance nonetheless. Yet another way her emotions were running wild today. Kathryn caught herself. *Don't be an idiot. You're disassociating, aren't you?*

That was exactly what she was doing—focusing on this way-too-interesting stranger instead of doing the hard work of acknowledging what had happened here. She'd almost killed her family, for God's sake! Kathryn stubbornly pushed this silly whatever-it-was out of her mind, focusing instead on getting her wounds clean.

She pointed to a cut he'd missed, over by her right ear. "Don't forget this one, please."

He nodded and began dabbing at that one too. "You're lucky, you know. The bleeding has pretty much clotted up. It's really just a matter of cleaning you up now."

Holding up his fingers, he asked her how many there were. She must have given him the right answer, because he seemed pleased.

With the bleeding now stopped, tow truck guy dumped disinfectant on the rag and diligently cleaned her cuts. It burned, but she was deeply thankful for his help. Between winces, she peered steadily at him, but apparently, he was trying not to engage her in any way. The silence was deafening. What was making him so standoffish?

Somehow, she had the overwhelming desire to cut the chitchat and *connect* with this stranger. She wasn't sure why, exactly. Maybe she didn't want to be alone after what she'd been through. Or maybe the silence was simply getting to her.

"You saved the lives of my whole family today." Kathryn finally sighed. "You know that, don't you? It's like you're our guardian angel or something."

He shrugged, still not making eye contact. "I'm no angel. I was only doing my job, and this is a part of it."

"No, it's not. Nobody called you. You didn't have to stop. But since you're obviously being noble about it, I won't embarrass you by sitting here and arguing with you." Not willing to leave it at that, Kathryn kept her eyes right on his face until the man finally stopped what he was doing. She kicked up her chin as their gaze locked. "You know, I don't even have your name."

The eye contact seemed to shock him somehow. His pupils dilated immediately, and some kind of sharp, almost *visceral* charge passed between them. Again.

Was that a good charge or a bad one? Kathryn honestly couldn't tell.

Still locked on her eyes, he stopped short and gasped. He stared at her, tension working at his jaw. *What in the world?* His face went chalky white, and he actually, visibly shuddered.

Come on, I can't look that bad, can I, that I'm scaring a perfect stranger?

The man swallowed and recovered himself, though he still seemed terribly shaky. "I'm Hunter Holliday, ma'am." He stared hard at her cuts now and not her eyes. "I own Holliday Hot Rods and Collision Repair, over in Lewisburg." He brusquely pointed to the logo on the side of his truck for proof. "You're lucky I came by when I did. I'm not normally out here. My shop is closed for Christmas break, but I still answer distress calls when we have weather emergencies. I'd already finished my last run of the day."

Kathryn held out her hand for him to shake, and he stared blankly at it for a moment, as if it took a moment to register. But then he seemed to remember his manners, dropped his rag on his leg, and took off his bloody work gloves. He closed both of his hands over hers. They were a working man's hands—calloused, no rings, with clean nails cut down to the quick. His hands were hard, yes, but surprisingly warm, wrapped over hers with a kind of tender respect she didn't expect, as if he were afraid she would break. And it felt *good*, having her hand wrapped in his, if she was going to be honest about it.

For his part, Hunter shook her hand up and down, searching her face for a beat or two too long. He suddenly looked away.

But Kathryn wouldn't let him pull away from her, not yet. She set her free hand on top of his, keeping up the eye contact until she forced him to meet her gaze again. "Thank you, Mr. Holliday. There really are no words to say how grateful I am to you. Until the moment you showed up, I was sure we were all going to die."

Hunter dropped her hands, but he still didn't speak. Instead, he ran his fingers through the front of her hair, moving the sodden strands around gently to ensure the bleeding had truly stopped. Then he dragged the rag down her cheek to catch the last of the blood.

His eyes locked with hers again, and he drew an unsteady breath. "You're welcome," he finally bit out. Actively frowning now, Hunter stood up abruptly and began quickly putting away his first aid gear. "It's too cold out here for small talk. This storm has been unusually bad, even for this time of year. We need to get going before the next front comes in. Go on and get in the truck. It's warm in there. I'll finish up out here, and...be ready in a minute."

Feeling strangely like she was being dismissed, Kathryn

raised her eyebrows. "Okay. Do you need me to help you gather up—"

"No," he huffed, a clear note of irritation in his voice. "Get in the truck, Kathryn. Now."

Well, there's no reason to be so snippy. Kathryn couldn't figure out what was making Hunter so brisk and uncommunicative to her, especially when he'd been gentle and talkative with Daddy and Wilson.

But as she got up to leave, she saw his jaw still clenching with—what? Fear? Was he having some kind of delayed reaction? Kathryn reluctantly got into the truck and waited.

"That Hunter is a nice fella," Daddy said. "Good of him to wrap up my arm like that."

"Yes, it was," Kathryn replied, not wanting to go on and on about their incredible rescue. She didn't want to add underlines to how truly dire their situation had been. It was important to her that Wilson knew she could keep him safe, even when really bad things happened. Her ex-husband was protective of his son, too, of course. As exes, they were friendly enough still, in spite of everything. But she knew, when push came to shove, she was a single mom. In every way that mattered, it was all on her, especially at times like this.

Daddy and Wilson snuggled up in the truck's surprisingly roomy backseat while they took turns playing Wilson's hand-held game console. Kathryn listened to their playful banter, relieved that her shivering seemed to finally be dying down and her heart rate was settling. But still, she couldn't manage to relax, even in the nicest tow truck she'd ever seen. The leather upholstery was black and plush, and the dash reminded her of the sort of polished, technologically tricked-out features you might see in a luxury sedan. The heated seats kept them warm as toast. But the silence from Hunter dragged on. What could he possibly be doing? After all, the Suburban was already secured to the flatbed.

A quick peek out the window, and she spotted Hunter sitting on one of the platform steps. Lord, the man looked like death on a biscuit. Even from this distance, she could tell he was even paler than before. Hunter jittered his knees up and down and curled his fists over his eyes.

A fresh ball of anxiety unwound in Kathryn's stomach. *Uh-oh. Something's wrong—really wrong.*

All her professional instincts kicked in as she jumped back out of the cab and went to Hunter. This kind, strong man was clearly in the grip of something. She crouched in front of him and, with some effort, pulled his stiff, clenched fists down from his forehead. Hunter was sweating and his eyes were dilated. The anguish in his eyes sent an answering wave of sadness through her too. *What has this man been through?*

"Hunter, I need you to look at me," she soothed.

He did—his eyes slowly, slowly clearing enough to focus on her. "I'm sorry, I'm sorry—" he groaned.

"It's okay. We all have our moments sometimes. What happened back there was pretty scary. Maybe you're having a delayed fear response. It's not all that uncommon."

He shook his head, puffing out shallow, uneven breaths. "It's j-just that I was in a b-bad accident like this a couple of years ago, really bad, and it was a lot like this..."

Kathryn could see Hunter was in no shape for talking. That crash he was in must have been horrendous. In fact, it must have been a life-altering event to evoke this panicked reaction. Had he lost someone? Her heart sank as the realization hit her. Hunter had a prolonged case of PTSD, and *her* crash had been his trigger. He was having flashbacks and, most likely, a panic attack.

Her heart sank in sympathy for him. But Kathryn

steeled her nerve. Her training could get him through this. She continued the eye contact, making sure to keep her voice even, soothing, and warm. "Keep your eyes right on me, okay? You're safe. We're all safe today, thanks to you. You did that. You took control. You can take it back again now. If you regulate your breathing, you can work through your panic faster. Come on. Breathe with me, in through the nose and out through the mouth. I'm going to count it off. Blow out to the count of six and in to the count of six. Got it?"

Hunter's eyes were wild, but he tried his best to work with her anyway, doing exactly what she asked. They held hands for five long, terrible minutes. Kathryn timed it on her watch, the second hand passing over the numbers again and again. The seconds seemed to drag on in agonized silence, as if time itself had slowed to wait for them. Still, they breathed together, in and out, until the panic slowly slid its grip from him. The tension in his forehead loosened, and the color began returning to his face. She moved her finger around to check his pulse without him catching on.

Ah good, it's slowing. He's through the worst. Kathryn finally stood up, pulled a bottle of water out of his pack, and tossed it over to him. Hunter cracked it open and guzzled a long draught, wiping his mouth with his arm. "You have these flashbacks often?" she asked.

Hunter grimaced, obviously embarrassed. "At first, several times a day. But now? I haven't had one in about six months. But today was so, so—"

"Familiar," Kathryn answered, grabbing his hand again to give it a quick squeeze. "I'm really sorry you got dragged into all this."

"No," he ground out. "I was able to *save* you. That's one story I was able to make come out right, anyway."

She wanted to ask him more questions about the crash

itself. There was a story there, and probably a sad one. But now clearly wasn't the time. "Has the PTSD been diagnosed? Have you been prescribed Prozac? Or Prazosin, maybe? You'd be surprised how much they could ease your symptoms."

Surprise flared in his eyes. "What, are you some kind of shrink?"

"Guilty as charged." Taking care with her bloody fingers, Kathryn fished a card out of her pocket and handed it to him. "I'm a clinical psychologist. I have a practice in Roanoke, Virginia."

He blew out a breath, stunned and obviously a bit chastened. "To answer your question, no. I don't need pills. I'll be fine." Standing up, he slid the card into his coat pocket and yanked on the chain holding her truck, making sure it was secure. "Right now, all I need to do is get you to safety. Where is that, anyway?"

"The Greenbrier Resort. We have reservations to celebrate Christmas there, so we planned to stay for a week."

Hunter's face brightened. "You're in luck then. My body shop is nearby. It might take me a couple of weeks to get the parts for a truck this old, but I can get a big chunk of the repairs done while you're vacationing."

Kathryn seriously doubted that. The whole grill of her truck was caved in. Her Suburban was fifteen years old and had more than 175,000 miles on it. This was her second car, actually, one she kept at home for hauling stuff and special trips like this. She could easily afford to replace it with a better one. But truthfully, she kept the Suburban for sentimental reasons, as it had been a present from her parents when she'd graduated a year early with her bachelor's degree. It had hauled many a load for her while she'd been moving apartments during her PhD studies. No, she wasn't ready to give the endearing old beater up yet.

She agreed to let Hunter work on it, thanking him profusely for taking it on during the holidays.

"I wouldn't have it any other way. Besides, my team likes jobs like this. They're a—a *challenge*, you could say."

Kathryn chuckled at that. "A challenge. Is that what we're calling it these days?"

Hunter chuckled softly, his eyes twinkling with amusement. Maybe he wasn't doing this out of obligation, after all. This was the first time Kathryn had seen him smile—*really* smile—and she had to admit, it was enchanting. Not that this was one of those false, show-me-all-your-teeth affairs. No, it was a smaller, quiet, self-effacing kind of grin that had a world of thoughts behind it. It carved deep dimples into his wind-stung cheeks and crinkles at the corners of his eyes. *Ah, those kind brown eyes again, the color of fine whiskey...*

Oh no, she couldn't help it. Here, in the freezing cold wind, Hunter Holliday actually made her warm, all the way down to her boots. Now Kathryn was the one staring, and that unsettled her.

Hunter patted her lightly on the shoulder as he walked by. "Come on. We'd better get a move on. There's no telling what'll happen when this storm rolls in."

Kathryn could hardly argue with that. She took his hand as he helped her up into the truck. Surely anything this storm could brew up couldn't be worse than what they'd been through.

Or so she hoped.

CHAPTER 3

HUNTER TURNED over the ignition in his tow truck, relieved to be back on the road. But he was still too riled up to hardly think.

Guardian angel—was that what Kathryn had called him? Some guardian. Yeah, he might have had enough wits about him to hook her Suburban to tow, but that stupid breakdown of his? That had never, *ever* happened. Not in public, anyway. He'd always been able to hide the swells of panic and the terrifying memories playing out in his head. But seeing Kathryn like that, with her face all bloody? It had taken him right back to hell.

The images had come rushing back to him then, cutting through his mind like an unforgiving winter wind.

He's trapped again, helpless. The busted dashboard has him pinned, and the scream. Oh God, the scream...

Laney's scream.

Hunter took a rattling breath and cursed himself. *Not again!* With a hard inward shake, he slowly white-knuckled himself back to the present.

Some days, he really hated what he'd become. Icy heart-sickness had overwhelmed him after the crash, but it had dulled over time, stubbornly scarring over to a numb hollow-ness. Truthfully, he'd left the most important part of himself by the side of that snowy road. Three years later, the loss of his wife still gripped him like a tangible, physical ache. The ache was all that was left of him. The rest just felt empty, as if his heart had been scooped out and the contents thrown over the hill somewhere. Most of the time, he did a pretty good job of managing it. But this wasn't one of those days. He'd let his grief and weakness make this poor family's bad day even worse. Jesus, Kathryn had to make him count so he could *breathe!*

Time to man up, Hunter. These people have enough troubles of their own.

Hunter ground his teeth, willing himself to get his mind back on task. Right now, he'd promised to get these folks to safety, and by God, that was what he'd do. Now, if only the weather would cooperate. He turned on his windshield wipers to push aside the fat, wet snowflakes that had kicked up in this sudden, gusty squall.

"How long will it take?" Wilson piped up from the back seat.

"How long will *what* take?" Hunter quipped, trying to keep things playful.

Wilson rolled his eyes. "How long will it take to *get* there?"

Hunter grinned. "About a half-hour or so until we get to the Greenbrier Medical Center, I suspect. Could be a lot longer, though. It all depends on how bad these roads get."

Kathryn turned to him, the expression on her face clearly saying she hated that idea. "Oh no, you don't have to worry about getting us to the hospital. We can handle that once—"

"No," Hunter cut her off. He'd brook no argument about this. "Your dad needs stitches, and you need an x-ray to make sure you don't have a concussion. And I won't have you waiting an extra minute to get that care."

"Yes, but you'll have to sit with us," she protested. "It could take all day. I don't want to take so much of your time this close to the holiday. You should be at home putting your feet up and enjoying the Christmas spirit, not messing with this. The staff at the Greenbrier could arrange our transportation and—"

"I don't have anything planned or anyone waiting on me," Hunter interrupted. "I'm glad to do it."

Hunter turned to Kathryn again, and their lingering eye contact was almost painful. She nodded like she knew the truth—he was all alone this Christmas. There was no judgment there, or pity. But it made him damn uncomfortable anyway, facing those bottomless gray eyes of hers.

She hesitated, as if she might try negotiating with him. But then she clamped her jaw shut again, apparently thinking better of it. And all the while, she caught him in her gaze, her eyes shimmering in some kind of recognition. Maybe the lovely Ms. Winslow could tell that he wanted— no, *needed*—to see them through this.

What was it about this woman? When Kathryn turned those perceptive eyes on him, she saw everything—the good, the bad, and the ugly. It made him feel strangely exposed and raw. Even though he knew it wasn't possible, he had the unsettling sense that she knew him, and knew what he was about, even though they'd only just met.

As the drive wore on, he stole a few more glances at her, trying to be casual about it. Even banged up as she was, she was the most elegant woman he'd ever seen. Kathryn Winslow stood out as plainly as a gazelle in a field of common does. She was only medium height, really—maybe five foot seven or eight without those sky-high heels she had on. But she was reed thin and willowy, with the kind of long legs and long torso that added a supple grace to her every movement. He even liked the way she talked, with the light sweep of a Virginia drawl, her voice low and melodious with the faintest hint of a sexy rasp to it. Every time she opened her mouth to speak, her words practically rippled over his skin like a caress.

Kathryn took off her coat and began scrubbing at the bloodstains on it with the wet rag he'd given her. She wasn't succeeding, of course, but she kicked her chin up in determination anyway. Digging around in the bottom of her enormous purse, she finally found a big tortoiseshell clip and pinned up her bloody hair, exposing the graceful line of her neck. Then she went back to work on the coat. Even now, even at her worst, everything about her was classy, from the intelligence in her eyes to the regal way she held her head. Her clothing only emphasized that fact.

The charcoal-gray dress she had on matched her eyes and was clearly expensive, like soft, touchable cashmere. He'd bet it was. Her clothes fit so perfectly, they could easily be custom made. She wore a sexy-as-hell, polished-silver thumb ring on her left hand that went from knuckle to knuckle, and an amethyst ring on her third finger of her right hand, but no wedding ring.

Hunter winced. *Ah, for Christ's sake, why did I have to notice that?*

Hunter shifted uncomfortably in his seat. Dammit, he had a hard time keeping his mind on task, what with the way the seat belt hugged her sweet little body, bringing out her gentle, perfect, tempting curves. Good God, it killed him, just being here in the truck with her, breathing the faint scent of jasmine she brought to the air. His whole body tuned in to her, responding in ways he really wished he wasn't right now.

He'd have laughed out loud if he could've. This whole

thing was friggin' *ridiculous*, really. Three years of numbness after the crash, and he picked *now* to notice a woman? But it was impossible not to, wasn't it? Even bloodstained and exhausted, Kathryn Winslow was seriously distracting.

She worried her plush bottom lip with her teeth as she scrubbed away. Before he could banish the idea, he pictured himself running his thumb along the sensual curl of that lip, testing it, tasting it, seeing if it was as soft and pliant as it looked. He'd bet it was. He'd bet she tasted like heaven.

Shifting in his seat again, Hunter bit back a groan. *Since when did I become such a horn dog? What in the hell is wrong with me?*

This woman had been through hell and back today!

Getting more disgusted with himself by the minute, he tried his damnedest to shake off the tingling awareness of her, reminding himself that a woman like Kathryn would never go for a grease monkey like him, anyway. Not that he'd be much use to any woman, as fucked up as he was.

Thankfully, Kathryn's father broke the silence. "If I haven't said this yet, I want you to know that we're damn grateful. I don't know what would've become of us if you hadn't shown up."

"I'm glad I could be in the right place at the right time, Mr. Wilson."

"Call me Huck. Everybody does."

"Okay, Huck." Hunter smiled. "That your real name or a nickname?"

"Nickname. Got it as a kid. I was always building rafts and going down the river. I guess it stuck, 'cause Lord knows, I'm still finding ways to run off to new adventures even in my old age."

"That so?" Hunter grinned back at him.

Kathryn rolled her eyes. "Oh, come on, Daddy. You're only sixty. You're not that old." She shot Hunter a conspiratorial wink. "He loves to play the doddering coot, though he's far from one. Daddy owns about forty gas stations throughout Virginia. Don't let him fool you. He's a busy guy."

"I don't doubt it," Hunter replied, amused at the man's broad smile, twitching under his white beard. Huck Wilson was full of piss and vinegar, in all the best ways.

"I may be busy now, but not as busy as I was as a kid, though." Huck chuckled, rapping his grandson on the arm. "Hey, Wilson, did I ever tell you about the time I blew up your great-grandpap's shed?"

Wilson glanced up from his video game. "What? No way!"

Kathryn groaned and pinched the bridge of her nose. "Oh no. Here he goes," she muttered, shaking her head in a cute, bemused way.

"I made myself a torch so I could go running around in the night like a real adventurer would!" Huck exclaimed, using his hands for emphasis like a man who was used to spinning a good yarn. "I went to soak the end of it in gasoline, but I got a sloppy about it. Turned out, I'd dripped gasoline all around and I didn't know it. When I lit that daggone torch, the ground started burning at my feet too. Then I got scared and dropped the torch, and *boom!*"

Hunter checked through his rearview mirror and laughed to see how wide Wilson's eyes had gotten. "What happened?" Wilson breathed.

"The whole storage shed went up, with all my daddy's tools in it. And all his fireworks he'd bought for our Fourth of July party."

"Cool!" Wilson cried.

"That's what I thought!" Huck crowed. "Except I was kinda sorry about frying the hair off the cat. Have you ever seen a cat with a bald butt? He was shiny as a brass knob, that one. Never did look right after that, the poor thing. I never heard my daddy say so many cuss words at once. Tanned my hide, let me tell you. But it never did stop me. Did I ever tell you about the time I..."

Hunter turned to Kathryn, and she turned to him. And they laughed. Lord, it felt good to laugh with someone. He couldn't remember the last time he had. Tension slowly unwound a bit in his shoulders.

They settled in to letting Huck tell his childhood tales as they rumbled down the road, Kathryn only interrupting occasionally to ask a question or challenge an overdrawn point in the story. Hunter had to admit, the old guy had a knack for lightening the mood with a good tale. Huck had quite a collection of them. The old guy cycled through some real gems Hunter suspected were heavily embellished, such as "the time I fell asleep on my raft and floated all the way to Louisville," "why potty-training little brothers and pet frogs shouldn't share the same toilet," and the unforgettable "why you should never open a jar of live June bugs at show and tell."

It was easy to slip into the rhythm of Huck's stories and Wilson's squeals of laughter. But Hunter couldn't stop the growing sense of foreboding in his gut over the driving conditions. Driving on these mountain roads in wintertime always took an expert touch. Luckily, Hunter knew every curve and twist on this particular stretch of narrow two-lane road. But the snow was coming down hard now, to near whiteout conditions. This snowstorm had been preceded by several days of cold, driving rain. The pavement glistened in that terrible stage between slush and a thick, stubborn glare of ice. By his guess, this freakishly bad storm had dropped a foot or more of snow in the last couple of hours, and there hadn't been a grain of salt or a snowplow in sight. Even the chains on the top of his commercial-grade tires couldn't get good traction in these conditions. It was all he could do to keep his back end from kicking out as they crept around the treacherous mountain curves.

As dusk dropped its darkening veil over the day, the rugged peaks and hushed, glittering valleys embraced the storm, stopping it and slowing its progress, as mountains did. The temperatures plunged as the minutes wore on. Dammit, he needed to get them to the hospital, and then to The Greenbrier by nightfall. At the rate they were inching along, they'd never make it.

The snow kicked up so suddenly, it actually made Hunter flinch. *Shit, that was one hellacious blast.* The blizzard formed like a cyclone, swirling around them in angry, oddly circular bursts. Hunter gripped the wheel in the ten o'clock and two o'clock position until his knuckles were white, stifling the urge to let out a string of curses. Hunter had driven in winter weather in these parts, but nothing had prepared him for this. They were having every kind of weather at once—high winds, horizontal sleet, blinding snow and, god help them, loud, ominous thunder. His wide, lumbering tow truck already swallowed up more than his lane on these narrow, shoulderless mountain roads. If another car came around the bend, its driver wouldn't have a prayer of seeing them in time to stop. Hunter turned on his emergency flashers and slowed even more. Visibility went down pretty much to zero. He couldn't see a thing. Not the next tree, the next turn...*nothing.*

Suddenly, lightning split the sky—blazing so hot and so close, it buckled the asphalt right in front of them. His ears rang and his teeth rattled in the aftermath of the blinding flash, stuttering his control on the wheel.

Goddammit!

They were sliding now. As their wheels left the pavement, his passengers held on tight and whimpered. But somehow, a strange calm descended over Hunter. They were toward the bottom of the mountain and about to start up another one, so the chances of them dying in a downhill crash were nil. Even as they jackknifed off the end of the road and started crashing through undergrowth he was sure his big truck could take the abuse. They eventually skidded to a stop in a stand of bushes.

Hunter grinned at all of them and shrugged. "Guess we found a detour."

Kathryn fixed him with an ironic stare. "You know, you're really not funny."

Hunter chuckled. "When I said I'd keep you safe, I meant it. Besides, we'll be back on the road in a second."

True to his word, Hunter spun his wheels, kicked up the gear, and got them back up and onto the pavement. Visibility was still horrendous, but he made slow, steady progress. The snow was so bad that he could hardly tell whether he was up or down. It was like they were driving into some kind of spiraling tunnel of snow.

"I sure wish we could get to that hospital," Huck grumbled. "My arm is hurting like the devil, and I've got a hankering for a buxom nurse serving me donuts and coffee on a tray."

Hunter chuckled. "Yeah, don't we all want that, Huck?"

Kathryn giggled as she punched him in the arm. "Don't encourage him."

Wilson popped his head up. "What does 'buxom' mean, Grandpa?"

"Well-endowed," Huck replied. "You know—a nicely turned-out woman."

"What does 'well-endowed' mean?" Wilson countered.

"It means she's got nice, big—"

"Pretty," Kathryn cut him off. "It means she's pretty."

"Oh. Huh," Wilson huffed, considering that.

Kathryn turned to Hunter, and they both snickered under their breath. He was glad to see her family smiling again after their last scare.

Suddenly the wall of snow gave a big burst, then mysteriously stopped. Somehow the blinding snow had instantly subsided into light, manageable flurries. In the distance, a big, lighted Red Cross sign appeared with the word *Hospital* underneath. He clenched his jaw shut, to keep from gaping like an idiot.

What in the— What is this place?

Hunter knew damn well the only medical center in these parts was Greenbrier Valley Medical Center, and that was miles from here. Had a new one opened up without him knowing?

Hunter pulled alongside the hospital, and it appeared to be a going concern, with gleaming, brand-new construction and a big emergency bay. Hunter stared in amazement as he turned in. "You must be getting your wish, Huck."

Everybody cheered as Hunter pulled under the emergency bay awning. Staff came running up with two wheelchairs for Kathryn and Huck. Hunter stood in amazement as the staff hit a few buttons on their tablet computers and pulled up Kathryn and Huck's medical records, approved their insurance, and shuttled them along right away for treatment. This wasn't like any emergency room he'd ever seen. No wait? *At all?*

Though he should've had a seat in the waiting room, Hunter couldn't stop himself from following the family back through the hall to the examining rooms. Hunter gaped in wonder as he walked. It was the craziest hospital he'd ever seen. If it were possible to say this about a hospital, he would've called it *plush*. This ER was less like a medical establishment and more like a cigar bar that had been retrofitted with medical equipment. The cherry-paneled walls were plastered with vintage pin-up art from the 1940s. The exam bays didn't have exam tables, but oversized black leather recliners instead. Big flat-screen televisions played the fishing and classic movie channels in every exam area.

Even Wilson was overawed at the place. Reassuring everyone he was perfectly fine, the boy darted off to an enormous, supervised children's gym that featured a monster slide, foam pits for jumping in, climbing walls, and virtual reality skiing.

But the tricked-out play center wasn't even the most alarming thing about the place. It was the staff. Every single nurse looked like a centerfold for a girlie magazine, all of them walking around in old-fashioned white nurse dresses that cut off above the knee and zipped up the front. Not that they were keeping the zippers up at anything resembling a decent angle.

Yet, the staff really did appear to know what they were doing. While one of the nurses bent forward, giving Huck a bird's eye view of her assets while she served him—honest to God—donuts off a silver platter, the other nurse gave the man shots of topical anesthetic. Huck was so entertained, he barely noticed the needle. The old guy happily ogled the *buxom* staff and wolfed down crullers.

Hunter watched, his eyes bugging out in amazement as Huck's doctor came by. She was every inch the sexy school-teacher fantasy, but wearing a white doctor's jacket. Dr. Whoever-she-was had raven hair scooped up in a loose bun, one of those little straight skirts, a ribbed turtleneck so tight it left nothing to the imagination, and high heels so pitched, he wondered how she walked at all. And of course, she had to have thick-framed glasses. Hunter chuckled under his breath as Huck launched into full-on charm mode. The doctor chuckled good-naturedly at Huck's shenanigans, and pulled out one of those creepy curved needles to start stitching the old guy up.

Hunter immediately got too queasy to continue his gawking. Opting to get out of there stat, he casually cruised on over to where Kathryn was being treated instead. Hunter groaned at the sight. Kathryn was sharing a med-school joke with Dr. Dreamy McDreamface over there. Ugh, Kathryn was batting her eyelashes at the man. And Hunter couldn't exactly say he blamed her. The guy was ridiculously hand-some, with muscles like a pro wrestler, kind, emo eyes, and evidently, Mensa-level skills at intelligent conversation. Even his teeth were dazzling. And to really stick a fork in it, the little shit had an English accent.

Hunter didn't know why it pissed him off so much to see her with this cheese daddy, but it did.

Kathryn finally caught sight of Hunter brooding in the corner and turned her sparkling eyes in his direction. "Oh! Hey, Hunter."

"Hey," Hunter answered, suppressing the urge to sigh.

Kathryn's doctor turned to him. "You'll be glad to know your girl isn't all that worse for the wear."

"Oh, she's not—um, she's not my girl," Hunter sput-tered. "I'm only giving her a ride into town."

"Oh, really?" The doctor cocked an eyebrow. "She's been going on and on about her rescue. She made you sound like a knight of the realm. I suppose I jumped to conclusions."

Hunter silently told himself he wasn't pleased by that compliment. But he was. "So, no concussion then?"

"No, everything's all clear. She has some bumps and a contusion on her forehead. We glued up her cuts, as they weren't particularly deep. She can cover most of the damage with a few feminine tricks." The doctor turned to Kathryn. "Matter of fact, why don't you step over into our salon?

They can fix up your hair and makeup. No reason why we shouldn't send you out into the street looking smart, am I right?"

Kathryn's jaw dropped. "You have a salon...*in the ER?* Are you making some kind of joke?"

As if on cue, a matronly, uniformed stylist breezed in, carrying a big, round brush. "Oh, it's no joke," the woman chirped. "This is a big tourist area, so we do things differently here. We're more service-oriented. We find that when you look good, you feel better. Isn't that right, doctor?"

Dr. McDreamy flashed his blinding, artificially whitened smile at Kathryn. "Capital, isn't it? We don't even bill your insurance. It's a free concierge service. Go on, there's a chair open for you."

Of course there is. Hunter shook his head. Why not? The day couldn't get any weirder, could it? The stylist shuttled a bewildered Kathryn into another room, muttering something about a shampoo and a French blowout.

Not knowing what else to do, Hunter wandered over to the waiting room. He ordered up a large coffee and a fresh-baked chocolate cookie from the barista in the hospital's *complimentary coffee bar*. Of course, it was one of the best cookies he'd ever eaten in his life, and piping hot from the oven. Hunter settled into one of their leather couches with the tiny buttons on the back and big turned arms. When he scanned the room, he suddenly noticed a novel on the end table beside him. Funny, he hadn't noticed it before. It was a thriller from one of Hunter's favorite authors that he'd been meaning to read. No battered magazines for *this* place, apparently. Still, he peered suspiciously at this very pristine, brand-new hardback. Oddly convenient and specific to him, wasn't it? He picked it up anyway and turned the page. And he tried to read it—he really did. But no matter how much coffee he swilled down and how hard he concentrated on the text, he just kept reading the same paragraph over and over.

Yeah, this place *definitely* gave him the creeps, and he couldn't quite figure out why. Maybe it was because everything about this strange hospital seemed too good to be true. As a matter of fact, it was beyond belief. Hunter wished he could figure out what in the hell was the deal. His stomach lurched with uneasiness. Any other person would be thanking their lucky stars to get such good, quick medical attention so close to the holidays. But the prickling sense of unease wouldn't let him go. Was this what a bug felt like, sitting on the edge of a Venus flytrap? Were they being lured into something?

No, we couldn't be. That would be ridiculous, right?

Hunter fidgeted in his chair and sent up appeals to various higher powers while he waited, not managing to read a damn thing. Thankfully, in no time, Kathryn stepped back out to the waiting room.

Holy hell.

Nothing could have prepared him for the sight of Kathryn Winslow all cleaned up. Hunter sucked in a breath. His brain was telling him to play it cool. She was just another customer. But his heart had other ideas. Dammit, she was so beautiful that it hurt him to breathe. Her long blonde hair was brushed back from her forehead down to its precise, blunt tips. Kathryn's cuts weren't even visible under her makeup. In fact, the makeup had the effect of making her high cheekbones more refined and her gray eyes smokier and more penetrating. Her small mouth was drawn up like the bow on a very pretty package. And her skin was china doll perfect, pale ivory tinged with pink. God, how that creamy, satiny skin would feel under his rough hands... Skin like that would glow, wouldn't it, against a white sheet, shimmering in the morning light?

Jesus. Get yourself under control, you moron.

Hunter bit back another groan. God, he was hopeless. He had no business wanting this woman, and he'd do well not to torture himself. After all, he was only dropping her off and fixing her car, and that would be it.

Apparently noting his staring, Kathryn furrowed her brows. She touched her hand to the tips of her hair and locked eyes on him again. "Do I look okay?"

"Better than okay," Hunter replied, his voice sounding gruffer than he'd intended. He hoped to God his face hadn't reddened up when he said it, but he felt like it might have.

"Good." Kathryn shrugged on her coat. "Can you believe they even got the stains out this thing? I'd always heard the service around here was beyond reproach, but who knew it would be like this? Come on, we'd better find Daddy before he gets himself into more trouble."

They caught up with Huck, still in his bay, all stitched up, and grinning like a Cheshire cat while he received a neck massage from one very attractive massage therapist. Huck was by any definition a big, burly guy, with longish, snow-white hair tucked back behind his ears, a straggly white beard, and a mat of thick white hair covering his chest. When Huck saw them walking in, he reluctantly pulled on his undershirt and stuffed himself back into his fancy white dress shirt. The hospital staff had brought it to the man, freshly laundered, pressed crisp, and missing a whole sleeve's worth of bloodstains. And that wasn't the only strange part of this scene. Huck was obviously a real salt-of-the-earth kind of guy. But yet, his personal trappings of success—the black snakeskin cowboy boots, the black dress pants, the turquoise bolo tie, the big rings, all seemed like they belonged to somebody else. The clothes were wearing Huck, and not the other way around.

Huck turned to them, excitedly showing off all twenty-eight stitches on his forearm. The donuts, it appeared, had done the man wonders.

Together, they went to fetch Wilson out of the fun zone. A fit, active kid, Wilson was clearly in no mood to call it a day. The boy's blue eyes were bright and his cheeks were flushed with play as he bounced all around the place. Hunter couldn't help but notice Wilson had his mother's cute smile and appraising gaze, but the resemblance ended there. The child must favor his father. Considering Wilson's strong jaw, straight nose, and athletic build, his father is surely a pretty nice-looking guy—*and a lowlife idiot.* From the obvious lack of a husband and a wedding ring at Christmas time, Hunter had to assume that Kathryn was on her own.

Hunter couldn't imagine why a man would leave a son and wife like Kathryn and Wilson. Was she widowed? Divorced? Never married? If his father was alive, why in God's name would he ignore his own son at Christmas? It boggled Hunter's mind and nagged at him, not that it was any of his business.

Hunter laughed as poor Kathryn tried to fish a protest-ing, wriggling Wilson out of the foam pit. She was finally able to get the boy to mind by pointing out that if he wanted some dinner, he'd better move along. They had a reservation at the Greenbrier, after all.

The college-age attendant at the kids' area desk over-heard their conversation and hollered over to Kathryn. "Ma'am, I'm sorry to tell you this, but I don't believe you'll be getting to the Greenbrier today, or even any time soon. The severe weather after so much rain caused a rockslide, and then the heavy snow caused an avalanche on top of it. The roads are blocked off starting at the edges of town and continuing for a good mile or two in every direction. See?" she called, pointing to the television in the play area. The local news played with a ticker along the bottom. The state had closed all the roads in the area, it said, and they wouldn't be cleared for another five days.

Five. Days.

Hunter's heart sank. *So much for Kathryn's Christmas vacation.*

They were stranded. Hunter cussed himself for not being able to get them to the Greenbrier faster.

The attendant didn't seem too concerned, her blond, blue-eyed bounciness never dimming. "Don't worry! You're already in the best place on earth to celebrate the holidays. And hey, at least the roads in the main part of town are cleared."

Hunter felt a zing of panic at that. "Town? What town? I don't remember seeing one when we came in."

The girl chuckled and jangled the bell on the tip of her Santa hat. "Oh, sir, don't you know? You're in Christmas Pass—the cutest little tourist town you ever did see. There's absolutely no way you'll have a better Christmas than you can have here."

And with that, all of Hunter's protective instincts kicked into overdrive. This was *bullshit.* He grabbed up Kathryn and her family and shuttled them out to the parking lot as fast as he could. That girl had to be lying. But when they made their way to the parking lot, Hunter blinked with shock.

A big, painted sign greeted him, lit now so motorists could see it in the dark. "Welcome to Christmas Pass," it read. "Founded 1772." Painted in big, looping script below it was the slogan "Where Christmas Wishes Come True!"

Hunter blinked a few more times—slowly, to make sure he really was seeing this right. Stretched out in front of them, as far as the eye could see, was an almost unbearably quaint town. Hunter wouldn't call it small, necessarily, as it seemed to go on forever, with activity and sound coming from all up and down the mountainside. Impossibly cute shops dotted the streets, with their colorfully painted clapboard exteriors, delicate turned spindles, and gingerbread woodwork. Old-fashioned holiday displays arched over the streets, the kind that had greenery mixed in with lights that flickered to shapes, like angels and bells and holly leaves. Cars cruised along the city streets at an unhurried pace, and crowds of well-dressed tourists milled in and out of the storefronts.

Christmas Pass was *beautiful*. In fact, it was so perfectly decorated and well ordered, it almost hurt his eyes to look at it. The whole town sparkled with the new-fallen snow, as if it had been frosted with sugar.

Of course this place was beautiful. Hunter had lived in these hills all his life. He knew every inch of this land, and he knew how beautiful it could be.

And that was the problem.

He was pretty sure they were standing in a place that wasn't on any map. *God help us, there is no such place as Christmas Pass.*

But after everything they'd been through today, Hunter wasn't planning on telling Kathryn that.

CHAPTER 4

Considering that her plans for Christmas were completely ruined, Hunter was amazed that the indestructible Ms. Winslow took the news of their stranding in stride. Kathryn seemed genuinely charmed by Christmas Pass and shrugged, saying, "It's as good a place as any to be at this time of year." Hunter had to give her credit. Kathryn may look like a princess, but she didn't act like one.

At least their perky attendant could fill them in on where to go and what to do during their stay at "Christmas Pass." Honestly, he should use air quotes when then said the town name, because he couldn't explain any of this. Somehow, some way, they were standing in a place that didn't physically exist. And right now, it was scaring the ever-living crap out of him.

In fact, Hunter pulled out his phone and tried to confirm his suspicions. But it was dead as a brick, even though his phone was only a month old and it had been juicing on his car charger all day long.

Hunter scowled down at the black screen. "Kathryn? Huck? Are your phones working?"

Kathryn pulled hers out of her bag and hit the power

button. She huffed with disgust and threw it back in her bag. "Nope. It's dead. But I'm not surprised. It was nearly out of battery life before I left. Not to mention the beating it took in the crash."

After rattling around in his pockets, Huck finally pulled out his flip phone too. "Yeah, mine's deader than a doornail. Can't say it worries me much. I hate the damn thing."

"Mine too, Hunter," Wilson piped up, waving his flip phone in the air. "It's okay. The only person I ever call is Momma and Daddy. At least my Nintendo is still working."

To Hunter's consternation, their perky attendant had followed them all outside. "Oh no, sir," the girl chirped. "You won't be able to get any reception here. Something about the electrostatic fields bouncing off the mountains. We've never been able to get cell service in Christmas Pass. And besides, the avalanche took down our all the poles that held our landlines and internet connections. With the exception of satellite television, we're cut off until they get linemen out here to get us some new poles and run new line. I doubt that'll get fixed until well after New Year's Day."

Okay, he could buy that the telephone poles had been destroyed. But that was a load of horseshit about the cell service. Hunter's cell phone carrier had never let him down, no matter where he was in the state. But this *entire town* was a cellular dead zone? Hunter grimaced, deciding there was no point making an issue out of it. "I suppose it won't matter. My shop is closed down until January third, and no one is waiting for me."

"Same here." Kathryn groaned. "But I do worry about how this will impact Daddy's business. Won't your staff have to check in?"

Huck shifted uncomfortably but shook his head.

"There's good people in charge. They can get along without me."

They talked through their options. But it seemed they really only had one choice—waiting until the roads cleared at the Hollyberry Inn, which the staff at the hospital had praised to the skies. It had free breakfast and was right in the center of town, so they could walk everywhere they wanted to go.

So, that settled it. As they rumbled down the road toward the inn, Hunter couldn't get past this feeling that something was terribly wrong. But then again, maybe he was mistaken about Christmas Pass not existing. Maybe he'd missed it somehow, for all these years. How that was possible, he didn't know.

Hunter gritted his teeth. No matter what, there was no sense pitching a fit. He wasn't in a position to prove a damn thing at the moment.

Hunter chuckled to himself. Prove what? That they were in some kind of alternate dimension? That they'd somehow landed in a place or time that didn't exist? Now that he thought about it, it was pretty nuts, wasn't it? The stress of the day must have officially sent him 'round the bend. Besides, was it actually possible there were things about his home state, and places nearby to him, that he'd never heard about? Of course it was possible. One man couldn't know everything.

Still, how many hundreds of times had he driven this stretch of road? A hundred times? A thousand? Hunter would've had to be deaf, dumb, and blind to miss this place. But then again, had he gotten back on the right road after they had slid off? Was it a road he'd never been on? Was *that* the reason he'd never heard of Christmas Pass?

This whole thing was making his head hurt. Hunter decided to put all his niggling doubts behind him for the moment and go with the flow. He could always check into things later. For all its strangeness, Christmas Pass *did* seem like a really nice place. Maybe a Christmas spent with strangers might be exactly the escape he needed. It would certainly beat the Christmas Hunter had planned, alone in his cold, attic loft above Holliday Hot Rods.

When they pulled into the parking lot at the inn, they were all pretty shocked at how nice it was. The Hollyberry Inn was a sprawling, red brick Victorian mansion with a massive wrap-around porch. Wreaths decorated every window, and garland was draped over every flat surface that he could see.

A slim, authoritative older lady came to greet them at the door as they walked up. She wore a halfway tasteful Christmas sweater and jeans, with her long, white hair pulled up in a tight bun. The minute they crossed the threshold, she shot them an overly familiar, almost *knowing* look. For some reason, it set Hunter's teeth on edge. "Welcome everyone to Christmas Pass! I'm Miss Holly Berry, your host and the proprietress at this inn. So you must be the stranded travelers I've heard so much about!" She extended her hand, and they each shook it in turn. While they exchanged pleasantries, she shuttled them into a lobby with a roaring fireplace almost as tall as he was and rows of plush, cozy couches. There were so many Christmas decorations and twinkling lights, the entire place seemed ablaze with the Christmas spirit. It was almost obnoxious. *Almost.*

Hunter raised his eyebrows. "You knew we were coming?"

"Of course! No one new comes to Christmas Pass without us knowing."

Kathryn chuckled. "Then you knew before we did. We didn't have plans to stay here until ten minutes ago."

"I know that, too," she answered.

Kathryn's smile faded, and his did too. Okay, *that* wasn't creepy at all. How the hell had she heard about them coming without any working phones?

Miss Berry's response seemed to linger in the air, making the hairs on the back of his neck stand up. Seeing the uncomfortable glance he exchanged with Kathryn, Miss Berry recovered herself, smiling innocently. "Well, you know how it is. Word travels fast in a small town, doesn't it?" She clapped her hands together, as if to change the subject. "So how many rooms are you needing? One for the two of you and..." she said, pointing to Kathryn and Hunter.

Kathryn immediately jumped in, suddenly blushing. "Oh no, we're not together, per se."

Huck cackled. "Per se. I can understand why you'd make that mistake, hon. They do kinda seem like a matched set, don't they?"

Kathryn groaned. "Would you stop trying to stir up trouble, Daddy? Give us a room for me, a room for Mr. Holliday, and a room for my father and son to share. And put Mr. Holliday's room on my tab."

Hunter cocked an eyebrow. "What? Do I look like I need charity?"

"No! Of course not!" Kathryn insisted. "But this is an expense you shouldn't have to incur. You were only doing your job when you pulled us off the side of the mountain. Now you're stuck here with us, racking up bills over the holidays. I don't want to take advantage of you."

"Maybe I don't have anything better to do this Christmas," Hunter muttered. It was true. He had no one really. Years ago, his parents had moved from Lewisburg to Canada to be near his brother, his Canadian sister-in-law, and their grandkids. They routinely made an effort to get together, of course. But since the accident, the thought of traveling alone at Christmas was more than he could bear. And pretty much everyone in his extended family had left West Virginia long before that, chasing their careers. So there were no family celebrations to be had here.

Oh, he'd gotten a few invitations to Christmas dinner from his employees. But who was he to intrude like that? No, he really was alone this holiday. And Christmas Pass, suspicious as it was, was as good a way to spend his time as any. Besides, he didn't know what to make of this place. Until he had it figured out, he didn't want to let Kathryn or her family out of his sight.

Hunter handed his credit card to Miss Berry before Kathryn could protest. But Miss Berry handed it back to him. "Oh! You don't need one of those around here. All you need to do is sign the register." She shuttled them over to an expansive front desk paneled in mahogany. "You'll find all the establishments in Christmas Pass are like that. Your purchases are registered in the log, and it's sent to us here at the end of every day. We keep track of you." Miss Berry pointed to a leather-bound ledger with big parchment pages and gave him a fine fountain pen with an actual goddamn feather sticking out of the top.

How...*odd*.

He was the first one to sign a completely empty book.

"It's like Santa's book!" Wilson exclaimed. "You know, the one he uses for the naughty and nice list."

Huck snickered as he signed his name. "Well then, I know which side of the ledger I'm on."

When he was done, Kathryn signed too, smiling quizzically and shaking her head. "You really can track us with all this?"

Miss Berry regarded them with a carefully neutral expression. "Everyone works together. No matter where you shop here, your purchases get automatically delivered to your room as soon as you make them. Will you be dining with us this evening?"

"Yes," Kathryn replied, apparently still trying, and failing, to size Miss Berry up. Finally Kathryn shrugged. "Please make a reservation for four in about an hour."

Wow. Did Kathryn really want him to eat with them? Deep down, the idea pleased Hunter and made him nervous, all at the same time. He fidgeted a bit, and stared down at his feet. "Hey, don't feel like you have to babysit me. I can go grab a bite on my own."

But instead of being deterred, Kathryn walked right up to him and poked her finger in the middle of his chest. "I don't want to hear any arguing. You saved our lives, and I'm not leaving you to celebrate the holidays alone in a hotel room. From now on, you're with us. Understand?"

She gazed up at him with those big beautiful eyes again, and his breath hitched.

He surely hadn't expected any of this. He knew he should refuse and put some distance between them.

Who are you kidding? You can't say no to her any more than the sun could say no to the sunrise. Swallowing hard, Hunter decided not to fight her. "Understood."

Kathryn's triumphant grin lit up the room as she spun away to hand the bellhop the rest of their suitcases. And Hunter stared after her, smiling stupidly, and wondering how a woman like that could have been hanging off the side of a mountain, more or less alone. Kathryn Winslow had more heart and generosity than anyone he'd ever met.

With a crisp efficiency that was one part fairy godmother and one part drill sergeant, Miss Berry mobilized her staff, whisked her new guests up to their rooms, and got them settled.

Their three rooms were next door to each other, with a suite door that locked between his room and Kathryn's. He stood and stared at it for a moment, but he knew he wouldn't be opening *that* anytime soon. But *damn*, how he wished he could—just walk in and wrap his hand around the back of her neck and kiss her until neither of them could think anymore. He wished they could tangle themselves around each other until they forgot everything and drowned out every bad thing that had ever happened to either one of them.

Like that would ever happen.

Silently cussing his dumbassery, he distracted himself by taking stock of his new accommodations. Like everything else in this strange town, it was extraordinary. The room was surprisingly masculine, by bed and breakfast standards. Rustic and comfortable, the place was dominated by a tall brass bed covered with a thick paisley comforter and fake fur throws. A remote on the nightstand caught his attention enough for him to pick it up. Hunter pushed a couple of buttons. *Shit!* He jumped, then barked out a laugh when a tricked-out flat-screen TV rose up out of the bed's footboard. *Nice.* Walking around, he took a moment to appreciate the fireplace crackling in the corner, flanked by two reclining leather club chairs for reading. God bless it, there was a bottle of Maker's Mark—his favorite—on the fireside table. Even the bookcases flanking the fireplace were stuffed with all the thrillers and historical fiction he had on his online reading list, and a few he'd only been *thinking* about adding to it. There wasn't a single book here that *wasn't* something he'd actively wanted to read.

Creepy—that was what it was. Whether it was creepy bad, or creepy good, he couldn't tell. For right now, he decided he'd hope like hell for the latter, and not the former.

Hunter walked into the bathroom and decided it was past time to throw some water on his face and wash his hands. Gratefully, he opened up the hipster-worthy, full-size toiletries Miss Berry had sent up for him. They were a far cry from the drugstore crap he used at home. He chuckled over the "bourbon-infused" soap, some kind of weird pomade thing for his hair, and even the old-fashioned straight razor for shaving.

Since he had no clothes to change into for dinner, he unbuckled the top of his overalls from his pants, cinched up the belt, and tried his best to freshen his appearance. Whipping up the fancy shaving powder into a fluffy cream, he shaved off his stubble and cleaned up his hair a bit with the pomade. He huffed out a surprised chuckle. The strange stuff did actually give his haircut some definition and made his features seem sharper and more refined. Even that bit of effort gave him a boost after the long-ass day they'd had.

Hunter considered himself as he splashed on a bit of the pricey aftershave. He wasn't a bad-looking man, all things considered. He was only five years out of his twenties, but in some ways, he felt as old as Methuselah. Life had pretty much run him over and left him by the side of the road. Since the crash, his life had become nothing but a gray fog, the march of time marked only by the workaday tasks of keeping his shop running. He couldn't remember the last time he'd truly faced his reflection in the mirror, let alone actually attempted careful, deliberate grooming. It felt...*good*. He made a mental note to go shopping tomorrow for clothes that didn't make him look like he'd crawled out from underneath an oil pan.

To his shock, a soft knock sounded on the suite door between rooms. He carefully opened it, and sure enough, Kathryn was standing there, changed into a light blue simple wrap-around dress. For a woman who'd been through hell and back today, she looked amazing. But then, he'd bet she always looked amazing.

"You ready?" she asked.

"Yeah," he answered, swallowing hard. "I believe I am."

They locked up and made their way down to the dining room. Like everything else in this strange, strange town, the Inn's restaurant blew him away. Normally, an establishment like this would have only a few menu items made from seasonal produce. But this place appeared ready to serve any kind of food, fresh and expertly prepared at a minute's notice. A small army of chefs labored at show tables, cutting prime rib, searing planked salmon, tossing stir-fry dishes, hand-rolling fresh pasta, and even grilling up fat, delicious-smelling hamburgers. It must be good too. Every customer in the place sat perched in their quaint colonial-era chairs, eating with identical blissful expressions on their faces.

For his part, Hunter was ready to dig in. He'd been so busy pulling drivers out of snowdrifts that he hadn't eaten since morning. They were seated right away, and a waiter in a tuxedo-like uniform came by their table, handing them all a menu that was so thick, it resembled a telephone book. The waiter informed them they could order any of the hundreds of menu items, or they could simply hold out their plate to one of the working chefs to get their meal. By one accord, they made a beeline for the chef's tables.

When they got back to their seats, the variety of their picks was amusingly predictable. Hunter had gone for steak with bleu cheese and, similarly, Huck had loaded up on prime rib and shrimp cocktail. Kathryn had a more sensible plate of sushi and planked salmon. And Wilson had a plate stacked high with gooey mac and cheese. The boy grumbled but paid heed when Kathryn made him go back and get a dish of steamed broccoli. Wilson was angling to get permission to visit the chocolate fondue fountain later.

Hunter took his first bite of steak and groaned with bliss. Had he died and gone to heaven? He'd eaten at plenty of high-end steakhouses over the years. But no simple slab of grilled meat could taste like this. It was buttery soft on his tongue and packed with flavor. The sear on the outside was perfection itself, yet the inside was perfectly medium rare. The twice-baked potato was just as good. The waiter informed him it was made with white truffle oil. *My Lord.*

A glance at Kathryn and her family confirmed they were feeling it too. Kathryn pointed to Hunter's plate. "So, I can tell by the joy on your face you're a meat-and-potatoes man."

"Not really." Hunter shrugged. "I'm a *if someone else is making it, it's delicious* man. But if given a choice, I'll go for steak, every time. So, does what you're eating mean you're a health food nut?"

Kathryn gave him a rueful smirk. "My momma, God rest her soul, always taught me to eat like a lady. That generally meant not eating all that much. But the upside is I prefer lighter food now. So I suppose she did me a favor."

"How long has your momma been gone?" Hunter asked, immediately regretting the off-handed question when he saw the pained expressions on Huck and Kathryn's faces. They both practically winced in unison, and neither one of them appeared comfortable talking about it. Wilson seemed ready to say something, but his mouth clamped shut as he looked back and forth between Kathryn and his granddaddy.

Kathryn's jaw ticked, and she took another sip of her drink before she finally answered, "She passed last year, right around this time." She gently cleared her throat. "Momma was fifty-three." Eyes downcast, she went back to eating her meal.

Too young—she'd passed way too young. Hunter sat back in his seat, considering Kathryn. There was a story there, a story none of them wanted to tell. Good Lord, he understood that, better than most. He didn't want to talk about his losses, either. Some truths would always be too painful to speak aloud, as if putting words to it would somehow rip the lid off the pain. That was the thing about that kind of grief. It never went away. It stayed there, locked in a vault in your heart, getting bigger and accruing interest with every passing day. Your only defense was to keep it locked up tight.

Grief. How well I know it. Hunter's heart ached in sympathy for her. *Dammit, how did I let the conversation take this turn?* Embarrassed now, Hunter decided he had to lighten things up again.

What had they been talking about? Food?

Hunter cut off a big slice of his steak and playfully held up his fork to her. "I'll bet even your momma would approve of this steak. Meat like this could turn anybody to the dark side." He dangled it enticingly, waggling his eyebrows. "I dare you to try it."

A pleased, surprised expression crossed her face. Then she leaned forward, her lips curling mischievously. "You'd like turning me, wouldn't you?"

He waved the fork in front of her nose, and she giggled —a magical, lilting, sexy sound he could get used to hearing. "Come on." He smirked. "You know you want to."

"Challenge accepted," she declared. And to his amazement, she quickly nipped it right off the end of his fork. Kathryn's eyes closed and fluttered in satisfaction as she chewed. She even moaned—a beautiful, low purr from the back of her throat.

Lord have mercy.

Oh my freakin' God—that sound could launch a thousand dirty fantasies, and she didn't even realize it. He caught himself grinning at her like a hound. How he was going to control himself around her for four more days, he didn't know.

"You're right about that steak," she admitted, and hustled off to the bar to get herself her own serving. When she got back, she regarded her son, who was headfirst into his giant bowl. "How's yours, honey?"

"Why can't you make mac n' cheese like this?" Wilson grunted out between bites.

Kathryn raised her eyebrows. "Because I'm not a chef, that's why. Are you sayin' you don't like my mac n' cheese?"

"No. It's out of a box," Wilson shrugged. "But maybe I can tell Dad about it, and he can figure out the difference."

Kathryn snorted. "Your dad can't cook to save his life. It's more like Avery will figure it out, huh? I hate to tell you, buddy, but they don't have mac n' cheese in France."

"They don't?" Wilson replied, his eyes wide.

"Nope!" Huck chimed in. "They're gonna make you eat snails! They call it es-car-gooo, kiddo. You'll have to pour butter all over it and act like it's the most delicious thing on earth."

"Would you stop it?" Kathryn rapped her father on the arm, giving him a playful glare. "You're going to scare him."

Hunter furrowed his brows in confusion. "Am I missing something? Are you sending Wilson to France?"

Huck rolled his eyes and pushed back from his plate. "Not exactly. Wilson's dad is moving to France, and Wilson will go visit him from time to time."

"Dad is going to let me stay the whole summer!" Wilson exclaimed.

Kathryn groaned and launched into an explanation. "Wilson's father and I have been divorced now for about five years. And my ex has found a new beloved. His betrothed, Avery, was born in France and has a dual citizenship. This year, they decided to up and move there permanently, to be closer to Avery's aging parents. I think éclairs and free government healthcare may have also had something to do with it."

"And you're okay with this?" Hunter asked, a little incredulous on her behalf.

She shrugged. "Do I have a choice? Sterling has always done what Sterling wants to do. I try to focus on the bright side. This is a great opportunity for Wilson to broaden his horizons and become bilingual at an early age."

Kathryn was smiling and upbeat. Why was that? Most women he knew would be beyond furious to have this situation shoved on them. And then it occurred to him—Kathryn was the sort of person who considered it her job to make sure everyone around her was okay. She kept the peace and smoothed out the bumps in the road, even if it meant putting herself and her needs behind everybody else's. Sure, he was making assumptions here and connecting the dots. But he'd bet he was right. It was obvious. She'd set her own needs aside a bunch of times already today.

Hunter decided to drop this line of questioning. He could see it was starting to make her squirm, and it wasn't any of his business anyway. But now he could clearly understand how Kathryn had ended up here. Her mother had passed away, and her ex was out of the country. This vacation must have been a desperately needed change of scenery for her. But while he couldn't figure her completely out, he could see some, if not all, of the bigger picture.

Hunter took a sip of his drink and quietly considered her. Maybe he'd been thrown into Kathryn's life by accident, but he felt a strange pang. He wanted to help her somehow and make sure a smile stayed on that pretty face. If anyone deserved some Christmas magic, it was Kathryn. Weird and potentially creepy as it was, this Christmas Pass place sure had *that* in spades.

Wilson was dancing around a bit in his seat. The boy

asked if anybody knew where the bathroom was. Saying she needed to go too, Kathryn shepherded her son away with her. They disappeared around the corner. Checking over his shoulder to make sure they were good and gone, Huck pulled a very large flask out of his pocket. He poured about six shots worth of vodka into the remnants of his Coke.

Hunter didn't raise his eyebrows or comment on the man's obvious drinking issues. But his eyes widened when Huck ditched the straw and chugged down the entire boozy concoction in about sixty seconds. Then old guy hailed over the waiter, handed him his glass, and asked for a new glass of Coke to replace it. Huck tossed some breath mints in his mouth, crunching them quickly with his teeth. *Damn.* Now there was a man with a *habit*, one he went to great lengths to hide from his family. Kathryn had to know Huck had a drinking problem. She was way too smart not to. Maybe that was why Kathryn wanted her daddy out of town and safe with her over the holidays.

To his amazement, Huck continued on as if nothing had happened, like downing two days' worth of alcohol in one long swallow was the sort of thing he did on the regular. Which, of course, had to be true. Nobody drank like that *on occasion.* Had Huck been born with his broad, country-fried charm, or was an act that he'd developed over the years? Was it a mask that helped him hide that he was half-crocked most of the time? If it was, Hunter had to give the man credit. Huck hid it pretty doggone well.

Huck sat back in his chair and took a long drag through his straw, picking up the thread of their conversation like nothing was amiss. "I always hated that Sterling. Prissy little shit. But I have to give him credit. He did marry Kathryn when he got her knocked up. Problem was, he didn't know what to do with a good thing when he had it."

Hunter didn't want to get the old guy on a roll. He

shifted his next question to safer ground. "What does Sterling do for a living?"

"He's an anesthesiologist. Puts people to sleep for a living. Seems somehow appropriate."

"And his fiancée?"

"A chef, and a choreographer, and a visual artist. Avery's all creative and dramatic and sophisticated." Huck snorted and shook his head. "Still not as good as my girl, if you ask me."

By the time Kathryn got back, Huck appeared to be innocently sipping his water. The man only appeared slightly buzzed, and you had to look hard to see it. Shit, the old guy must be built like a *tank*.

No sooner had Kathryn come back to her seat than the waiter came by with their checks. Again, all they had to do was sign the mysterious register. The waiter also handed them each a copy of *Christmas Pass Illustrated*, a very fancy magazine featuring all the attractions, food, and shopping in town.

They casually flipped through their copies. The choices were unbelievably diverse. Though he couldn't quite prove it, he could swear his pages magically populated with attractions he'd enjoy—outdoor living stores, steak restaurants, bookstores, country bars, snowmobile outfitters, skiing, you name it. When he checked over Kathryn's shoulder, *her* book was filled with fancy boutiques, fun gift stores, art galleries, theatrical productions, spas, and gyms. And Wilson was practically in orbit over his book, which touted a huge LEGO building event, competitive sledding through the city streets, a multi-story arcade, go carting, ice skating, and more.

Comparing the magazines, Kathryn scratched her head. "Boy, that's odd. How in the world could a town this size support so many entertainment options? And how could they afford to print so many versions of this magazine? I've never seen a place like this."

Hunter silently agreed with her. How was this whole place so packed with tourists when he'd never heard even a whisper about the place? How did he not know people who were employed at this place? He'd grown up not even twenty miles from here! He played dumb for Kathryn's benefit. "'Ours is not to wonder why,' I guess. Too many questions can keep you from enjoying things."

He waited for Kathryn to keep pulling on that thread, but he was relieved when she didn't. There was no call to scare them all with his bizarre suspicions.

Hunter must have been nervously scowling at the pages. Kathryn called him on it, playfully putting her elbow on the table, resting her pretty head on her hand, and batting her eyelashes at him. "What's with the glum face? You can't find something you want to do out of all that?"

"It's not that. It's just..." Honestly, it took his breath away having her so close. Her face was inches from his, and lit with happiness and Christmas spirit. Who was he to mess with that? And besides, if he went with all this, he'd have a better chance of keeping them safe if this place turned out to be as weird as he thought. He sighed in resignation. "I can't pick. Everything seems fun."

They began gathering their things to leave. "Good. That's what I want to hear, because you're coming with us tomorrow, and we're going to have the hap-happiest Christmas season ever. It may not be what any of us planned, but I think Christmas Pass may be what we all need."

Hunter swallowed hard. Whether he agreed with her or not, he couldn't yet say. But for her sake, he'd play along.

They migrated to the lobby and took up residence on the overstuffed couches. A uniformed staff member convinced them to try their special hot chocolate. The man brought each of them piping mugs of steamed cream and two big squares of Belgian chocolate, which they stirred into their own cups. They chatted companionably for a while, taking turns moaning and groaning over the best hot chocolate any of them had ever had.

Hunter had a great time telling tales about the high-end custom hot rods he'd built, and what it was like at hot rod competitions. Huck answered his questions about how he'd built his chain of gas stations. Wilson talked about his favorite video games, and scouts, and their recent trip to Disney. Kathryn demurred, saying all her best stories were about her patients and she couldn't talk about them. That made Hunter smile, thinking about what some of those stories might be. It was surprising, really, how he could be so comfortable with perfect strangers. Hell, he didn't even talk this much to his friends.

But as fun as it was, Wilson's head was starting to droop. Huck shuttled the boy to his feet and took him back to their room. Deciding to call it a night too, he and Kathryn took their good, sweet time walking back up the stairs. They lingered a bit in the hall outside her door, unwilling to let the day end. Truthfully, he was a tiny bit sad to be saying goodnight to her, even though he should be exhausted after the horrible day they'd all had. But the normalcy of drinking hot chocolate and making light conversation with Kathryn's family had grounded and centered him in a way he hadn't felt in a while. And he didn't want to stop looking at her, if he had to be honest.

Hunter turned for his room, but Kathryn stopped him, grabbing his hand, and hesitated, just for a moment. He was too busy feeling the electric jolt of their linked fingers to see her coming with the hug. As if it were simple, as if it was the easiest thing to do in the world, she pushed up on her toes and threw her arms around his neck. Soft. Sweet. He inhaled sharply, trying not to gasp. And before he even realized what he was doing, Hunter slid his arms around her and tucked her against him.

So good. So perfect.

Every feminine swell of her body was *right there*, pressed against him. His hand fit perfectly in the graceful dip in the small of her back. All his senses roared to back to life with the shock of her, cradled there in his arms. Ah, that jasmine scent was a perfume, wasn't it? Its delicious, subtle scent concentrated here, at the base of her neck, right below her pulse point. Hunter breathed in deep, lost for a moment.

Almost four years now. That was how long it had been since he'd held a woman in any way. And now that deprivation hit him like a sharp, unwelcome ache. Like a reminder of everything he'd lost and everything he'd never have again. Against his will, his body reacted, his groin tightening and his heart thumping uncomfortably in his chest.

But almost as soon as she'd leaped in his arms, Kathryn gave him a squeeze and an innocent peck on the cheek, and backed away. As well she should.

Hunter reminded himself that was only a friendly hug. But when he looked down at her, he could almost swear he saw a flash of something on Kathryn's face. Had she enjoyed that hug as much as he had? She seemed flustered. A beautiful shell-pink blush bloomed over her cheeks. But she quickly schooled her expression.

"Thank you," she murmured, never taking her eyes from his face.

"Didn't we discuss this? You don't have to keep thanking me. I'm so glad I could be there when you needed me."

"Not for that, silly. For this," she answered, motioning

to the building around her. "Thank you for being such a good sport about being stranded and all, and for being such good company. I don't know anyone who'd be so great about all this as you've been. I'm so, so sorry we ruined your Christmas. And I—I want you to know that I think you deserve to have a good holiday as much or more as we do. So, I hope when you come out with us, you won't be shy about saying what you want. We *all* will have a good holiday, okay?"

A woman like her could almost make him believe it too. "I think I can manage that."

"Good." Kathryn tapped his arm, smiling up at him. "I'll hold you to it." She disappeared through her door.

And Hunter couldn't do a thing but stand there and smile after her.

CHAPTER 5

HUNTER WOKE to a soft knock on his door. Cursing under his breath, he struggled to pull his head from the pillow. Last night had been the best sleep he'd had in years.

"Mr. Holliday?" the tentative voice said. "It's Miss Berry. I have a special delivery for you."

Groaning, he wrapped his nude, pajama-deprived self in one of the inn's fluffy Turkish robes and answered the door. He blinked stupidly at the sight of Miss Berry standing there with a large stack of bundles covered in plain brown wrap and string. He took them from her, and offered her a tip, which she refused. He walked the packages back to his bed, eyeing them warily,

What in the world?

A note rested on top of the stack, with the words "for Hunter" written on the envelope in a light, feminine script. Intrigued, he opened it up. It was from Kathryn.

We have suitcases of clothes to wear, but you don't. I didn't want to stick you with that burden too. So I made some executive decisions. I hope you like what I picked. My granddaddy on my mother's side was a tailor, and he taught me how to size up a man's inseam. If you don't like these, the

mercantile across the street will take the returns, no questions asked. When you're done getting dressed, meet us for pancakes downstairs! —Kathryn.

Hunter quickly unwrapped the packages and was amazed by what he saw. She had him figured out, all right. Each package held exactly the kind of clothes he might have bought for himself, in all the right sizes. Except these garments were much better quality than he usually wore. There were three pairs of dark blue jeans, made from the thickest, softest denim he'd ever seen, and a pair of slim-fitting khakis too. The same went for the finely woven, combed flannel shirts, the fitted Henley shirts, the chocolate-brown half-zip sweater with the subtle herringbone pattern, the wicking wool socks, the finely milled undershirts. He gulped as he realized she'd even thrown in underwear—colorful, clingy boxer briefs. Good God, she'd even bought him a new pair of high-quality hiking boots. Size twelve—his size, exactly.

He rolled his eyes at the labels. "Made by the elves in Christmas Pass," they said. *Yeah, right.* They really got into their branding around here, didn't they? Even the rivets had teeny-tiny Christmas wreaths stamped on them. It was subtle, though. You had to squint to even see them.

I shouldn't be accepting this. Why does Kathryn think she has to take care of me?

Honestly, the whole thing stuck in his craw. But Hunter had to admit—she'd put a lot of thought into this gift. And it was exactly what he needed, when he needed it. Maybe he'd make an exception, just this once.

He took a quick shower, dried off, and pulled on the boxer briefs. Honestly, they were a bit out of his comfort zone, since he'd always worn baggy traditional boxers. But damn if this new option didn't make him look almost kinda hot. After the crash, he'd thrown himself into his work, and the hard physical labor of it. And he'd skipped more than his share of meals too. He hadn't realized it until this moment, but the extra work had brought out the planes and angles of his body. The fabric clung to him in all the right spots.

He pulled on the jeans and buttoned up the fly. They were soft and supple and fit him like they'd been made for him—better than any pair he'd ever had. Even the sage-colored flannel fit like a glove, with luxurious deep seams and plackets. The color was great on him, and the fabric molded to his body, emphasizing the muscles in his chest and arms. He buckled on the hand-tooled leather belt Kathryn had sent. Its western-style silver buckle hung low on his hips. Not bad, if he did say so himself. These clothes were a far cry from the raggedy T-shirts and baggy jeans he'd been wearing lately, barely bothering to match his socks. These past few years, he'd told himself he didn't need anything, didn't have a reason to make a fuss in any way. But the truth was staring him right in the face. He really had been letting himself go, hadn't he?

Hunter stood taking his measure in the mirror—something he'd barely done in months, if not years. This gift of Kathryn's was more than nice. It was *flattering*. He marveled at how a woman he'd just met could have such an accurate eye for what would be good on his body. But more than that, she had a real sense for what would make him look confident and, well...*sexy*.

He didn't want to read too much into all this. But Kathryn had sized him up in more ways than one. She saw him—truly saw him—for the man he was. For the first time in a long time, he was at peace with the man looking back at him.

※

Kathryn had been certain Hunter would return those clothes, being a man who probably didn't want to accept a big gift from someone he barely knew. But she was so glad he didn't. It was the least she could do for him, after all. Oh, he complained and grumbled all through breakfast, insisting she didn't need to do it. But deep down, she knew he appreciated the gesture. She couldn't believe her luck when she'd found out how early Christmas Pass opened its stores in the morning. The mercantile across the street had an astonishing array of men's clothes, nearly all of them perfect for Hunter. In minutes she'd been able to outfit him in style.

And, man, Hunter sure was something in those clothes. Now that he was out of those baggy, padded work clothes, she could actually appreciate the man's body. What a transformation. Never had a pair of jeans fit a man so perfectly, hugging so right over his powerful thighs and muscular backside. She'd guessed that he had an amazing body underneath those coveralls, and she was right. He was wearing her favorite today—the sage-green shirt. The fine-combed fabric looked so soft and touchable stretched over his surprisingly chiseled frame. Her fingers itched to spread her hands over his pecs and feel for herself how the soft fabric pulled over the hardness of his chest.

Chastising herself for her ogling, she sipped on her water, hoping the glass would hide the heat that had risen to her cheeks. From the slightly cocky way he draped himself in his chair, Hunter knew he was looking damn fine this morning. But when met her gaze, his expression seemed a bit shy and unsure—like he was rusty at this whole flirting thing.

Wait—*flirting? Is that what he's doing?*
Is that what I'm doing?

How could she deny it? Hunter Holliday was appealing. So appealing, the flirting seemed to be practically

65

leaching out of her pores. She worried the whole thing with the clothes would make her seem desperate for his approval, like she was throwing herself at him. She didn't want to seem like some clingy, predatory spinster, after all.

Dammit, I can't afford to have these thoughts about him, can I?

They were two people from different towns and different worlds, stuck together for a very short time. But she was on vacation. And she'd have to be blind not to notice him. Not when all that rugged sensuality was trained in her direction. That subtle tremor of uncertainty in his eyes only heightened the effect.

They finished their breakfast and headed out for a day of adventure in Christmas Pass. Despite her best efforts, she couldn't seem to keep her eyes from drifting to him all morning long. As they walked around town, Kathryn secretly studied him—his easy, loping gait, his gentle mountain charm, and especially his shy smiles. Hunter wore his masculinity well. How different he was from the cerebral, often preening men she'd had in her life. Hunter was obviously smart and most likely ambitious, but he showed it differently—in a natural, unaffected way that suggested he wasn't trying to prove anything to anyone. He was a man who knew who he was, and where he belonged in the world.

Does he ever let anyone into that world?

"So, what should we do?" Hunter asked.

Kathryn reluctantly snapped out of her reverie. "Hmm? Oh, I don't really have anything specific in mind. Do you?"

"Hey, I'm going with the flow." Hunter offered up another one of his shy half smiles and jammed his hands into his front pockets. He hooked his thumbs casually through his belt loops as he walked along. Kathryn did her best not to let her eyes linger on that movement. She lost.

"I *wish* I knew where that big sled thing was that I saw in the magazine last night," Wilson whined. He trudged along with a fitful air, as if he was certain he'd be forced into some kind of terrible adult activity like shopping or going to a museum. But the buzz of a crowd beckoned from around the corner. Soon, his eyes widened. "There it is! There it is!" The boy tore off to the sign-up counter as fast as his legs would carry him.

Kathryn stopped in her tracks, taking in the scene on the next street over with more than a small amount of dismay.

Daddy guffawed. "Oh, no. Wilson's going to be like a pig in slop."

"Ya think?" Kathryn groaned as she took in the cheerful pandemonium at the entrance to the "Christmas Pass Annual Street Sled Races."

The place was packed, thrumming with a kind of contained chaos that promised chills, spills and, most likely, broken bones. It was the kind of scene engineered to make a mother squirm and a boy beg to try it. The intensely steep center of this mountain town was cordoned off, and officials had iced the streets until they were as slick and shiny as a hockey rink. Then snow was packed down tight on top and layered up the sides to make retaining walls and areas called, ominously, *spill zones*.

This was no "slide from the top to the bottom" affair. No, this took some measure of skill. Contestants had their choice of one- or two-person inner tubes. They would then be required to hurl themselves down what was clearly a formidable obstacle course, not unlike a pinball machine, with banks and curves and ramps designed to throw the riders in the air. Nowhere on this course was the angle any flatter than forty-five degrees. There were several courses and various types and lengths of races—enough for it to go on all morning and into the afternoon. The grand prize was a trophy nearly as tall as Wilson himself.

Wilson danced around the sign-up booth. "Can we enter? *Pleeeeaaase?"*

"After what we went through yesterday, you want to get knocked around some more?" Kathryn cried.

"I'd do it," Daddy offered, rubbing his hands together with glee. "Seems like fun."

"Daddy!" Kathryn yelped. "You can't be serious! You have twenty-eight stiches and God knows how many fresh bumps on your head!"

"So what's one more?" He shrugged.

There was no way she was going to allow this. But Kathryn found herself asking the prim young woman behind the sign-up desk about the age limits for the races, thinking that would surely disqualify Wilson.

"Oh, no," little Miss oh-so-helpful cried. "We have all kinds of races. An eight-year-old could compete in the eight-to twelve-year-old division. Or, he could be an entrant in our tandem races—you know, for two riders."

"Woot!" Daddy hollered, high-fiving Wilson. "You're on my team, buddy." He strode up to the counter and started filling out his application and signing for the fee.

"Daddy!" Kathryn squealed. "No! It's too dangerous!" But Daddy flashed another of his roguish grins and ignored her, as usual.

The woman behind the desk assured her everything was perfectly safe and bumpered to prevent excessive injury.

Kathryn took note of that surgically careful, legal use of the word *excessive,* and sighed. The entry fee was twenty dollars per rider, the woman continued, and all the money went to help the local humane society keep their shelter open.

So *great*, if she said no, she was the worst kind of over-protective parent—the kind who denied her child age-appropriate amusements and begrudged helping puppies. She moaned and massaged her temples, realizing she was beaten.

"Oh, come on." Hunter chuckled, nudging her with his shoulder. "Don't worry. I used to do these kinds of races all the time when I was his age. There's nothing like it, hurtling through space at twenty miles an hour. It's kinda like bumper cars, but on ice and, sometimes, in the air."

"You're not helping," Kathryn answered drily.

"He'll be fine. And so will Huck. You'll see."

She wasn't so sure about that. Daddy and Wilson trekked up the city's steepest slope and settled into their two-man inner tube. Wilson waved excitedly at her. And before she knew it, the sounding bell went off.

Kathryn watched with a competing mixture of queasiness and pride as they tore off down the slope. The event had all the finesse of a roller derby match, with riders trying to bump each other out of bounds and out of the race. Her son's tube bounced off the sides twice, but Wilson soon leaned hard enough to straighten out their path. When another rider jammed in front of them, they veered left and took a ramp that launched them into the air, and over not one but two other tubes!

Their sideways landing made her stomach lurch. And their unceremonious splat landed them in a pile of deep snow in the spill zone. But they jumped right up again and recovered quickly, Daddy giving them a running push worthy of any bobsled team. Daddy jumped back on, and the momentum from his running leap shot them out far. Sawing at the ground, they pushed themselves along until they were practically hurtling down the final stretch.

"They're pulling ahead!" Kathryn cheered. Somehow

they'd taken the lead. But at the last moment, another rider tapped them and sent the heavy, figure-eight construction of their tube spinning. Grandpa and Grandson spun across the finish line in fourth place.

Wilson jumped up and whooped, even though they'd barely missed placing, and ran over to her waiting place at the finish line. "Can we do it again, Momma? That was so awesome!" he begged.

Kathryn hugged Daddy. "You practically gave me a heart attack there for a minute on that spill."

"'Bout gave myself a heart attack," he chuckled. "But I'd do it again for him. It was fun. You could stand to have some fun, Katie-belle. You should try it."

"Oh, no. No way." She waved off that idea. "I'd be too scared."

"I'll go down the hill with you," Hunter offered.

She spat out an incredulous squeak.

Hunter snickered. "My God. I think your eyebrows disappeared under your hairline, you're so scandalized."

"What made you think I'd do such a thing? I'd be petrified!"

"Yes, but you'd be with me. And I have a lot of experience with these kinds of things."

Experience. *Riiiiight.*

"But I'm not dressed for it!" she protested, scowling down at her outfit. And for the record, it *was* a pretty cute ensemble. She was wearing a trim, shimmery, champagne-colored parka with a fluffy faux-fur lined hood, coordinating quilted snow boots with a tassel and a tall wedge heel, rose-colored leggings, a rose-colored angora sweater, and a short, wrap-around ivory knit skirt embroidered with a snowflake design.

No two ways about it, she was too cute to scoot.

But Hunter was having none of it. "What's the matter?"

He leaned in to murmur in her ear, brushing his stubbled jaw against her cheek as he did. "You chicken?"

"No, I'm not!" she sputtered, getting flustered at his closeness. "It's just that I—"

"Don't want to break a fingernail? Are you really that much of a princess?"

"I'm *not* a princess!"

He pushed his chest against her back, and squeezed her shoulders, as if he knew darn well the effect he was having on her. Oh, he didn't play fair! "But you're too dainty to go down a slope on a silly two-man inner tube. Sounds pretty princess-y to me. Or maybe you really are too chicken."

He tilted his head to consider her, and she turned, trying not to smile too. She swallowed. His mouth was *right there* by hers.

"Bock, bock!" he cackled.

"Oh, all right!" Kathryn grumbled. "I'll do it. But only if you steer the thing. I'd be hopeless."

They paid their entry fee and made their way to the top of the hill. Kathryn gulped as she previewed the course from this vantage point. It was a long, *long* way down.

"If we don't die doing this," she stabbed a finger at him, "remind me to kill you."

His face lit with triumph and he turned to grab the last two-man tube. But before he could get his hand on it, another couple snatched it away. Frowning, he searched for another one. "Man," he muttered. "I wish there was another—"

But then, lo and behold, Hunter spotted a *one-ma*n tube right near them. Apparently, the tiny thing was the last tube available. *Great.*

"Over here," he cried, sitting down and wedging himself against the back of the tube to make space for her. "We can ride this together!"

"But it's too dangerous! I'll get thrown—"

The starting buzzer sounded.

"There's no time!" Hunter commanded. "Get on!"

He yanked her arm, and she tumbled onto his lap as he pulled her tight against him. Folded in the hollow of his legs, she could very nearly wrap herself up in his open coat. The heat and the hard planes of his chest felt *way* too good. She shook her head to focus herself on the death ride in front of them. They both pumped with their arms, pushing themselves off to a flying start.

Wedged in with the other riders, they fell more than rode down the hill at breakneck speed. Rounding the curve, they bounced up onto their side and slid through a looping, curved tunnel. Kathryn screamed, and Hunter tightened his arms around her, cinching her against him. Even in her panicked state, she still could feel every ripple of his hard muscles under his shirt.

"Don't worry, I've got you," he hollered.

"That better be true!" she hollered back.

They pulled into a clearing and the top of another incline. Kathryn's stomach lurched as she comprehended the precipitous drop. If it wasn't a ninety-degree angle, it sure as heck seemed like one. They teetered, half over the edge and half not. Jesus, her feet were dangling in the thin air!

Kathryn hated heights.

She really, *really* hated heights.

"No. No way, Hunter! We cannot—"

"Too late now!"

"No!" she squealed.

"Yes!" He bellowed out a long, annoying *yeeee-haawwww* as he heaved them off over the side.

She burrowed back against him and howled as they hurtled down the slope. They went so fast they barely touched the ground. Falling, turning, twisting together, his arms locked around her like steel bands. Kathryn dug her fingers into Hunter's meaty biceps, hanging on for dear life. They skidded up against a crash wall made of inner tubes, and the velocity of it bounced them directly into the path of oncoming riders. But they were going too fast to hit them. Instead, they careened diagonally across the course and flew over an embankment and into a deep snowdrift. The tube crashed and rolled, tossing them both through the air.

Kathryn landed ass up, dammit, her head and hands stuck in a snowdrift up to her waist. Coughing and sputtering, she opened her eyes to nothing but white, fluffy snow. Thank God, this was the lightweight kind of snow that was probably made with a snow machine. She was able to move her arms and was halfway to freeing herself when she heard Hunter's amused voice behind her.

Hunter swiftly pulled her backward out of the snow by her hips, then flopped her over and began patting her down, trying to brush off the snow. She gulped. Here she was, laying on her back, with Hunter leaning over her, his hands all over her.

Patting her down—*helpfully*, of course.

His eyes were bright with the excitement of the race. And he was laughing outright at her ridiculous, bedraggled self. Suddenly, she didn't care how dirty she was if Hunter would keep looking at her like that. As if she were a different person. Not boring, predictable Kathryn, but a vibrant, sexy woman—someone who was fun, and funny, and desirable...and—and *happy*. The idea stopped her, and she nearly sighed in wonderment. Right now, maybe *wa*s happy, in all her happy places.

"You okay?" He smirked, at least trying to sound concerned through his snickering. "Nothing broken?"

"Just my pride," she muttered, trying her best to scowl. Truthfully, he was too cute to be mad at.

She sat up, and Hunter reached a gloved hand up to her face, shaking the worst of the snow from her hair with his fingers. "You did land butter-side down, didn't you?"

Their eyes caught for a long moment, and then she shoved at him in mock exasperation. "I think you did that on purpose."

He giggled and snorted as she struggled, his smile lighting up his whole face. Her shoving didn't budge him. "I guess you'll never know." He grinned, still staring at her face, her eyes, her mouth. She stopped her struggling, and settled for scowling at him instead.

And in the silence, a flicker of intention crossed Hunter's face. For a moment, the man's entire demeanor changed—his eyes going dreamy and dark with a slash of color rising across his cheekbones. Was he going to kiss her? God, she wished he would. Even under her coat, the hairs rose up on her arm, and she trembled with a kind of hot, physical awareness of him that made her breaths come in short. Hunter leaned dangerously close to her lips, but then no. She must have been mistaken. He pushed himself up to his feet abruptly, holding his hand out to pull her up. She didn't want to admit it, but she felt a bit...

You're disappointed, aren't you?

Yes, she was. She could practically draw a heat map on her body of every place he'd touched her. And the thought of laying a scorching hot kiss on him was unbearably tempting. But he'd pulled away.

Why?

Should she just grab him and steal a kiss? No—no, she wouldn't. She promised herself she'd never beg a man for his affections again, and she meant it. So she settled for searching Hunter's eyes for an answer. As she met his gaze, another flash of heat and vulnerability crackled across his expression, and then it was gone.

Hunter stepped away for a second, and came back holding her sodden wrap-around skirt in his hands. He looked like the cat that swallowed the canary. "I think you dropped this."

Heat rose to her cheeks as she yanked it out of his hands. She didn't know why she was so embarrassed. She was still covered with her tights, which were thick and lined and practically pants in their own right anyway. But Hunter seemed to be enjoying the view and watching her squirm, nonetheless.

Kathryn grumbled while she tied the bedraggled rag back around her waist. "Don't think your dimples are going to get you out of this one." She sniffed.

To his credit, Hunter stifled his snickering. But then he smiled even more, the expression lighting up his whole face. God, what glorious sight it was to see him so carefree. The tiny crease perpetually between his eyebrows seemed to fade away. Maybe it was almost worth her ruined outfit to see him finally relax. *Almost.*

"Come on." He grabbed her hand. "We'd better get back down the hill before they send out a search party."

Once they managed to find Daddy and Wilson in the crowd, they returned their inner tube. Then they hit one of the food trucks for mulled cider and some roasted sugar almonds, served in cute paper cones. They started to roam the streets again, but it was no time before Wilson spotted another of his anticipated Christmas Pass events, the "Crazy Christmas Robot Build." Teams were signing up to put together robots that would battle each other on the arena floor. The entire event was designed for adults to work together with the kids to create the entries. Most included simple click-to-build pieces, but for people with more advanced circuit board and mechanical skills, the event offered a "masters" category.

Hunter stopped in front of the sign, his eyes twinkling with interest. "Would you want to enter as a team, Wilson? You know, I build and fix cars for a living. I think if we all worked together, we'd have a real shot."

Wilson's eyes grew wide. "You'd do that?"

Hunter clapped Wilson on the back. "Sure, buddy. Sounds like my idea of a fun afternoon, we all could do it."

Daddy whooped. "I'm in. I love to tinker."

Kathryn scanned the schedule. It was two in the afternoon, and the bell for the start of the building phase would be ringing any minute now. At five, the bot battles would begin. "I'd help you guys, but I can barely hammer a nail, let alone build a robot. I'd be in the way. How about I let you boys get everything built, and I'll come to watch the competition when it starts? I'll shop around and relax. I could use the break."

Wilson ran up to her and threw his arms around her waist. "Thanks, Momma! This is going to be so cool! This is the best Christmas ever!"

She caught Hunter's eye and mouthed *thank you*.

Hunter inclined his head, as if he were tipping an imaginary hat. And, dammit, her heart practically turned over in her chest.

"Come on, kiddo." Daddy rapped Wilson's arm. "Let's go and let your momma do girl stuff."

"To guy stuff!" Wilson roared, and she smiled at the sound of them cheering as she sauntered away.

Kathryn walked back down onto Main Street and strolled along block after bedecked block lined with perfect boutiques, quaint gift shops, art galleries, restaurants, and more. Maybe she could find some distractions to keep her mind off Hunter, who was getting more damned attractive by the minute. Her mind turned back to that sled race. Even though it had scared her witless, she had to admit it had been exhilarating, as much for the adrenalin bath as for the sensation of being snuggled up underneath Hunter's coat. He was clearly trying to keep the day flirty and fun. And really, she could get on board with that. How long had it been since she'd felt that way? Come to think of it—had she *ever been* flirty and fun?

It pained her to admit it, but the answer was no. She'd always been so serious all the time, so focused on school, or her job, or her son. When she wasn't doing that, she was perpetually putting out some kind of fire with her family. But then Hunter had come along, completely out of the blue, making her feel *better*. Desirable. Maybe even...*carefree*.

Wasn't that the way you were supposed to be on vacation?

Kathryn's thoughts turned wistful as she walked along. Though she owed Hunter a debt of gratitude for saving their lives, she owed him more for the way he made her see herself—like a woman whose sexuality might burst into flame at any moment. Not that she had the faintest idea what she was going to do about that.

Cutting off those futile thoughts, Kathryn turned her attention back to the street around her. Every single store was interesting. She could spend a couple of weeks here, she'd bet, and never run out of great options for spending her time and money. But as she walked, she caught her reflection in one of the shop windows. Shocked, she stood and stared at herself, unable to look away.

Lord, she was a sight. Her tights were all muddy and damp, and her hair, still wet, lay stringy all along the sides of her face. Her eyes were huge and her ears stuck out. No wonder nobody had protested when she'd asked for some "me" time.

But that wasn't what had stopped her in her tracks. It was the lines and shapes of the face staring back at her in the glass. She'd always known she resembled her mother. But facing her reflection now, it hit her all over again, rolling over her in a bittersweet wave.

Momma.

My God, I resemble Momma in almost every way, don't I?

She touched her hand to the long strands of her platinum-blonde hair, a too-pale but distinctive shade she'd never had to dye. All she'd have to do was pull a few locks back from her face, flip up the ends, and she'd be her mother's carbon copy.

That was what mother had always wanted, wasn't it—a beautiful girl she could parade around? Mother had been so determined to teach Kathryn how to be the perfect Southern lady. She had no doubt that her momma had loved her, in her way. But Kathryn's childhood had been nothing but one big finishing school, with incessant lessons in how to stand, how to sit, how to walk, how to make charming conversation, how to mix the perfect sweet tea. As she'd gotten older, that had been followed with daily lectures on where to go, what to do, who to be friends with, what opinions to espouse, where to go to college, and, of course, how to snag the "right" man, among Momma's greatest hits. To this day, Kathryn could walk in high heels perfectly balancing a stack of books on her head, play the piano passably with her hands arched high over the keys, and arrange cut flowers like a professional. She could do those and a thousand other things that "ladies" were supposed to do to be happy, loved, and respected in their lives.

Funny, wasn't it, how none of that had worked—not for her, and definitely not for her momma.

As she stood there, starting blindly into the shop window, restless memories asserted themselves. Images flashed of Momma brushing Kathryn's hair on her wedding day, the emotions they evoked as fresh and clear as if she were there again. Even now, Kathryn could almost feel the crisp tugs on her scalp...just like she had that day...

Momma pulled Kathryn's shoulders around to face her as she finished pinning down the pearl-studded tiara that held Kathryn's long, cathedral-length veil.

No fewer than eight bridesmaids had littered the room, a hastily assembled crew of cousins and sorority sisters nervously pacing around in tasteful lavender satin dresses. Her beleaguered wedding planner and photographers and string/brass combo flitted about like so many gadflies. But Kathryn couldn't focus on the controlled chaos in the stuffy room, or the prospect of the four hundred guests waiting patiently for her in the church for this very hastily prepared wedding of the year.

She'd barely hidden the fact that she was four months pregnant under her designer gown, and she hadn't felt like she knew her groom nearly well enough. Her stomach churned with anxiety. Momma pulled the veil down over her face, and their eyes had met. And Kathryn had known, in an instant, that her mother could see Kathryn's fears went well beyond wedding-day jitters. It was perhaps the most real moment they'd ever shared. As she locked eyes with her momma that day, Kathryn's face flushed and her eyes had welled up with tears. But she battled them back, determined to marry the man who'd fathered her unborn child. Kathryn struggled for a moment to collect herself, but she had.

And Momma's face softened with something Kathryn

hadn't often seen from her—sympathy. "Baby girl," Momma breathed and reached out to grab her hands.

Finally, Kathryn worked up the courage to ask, "Will I be happy, Momma?"

Momma chuckled softly. "Oh, my darling, don't you know? Life isn't about being happy. Life is about being you—the real you—with every step and every choice you make. Don't you know, no man, no other person, can make those choices but you? Lord knows my life hasn't always been the best. But it's mine, and I've lived it, right or wrong, one choice at a time. When you walk down that aisle today, you'll step out into your life. Yours. You make it what it's going to be. Make it count."

How ironic. After a lifetime of telling her what to do, her momma had finally admitted that her daughter's life was her own, to screw up or enjoy as she saw fit.

The memory faded, and Kathryn realized it might have been the wisest piece of advice she'd ever gotten. Only she could choose her life. Only she could make it count. But had she? Or was she so focused on the grind of living and working and doing all the things she was supposed to do that she'd neglected her true self? Who was she even, once you stripped the professional designations away? A mother? A daughter?

Was that all?

Was it enough?

Kathryn wished, with all her heart, that she could find herself again, whoever that person may be. She wished she could break out, make a new start, and learn to live on her own terms. Maybe she could even find true love, if such a thing existed.

She'd been standing here, staring at herself for far too long. A bit self-conscious now, she turned to cross the street. But straight ahead, a bright, flashing sign glowed like the answer to a silent prayer, lighting the entrance to an adorable day spa and salon. "Walk-ins welcome," the sign said. Generally, spas weren't the kind of place she had time to visit. But she was a bit of a mess.

And maybe a change was what she needed—new day, new Kathryn, new choices. She walked up to the spa, gave the door a push, and walked in.

CHAPTER 6

Luckily for Hunter, one of his favorite guilty pleasures was watching *Bot Wars* on cable television. The gladiator-style robotic smack-downs on that show gave him a few ideas about how they should put their entry together now.

Not that this competition was as intense as the show. Hunter was a bit hamstrung by the time limit, and the fact that they couldn't weld and had to choose from some pre-made parts. But with all of them putting their heads together, they'd managed to come up with Black Lightning, the name of the bot they'd built. The name was perfect. The bugger was fast and lethal. It could be a fierce competitor.

Smiling with excitement, Wilson beamed up at him as he worked. Hunter ruffled the boy's hair and felt something almost like contentment and...*pride*. Just as quickly, he found himself nearly paralyzed by an overwhelming wave of regret that traveled through his chest. *Is this what it feels like to be a father?*

Hunter rubbed his chest a bit and looked away. There was no need to dredge up the past. Chances were slim to none that he'd ever have kids of his own. It was a shame, really. He loved kids, though he rarely got to spend much time around them. He especially enjoyed the antics of his young nephew and niece. He didn't get to see them nearly enough. But those two still weren't even in kindergarten yet.

This afternoon with Wilson was wonderfully different. The kid was smart as a whip and full of energy. Once they got their parts out in front of them and made a plan, the boy gave it a hundred percent. Wilson asked lots of questions and seemed to absorb everything Hunter and Huck were showing him. Some of the wiring they needed to do was too complex for him yet. But the child dove right in anyway, helping them assemble all the metal pieces. He was a cute little thing, puffing out his chest with accomplishment every time he finished a task.

While Wilson bounced around a lot, it was deceiving. He was unusually mature for his age, with a considered way of studying people that was exactly like his mother. A lot of other kids would've wandered off or whined to play some handheld video game after a few minutes. But Wilson stayed riveted on task. He watched Hunter intently as he showed the boy how to click the pieces of their circuit board in place and attach the tiny wiring. And with focus like that, Hunter would bet Wilson would be doing something like this all by himself in a year or two.

Huck gathered up all the rest of their spare parts and ran off to return the bits back to the contest organizers. Meanwhile, Hunter and Wilson worked together to click the last parts into place. Black Lightning wasn't flashy, but that was the point. It was very low to the ground, with a deep wedge cut across the front that was designed to flip its rivals over. Then an arm extended with a heavy mallet that could smash competitors to pieces. Hunter flipped the power switch on the remote control and gave it to Wilson.

The boy's eyes lit up. "Do you think it'll work?"

Huck gave his grandson an encouraging pat on the back. "Let's find out!"

Hunter opened his mouth to give Wilson a pointer or two about how the control worked, but like most kids, the child was a natural with a joystick. Wilson was overjoyed to see it could spin, charge, and parry with the best of them. Satisfied they had a working entry, Huck wandered off to gather up and dispose of all their garbage, still sipping from an ever-present coffee cup. How much booze had Huck had been "adding" into that cup throughout the afternoon? But it wasn't any business of his.

Hunter hadn't realized he'd been staring after Huck until Wilson tugged on his sleeve. The boy stood there, peering up at him as if he were trying to decide what to say. Then the child hurriedly looked at the ground.

Finally, Hunter patted him on the shoulder. "The match is coming up. Don't you want to keep practicing, buddy?"

Wilson's pure, earnest expression caught Hunter off guard. The child took a deep breath and stuck out his hand for Hunter to shake. "I haven't thanked you yet for saving us and all."

Hunter returned the handshake, but he sighed. "I keep telling y'all, you don't have to keep thanking me. I was happy to help you off that hill. I bought that tow truck for that very reason—to haul people out who need it."

"I know, Mr. Holliday, but—"

"Hunter. Call me Hunter."

"Okay, *Hunter*." Wilson nodded respectfully. "I want you to know that for a couple of minutes up there, Momma and Granddaddy wouldn't wake up. You know, Momma always says what doesn't kill you makes you stronger. But I guess I didn't see how we could get any stronger if we all were gonna be dead. Ugh, I'm not making any of this come out right. But I—I wanna say I'm glad we're not dead. And I'm glad you came along when you did, and I'm real, real glad you're spending your Christmas with us. It's been super cool so far."

And then the boy impetuously threw his arms around him and gave him a big bear hug. Hunter froze for a moment, shocked by the boy's sudden burst of affection, then relaxed into the embrace. He reminded himself again that this child wasn't his. But the bittersweet pang stung his chest, anyway. "You're welcome," he answered, ruffling Wilson's hair again. The boy ran off with his granddaddy to get in the last of his practice. Hunter found himself grinning as he watched the child go. What an afternoon this had been. He'd enjoyed it more than he realized he would.

"Awww, now that was cute," Hunter heard coming from behind him. That sultry Southern lilt could only be Kathryn.

But when he turned, he blinked in surprise. *My God. Is that really her? She's...oh, Lord, she's...*

She'd always been beautiful—perfectly styled and so elegant, she resembled some kind of unapproachable, pale fairy. But now? Now she was completely different—sporty and playful and so damn sexy, he could hardly hold himself together in one piece. She must've gotten a complete makeover while she was out. Her long hair was short now—a move he generally wouldn't have liked. But the short, shaggy cut only made her appealingly tumbled and achingly sexy. Her hair wasn't that icy blonde anymore, but a warm mix of honey-colored tones, and her brows and eyelashes were darker too. The cut, going up over her ears and down to a point at the nape, made her high cheekbones and long neck even more extraordinary. But it was the tumble of loose waves over her forehead he liked the best. It warmed up her whole face. Her eyes appeared bolder too, now that she was wearing glasses—a pair with turquoise frames that were big and round, with a bit of a point at the corners.

Though he was sure she hadn't dressed for his benefit, everything about what she was wearing was a turn-on designed to torture his dreams—blue jeans that clung to her lean legs, high-heeled turquoise cowboy boots, and that same, form fitting fuzzy sweater from before.

He flexed his hands absently, wondering how those downy fibers would feel under his fingertips. He'd bet she'd be so warm, and soft, and perfect, her breasts arching under his roaming hands...

He stifled the urge to groan. Again.

He hadn't a clue what to say to the woman. Hunter cleared his throat and shoved his hands in his pockets. "I never knew you wore glasses," he finally managed to say.

Kathryn never missed a trick. She looked like she was trying not to smirk, probably because he was so obviously flustered. "I wear contacts mostly," she answered. "But it's been so cold and windy. They were starting to bug me. Thank goodness the spa was connected to an optometrist's shop. I picked out the frames on a whim, and they were able to pop in a lens fitted exactly to my rather complex prescription while I got my hair done, if you can believe that. The service in this place is truly beyond belief. I felt like a racecar in the pit at the Indy 500. There was a whole team of people buffing and polishing and fixing me up, sometimes all at once. I still can't believe they got all that done in two hours. It's quite a change. Do you like it?" she asked, twirling around so he could soak up the whole effect.

"Yes," he answered, swallowing hard. God, her ass in those jeans...His throat went dry with desire, thoughts of touching her, undressing her crowding his mind. What was *wrong* with him? He couldn't look at a woman in a pair of *jeans* now without losing his ever-lovin' mind?

Kathryn caught him gawking. Her mouth curled up at the corners, and she couldn't tear her gaze away. Finally, she muttered "I—I suppose I'd better get up to the spectator seats."

He watched her as she got herself seated near their competition area. It took some waiting, but before he knew it, Wilson got his big chance to compete.

Hunter and Huck stayed down on the competition floor with the boy, yelling suggestions, cheering him on, and trying to offer as much support as they could. Surprisingly, his heart was in his throat as he watched Wilson go. But, as it turned out, Wilson didn't need anybody worrying about him. He won his first match handily, tossing over another much-bigger robot, like they'd practiced. They jumped and cheered and high-fived each other with abandon. Then the next match came, and the next. And Wilson kept winning, moving the robot with a remarkable, deadly efficiency for a boy of his age. The boy managed to stay in the game until the qualifier for the semi-final, when a robot with a saw attachment cut Black Lightning right through the middle.

Poor Wilson. The kid seemed more upset about the robot being bisected than he did about getting knocked out of the competition. He came running up to Hunter with the remains of the thing clutched in his hands. "It's busted!" Wilson moaned. "I was hoping I could take it home and keep it, but...we'll never fix it now."

Hunter took the broken bot out of the boy's hands and turned it over to inspect the damage. "It's not dead yet. I could take this back to my shop and fix it up so it'll be sturdier, and reinforce it. Maybe you could even suggest some new design elements."

Wilson's eyes got wide. "Really? You'd do that?"

"Sure. You'll have the toughest robot around," Hunter replied.

He felt Kathryn's hand on his arm. "Hunter! You don't have to go to all that trouble! I'm sure you have so many real customers..."

He laid his hand over hers. Her expression was uncertain, as if he were crossing some kind of magic line, showing such interest in Wilson. But he surprised himself by suddenly picking up her hand, and pressing a courtly kiss on the top of it. She was obviously flustered by the gesture, but she smiled brilliantly.

"I want to. It'll be fun," he insisted. "I can get started on it as soon as the roads get cleared and I can get back to my shop."

"Can I come too?" Wilson cried. "I want to work on it with you!"

"That depends on how many days it takes us to get out of Christmas Pass. But don't worry. One way or another, we'll get it done—even if we have to finish once you've gone back to school."

"You promise? For *real*?" Wilson jumped up and down with excitement.

"For real," Hunter promised, holding out his hand for Wilson to shake. Wilson took it, seeming truly overjoyed at the turn of events. As he watched Wilson scamper off, Hunter swallowed against the growing lump in his throat. He'd made the kid happy. And it felt nice to do something out of the ordinary for someone. It made him feel, well, almost Christmas-y.

Gratitude glowed in Kathryn's smile. "It appears you made a friend there. I hope this isn't all too much trouble."

"It isn't. A kid like that is a pleasure—smart, mature for his age and dying to learn. No, I wouldn't mind having a new apprentice."

Kathryn gave him another one of her long, appraising looks. "You like kids. I'll bet you're the kind of man who's always wanted a house full of children. Am I right?"

Hunter was quickly learning that Kathryn had the ability to see right through to the heart of things. He hadn't been prepared for it this time. The question brought him up short, and he winced. "Yes," he rasped out, his throat tightening with the memory. "But it never worked out." That was an understatement, but he hardly felt like getting into the whole sad story right now. He and Laney had tried and tried for years, but no luck. Hunter had wanted her to try fertility treatments, had the money set aside and everything. But his wife had refused. As a labor and delivery nurse, Laney had known well what couples went through to get those treatments. She'd always said if she couldn't have a child by the time she was thirty-five, she'd adopt. But she'd died when she was thirty-one. And in that time, she'd had two miscarriages. Yeah, motherhood was another thing he'd failed to do for her, and, honestly, it made his heart lurch uncomfortably in his chest every time he thought about it. He could see that Kathryn hoped he'd talk some more, maybe explain his answer about the whys or why nots. But he...*couldn't*. His mouth had clamped shut like a vise.

Kathryn gently put her hand on his arm again, a movement that seemed to say she understood his need to change the subject. "Come on. I'm starved. I bet you are too. Let's see if we can get something to eat."

They set off walking through town, searching for something they'd all like. They passed several restaurants that would appeal to Kathryn—sushi bars, seafood restaurants, and other healthy eating establishments. But the men in the delegation vetoed those choices, especially Wilson, who made loud gagging noises at the suggestion. As much as they liked the inn, they decided they preferred something new and different tonight.

Kathryn stopped, and scanned the street ahead of them. "You know what we need? Some kind of a country diner. You know, some place that's big and noisy and sells home-style food."

"Yeah!" Wilson piped up. "Some place with a mechanical bull! I've always wished I could ride a mechanical bull!"

"Good God." Huck snickered, patting his grandson on the back. "I admire your get up and go, kiddo. But the last time I saw a mechanical bull was in the movies. I doubt very seriously we're going to be finding any place with one of those. And even if there was a restaurant around here that had one, you'd probably have to be over eighteen to ride it."

"Yeah," Kathryn called back to them. "I can't think of a faster way to break your ne—"

But then she stopped dead in her tracks, her mouth open. The rest of them walked up behind and they were too shocked to say a word. They'd turned a corner, only to come up to a brightly lit, timber frame building with a big wrap-around porch. *Hoot n'Annie's*, the sign said. There were several other promotional signs too—*Chicken-Fried Family Fun* and *Home of the Hillbilly Bison Burger* and, most tellingly, *Can you Best Bessie, our Mechanical Bull?*

Hunter shook his head. Here it was, yet another example of someone saying the word "wish" and it getting fulfilled, exactly to order. Was he the only one noticing this?

Her eyes were round with amazement, but Kathryn chuckled.

Christmas Pass was absolutely, positively spooking him out. But at least they'd figured out where they going to dinner.

CHAPTER 7

By the time Kathryn finished her plate of ribs and helped Wilson polish off his chocolate brownie sundae, she felt like a beached whale. But she could hardly say she regretted it. She'd never had ribs that good. They were so succulent and fall-off-the-bone perfect that her self-control deserted her. Now she was stuffed. She consoled herself that at least she'd replaced the fries with a plate of kale. She made a mental note to get an early wakeup call tomorrow so she could try out the inn's extensive gym setup.

Just then, a middle-aged couple walked up to their table, brimming with welcomes and howdy-dos. The man was mostly bald but had a brushy white mustache and beard so thick, it seemed like all the hair on his head had decided to migrate to his upper lip for the winter. His eyes twinkled and he wore a bow tie that had flashing red Christmas lights on it. The plump, kindly woman with him, not one to be outdone, wore a tinsel necklace, a Christmas sweater, and a headband with sequined reindeer antlers twinkling with tiny LED lights.

The man introduced himself as Hoot, and his wife as

Annie, hence the restaurant's name. "We thought we'd come say hello and see how your meal is treatin' you."

"Like the stuffing in the Christmas goose." Kathryn groaned.

"I think that means she liked it," Daddy quipped, and Annie beamed with genuine pleasure in response.

Kathryn pushed her plate away, stealing another glance at the thick, pickled wood paneling and the hunting trophies hanging all around. In between the animal heads were bar lights, cheap oil paintings of mountain scenes, and assorted bric-a-brac. It was a quirky, quaint place, and the food was phenomenal. It was no wonder why Hoot n' Annie's was jam-packed.

"That was one fine meal," Hunter declared. "This place is quite the local institution. How long have you been running it?"

Annie linked her arm with her husband and cocked her head proudly. "Me and Hoot opened many years ago. We don't know anything else."

"Is Hoot your real name?" Wilson piped up.

"Nah." The man bowed. "Real name's Owsley Winter-white. Everyone calls me Hoot and always has. Can't remember when it started."

"Are you from around here?" Hunter jumped in. "Did you grow up in Christmas Pass?"

"Goodness, yes." Annie canted her head at them. Evidently, the woman was confused by their question. "Where else would we be from? We're all part of that small-town Christmas tradition."

How odd. So the only outsiders here were the tourists? Annie made it sound as if they'd never set foot past the city limits. Something about that made Kathryn distinctly uneasy. "So everyone who lives here has been here for generations, is that what you're telling me?"

"Yes," Annie answered.

"Does anyone ever leave?" Kathryn pressed. "You know, move away to pursue their fortune elsewhere?"

Annie seemed truly confused at her question. "No, of course not. We've never wanted to leave. Why would we, when everything you could wish for is right here?"

Kathryn exchanged a look with Hunter. He rolled his eyes, making light of it. But as nice as Hoot and Annie were, there was something about them that made the hairs stand up on the base of her neck. It was silly, really. They were only snowed in for a couple of days, not stranded for all eternity. Still, she couldn't quite put her finger on it...

Wilson distracted Kathryn from asking more questions. Seeing his opportunity to get his bull ride, he launched into asking a thousand questions about the mechanical bull, begging passionately to ride it.

Kathryn crossed her arms over her chest. "Wilson! If you think I'm letting you ride a mechanical bull, right after you've stuffed yourself with a big dinner, you've got another thing coming."

"Oh, ma'am, he wouldn't ride Bessie anyway. His legs aren't big enough to get a hold on it," Hoot answered. "We have a kid-sized bull right next to it that's every bit as challenging. We could put it on the slow cycle."

Kathryn gazed into Hoot and Annie's guileless faces and wondered if this would be the thing that finally did her son in for the day. He never did know when to quit. But Wilson was getting older. Children needed to explore their limits to develop and grow, right? Maybe she could loosen up. He'd done okay with the sledding, hadn't he? "All right. I'll allow it. But only on the slow setting, okay?"

"Woo-hoo!" Wilson hollered, hopping over the fence and bounding over to the mechanical bull setup.

They followed him to the ring, leaning against the fence

to cheer him on. Hoot strapped the boy to the bull and showed him how to wrap the strap around his wrist to hold on. Wilson grinned from ear to ear as the bull rumbled to life. Though it made her hold her breath with apprehension, it was fun to see Wilson so excited. The "bull" moved up and down, rolling slowly from front to back.

Okay, that's tame enough.

But Wilson frowned. "Oh, come on. That's it? This ain't nothin', Momma. It's like one of those stupid penny horses they have at the grocery store. Can't I go faster? Please?"

Kathryn looked to Daddy and Hunter to see if they had an opinion. But they only shrugged. "Okay, I'll let you up one level if you correct your speech. A Winslow doesn't use ain't, or double negatives."

Wilson rolled his eyes. "It *isn't anything*. There, now faster, Momma!"

Kathryn waved to Hoot. "One more level."

Hoot complied, and now, the bull was rolling in earnest and doing small half turns.

Wilson was ecstatic. "Hey, Momma! I'm in the rodeo!" Her boy showed no signs of falling off. In fact, he was doing great, gripping the sides of the pommel with his legs and keeping his grip firm on the strap.

"I think he can do one more," Annie urged. "Why don't you let him try it?"

Kathryn agreed, but she soon wished she hadn't. Stunned, she could only stand there in shock as the ride went from manageable to el Diablo on steroids. The machine whipped around in 180-degree turns, first one way, then the next. And the bucking action was tremendous, bouncing Wilson several inches up off his seat with each twist and turn.

"Uh-oh," Huck uttered. "You'd better—"

"Momma!" Wilson cried out. "Make it stop! Make it—" Wilson froze in fear, hunching up over the saddle horn with his eyes squeezed shut.

"You heard him!" Hunter barked before Kathryn could even open her mouth. "Stop the thing!"

Hoot reached for the lever to stop the machine, but the control bar snapped off in his hands. "Oh no! It's stuck!"

Trying not to panic, Kathryn yelled out encouragements to her boy to keep him calm. Hunter vaulted over the railing. Though he tried to pull Wilson off, the turning, whipping motion of the bull made it impossible.

Daddy, thankfully, saved the day. While Hoot and Annie tried to work the stuck lever, he was smart enough to follow the cord to where the bull was plugged in and yank it out of the wall. The bull slowed, and Hunter quickly pulled him off, setting her boy down on his wobbling feet.

Hoot and Annie rushed over, full of apologies that Kathryn was in no mood to hear. She was mad at them for portraying this ride as harmless when clearly it wasn't. And she was mad at herself for letting her guard down. Wasn't this what happened whenever she tried to loosen things up? Somebody got hurt. Now her son was standing in front of her, his eyes practically spinning in his head. The poor kid was desperately green around the gills.

"My stomach hurts," he wailed. "Why is everything spinning?"

"Because *you* were spinning, pumpkin, and now you're not," Kathryn soothed, patting Wilson's head and holding him tight—from behind. She'd bet the boy would be puking within the hour. Or maybe not, if they could get him back to the inn, and to bed.

It had been too much excitement for one day. But she could hardly blame the child. Christmas Pass was packed so full of fun choices, it was hard not to binge on the buffet.

Even she—careful, responsible, boring Kathryn—had been pulled into it. It was only eight-thirty at night, still pretty early. But she supposed they should call it a night.

"Let's get our coats and go back. Come on, son. You need to lie down and get a good night's rest before you barf up your socks."

Wilson didn't protest when she walked him back to their booth and pulled his limp arms into his parka.

"You two don't have to turn in so early," Daddy offered. "Let me take him back. It only takes one person to take care of a pukey kid."

Kathryn opened her mouth to protest but before she could get a word in edgewise, Annie came scurrying over. "Oh, ma'am, we are so sorry. I don't know what happened to our controls. We've taken the bull down for repairs. I'm heartbroken we made your dear boy sick. Let us make it up to you. Are you staying at the inn? For how long?"

Kathryn shrugged. "Probably four more days, or until the roads are plowed out, whichever comes first."

"Then for as long as you stay here, you can eat or drink here anytime, at no charge. We have a hundred percent satisfaction guarantee here at Christmas Pass. And I'll be darned if you leave here thinking like we didn't do right by you."

Kathryn waved away Annie's concern. "Oh, that's very kind but, really, it was an accident. You don't have to—"

"Matter of fact, why don't you and your gentleman friend here stay for drinks?" Annie interrupted. "It will be a good way to unwind at the end of the day. I'll bring out some of our best Irish Cream drinks. It's good for what ails ya."

Before Kathryn could argue, Daddy was out the door with Wilson, and Annie had shuttled Kathryn and Hunter into an intimate, half-circle booth for two.

Hunter shook his head in that bemused way of his. "Boy, Hoot and Annie don't take no for an answer, do they?"

"That's okay." Kathryn shrugged, stretching herself out in the booth. "It's nice to relax with adult conversation at the end of the day. Don't get me wrong. I love my son to pieces. But it is good to get a break from mom duty every now and then."

Annie hustled up with their drinks—two of the most impressive coffees she'd ever seen, served in enormous red and white speckled tin mugs with a towering stack of whipped cream and crushed peppermints. "Now remember, y'all, that's on the house." She motioned to the cup. "Go on, and tell me what you think."

Kathryn took a long pull of the steaming, decadent concoction and groaned with pleasure. "My God, that may be the best coffee I've ever had. What's in it again?"

Annie winked. "A double serving of Christmas magic, that's what."

Kathryn and Hunter rolled their eyes and exchanged an amused look.

Annie stuck her hands on her hips and did her best to appear affronted, but the blinking lights on her antler headband made it funnier. "Now, don't you laugh at me. The only way to get Christmas magic is if you *believe*, you know."

Kathryn grinned apologetically and wiped a blot of whipped cream off her nose. "If you can mix drinks like this, then I promise, we'll believe."

"That's what I want to hear, dear." Annie patted her on the shoulder and walked off to tend to other customers.

Kathryn rolled her shoulders and willed herself to simply enjoy this winter's night. She'd let too many things crowd her mind today. Truth be told, she couldn't wait to spend some alone time unwinding with Hunter. For some reason, this man's presence calmed and centered her. She couldn't say why that was, really. Maybe it had something to do with the rescue. But Kathryn suspected there was more to it. What that "it" was, "it" was too early to say.

And as they sat there, quietly sipping their drinks, Kathryn gradually became acutely aware of Hunter's big, masculine presence in the booth, and the heat radiating from his leg and shoulder as it brushed against hers. He had a certain ruggedness about him that was almost hardened, but yet, there was an undeniable warmth and self-effacing, unaffected charm that seemed to soften those hard edges. How different he was from her ex-husband, who was so polished, he practically glowed with the force of impeccable grooming, a well-considered wardrobe, and practiced Southern manners.

Hunter Holiday was everything that Sterling Winslow wasn't. And yet, even though they'd really only spent thirty-six hours together, Kathryn found herself drawn to this man in every possible way.

Yeah, that's right. The man is temptation on a silver platter.

Exhibit A: the way Hunter drank that frothy coffee. He hummed with delight as he tilted back his cup, tipping his head back to expose his strong, muscled neck. Having wrung out the last drop, he sat down his cup and gave her a long, considered perusal with those arresting, expressive eyes of his.

Ah, there it was again—that feeling he gave her whenever he held his eyes on her. Heat traveled through her body from her head to her toes. She couldn't deny it. No matter how much she tried to keep her mind on other things, Kathryn couldn't help but notice everything about him—especially the way he cocked his head and listened attentively to whatever she had to say, giving her every bit of his attention. And that was to say nothing about the way his broad-shouldered back tapered down into a perfect vee, or how his jeans rode so perfectly over his very enticing posterior. He'd be as fun to touch and taste as he was to look at. She was sure of it.

But it was about more than the sexy way he made her feel. He was a good friend to her family too, wasn't he? She couldn't discount his easy rapport with Wilson, or how he'd even managed to find Daddy's pugnacious charm amusing. When it came to attractiveness, Hunter Holliday ticked off boxes she hadn't even known she had.

So strange, isn't it, feeling this way? A little breathless and befuddled...

"So, are you regretting being stranded in the middle of nowhere with a total stranger yet?" Hunter asked, snapping her out of her thoughts.

"I'd have to find you strange for you to be a stranger, wouldn't I?"

Hunter chuckled. "Fair enough." He crossed his arms on the table and leaned in. "I gotta tell you, you've been nothing but one big surprise after another, from the moment I found you on that hill."

"Really?" She snorted. "'Surprising' isn't a word that's ever been used in the same sentence as my name. It's more like 'reliable, predictable, steady Kathryn' on most days. So, what has surprised you?"

"I would've expected someone who had such expensive reservations at the Greenbrier to be in a total snit over being stranded. But you shrugged. And then there was the spill you took sledding today. Most women who took the time to pretty themselves up in the morning wouldn't have been able take a ruined outfit in stride. And instead of going back to your room and changing, you came back with a total makeover. That was a pretty adventuresome choice. And I didn't expect you to cave on the bull riding thing, either."

"That last one was a mistake."

"Maybe, maybe not." He shrugged "But it was a call not a lot of mothers would've made. I doubt Wilson will ever forget it."

Kathryn winced. "Yeah, and not in a good way, unfortunately. So, you're saying you didn't expect me to be a permissive mother?"

He picked up her hand, inspecting her sparkly pink manicure and lightly toying with her fingertips. "No, I expected you to be a princess. And you're not."

He was dangerously close to holding her hand now, just for the pleasure of it. Kathryn huffed out a nervous chuckle. "Alas, I may give the appearance of being a princess, but I lack the requisite princess accessories—the adoring court, the fairy godmother, Prince Charming, for instance."

"I take it your ex wasn't Prince Charming, then."

Kathryn blanched, wanting to smack herself for walking right into that question. She'd promised herself she'd never be one of those bitter exes, for her sake and for Wilson's. "No, he wasn't." She groaned. "But he wasn't so terrible, either. He and I weren't— Well, we weren't *compatible*. He couldn't help it, and neither could I. It was better for everyone if we parted ways. That was five years ago. He's still a good dad to Wilson, and we're firm friends in spite of it all."

The interest in Hunter's eyes suggested that her breakup with Sterling was a thread he wanted to keep pulling. Kathryn cast her eyes down to the table and fiddled with her coffee cup, bracing herself for follow up questions. They never came. Hunter must have realized he was wading into painful territory.

Kathryn took another sip of her coffee, grateful for

Hunter's restraint. It seemed like the *so- why-did-you-get-divorced* question was the first topic of conversation when she went out on the rare date. Her divorce should be ancient history by now. But if she allowed herself to dwell on her failed marriage, her chest would end up aching with a strange, hollow disappointment. And she'd had all the heartache she could take. Sterling wasn't exactly her favorite topic.

Hunter laced his fingers through hers, and Kathryn was so fixated on the sensation of his strong hand wrapped around hers, that she almost didn't hear him ask, "So, have you had much luck on the dating scene since then?"

The question brought her up short. Kathryn considered Hunter for a second, gazing into his expectant eyes. *Wow, there it is, as clear as if he'd planted a flag in the ground. He's interested.*

Kathryn swallowed hard, wishing she knew how to answer the man. She wanted to paint a picture of some alluring, exciting dating life she'd had. But she thought back over the overall hot mess she'd encountered in the dating market—the ghosting, the bread-crumbing, and the near-endless variety of passive-aggressive selfishness that pretty much screamed *he's just not that into you*. It was hardly a ringing endorsement of her desirability. For a while, she'd wondered what was wrong with her, really, that she couldn't seem to keep a man's interest. Her paramours all seemed to fade away without an explanation, whether she was sleeping with them or not. Then, she'd finally gotten disgusted. She'd sworn off the whole mess about a year ago, vowing she'd never use another dating app, website, or matchmaking service again. And the crickets had been chirping in her bedroom, metaphorically speaking, ever since.

Kathryn curled her lip with a wryness she hoped didn't

appear bitter. "I believe that luck has eluded me, Hunter. Let's leave it at that."

Hunter huffed out a rueful sound. "Can't say I've had much luck, either. Not that I've really given it much of a try."

She studied his pained expression. *There's more to that story, isn't there?* After a few moments, she rested her hand over top of his to remind him he wasn't alone. And, she had to admit, to remind *herself* that she wasn't alone.

"You lost a wife in that crash, didn't you?"

He sucked in a breath. She'd surprised him again, apparently. "How did you—"

"A hunch. You're so protective and easy to be with. You're a good companion, too—the sort of man who falls into that role as if it's second nature. You'd be surprised how very many men don't have that core set of skills. And the way you reacted to the blood on my face, it told me you had to have lost someone in that crash. You wouldn't have had those kind of lingering effects if it'd only been you in that car. It didn't take a PhD in psychology to figure it out."

Hunter locked eyes with her, as if he were transfixed and utterly at a loss for what to say. But as she'd frequently found in her practice, the best way out of these situations was through.

She continued to press. "It was a good marriage, wasn't it, Hunter?"

"Yes," he whispered, "the best. She was my everything."

"You were married a long time?"

"Nine years. But we were together a lot longer than that. Our first date was junior prom, and we never stopped after that."

"What was her name?"

Hunter met her gaze with effort. "Laney," he answered,

grimacing at the pronounced break in his voice. He cleared his throat. "Her name was Laney."

There was a world of pain behind those eyes, pain she wished for all the world that she could lift from him. Whatever it was that he was beating himself up about, she was sure he didn't deserve it. But she sensed that pushing him more on the subject would be unwise and, most likely, rude. Hunter had his stories, and she had hers. She'd respect that.

Steering the conversation to safer ground, Kathryn asked him about Holliday Hot Rods. As Hunter described it, the shop was a surprisingly large enterprise he'd inherited in Lewisburg. Though Hunter had talked some about it before, he really lit up this evening. He told her all the ins and outs of his operation. Holliday Hot Rods had five full-time employees and a few hourly employees, the business attracting clients from all over the world who wanted high-end restorations of vintage cars. West Virginia wasn't such an odd place to have such an operation, he explained, because it allowed Hunter to keep his operating expenses low, while keeping him close enough to his big-money contacts in D.C. and up the eastern seaboard.

Hunter didn't have pictures to show her because of their dead phones—another unaccountably bizarre Christmas Pass phenomenon. But Hunter had such a beguiling way of describing the cars—the showy, artistic paint jobs, the thrill of hearing one of his engines fire for the first time, the excitement of putting his hands on the steering wheel and rolling down the highway. She asked him question after question. Kathryn could have listened to him all day, his stories making her feel like she was in the seat beside him, taking off for adventure, right then and there, on the open road.

How nice it was to see a man who so thoroughly loved

his job. "You know, I've always had a fondness for flashy cars. Does that surprise you?"

"What, you're not driving a ten-year-old Volvo?"

Kathryn pantomimed as if she were removing an imaginary knife from her chest. "Ugh! You wound me! Don't let that beat-up Suburban fool you. My main ride back home is a flashy Mini Cooper Countryman. It's ivory with black stripes down the hood, with a black top."

Hunter chuckled. "Hey, there's nothing wrong with a Mini Cooper. It's the sort of car that's cute. But in my world, that's not flashy. That's off the rack."

"But I bought the door lights that flash the mini logo on the ground when you open the door!" she protested.

He snorted. "So now it's cute. As the dickens."

She slapped his arm. "So what do you think I should drive, then?"

And just like that, the air shifted, as if the energy that always thrummed between them intensified somehow.

He unlaced his hands from hers, and slid his arm around her shoulders. "I'd do you up a 1970 MG Midget, something kind of racy and exciting. I'd use misty grey paint, to match your eyes. On the inside, there'd be a curly maple dash and soft, ivory leather that's impossibly silky under your hand. I'd set it off with some blush pink piping, for an accent. Once you took a ride in it, you'd never want anything else."

Oh. My. Lord. Did he know how sexy that sounded?
Yes—oh, *yes he did.*

Hunter's eyes crinkled with amusement at the edges, but his eyes radiated heat.

Her throat went dry with desire. "It sounds beautiful," she croaked. "The perfect ride."

"It would suit you," he answered, never taking his eyes off hers.

Is it getting hot in here?

Eager to lighten the sexual tension, Kathryn chuckled. "It may. But a hot number like an MG might be a bit too much for the boring life I lead. Seems like it would be a waste to leave it in the parking lot at the school or at the grocery store."

Hunter grinned at her as he leaned back in his seat. "Ah, yes, but you could put on a neck scarf and sunglasses and convince everyone you're Grace Kelly while you're doing it."

"Not terribly likely," Kathryn scoffed.

Hunter stopped and considered her again for a moment. "Tell me about your life, Kathryn. Is it really that boring?"

"Spectacularly. But not terribly unhappy, either."

Kathryn proceeded to regale him with tales about her adventures as a clinical psychologist, since there was hardly any time in her life for anything else besides her job and her son. In her affluent end of Roanoke, she tended to see a lot of people with failing marriages, mid-life crises, and persistent family dysfunctions. Most of her patients mainly needed someone objective to talk to, someone who'd listen without judgment. Of course, she did see patients with significant depression, illnesses like schizophrenia, and such. For them, it was a matter of staying on the right medicine, having healthy habits, and avoiding triggering circumstances.

"Is it like the counselors you often see in the movies, you know, where you sit with your tablet on your lap and answer all the questions with another question?"

She smirked. "Sometimes. But mostly it's not. Sometimes, you may be the only thing standing between that patient and despair, or a descent into very serious mental health issues, or dysfunctional patterns in their relationships."

"You love your work, don't you?"

"I suppose I do. It's important work for my patients, and for me. Our office building is in the restored historic part of downtown. It's a big, beautiful old building. The partners and I have our offices on the bottom floor, and Wilson and I live in the condo on the upper floor. The building is stately and full of character. All I have to do is walk a few steps to get to work each day."

He clucked in surprise. "I live over top of my shop too. We're in a repurposed factory. There's a small garret upstairs I've redone to be like an industrial loft. It's not much, but it's all I need. I used to live in a bigger house, but I rent it out now. I don't want to deal with all that space."

"Why not sell it?"

Hunter's mouth clamped shut, and a faint tick bounced on his jaw. Was that the house he shared with Laney? It must have been. "It belonged to my grandparents, and then my parents," he finally admitted. "But it's been in the family for a few generations. It's a Victorian farmhouse with a hundred and five acres of land attached."

"Sounds marvelous."

"It is." He sighed heavily. "But it's not who I am now."

"So...who are you then, Hunter Holliday?"

Hunter gave her a wry smile, but she could see how deeply unsettled the question made him. "I can see why you're a psychologist, Kathryn. You always know how to ask those hard questions, don't you?"

She felt an immediate stab of remorse. "I'm—I'm sorry, Hunter. I've got no right to pepper you with intrusive questions."

He answered with a rueful shrug. "Oh, it's all right. I only wish I knew how to answer you. Some days, I know who I am and what I'm about, and some days, I don't."

"Hunter, I think every person alive could say the same thing."

His expression got a little introspective, and he traced little circles on the top of her hand. After all the hours they'd spent together, and all the activities they'd shared today, both of them seemed at a loss for what to say next.

Kathryn let her gaze travel around the room. It was a big place—one enormous room filled with booths and sturdy pine tables. The crowd had thinned out considerably since they'd come in. Apparently, Hoot n'Annie's was winding down for the night. Maybe it would be closing down soon.

"It's funny," Kathryn sighed. "This place in so many ways seems like it's right out of Texas or something—like a cross between a honky tonk and a Cracker Barrel. You'd think they'd have a band, or dancing or something."

Hunter cocked an eyebrow. "Do you like to dance?"

"Yes, but most of the time, it's been general dancing in a club, or a bit of the shag or swing at a charity benefit. I've always wished I could line dance in a real honky tonk. Sterling would have died before he set foot in one, though."

She studied Hunter's face, which had suddenly gone still, completely thunderstruck by something that was happening right behind her. He was white-faced even, and grim.

Turning around, she blinked, not quite believing what she was seeing. *It couldn't be.* Hoot and Annie must have pulled back an extra wall or something, because behind her, a band began warming up on stage, and people shuffled up to an expansive wooden dance floor. Colored lights swirled over it, and the band broke into a fast instrumental that had patrons queuing up for line dancing.

She turned back to Hunter, whose color seemed to be returning now. "Do you know how to dance, Hunter?"

"Yeah, um, yeah," he muttered absently, still seeming

confused. "My mother ran a dance studio in our garage for kids. She made me learn the steps to everything. I had to be a partner to all her students."

How perfect! "Oh, please, please will you show me?"

Hunter swallowed hard, apparently a bit nervous about it. But he agreed. Her stomach fluttered, actually *fluttered* at the idea of him holding her. Kathryn almost laughed out loud at the surprise of it. *Oh yes, I'm going to do this, and I'm going to enjoy it.*

He wrapped his big, strong hand around hers, giving her a couple of his heart-stopping shy smiles as they made their way to the dance floor. And oh, when the music started, dancing with Hunter was even more glorious than she'd expected. The man was a fabulous teacher, helping her get into step quickly for the electric slide. She squealed with delight as she turned and scuffed and shimmied in her new cowgirl boots. And he laughed with her, happiness shining in his eyes.

Kathryn was a passable dancer, but she couldn't match the surprising grace of Hunter Holliday on the dance floor. His form was great, his movements fluid but masculine. He never slouched, or hunched over, or got off the beat like so many men often do. They did line dance after line dance, and even a round of Texas two-step, which left her breathless and giggling. His sure hands guided her through turn after complicated turn with a lead so strong, she didn't have to think about a thing but moving her feet in time. They actually felt light moving across the floor—a sensation she'd never felt before—as if the music was a current that thrummed just through them.

Then the band slowed down even more, covering a familiar tune—was that "Bless the Broken Road" by Rascal Flatts? All the couples paired up, wrapped their arms around each other, and started slow dancing. She fully expected Hunter to leave the floor, and she started to. But he grabbed her hand and pulled her back with a flourish.

She twirled into his rock-hard chest, and he circled his arms around her, cinching her to him from hip to shoulder. The intense contact shocked her senses, making her breath catch in her throat. But she couldn't say she was upset. Oh no, he smelled and felt far too good for that.

"Come on, Kathryn, you said you wanted the full country dancing experience," he rasped, soft and silky against her ear. "Wrap your arms around my neck."

Kathryn did as she was told, sliding her hands up his chest until they came to rest at the firm sinews at the base of his neck. She slid her fingertips over the neatly trimmed ridge of his hair as it tapered down to his collar. He still smelled like coffee, and the heat of his skin radiated through his shirt, no doubt from all their dancing.

She tilted her hips against his, molding herself to him. Hunter's breath hitched from the contact, and he smirked down at her. She was playing with fire. She knew it. But she couldn't stop herself. All her instincts were screaming for her to get more of his touch, his feel, and his unique, woodsy scent. Even now, he still smelled like the mountains to her—something so rich and elemental and earthy, there wasn't a word she could think of that would define it.

Hunter held his mouth close to her ear and murmured, "So, did I fulfill your honky-tonk fantasy?"

She didn't have to see him. She could hear the sexy smirk on his face. "The judge's table gives you a ten on expression, but an eight for form."

"Only an eight, huh? Why?"

"Your partner was slowing down your vibe."

"Really?" He unexpectedly twirled her out and right back to him. Then he scooped her down into a dip and whipped her back up while she panted and squealed with laughter. He put both hands on her hips now, lightly bending his knee between hers and swiveling a bit as he pulled her hard against him. He tilted his forehead against hers as they swayed together to the beat. God, Hunter Holliday was so sexy, she just might spontaneously combust.

"See?" he breathed. "Nothing about you slows down my vibe, Kathryn."

Hunter circled his arms tighter around her, and they settled back into a slow sway. Moving together in time, she could practically feel every muscle working in his back and chest and legs as he held her. They moved around the dance floor so effortlessly, she wasn't even aware of her feet hitting the floor. Restless energy rippled under his skin, tingling her fingertips. God, the pure electricity of him—had she ever been this aroused by a man's sheer presence? All her senses crackled to life, as if they'd lain dormant all these years, waiting to be called to the surface.

As they moved, he pressed his cheek against hers, his stubble rasping gently. Kathryn's whole body felt jangled, like it was humming on a different frequency. Her pulse kicked up, her heartbeat hammering against her ribs. Something was happening between them—something perfect and strong and...*absolutely undeniable.*

Hunter regarded her with eyes dark with...with what? Desire? Tenderness?

God, she hoped so. She needed him to feel it too. She needed him close to her, in ways she couldn't quite explain to herself. Without words, without warning, he tipped the warmth of his mouth to hers, brushing his lips against hers, as if inviting her to have a very, very sensual conversation. And she shuddered at the sharp, delicious frisson of heat that coursed between them. Before her mind could register what she was doing, she kissed him back, exploring him with a curious intensity she'd never felt before. His mouth was drugging, insistent but tender, feathering kisses against her with exquisite care. And then their lips parted, and he gave her more. Nothing could be more perfect, more intimate, than this. The dizzying taste of him filled her—salty sweat and boozy coffee and *man*. She tightened her arms around his neck and arched herself against him, pulling him down to her, kissing him deeper, harder.

Kathryn knew she was taking it up a notch, and she didn't care. Hunter chuckled softly against her lips and answered her challenge, his mouth demanding, claiming. A powerful shiver passed down Hunter's back as he planted hot, lingering kisses on the hollows of her shoulder, her throat. He wanted her. Neither one of them could deny it. The enormous, bulging evidence of it was obvious, pressing against her hip. Good God, picturing *that* made her head spin.

Could boring old Kathryn really be turning on a man like big, strappin' Hunter Holliday?

Hunter pulled his head back and stared down at her, softly stroking her cheek with his thumb. He seemed to be trying to put on the brakes, to compose himself. The way his brows were bunched up, he seemed surprised and almost concerned at the strength of his reaction to her. So was she.

"Lord," he huffed out between panting breaths. "You're full of surprises."

She ran the backs of her knuckles over the shadow of stubble along his jaw. "So are you."

The song, at long last, ended. Chastened by the incredible, overwhelming experience they'd both clearly had, they reluctantly left the dance floor. The band had kicked back up to a fast song anyway. By mutual assent, they decided it was time to head back to the inn. They walked back in weighty but companionable silence. Neither one of them seemed particularly inclined to talk about what had happened between them, as if by putting words to it, they'd somehow break the connection. They walked in silence, hand in hand, until they got to her door.

Kathryn leaned back against the doorjamb, considering him. Then she wrapped her arms around Hunter's waist and cinched him in tight. "Thank you," she whispered.

He grimaced. "I keep telling you, you can stop thanking me for towing you."

"Not for that, silly. For this."

And then she kissed him again, slow and dreamy this time, pulsing into his mouth with long, languid strokes, tasting and tempting until they both were breathless and burning up with heat. She couldn't help it—she ran her hands over the hard plane of his back and twisted his flannel shirt in her fist, pulling him to her. And Hunter leaned into her, kissing her harder, more desperately, one hand against the door by her head. His whole body tensed with it, deep, heavy breaths shuddering through him.

Mmmmm, she needed him—too much.

Desperate longing spiked through her, and God knew how many moans. But she stopped herself, struggling for some kind of control so she wouldn't seem like some kind of hard-up lonely heart.

Even if, right then, that was exactly what she was.

Kathryn raised her hand to stroke his jaw again while they leaned their foreheads together, trying to catch their breath. Finally, she summoned the effort to move her hand to the doorknob behind her, and he took the cue, stepping respectfully back.

"Good night, Hunter." She tipped her fingertip into the cleft on his chin. "Thanks for waking me up."

He quirked up the corner of his mouth and shook his head in that cute way that he had. And she slipped quietly through her door.

CHAPTER 8

Hunter tossed and turned in his bed. The blackness sucked him under, and hazy images flickered like an old film in the theater of his mind. Dammit. Another nightmare— again! Even in his sleep-addled state, he tried to claw his way back from the darkness, but he couldn't shake himself awake. Not this time.

It pulled him down-down-down.

And he was there.

Hunter rolled his eyes. Laney was singing along with the radio again. Today's rendition—"Rockin' Around the Christmas Tree." Bemused, he shook his head. "Do you even know what key that's in?"

His wife turned her pretty head to him and narrowed her big green eyes. "I don't have to know. I sing with feeling."

He grinned. "Is that what we're calling it these days?"

She smacked him playfully on the leg. "Oh, stop it. You know you love it."

"I love you, but I don't love your singing." Hunter leaned over to give her a quick peck on the side of her neck, even though he was driving the car. His wife may have a singing voice that sounded roughly like cats in a bag, but her

darlin' goofiness lifted his spirits, regardless. Life couldn't get any better as far as he was concerned. They were making the most of their extended Christmas holiday with a nice, romantic dinner out. He was all dressed up and hitting the town with the most beautiful woman in the world on his arm. They drove toward downtown Lewisburg in his latest creation—his red, recently restored 1970 Corvette with a kick-ass dragon painted on the hood. People pointed and waved as they went by.

They were all checking out his car. But he was checking out his girl. Damn, she looked fine tonight. Laney's glorious auburn hair fell down in thick waves over the top of her strapless wine-red dress. Her lush, beautiful breasts practically spilled out of the top of the fitted satin. She flexed her sleek, toned legs while she tapped her black peep-toe sandals on the floor to the time of the music. Damn, he felt like he had his very own 1940s pinup for the evening. Any man would have to be half dead not to steal glances at her. She was unbelievably gorgeous, and still, after all these years, it made his chest bow with pride to know she was his.

Laney caught him ogling her, of course. She made that purring sound in the back of her throat that he loved so much. "Mmmmm, you like what you see tonight, Hunter?" She trailed her clever fingers up his thigh, making him jump with ticklishness.

He turned to look at her again, this time with enough heat in his gaze to let her know exactly what he wanted to do with her when they got home. "Always, Redbird. You know me."

"Yes, I do." She hummed, slowly pulling up the hem of her dress to reveal the red garter holding up her fishnet stockings.

He groaned. He was hard as a rock now. She was going to

torture him all night, wasn't she? "Oh man, not garters. Awww, hell, you're making me sweat, girl. Are they new?"

"Uh-huh," she hummed. "New fishnets, new garters, new corset. Consider it your New Year's present. I have more presents waiting for you when you get home. Let that be something to keep your brain busy over dinner."

"Somehow, I don't think it's my brain that will be involved. Seriously, am I supposed to eat after that? Can't I skip to dessert first?" He slipped one hand free of the wheel so he could explore the enticing way the fishnet pulled taut over her leg. His fingertips grazed the garter, but she smacked his hand.

Laney pretended to give him a stern stare. "We have reservations."

Oh no, he wasn't moving his hand yet. He twirled his fingers in lazy circles on her thigh. Just then, the Corvette gave a sideways lurch, skittering across the ice. He quickly righted the car.

"Hunter! Keep your hands on the wheel, for Pete's sake!"

"Don't worry, I've got it," he muttered, putting his hands back where they belonged.

Laney scowled. "You know we shouldn't have taken the Corvette out after the ice storm. They still haven't gotten everything scraped up. You should've taken my truck."

"Come on, babe, how long have you known me? Has there ever been a time I haven't protected you? Besides, I put on brand-new snow tires. This car's as good as any."

Laney shook her head and started singing along again. This time "All I Want for Christmas Is You" pounded through the speakers. Hunter laughed at her again, wincing at her attempt at Mariah's high notes. But then the wheels began to spin.

They were sliding again, the car lurching hard against his efforts to steer. He yanked the wheel— Shit!

His tires lost all traction, skating them across the road diagonally, over the yellow line. He pulled the wheel with all his might back the other way, but they were spinning now, turning so fast, he didn't know which direction they were going. The car turned once, twice...

They squealed to a hard stop, cutting horizontally across the opposite lane. Laney stopped screaming and turned her beautiful face to him.

But he couldn't get a word out. There was no time. Behind her, a coal truck careened straight toward them, flying down the icy hill, its brakes whining as its steaming, mud-splattered grill hurtled closer.

It only took a split second, but he saw it all in the most horrifying slow motion possible, like a series of stop-action photographs burned in his brain.

The truck driver's panicked eyes as he tried in vain to swerve...

Laney's relieved expression as she thought they'd stopped and were out of danger...

And the gut-wrenching agony of watching the truck bear down on them at what had to be over forty miles an hour. One glance at the truck driver's face told Hunter the man had lost control, lost his ability to stop as he slid down off the hill Now his wife sat unsuspecting and perfectly centered in the middle of a deadly target, smack in the middle of Washington Street.

Laney's scream ripped through the air at the impact. That coal truck crushed their sports car like a tin can. Glass sprayed, metal shrieked and groaned, hot radiator steam hissed. And worst of all, vinyl cracked as the dashboard popped up and landed in his lap, trapping his legs beyond any hope of moving them.

He looked over at Laney.

No. NO!

She was pinned back against her seat, her seat belt still perfectly in place. But the dashboard had crushed her from her chest to her hips. Blood poured down her face from where her head hit the side window. But somehow, she was still breathing. Barely.

Laney's head lolled in his direction, but she didn't appear conscious. Hunter struggled and writhed and beat the dash with all his might. But he couldn't pull either of them free. Oh Jesus, no-no-no-no-no-no! He had to get them out! Dimly he heard the voices of good Samaritans outside, pounding on the doors, unable to open them. He bellowed in frustration, a soul-deep howl.

But in the silence that followed, Laney took a rattling breath. "No, don't." Her weak, thready voice was barely audible.

Laney!

He reached his arm over to his wife and cupped her precious, precious face in his hand.

Her eyelids fluttered, but she was able to focus on him.

His heart leaped. "Stay with me, baby," Hunter wailed. "Don't you die on me, you hear? There's people out there trying to help us. An ambulance is on its way, babe. You've got to stay awake and stay strong for me. We're going to get through—"

"Hunter, no," she whispered, the air whistling through her chest. She groaned with agony but managed another shuddering breath. "It's my time to go. I love you, babe. Don't be sad for me...let me go..." Her voice trailed off. She took one last shallow breath, and then one long, long exhale. And then...nothing. There was no other breath. He begged. He pleaded. But there was only silence.

And that was it. Just like that. The center of his whole world, and everything he'd ever cared about—gone.

No. No-no-no-no-no. LANEY!

. . .

Hunter sat bolt upright in the bed, flying across it as if he were still trying to get to her. *If only I could get to her.*

Hunter scrambled and scrabbled but stopped before he threw himself over the side of the bed. His heart raced, and his guts felt as if they were being pulled out of his body by some unseen hand. The sheets were tangled in knots and soaked with his sweat. And of course, he was shaking uncontrollably. *Again.* At least this time, he hadn't screamed when he'd woken up. All these years of flashbacks had trained him to do that much, at least.

He ran a trembling hand over his face, trying to reassure himself that he was really here in The Hollyberry Inn and not back there again, watching his beautiful wife bleed to death before his eyes. He couldn't even hold her in his arms at the last. That was the hell of it. He hadn't even had time to tell her he loved her one last time, to say goodbye, to kiss her lips. She'd died, just out of his reach.

Hunter sat on the bed, his arms clasped around his knees, rocking himself back and forth until his panic slowly, steadily subsided. He wasn't really sure how to describe what had happened. He wasn't sure whether he could call these episodes nightmares, or visions, or flashbacks. Maybe they were all three. But he was sure of one thing. It was like being there all over again. Like he was reliving it in lurid technicolor, the dreams were so strong he could feel them, smell them, and taste them. If he ever died and went to hell, this was what it would be—to live an endless loop of losing Laney, over and over again.

Laney. My girl. My world.

But she was gone now. He had to accept that. Hell, she'd *asked* him to accept that.

He *had*, hadn't he? But now...

Goddammit! If only he could stop the images in his head. After so many months of not a single incident he was starting to believe he'd finally kicked them. But now they were back.

Hunter peered out his window at the sun beginning to rise over the wintry horizon. It must've been the kiss. There was all the holiday spirit, and the rescue, and then Kathryn, so damn sexy and wonderful and vulnerable in his arms. Had it been any wonder that the flashbacks had come back? It had all been one big recipe for a trigger. He shouldn't be surprised by any of it.

Hunter groaned and rubbed his hands over his face again. Was this his future? Would he fall apart every time he reached out to a woman? Laney wouldn't want that. Hell, she'd told him so, with her dying breath.

No, he'd have to power through these flashbacks, like he'd powered through everything else. Long ago, he'd accepted that his life would most likely be lived in the shadows, never getting close to anyone or anything again. A week ago, the notion of marching through the days, doing what had to be done, would've been okay, maybe even desirable. But there was something about Kathryn that made him question that. She made him want more.

He could chalk it up to lust, and going too long without a woman in his life. But it was so, so much more than that.

She's special, and you know it.

Yes, yes, she was. He couldn't deny it. Kathryn Winslow was a fascinating interplay of opposites—vulnerable, yet strong as a steel magnolia. She was properly lady-like, yet so direct sometimes it took his breath away. And, of course, she was brilliantly smart. But thankfully, she had none of the smug arrogance you often saw in the highly educated. She didn't seem put off by his trade school degree. If anything, she seemed to respect his blue-collar skills and be genuinely interested in his business. And those kisses—my Lord, a man could get lost in those kisses. The girl lit him up like a Roman candle.

Jesus, when did Kathryn get under my skin like this?

Hunter walked on shaky legs over to the minibar in his room. His emotions were jangled and his bones ached from what surely must have been a night of turning and twisting in the bed. His mouth was dry, too, probably from all the labored breathing while he'd "slept." Lord, he needed a drink. Rooting around in his mini-fridge, he found an over-priced bottle of orange juice, cracked it open, and took a few sips. Though he really wasn't all that much of a drinking man, he considered pouring the tiny bottle of vodka into it. *Ah, forget it.* Getting buzzed at freakin' sunrise wouldn't help.

Miserable now, he flopped back down on the bed and pulled up his television. Turning it to the news channel, Hunter turned down the volume and stared at the ticker going by. According to their reports, the state was no closer to getting the roads cleared. They still estimated the road to Christmas Pass would be cleared three days from now, the day after Christmas.

There was no two ways about it. They were stuck in Christmas Pass, and he couldn't pretend to be upset about that. More days here meant more Christmas magic, and more days to explore whatever this thing was with Kathryn. And God knew he wanted to. Oh yes, he wanted Kathryn Winslow, more than he'd wanted anything in a long, long time. The way she'd kissed him, it had taken all his strength not to throw her over his shoulder and drag her off to his room like some kind of fuckin' Neanderthal.

And Kathryn deserved better than that. She deserved a man who was strong, and sure, and not plagued with violent nightmares when he closed his eyes. She deserved someone who wasn't haunted by the ghosts of his regrets every minute of every goddamn day.

But as much as he believed that, he knew he was drawn to that woman like a moth to the flame. He'd never be able to resist her, especially when the Christmas magic in this place seemed to be conspiring to push them together. There was no way you'd get him to believe that whole thing at Hoot n' Annie's hadn't somehow been engineered.

By who—or what? That was the question, wasn't it?

Hunter turned off the television with a decisive click. What was it about this place? Something about it wasn't right. And it wasn't only because he hadn't heard of it before.

Hunter laid there in the twilight, mulling over their stay so far. Everything was a bit too convenient, wasn't it? Anytime anyone wanted something, there it seemed to be— a restaurant with a mechanical bull...the sledding run...and who could forget Huck's buxom nurses?

And even then, he still would've chalked it up to a coincidence. But last night, at Hoot n' Annie's, he'd seen something. Or, he thought he'd seen something. Okay, okay, he *knew* he'd seen something. But it didn't make a damn bit of sense. He'd been talking to Kathryn, and when she'd said, "I wish they had line dancing," the back wall of the restaurant had started to shimmer, like a watery, silvery veil. And then, almost as fast as it had appeared, the veil had evaporated. And in its place had stood an entirely new dance hall. It hadn't been there before. It hadn't! He'd been looking right at the wall!

Thinking back clearly about the night now, he couldn't believe he hadn't just gathered Kathryn up and run out of that place as fast as he could right then. He probably should've. But there was something about the place, an irresistible, almost cloying sweetness that made you want to stay and wrap yourself up in it like a warm, comforting blanket.

Shit, who am I kidding? I stayed because of Kathryn.

He'd wanted to show off, impress her and, yeah, maybe even turn her on. Maybe his plan had worked too well. God, she was so perfect, the way she'd molded against his whole body, moving to the music. She'd flamed to life under his touch. His libido had roared back to life, making him forget everything—his pain, his misgivings. Hell, the bold way she'd taken his mouth, he'd forgotten his own name. The world had stood still, and there was nothing but the two of them, and that single, unforgettable kiss.

God, the things I want to do to her.

And his mind went straight to his cock. Again, dammit.

Mind on task, Hunter. He huffed out a breath, burrowed back onto the pillow, and threw his arm up over his eyes. What was the task, anyway? What was he supposed to do?

Okay, last night had proven to him, anyway, that there was some kind of magical mojo to Christmas Pass. The sign at the town's entrance had read, "Where your Christmas wishes come true." And that promise was powered by a lot more than extreme devotion to customer service. But how could he *prove* it? And what would he do about it once he did?

One thing was for sure—he had to find out more about Christmas Pass. Maybe he should do some sleuthing on his own today. Yeah, he really needed to do that, didn't he? He had to protect Kathryn and her family, no matter what. And he couldn't do that blind.

Hunter rolled over and fished around in the nightstand until he could find a notepad and pen. Then he wrote out a brief note.

Kathryn,

Wasn't sure what your plans were for the day, but I'd like to come along. But I need to do a couple things first on my own today. Can I meet you on the benches in the town square at three o'clock?

—Hunter.

He hesitated a moment and screwed up his nerve before he added the last line.

P.S. I enjoyed our time together last night. I hope you did too.

Since it was too early to go knocking, he slid the note under the door that separated their two bedrooms. And he flopped back down on the bed. There. Maybe now, he'd be able to get the sleep he desperately needed.

Hunter woke again, blinking against the slanting morning sun filtering through the curtains. He glanced over at the clock. *Ten o'clock in the morning—perfect.* He stretched, amazed and thankful that he'd been able to sleep without incident. He felt about as rested as he was going to get, considering.

Ambling over to his bathroom, he saw his note, pushed back under the suite door. Kathryn had written a return message.

Of course I enjoyed it. You're a very good kisser, Hunter Holliday. See you at three.

—Kathryn.

Blinking with disbelief for a moment, Hunter read the note again, hardly able to believe his luck. Leave it to Kathryn to lay it all out there. Everything about this woman excited and entertained him. Maybe being stranded here with her was exactly what he needed, weird mystery vibes notwithstanding.

He showered and shaved and picked out a couple of items from the soft, form-fitting clothes Kathryn had bought him. He pulled a red Henley shirt over his head and grinned. Oh yeah, this shirt pulled just right over his pecs and biceps. Would Kathryn notice?

He grabbed his coat and trotted down the steps and into the lobby. From the sugary smell of waffles still wafting from the inn's sprawling restaurant, the place apparently had a big trade in brunch.

Miss Berry stood behind the front desk. "Good morning, Mr. Holliday," she chirped. "I hope your accommodations have been everything you're wishing for. I know it's a bit of a hardship being stranded over the Christmas holiday."

Hunter stopped, caught by that turn of phrase. *Wishing for...* "Not at all." He inclined his head, being carefully polite. "My own family doesn't live close anymore, and I've been enjoying my time with Kathryn and her family. And Christmas Pass is pretty incredible. I can't believe I grew up so close to here and never heard of this place."

Miss Berry's bland, poker-faced expression gave nothing away. "We've been fortunate enough never to have to advertise. When people need us, they tend to find us. We have people here from all over the world."

As if to demonstrate, a flock of oddly identical, chattering Chinese tourists passed by them on their way out the door.

Hunter turned his attention back to her. "Impressive. That's a lot of business, considering I've never seen as much as a single billboard or rest stop brochure about this place. The inn is packed. Maybe I should start chatting up some of your patrons about what brought them here. It would be interesting to see why people enjoy coming to the mountain state."

A flustered expression passed over Miss Berry's face. But the woman collected herself, smoothing out her apron. "Oh, I think you'll find our visitors to be a pretty circumspect bunch. Most people are pretty private, I've found. They want to have their time away from it all, you know."

Hunter furrowed his brows at that. He'd often found the exact opposite to be true when people were on vacation. With extra time on their hands, they were often friendlier than usual and eager to exchange stories. He needed to find a place where he could hear stories about Christmas Pass. And it would be better, even, if he could find a place to talk to locals. That was probably the only way he could get to the bottom of all this.

Sensing he'd get no more information from Miss Berry today, he decided he'd find another place to eat and press its patrons for information. He stood on the sidewalk outside the inn and looked up and down the street. Unfortunately, he saw more tourist stores, bookstores, and movie theaters than the hole-in-the-wall diner he needed. There might be the right place around the corner if he kept on walking. But rather than do that, he decided to test out a theory.

Looking around to make sure no one could watch him talk to himself, he let his voice ring out nice and clear. "I wish I could find a great local breakfast spot, where I could hang out and talk to people from Christmas Pass."

Hunter closed his eyes, scrunching them tight. Then he slowly, slowly opened them again. And he stood there, slack-jawed, rooted to the spot in shock. There, directly in front of him, was an old-timey breakfast diner called Flapjacks. The place had most definitely *not been there* moments before. Yet customers walked out patting their bellies, and the greasy spoon was lined with customers. *How can I possibly be seeing this?*

It was enough to make him doubt his own senses. For a

small storefront, this restaurant was bustling. People sat in booths up against the plate glass windows, eagerly forking up stacks of pancakes and piles of eggs. The windows were hand painted with pictures of their best-selling items— western scramble, waffles, and such. Evidently, it hadn't been redecorated since the 1930s.

Was it real? How could it be? *It appeared out of thin air!*

Swallowing down his better judgment, Hunter tentatively stepped inside. The bell on the door clattered behind him. He marveled at the battered not-real pressed-tin ceiling, the not-real wooden booths, and the not-real turquoise Formica counter, where he sat down on the last empty, not-real swiveling stool.

Jesus Christ, I did this. I'm sitting here in a place that somehow, some way, I wished into existence.

Hunter's heart hammered against his ribs as he gawked in wonder at the place.

A not-real waiter came up to him, an older man wearing a grimy white apron around his waist. The waiter didn't *seem* like a figment of his imagination. A nondescript, brown-haired, middle-aged man, the waiter was a bit weathered looking in the way people from West Virginia sometimes were. "Blowed in here out of the cold, did ya?" the man crooned. "Wanna warm up with some coffee?"

Hunter said yes, and the man turned a clean white ceramic coffee cup over into its saucer and began filling it. Sitting the cup on a scalloped white paper placemat in front of him, he offered Hunter a disposable coffee creamer.

Hunter shook his head and tentatively took a sip of the grog. Was this not-real too? It *tasted* real, exactly like every kind of black coffee-machine coffee he'd ever had in places like this.

"I'm Bob Sledde, by the way," the man offered. "I've

never seen you around before. You visitin'? Staying at the inn?"

Hunter bit back the urge to comment on his not-real waiter's ridiculous name. Bob handed him a two-sided menu in a plastic sleeve. After a short conversation, Hunter ordered up some blueberry pancakes. Hopefully those were real too, because he was starving. "Do y'all have a morning newspaper I can read?"

Bob wordlessly handed him a folded-up paper from behind the counter. Expecting to be given the area's *West Virginia Daily News*, or the *Mountain Messenger*, Hunter raised his eyebrows when the masthead said *The Christmas Herald.* "*Serving Christmas Pass since 1893.*"

Bullshit. There's no such paper.

Yet here he was, holding it in his hand.

Hunter paged through it. This community news rag struck him as distinctly strange. It was filled with happy-face news stories and previews of what was happening at upcoming attractions. There were a few wedding announcements—all with names like "Snow-Flake to Wed in New Year's Nuptials" or "Ice-Crystalle Engagement Set." But, even though the paper was relatively thick, there were notable omissions—local school news and high school sports scores, crime stories, or obituaries and birth announcements, for instance. Come to think of it, he hadn't seen a single school or day care center anywhere, even though there were plenty of kids about.

Bob stopped by with Hunter's order, a fluffy pile of the most beautiful pancakes he'd ever seen, smothered in blue-berry syrup. He sliced off a piece and groaned apprecia-tively the second the not-real breakfast hit his mouth.

An older gentleman in a Marshall University sweatshirt sat on the stool beside him and tipped his ball hat in Hunter's direction. "Yeah, it's pretty good, innit?"

"I didn't think it was possible for pancakes to taste this good," Hunter marveled. "Is all the food in Christmas Pass like this? Perfect? I haven't had a mediocre bite since I came here."

The man cackled. "Pretty much. Always has been, always will be."

"So." Hunter leaned in, trying not to betray how intense his interest was. "You obviously know a lot about Christmas Pass. What can you tell me about the history of the place?"

The kindly, bright-eyed man introduced himself as Peter Pine, and his companions around the side of the counter as Herb Holly and Ian Ivy, respectively. And they seemed all too eager to talk about their hometown. But there was something very odd about them. Maybe it was their ridiculous names. But then again, everyone here seemed to have these super obvious, totally unlikely Christmas-themed names. Maybe it was part of the local culture around here?

Yeah, that didn't wash, especially when Hunter factored in how strangely similar the men were—all wearing local college sweats, all balding in the same way, all three with similar expressions that showed they were crusty old coots who probably hung out at the counter all morning, every morning. They were practically interchangeable, and thrilled that they had someone new they could regale with their stories. Were they some kind of actors, or something? Had he poofed them up with his wishes, too? Hunter had the sudden urge to flee. But he kept his butt glued in the seat anyway. He wished for this place. He might as well get his answers while he was at it.

Herb was the first to start, putting down his coffee meaningfully and taking a big breath. "People first started migrating to this place in serious numbers shortly before the Revolutionary War," Herb offered. "My folk were among them. They were fleeing attacks by the Lakota Indians. Legend states that they fought off no less than Sitting Bull himself! The first Fort Christmas was erected on Christmas Day by William Pitt."

Who builds a fort in the middle of winter? And besides, that *couldn't* have been William Pitt. Hunter raised his brows in astonishment. "William Pitt? What, you mean the man who founded Pittsburgh, Pennsylvania?"

"He founded Christmas Pass first," Ian jumped in. "We were his first project, and he moved on."

The men went on and on with their bullshit stories. Hunter was too dumbfounded by this steaming pile of lies they were telling him to even answer them. Where in the hell did they get this garbage? First of all, the Lakota couldn't have attacked. They were a *Western* tribe. This area had been full of Shawnee Indians back then, for crying out loud. Sitting Bull wouldn't have even been born for another hundred years.

Holy shit, they were making the town history up out of whole cloth!

The men went on to tell him one fractured tale after another. They sounded plausible enough, maybe to a foreign tourist. But Hunter was a history buff. He always had been. In fact, in eighth grade, he'd become a Knight of the Golden Horseshoe—a feat only two hundred students each year managed by getting top scores on a West Virginia history test. He'd studied for months for that doggone exam. He didn't memorize facts easily, but once they were in there, they were in there for life. And he knew, beyond a shadow of a doubt, he was being had.

Hunter swallowed hard and tried to make polite conversation. Honestly, he was too shell-shocked to do much of anything else. Shoveling in all the pancakes his stomach could hold, Hunter stayed and listened to the old codgers tell stories all morning. Between the three of them, they managed to butcher, cut, and paste bits of West Virginia history into a Frankenstein's monster of fractured cultural facts. Midway through, he stopped listening very hard. There was hardly any point. Instead, he spent his time observing details in a scene he could only describe as "off."

Though it seemed completely irrational, even to him, he felt like this place and these people wouldn't exist if he weren't looking right at them. Somehow, when he looked at them, he could see flashes in his peripheral vision.

Come on, I'm not really seeing that, am I?

Hunter kept casing the place, and the strange sensation passed.

He rubbed his hands over his face and took his last sip of coffee. One thing was for sure. He had some crazy theories. But he needed more proof.

"Wow, fellas, you sure have given me some things to think about. Who knew this place was so steeped in history?" Hunter motioned over to Bob so he could sign for his bill.

Peter clapped him on the back. "It's nice to see a West Virginia boy like you in here. Most people don't have an appreciation for the history of this place. These hills played a big, big part in the early history of America."

That was the one true statement he'd heard out of the lot of them all morning.

Hunter asked the men if there was a place he could go to read up from official documents about the place. They directed him to the town's library, which—imagine that— had somehow magically appeared across the street. Hunter squelched the urge to laugh helplessly at its sudden appearance. But he signed the ledger to "pay" for his food and walked across the road to the big, gray-columned library.

The place was ornate, with stained glass windows and

acres of mahogany library tables for spreading out with your finds. This library was easily ten times bigger than it should be for a town of this size. But Hunter was grateful for the vast troves of microfiche, the endlessly helpful library staff, and the collections of historic documents that were stored here.

He spent a couple of hours digging through the archives. It was entertaining reading. But here was the thing—all the stories were as effed up as the ones he heard at Flapjacks. For instance, the people listed in the "founding families" of Christmas Pass were actually founders of *other* towns in the state—Morgan Morgan, the founder of Morgantown, for instance, and Collis Huntington, the founder of Huntington. All these guys were supposed to be original settlers in Christmas Pass? It wasn't even physically possible! Jesus, if they were going to tell such outright lies, you'd think they wouldn't be so obvious about it.

Was someone, or some *thing*, daring him to figure it all out?

Hunter read and read, hoping against hope that he'd find something somewhere that made any sense. But the longer he investigated Christmas Pass, the more upset he became. What kind of place was this? Where were they, really?

Was this some kind of bad *Fantasy Island* rerun? Or worse, were they in purgatory, like an episode of *Lost?* Jesus Christ, had they all died on that mountain? He patted himself down. No, he doubted it. He felt too solid to be dead.

Hunter scrubbed his shaking hands through his hair and willed himself to calm his shit down. He was being ridiculous. There was nothing about this place, weird as it may be, that suggested it was sinister. They'd said they'd be able to

131

leave in three more days, right? They wouldn't be trapped here forever, right?

Whether Christmas Pass was real or not, magical or not, dangerous or not, he needed to be careful. Because if there was one thing he knew for certain, Kathryn and Huck and Wilson were real. And they were here with him, too. It was up to Hunter, more than anyone, to make sure they all came out of this in one piece.

Kathryn. She needed him. And, God help him, maybe he needed her too.

Oh no—Kathryn! Shit! It was five to three! He was supposed to meet her! Hunter pushed himself back from the table and practically ran out of there. He had to get to Kathryn and stick to them all like glue until they could get out of this weird-ass place for good.

As he hurried off to the town square, more doubts clouded his mind. Should he tell Kathryn what he'd learned about the town's history? Should he tell her what he'd seen at Hoot n'Annie's? Should he tell her his theory about how wishing for things here could make them happen?

He turned the corner and spotted Kathryn pacing in front of the gazebo in center of the square. To his surprise, she came running up to him and practically launched herself into his arms. Alarm registered in his gut when he saw Kathryn's stricken face. She looked like she'd burst into tears at any moment.

Before he could even open his mouth to ask her what had happened, she blurted out, "I can't find Daddy or Wilson! They're *gone!*"

CHAPTER 9

KATHRYN KNEW SHE WAS PANICKING. And panic never solved anything. She tried to take deep, calming breaths. Then she tried to think through her situation logically and set her worst fears to the side as unfounded or unwanted. Over the last hour, she'd tried every cognitive trick she knew to pull herself together. But as she'd stood alone in the middle of this strange city, dread had her gripped so tight she couldn't think straight.

When Hunter showed up, she was so relieved, she could've cried. Kathryn ran into his arms instinctively, not even realizing what she'd done until he wrapped his arms around her back. The care and concern on his face steadied her.

He braced his hands on her shoulders. "Tell me what happened, step by step."

"I—I needed to do some last-minute shopping, and Daddy, he agreed to take Wilson over to this laser tag place. Daddy was supposed to take care of him! But now they're both gone. *Gone!* I've been at it for hours, going in and out of every store. I even went back to the inn. It's like they vanished into thin air!"

"Are you sure they haven't gotten distracted?"

"No. It's not like them. They've never been late like this before."

She knew what he was saying. A normal parent might not be so worried. Wilson was with his grandfather, after all. But Daddy was a high-functioning alcoholic, and that made him unreliable. Her father had been going to Alcoholics Anonymous and was back on the wagon now. *Supposedly*. But what if Daddy had gotten them both into hot water somehow?

The thought made her sick to her stomach.

She wasn't sure what Hunter could do that she hadn't tried, but having another person to help her figure her way through a crisis was more than she'd ever had.

Kathryn took a deep breath, and the knot in her chest loosened a few degrees. "Wilson wanted to go to a laser tag arcade up the street. We agreed we'd all meet back here two hours ago."

"And there's been no sign of them? Has anyone seen them?"

Kathryn shook her head, pulling away. "No! And that's what's got me so scared. The attendant at the arcade said that Daddy came in with Wilson, but he left him there as soon as Daddy signed for the entrance fee. When his session was up, Wilson waited for him like he was supposed to, but finally he left all by himself."

"Surely they couldn't have gotten far. Let's think this through. What about Huck? Have you tried going to the places he might've gone?"

The suggestion stopped her. Surely Daddy wouldn't have started drinking again in the middle of the day, at least. He wouldn't do that to her, would he?

Hunter pushed his hands in his pockets and calmly

scanned the landscape. Then he slowly said, "I sure wish we could figure out where Huck went."

Kathryn scanned the street around them. And almost like magic, she spotted her daddy. Her heart leaped in relief, only to plummet to the pit of her stomach. Daddy was stumbling, staggering so hard he almost wiped out in the middle of the sidewalk. He'd tumbled out of the doorway of a particularly vile dive called Nogg's. The plate-glass windows were painted black and the crusty wood door looked like it'd kicked in and reassembled a few times, shard by shard.

When Daddy finally saw her standing there, his bloated, reddened face flushed with panic. As she stormed across the street, he turned as if he could somehow run from her.

Kathryn pounded up behind him, with Hunter right on her heels. She grabbed her father's coat sleeve and whipped him around. "Dammit, Daddy, where's Wilson?"

He teetered on unsteady legs as he answered her, grabbing a lamppost to help him stand. "Aww, he's s'okay. The boy's having the time of his life, ya know. I'm going down to the arcade to get him. I'll have him back here in juuust a minute." And he turned, as if he was going to get away again.

Kathryn ran around in front of him, blocking his way, while Hunter stood behind him. "That session was over a long time ago! I went over there myself, and they said Wilson waited and waited but you never came. He's gone now, Daddy!"

Daddy laughed. The man actually had the unmitigated gall to *laugh*. "What are you looking at me for? How am I s'posed to know where the boy went?"

Kathryn went rigid with fury. She scowled at her father for one long, long moment. And then she slapped him—

hard and fast, so hard her hand hurt and her father's face actually snapped to the side. "You're *drunk*," she thundered. She was shaking so hard, she could hardly say anything else.

Daddy held his hand up to his face in shock, his eyes wide. His only daughter had never, ever done anything like this before. But something about this had stepped over a bright red line for her. How many times had she covered for him? How many times had she scraped him off the floor when he'd gone on one of his binges? She realized in this moment that she'd never known anything else. And now, he was dragging Wilson's safety into it.

"So, *Daddy*," she spat, "how many highball glasses of vodka did they let you have before they kicked you out this time? Ten? Fifteen? Or did you buy the whole bottle so you could pour it straight down your own goddamn throat?"

Round-eyed with regret, Daddy blanched. His eyes filled up with tears, and the expression on his face was so confused and hurt that suddenly *he* resembled a lost child. "I—I don't know. I'm—I'm sorry, Katie-belle."

Kathryn was in no mood to be moved. "*Sorry?*" She chuckled, and even she could hear the awful, bitter ring to it. "You don't know the meaning of the word. A man who's sorry realizes what he's done and takes responsibility. A man who's sorry tries to change. But you'll never change, will you? You won't change for your own sake, and certainly not for the sake of anyone else in your life. You love the bottle more than you *ever* loved any of us."

"Girl, you're makin' too much of this," Daddy stammered. He teetered over to a lamppost, wrapping both arms around it for protection, probably, as much as support. She glanced over at Hunter, who mouthed, "*What do you need?*" Kathryn held up a hand to let him know she needed to take the lead, and he stood back.

Daddy, for his part, didn't seem capable of much except

hugging the lamppost and groaning. "It's only a li'l slip. I was feeling low, and I needed to top myself off, that's all. I'll crawl back up on the wagon. You'll see."

Kathryn stormed over to her father and began furiously patting down his jacket, grunting with disgust when she heard a metallic hollow noise. Wrestling her hand under her father's jacket, she yanked out his flask. Daddy tried to wrestle it back, but his motor skills were shot. "A slip, huh?" Kathryn eyed his flask. "Wow, it's your extra-big one! How much does it hold? Two pints? Does that mean you've stopped keeping the small one in your boot, or have you decided to double up?"

She dove to his leg before he could stop her and, sure enough, found flask number two. She hurriedly unscrewed the lids and began pouring the stash down the storm sewer grate.

Daddy stared at her, shame twisting his features as he watched his precious hoard drain away.

Shame. Yeah, she knew that, too. It had been no fun weathering the reactions of friends and family every time her Daddy had to shamble off to rehab. She'd always reminded herself that Daddy's drinking wasn't about her. But in a way, it was, wasn't it? His drinking had blighted her life in so many ways. And now Hunter was standing here, watching yet another of her family tragedies play out before his eyes. What man would sign up for this kind of hazard duty? He'd be gone, too, the minute he could. She'd bet money on it. And the old familiar anger that she tried to reason away came roaring back to the surface.

Her jaw clenched with fury as she watched the alcohol mix with the dirty snow and snake its way into the sewer. "You know, the crazy part of all this is, I trusted you," Kathryn hissed. "All those months I spent nursing you through rehab, carefully working with the doctors on your anti-addiction meds, cleaning the house out, and teaming up with you to remove all the obstacles to your recovery. *God*...I really thought you *wanted* it this time!"

Kathryn's throat thickened with misery. "Every bit of that was a waste of time, wasn't it? Yep, just like all the other times—you went through the motions so I'd get off your back. You were biding your time until you could get right back to the bottle again. Weren't you? Come on! Be a man for once and admit it!"

The only sound now was the last drops of whiskey hitting the pavement. Kathryn shook the flasks dry and jammed them into her purse.

Daddy didn't answer her. He closed his eyes and held his stomach. Then he lunged at the garbage can and began violently retching into it. Kathryn stood there, watching in a kind of dull, wretched acceptance as the man who'd raised her threw up on a public street.

She was too numb to comfort him. This was one slip too many. The first time she'd helped Daddy after a bender, she'd been six years old, running to get him washcloths and glasses of water, even helping him find his way into bed. By the time she was ten or so, she'd learned to clean up the vomit without gagging herself. Mother had always claimed to be too squeamish and, of course, no one wanted the *housekeeper* to see it. Then people might *tell tales*, God forbid.

Kathryn cast another baleful look at her utterly wrecked father. She should probably pat his back and reassure him. But she couldn't. She just couldn't. Standing there, fists clenched, rage and hopelessness pounded in equal measure in her veins.

Kathryn was painfully aware of Hunter's watchful eye, taking this whole mess in. He leaned casually on the nearby mailbox, standing at a respectful distance but watching her with an intensity that caught her off guard. Their eyes met, and a world of meaning seemed to pass between them. So many emotions swirled in his gaze—pity, concern, and a respect she was, quite frankly, astounded to see. And there was something else there too, something warm, something...

Hunter crossed to her in two strides and gathered her to him, wrapping his arms around her in a tender, yet somehow commanding embrace. Guiding her head to rest against his strong chest, he nestled her perfectly in the cradle of his arms, as if he were silently ordering her to rest, to lay down her burdens. Kathryn let out a shaky breath and leaned into him, allowing the reassurance of his presence to slowly sink into her skin. Until this moment, she hadn't realized how she wore worry and heartache like a millstone around her neck every damn day. And without a word, Hunter took that burden on, his arms a perfect circle of defense against all that the world could throw at her. No one had ever offered her this kind of protectiveness—not her ex, not any boyfriend, and surely to God not her parents. It was the most precious gift anyone had ever given her, that look, that touch.

Ah, Hunter. Helpless tears overwhelmed her, and she realized she was sobbing—deep, guttural sobs she couldn't control. A lifetime of frustration and carefully buried resentment poured from her, just as toxic as the hooch she'd poured down the street.

None of this made sense. Hunter Holliday was practically a stranger. And yet here, wrapped in his protection, she felt the irrational hope that nothing bad could ever happen to her. He didn't even judge her for her crazy family, or for what probably seemed to the uninitiated like a stunning lack of compassion toward her father right now. No, he simply held her, whispering reassurances in her ear, telling her he was here for her.

I'm falling. Always falling, and he's catching me.

"Ah, Ryn," he murmured. "It's okay to cry. You can't hold up the world by yourself."

She huffed out a rueful laugh. "If I have been, I've been doing a pretty lousy job."

Slowly, slowly, the acute stab of pain drained away, replaced by a familiar, dull ache of fear. She pulled away from Hunter, drying the last of her tears with her sleeve. Daddy had collapsed onto the nearby bench, still conscious, thank God. Wearily she walked over and plunked herself down beside him. Checking his pupils, pulse, and breathing, Kathryn breathed a sigh of relief to see they were all regular. He wasn't too sweaty, either. So thankfully, they wouldn't need to take him to the hospital for alcohol poisoning this evening. Maybe all that puking had done him some good.

Hunter crouched down in front of them both. "Are you sure he's going to be okay?"

"Yeah," Kathryn groaned. "I need to put him to bed."

"All right then, while you're taking care of him, I'm going to find Wilson. And, Kathryn, I promise you—I *will* find him. I'll get the local police involved if I have to. You go back to the inn. I've got this." He twined his fingers with hers, and kissed the top of her hand.

A part of Kathryn wanted to insist on staying right there until her son was found, but Hunter had a point. And when it came right down to it, she trusted him. The man would do what he said.

Watching Hunter trot off around the corner, she hailed a bright yellow, old-fashioned cab. It was only a few blocks to the inn, but Daddy was in no shape to walk. She helped her father into the cab, and when they arrived at the inn, a staff member helped him stagger up to his room. Kathryn ordered a pitcher of ice water, helped him into his pajamas, and tucked him into his bed.

Pouring three tall glasses of water, she gave her father a stern stare. "I want you to drink one of these now, one if you wake up in the middle of the night, and another when you wake up. Don't forget, okay? It's important."

Daddy said he understood and began on the first glass. She started to darken the room, but he grabbed her hand before she could switch off the lamp. "I can't go to bed with my little girl mad at me," he pleaded, so contrite he seemed...*tortured.*

Kathryn swallowed hard. "I'm not mad, Daddy. I'm disappointed, and scared. There's a difference. You really want me to forgive you for today?"

"Yes." He let out a long, shaky sigh. "But I know I don't deserve it."

Kathryn pinched the bridge of her nose between her fingers. "All right then, forgiveness is on the table. But you're going to answer my questions. *All* of them."

He gulped, but didn't argue with her.

"Okay, let's start with the obvious. You said the rehab was working. But you stopped taking your meds, didn't you?"

He shot her another guilty glance and squirmed.

"Don't bother to open your mouth. You already answered me." She crossed her arms over her chest. "You want to explain why you stopped?"

Daddy rubbed his forehead as if he could wipe the misery away. "I got the anti-addiction injection, like you said to do. They gave it to me at the rehab center, after the worst of the withdrawal was over. Oh, sure, it took away my cravings for the sauce. But it made me all sick and jittery. I had headaches to beat the band. I couldn't sleep, and hell, I couldn't even get it up. All in all, I figured it was easier goin' around half-crocked than it was living like that."

Kathryn was almost too incredulous to answer him. "And you didn't think to tell me this, or your doctor?"

"Why? So I could get more drugs that would do the same thing? I read up about 'em on the internet. No matter which one you take, they have similar side effects. And half of them don't even test out good in studies. Besides, I figured I'd gotten through a month without a drink. I told myself that maybe I could get by without the addiction busters. And it worked, too, for a time."

As she heard his story, Kathryn's anger slowly drained away. Her Daddy might be high-functioning, but the stark reality was that he was an end-stage alcoholic. There was always a possibility they could pull him back from the brink, but the odds were long. He had to fight his way past strong, entrenched biological urges. No matter how desperate she was to help him, only he could do the real work. She reached out and placed her hand over his.

Gripping her hand hard, Daddy raised it up to his cheek in appreciation. And it broke her heart a little bit, like always.

"So, what happened? What bumped you off the wagon?"

He squirmed uncomfortably. "I came across a box of your momma's stuff."

Kathryn raised her eyebrows. She didn't see how that could be possible. After Momma's suicide, she'd taken pains to move all her personal items from the house, as they seemed to tip Daddy even deeper into despair. Everything was removed—her mother's Lily Pulitzer dress collection, her perfumes and delicate French powders, her mountains of cooking tools, her books and knickknacks and handmade laces. She'd only allowed Daddy to keep photos and a handful of items he wanted to remember his wife by. That was it.

Though she knew Daddy didn't want to talk anymore, she wasn't going to let him get off that easy. "And? What did you find?"

Daddy grabbed the glass of water and took a long swig before he began, to steady himself. "Right after Thanksgiving, I decided I wanted to decorate the house at Christmas. You know how my Evangeline loved Christmas. I figured that's what she would've wanted me to do."

Kathryn squirmed a little, listening to this. It was true, of course. But not in the way Daddy meant. Momma was a certified Christmas fanatic, one who often went to extreme lengths celebrating the holiday. Wincing, all-too-vivid memories came to mind—Momma's frenzied cooking sprees, the dangerous overspending on gifts, the over-commitment to charitable causes, and the hyper-competitive bouts of excessive decorating, as a start. Oh no, her bipolar momma had never been so dangerously manic as she'd been around the holidays. For a few weeks every year, Evangeline Wilson had become a tinsel-covered five-star general, barking at everyone until they'd helped her chase her elusive, over-inflated Christmas expectations.

"So I was digging around in a box with a bunch of busted-up Christmas tree lights," Daddy continued, "and I found a smaller box, one that was covered with fancy flowered wallpaper. Your momma must have had hid it in there, knowing how I always refused to mess around on a ladder, putting up Christmas lights. The box smelled like her, like her perfume, Clair de Lune. Do you remember?"

She did. She found the scent so evocative of her momma, it still had the power to bring tears to her eyes. Kathryn motioned for him to continue.

"I opened it up and found stacks of letters and journals

full of poetry. At first I was touched when I found a bunch of love poems she'd written. But they weren't for me. They were for some man she was having an affair with."

"Anyone you know?" She asked the question without a hint of surprise. Her parents' marriage had been tense and unhappy for as long as she could remember, even though she was sure her daddy truly did love his wife.

"He was a friend from her childhood," Daddy answered. "They'd have lunch and shop together from time to time. You remember the guy she had you call Uncle Miles?"

Kathryn searched her mind and vaguely remembered a blond, impeccably dressed man who would sometimes come in and help Momma with her decorating, or take her out for coffee and cake. Momma would call him every now and then when she needed an ear to complain about something. But Kathryn had never gotten a sense from him that he *loved* Momma, or even wanted her in any way other than a friend. Were they that good of actors? How could she have missed that?

Daddy clearly was wondering the same thing.

"They had us all fooled," he groaned. "When I read those poems and journal entries, I knew your momma wanted him a helluva lot more than she ever wanted me. I can't say I know why they didn't stay together. I can't say why she married me when she obviously wanted someone else. Here, I'd always thought I was her first choice. I guess I wasn't."

Kathryn's heart squeezed in pity for her Daddy. "What stopped it?"

"I don't know. I can't say that it ever stopped. I probably could've figured out how it ended if I kept reading her journals, but I didn't have the heart to. Do you recall him coming around? I think I remember him coming by about Thanksgiving of last year. Not that it really matters."

"I don't remember anything about his visits or calls there toward the end," Kathryn answered. And it was true. "But I do remember him being at Momma's memorial service. He sat in the back, not talking to anyone. He was pretty shaken up."

Daddy fell into a sullen silence.

Kathryn kept turning all she'd heard over in her mind. Was it really as bad as all that? Did it make any difference how long it all had gone on? Momma was gone, and she wasn't coming back. And who's to say what their relationship really was? "Maybe it wasn't as dire as all that," Kathryn offered. "Maybe it was something in her own head, something she never acted on. Momma stayed with you, don't forget that."

His bark of laughter sounded rusty and rueful. "She stayed with me because I stayed with her. I made plenty of money, and I put up with her shit."

"And she put up with yours."

His chin wobbled, and for a moment, she was afraid he would fall to pieces right in front of her. "I was a lousy husband and father, wasn't I, girl? I worked too hard and drank too much, and I was never home. The worse her illness got, the more I drank and the more I shut her out. I never understood her. But I never stopped loving her, girl. You have to believe that. I *loved* her—in spite of everything. Everything I did with the business, and buying a fine house, and the social climbing, was all for her. To give her what she deserved. Maybe because *I* wasn't what she deserved. Somehow, in my heart, I knew she was never really mine."

His eyes were wet with unshed tears. "I know she was often fightin' with you and me. But in my eyes, she never stopped bein' like a bright, shining angel, full of Southern charm and fancy dreams. Then I read those letters." His voice broke off, and he shook his head. "You know, I think she might have hated me a little bit. I was some kind of straw dog, the man she had to present in public as her husband when her heart belonged to somebody else." He started to cry then—a soundless wail that seemed to bubble up from the depth of him. "I couldn't bear it, Kathryn!"

She held her daddy as he sobbed in her arms. Patting his back, she reassured him that she loved him and would always be there for him. And as she did, the realization sank in that Momma had killed herself, and Daddy was killing himself now by degrees because of it.

"What if it was me? What if I'm the reason she put that gun in her mouth?" he quavered.

Oh, Lord. Oh, Daddy, please no.

The agony came off her father in waves, and it was killing her to see him like this. She pulled his face up so he could see her face, and she remembered those words of advice her momma had had told her so many years ago. "Momma told me once that your life was about your own choices, and nobody else's. She told me that on my wedding day. Did you know that? Momma chose to marry you. Momma chose to be in love with another man. And she chose to end her life. If you want someone to blame, blame her. Momma always took ownership of her choices. Let her take ownership now. But better yet, let her go, Daddy. She wanted to be gone. Let her be. Keep the best of her, the good memories, and let go of the pain. It's the only way."

"How do I do that?"

She smoothed back his hair, and patted his whiskery cheek. "When I figure that out, I'll be sure to tell you."

He chuckled softly. With no more words left to say between them, Daddy was too exhausted to do anything more than give her cheek a pat.

Kathryn grabbed his hand and kissed his knuckles. Then she pulled up his covers around him.

It frightened her to see him so utterly defeated. And even though the red mark from her slap had faded, she felt like it was still there, glaring at her like a brand. She never should have slapped him. For all his foibles and faults, her daddy had always been a vital, active man. Maybe she'd been too hard on him right now, and way too honest. Perhaps the kinder way would have been psychologist's answers that would most likely involve five steps to forgiveness and constructive empathy or some other such folderol. It would've been easy enough to say. But it was different when it was *your* heart and *your* loved ones. She had to be real with him. Forgiving yourself never came easy, or fast. Some people never found a way to accomplish that.

Yeah, she talked a big game. But she hadn't forgiven herself, either. Even with all her training, she still hadn't seen her mother's suicide coming. How could she forgive herself for that? So when it came to this healing business, it was really the blind leading the blind, wasn't it?

"Get some sleep, Daddy," she soothed. "Everything will be better in the morning."

It was something Momma always used to say. He smiled a soft, sad smile at that memory as she turned out the light.

Kathryn tiptoed back to her room, turned on all the lights, and flopped down on the bed. She stared at the ceiling. *What an afternoon.* She'd been nuts to think she'd ever have a stress-free holiday. And now with these horrible revelations...

See, that was the thing about traveling. No matter how far away you go, your baggage always hitches a ride with you.

Kathryn shut her eyes and let out a shaky breath. Fixing

everything for her daddy wasn't even possible. But oh, how she wanted that, with all her heart. A big part of her felt responsible for his emotional and physical wellbeing, even though she knew darn well that wasn't how it worked. She had to remember that Daddy's problems were his to bear, not hers. Though she could walk beside him on this journey, he'd have to do the hard work of recovery on his own.

Besides, she had her own heaping helping of pain and regret to swallow still. She checked her watch, willing herself to focus on the problems of today and not the past.

Where was Hunter? Had he found Wilson? This business of not having a phone was damned inconvenient. Right now, she'd settle for a carrier pigeon if that would help.

Just as her panic was starting to rise again, the sound of familiar footsteps rang out in the hall. *Wilson!*

Hunter pushed through her door, with her son right behind. Kathryn ran to her boy, hugging him and patting him up and down to make sure he was okay.

"Geez, Momma, I'm fine! Let me go! There was no reason to be so upset. I had everything under control." He wriggled.

Hunter rolled his eyes. "We found him at a chocolatier on a side street you missed. When he got out of laser tag, he was hungry. So naturally, he wanted candy for lunch. I think he's eaten a couple of pounds of peanut butter cups by now."

Kathryn couldn't find it in her heart to be too mad. After all, Wilson *had* waited for a pickup that had never come. "I'm going to let you off the hook for all this, Wilson, only because your granddaddy didn't hold up his end of the bargain. Hopefully next time this happens, you'll have a working phone and can call somebody. But if not, promise me you'll stay at your original meeting point. No wandering. Okay?"

"Okay, Momma." He gave her a big hug, probably in gratitude that she didn't take away his video games for the infraction.

A soft knock sounded on her door. Hunter rose to open it. Kathryn was shocked to see Miss Berry standing in the hallway, holding what appeared to be a full-size Christmas tree. A bellhop stood behind her with crates of decorations.

"Oh!" Miss Berry cried. "I didn't see you come in! We usually try to deliver these when our guests are out and about. It's time for our annual decking of the halls!"

Wilson danced on his toes with excitement. "Woo-hoo! Does every room get one of these?"

Miss Berry motioned the staff in. "We're not called Christmas Pass for nothing. Let me get it set up for you. We can have this decorated in a jiffy."

Wilson put on his most baleful, puppy-dog face. "Oh, Momma, can *we* decorate it? Pleeease? We didn't put up our tree at home."

Kathryn looked over at Hunter. "Would you mind?"

He shrugged. "It's been a while since I've had a tree. It might be nice."

After conferring a bit with Miss Berry, Kathryn made arrangements for the decorations to be left for them to do. Though, she did ask the staff to decorate Huck and Wilson's room tomorrow afternoon so Daddy could get some rest. And she made sure to order a thick Sicilian pizza from room service. They were all starving.

Kathryn couldn't help but be awed by the Christmas finery the staff was in the process of leaving with them. The tree was real—a beautiful, full blue spruce that unfurled to a perfect seven-foot height once its ropes were cut. House-keeping set it up in its stand and vacuumed up the stray needles.

When they were finally alone with all of it, Wilson tore

through the boxes. He found the string lights first—the old-fashioned kind, with big multi-colored bulbs. He seemed confused at first, holding them up as if he couldn't believe what he was seeing. "They're so *big*," he exclaimed.

"Oh, my Lord, the old C9 lights," Kathryn exclaimed. "My grandmomma used to have those on her tree. I didn't even think you could buy these anymore. Boy, does this take me back. You should have seen it, Wilson. Your Great-Granddaddy Weiss, your Grandmomma Wilson's daddy, used to string these over everything. He used to have a twenty-foot-tall hemlock tree outside his front window, and he'd get up on a big ladder and use a long stick to hang these lights up to the very top. Kids would come from all around the neighborhood to see it."

Hunter grabbed one end, and Wilson the other, and they quickly had them unrolled. Before long, the two were working in perfect harmony, wrapping the lights in concentric circles around the tree. It warmed her heart to see the two of them working so well together. Kathryn bent down and began categorizing the ornaments. They were gorgeous and, she guessed, antique.

They ate the pizza quickly and soon were back to work. Kathryn dug to the bottom of the last box and found that every item they'd given her for decorations was something her grandparents had also put on their tree—silvery strand tinsel, bubbling oil lights that looked like burning candles...

She stopped everyone and made them put the tinsel icicles on before the ornaments, to make it easier. They worked together, Wilson struggling until he figured out how to drape them without making big silvery clumps. Finally, they had it covered with the ethereal, shiny silver strands.

Kathryn dug around to make sure she'd gotten all the ornaments out. As she got down to the very bottom, she found a white box stamped with "made on December 23."

Had they sent dessert? She opened the box and sat there in stunned silence. The smell of anise assailed her nose, and she knew immediately what these were—embossed German springerle cookies.

Good Lord, how is it even possible? One of her very few fond childhood Christmas memories was working in the kitchen with her own Grandmomma Weiss, Momma's mother, to make these. Grandmomma would take Kathryn into her kitchen for lazy afternoons of baking while Momma was sponsoring a charity tea or running around shopping or such. Kathryn was too terrible at baking to be much help, but that never seemed to matter to her calm, kind, infinitely patient grandmomma. Together they'd roll out the buttery shortbread-style dough and stamp on the elaborate designs with her wooden molds. Kathryn often stayed at her grandmomma's house the whole weekend, because the cookie dough had to rest for a day before they could bake it. The next day, when the cookies were baked and cooled, she and grandmomma strung them with red ribbons and hung them on the tree, loading the fragrant cookies in gift boxes for friends too. To this day, the smell of anise cookies was the smell of Christmas to Kathryn.

What a shame Wilson would never know his Great-Grandmomma Weiss, who died when she was a teen. The boy had never seen a springerle cookie, either.

Considering his pitch perfect radar for sugar, Wilson was hanging over her shoulder in no time. He reached in and grabbed a cookie. "Oooo! Can we eat them?"

"No, baby." She snatched the cookie back. "There's an elaborate family tradition around these things. You hang them first. Then you eat them on Christmas Day."

"Awww," the boy whined.

But Kathryn reminded him that when it came to Christmas, some things were worth the wait. Before long, they had all the ornaments on.

Wilson fished out the top-of-the tree star, an old-fashioned one made with silver tinsel and multi-colored lights. His face fell as he held it in his hands. And his eyes glistened with unshed tears. "I miss my grandmomma. She was fun. She always used to lift me up so I could put the star on her tree. Why'd she have to die, Momma?"

The question stopped Kathryn in her tracks, and for more than the obvious reason. All at once, it occurred to Kathryn that Wilson saw Evangeline Wilson, her own complicated momma, like Kathryn saw her own sainted Grandmomma Weiss. And the thought shredded her, grief throbbing in her like a dull ache that would never be soothed.

Kathryn pulled her son to her and wrapped him in her arms. "I wish I understood why your grandmomma is gone, honey. But I don't. Sometimes life doesn't give you the answers you need most."

He nodded against her side, hugging her back.

Hunter crouched down in front of Wilson. "I can lift you up there if you want," he offered.

Wilson agreed. And as Kathryn watched Hunter lift her giggling son up to the top of the tree, she wondered how a man she'd met only two days ago could somehow sense just what they needed.

CHAPTER 10

It had been a long time since Hunter had seen a winter's night this beautiful. Wilson and Huck were safely asleep in their room upstairs. And he and Kathryn were the only two on the inn's back porch, enjoying the kind of view usually reserved for glitter-frosted Christmas cards. The cobbled patio was covered, and open on the sides. But thanks to a couple of nearby heaters and the roaring fire pit in front of them, they didn't really feel the chill. Snowflakes fell lazily from the sky, twirling in gentle currents of air until they settled softly to the ground. Except for the occasional puffy snow cloud, the sky was clear, dark, and luminous. A picture-perfect, fat little bunny hopped languidly through the inn's yard, making a snack of the grass sticking up through the snow. Hunter smiled. Even the rabbit seemed filled with the winter's calm.

Well played, Christmas Pass, well played.

Kathryn was quiet, seemingly lost in her thoughts after the rough day she'd had. Her nerves had to be shot. Yet, as she sat on the fancy outdoor couch beside him, she tucked her feet up underneath her and laid her head on his shoulder. He wrapped an arm around her and she sighed contentedly.

Being here for this woman...why is it so satisfying, so right?

The connection between them was undeniable. Which led him to another question. Should he tell Kathryn about all his research and his theories about the not-real Christmas Pass? Should he tell her about his morning? But how could he? His proof was weird, and not necessarily open and shut. Even if he was right, there wasn't a damn thing either one of them could do about it.

And what would happen if he told her? There was no scenario where that turned out well. He needed to think this through rationally. If his theory was correct, they were trapped in a beautiful place that populated around their wishes. He had no reason to believe that anything bad would happen to them here. Maybe this wasn't the time to panic. Maybe he'd decide to panic if, after the fifth day, they still couldn't get out.

Yeah, he could get behind that plan, because honestly, he didn't want any of this to end. Already he was addicted to Kathryn—her taste, her smell, the lithe warmth of her against his body. She had him so stirred up every minute of the day that he hardly knew what to do with himself.

"I'm not used to it, you know," Kathryn murmured, her voice shaking him out of his thoughts.

"Used to what?"

"Help."

He idly brushed the hair from her forehead and kissed it. "You don't have to keep thanking me, Kathryn."

"You keep saving us, over and over. I don't know what I would've done if you hadn't been there today. I couldn't have handled it all at once."

"I'm glad I could be there when you needed me."

"But you didn't have to be. You shouldn't have to put up with all my family's crazy—"

He popped his head around to shoot her a no-nonsense look, stopping her apology in its tracks. "You have your crazy, and I have mine. You know that more than anybody."

Their gaze held for a moment, then she cuddled up on his shoulder again.

They were quiet for a long time, watching the snow flutter down in lazy circles in the sky.

Despite her silence, Hunter sensed that Kathryn needed to talk to someone who could help her make sense of her day. So he was doin' it. He was wading in to the deep end. He cleared his throat. "About what Wilson said earlier —Kathryn, how did your momma die?"

She was quiet for a long moment, but she didn't flinch. "Suicide. Last year, the day after Christmas. She shot herself in the head, and I was the one to find her. Why do you think I was so desperate to get out of town for the holidays?"

Jesus. He twisted himself around so he could look her in the eye. But Kathryn was staring intently at the field in front of them, her eyes dry and full of a kind of hollow resignation. "And you really don't know why?" he finally asked.

"Oh, she left a note. But for all my degrees, I doubt I'll ever truly understand how she felt. Momma was bipolar, you see, and a pretty severe case too. She'd have these periods of mania, and when she hit her depression, she'd hardly be able to get out of bed. There wasn't much in between. She hated every psychiatrist I set her up with. She didn't like taking her medicine, either. I think I made her try every single one. But she said it dulled her to the rhythm of life, or some other kind of nonsense."

"And Huck? He always drank?"

She chuckled bitterly, and sighed. "Yeah. I can't

remember a time when he didn't. But he held it together most of the time. He ran his stations during the day and traveled a lot. He drank while he was out but he was never too sloppy to let it keep him from building his business. He'd save his worst drinking for when he was home. Thankfully, he was never a mean drunk. But he wasn't the sort of calm, steady father you'd want, either."

"And you were an only child caught in the middle of all that."

"Yes," she answered. But she didn't elaborate.

She didn't need to. It was easy enough to see the evidence of her childhood in the person she was now. He could imagine her playing the peacemaker, being the good child, trying so hard to understand what made her parents tick. It wasn't hard to see how she fell into the role of being a psychologist. The job must have come to her naturally.

"You're the strongest person I've ever met, Kathryn."

She snorted. "Me? Oh no, definitely not."

"No, I'm being serious. A lot of other people would have cut their parents out or found some other way of not having to deal with their problems. Or they simply would've fallen to pieces and become bitter and useless themselves. But what do you do? You meet things head on, without flinching, no matter what."

"I'm pretty sure I fell to pieces on that sidewalk today."

"And you picked yourself right up and helped your daddy. And then you put on enough of a brave face to make a nice Christmas memory for your son, decorating that tree."

"And you helped."

He tucked his chin over top of her blond waves. "Yeah, decorating again was nice. It's been a while since I've done anything like that. It seemed wrong to do it, somehow, when it was just for me."

156

She didn't need to say anything to let him know she understood. She wrapped her arms around his waist, and they were quiet again. Funny how he was as comfortable in the quiet with her as he was when they talked. Long moments ticked by, with only the crackle of the fire to punctuate the stillness. Watching the firelight cast shifting shadows over her face, he felt a pang of recognition. He'd been wrong about them being worlds apart, hadn't he? For all their differences, he and Kathryn were really the same. They both knew what it was like to live with crippling regret.

Finally, Miss Berry ambled onto the porch, picking up cups and tidying. The poor woman jumped a mile high when she saw them. "Goodness! I didn't see you two there. I was about ready to shut down the fire pit for the night."

"We were enjoying the view. It's so beautiful, it's hard to come in," Hunter explained. "I don't think I've ever seen a winter landscape so perfect. It's as pretty as a picture."

"Oh, if you think this is pretty, you should go walk on our scenic trail. It starts right over there." Miss Berry pointed to a clearing to the left. "It's beautiful at night, and it's not gotten too cold yet."

Kathryn seemed surprised but intrigued by the suggestion. "Sounds gorgeous. But isn't there supposed to be a big storm coming in?"

Miss Berry clucked her tongue. "I checked the weather reports a couple minutes ago. We're supposed to get another foot of snow, but it's not supposed to make Christmas Pass until about three in the morning. The path only takes about forty-five minutes to walk, and it'll give you some of the best overlooks in the region. You go up to the top of the mountain, and then around the other side. It's designed for nighttime walking—the whole path is lit with lights in the ground. It's very safe."

Hunter knitted his brows, wondering if the storm would make an early appearance.

Seeming to sense his unease, Miss Berry put her hands on her hips. "Now, Mr. Holliday, you know we'd never let anything happen to you out there. Our staff is very responsive."

Hunter still didn't answer, because he definitely wasn't so sure about Miss Berry. Hiking a mountain at ten o'clock at night with no cell phones didn't exactly seem to be a smart idea, either. "I dunno."

But Kathryn batted her big doe eyes at him hopefully, clearly latching on to the idea. "Oh, come on, baby, let's do it! Maybe we can rescue this day after all."

Did she call him *baby? Well now.*

He squinted out at the sky. It did seem reasonably tame out there, didn't it? Against his better judgment, he shrugged his assent. "Why not?" Kathryn surely deserved to do something just for her. Maybe he could use the break too.

They said goodnight to Miss Berry and set off through the clearing and onto the path, the snow crunching under their boots. Tall pine trees towered around them, and the LED lights that framed the path glowed red and green like glittering gems scattered in the snow. The night was hushed and still, except for the occasional rustle in the trees or the hoot of an owl. Kathryn laced her fingers with his, and they walked along hand in hand. She looked out over the trail ahead. He couldn't resist the urge to steal glances at her moonlit profile. The light bite of the winter wind had colored her cheeks, and made her eyes shine bright. The sight made his heart thump against his ribs.

God, she's so beautiful.

And she was smiling at him. *Smiling*—after the horrendous day she'd had. He'd made her happy, hadn't he? The idea warmed him.

Maybe I could be good for her, after all.

Smiling to himself now too, Hunter took note of how the path had been expertly cut in the hillside, allowing them to climb up the steep mountain as if it were a lazy walking path. The trail sloped reasonably all the way so they could pass along it side by side, hand in hand.

Kathryn grew introspective in the silence. "It's easy to forget there are places in the world like this. I spend so much of my day running around from building to building —office to home, home to shop, shop to gym. How much time have I spent listening to the world and what it's trying to tell me? How much time have I spent, just being still like this? Not nearly enough, I'd say."

"I've always enjoyed being out in the elements—camping, fishing, hiking, white water rafting. I was lucky when I was a kid. My mom and dad and brother and me were always out doing outdoorsy things. We had a great time. You know, typical wild, wonderful West Virginia stuff. I've kept it up as an adult. It's good for the soul."

"Do you hunt?" she asked.

"No," he replied flatly. "Ironic, isn't it, growing up in West Virginia with a name like Hunter? I'm a decent shot, but I can't bring myself to kill another living thing. I'll let other people deal with the deer overpopulation problem. I even throw the fish back when I fish."

She paused and gave him another one of her probing looks. "Do you miss your family?"

"Yeah, I do. Nobody expected my brother Joe to fall in love and move to Canada. And I sure as heck never expected my parents to follow him. But I'm still close to them anyway, because I'm running the shop now that my dad founded and I can carry on the Holliday name that way. I get up to see them when I can."

"But not over Christmas."

He looked away so she wouldn't see him grimace. "It wasn't always like that. I used to go up every year for the holidays, but now..."

Kathryn stopped walking and turned to him, not saying a word. And he stood there, staring at her like an idiot. Dammit, his throat was thick and his chest was tight. Honestly, he didn't know why discussing his family upset him all of a sudden. Truth was, he had a terrific family—one he should be excited to visit. But he couldn't tell her that the prospect of facing his family alone on the holidays was worse than actually *being* alone in his loft, watching the same Christmas movies over and over and eating cold pizza.

Good God, what have I been doing with my life?

Hunter found himself suddenly overwhelmed and completely at a loss for words. It was like this with Kathryn. At a moment's notice, she could reach inside his chest and squeeze. He stood there, trembling, but he couldn't wrench his gaze from her gentle gray eyes—eyes that, in the moonlight, seemed even more bottomless than usual. Unsaid words hung in the air between them. She was quiet for a long time. Then she squeezed his hand, as if to say *let's keep walking*. And at that moment, that was exactly the reaction he needed from her.

Letting out a shaky breath, he squeezed her hand back, grateful she could leave it at that. Hunter sensed that it was more than her psychologist's instincts that prompted her to stop. Kathryn knew pain when she saw it—knew what it was like to be seared so deep with it that you couldn't bring yourself to name it out loud.

They continued their walk up the mountain, not talking so much now. It seemed the right thing to do, to preserve the soothing shroud of nighttime all around them. The snow had picked up a bit, and the temperature had dropped sharply. But they'd gotten almost to the peak. A thinning tree line gave way to rugged mountain scrub, and the sharpness in the air made the colors around them vibrate with intensity.

They stopped at an outcropping that made the perfect overlook. Hunter moved behind Kathryn, snaking his arms around her waist, grateful that she granted him these little intimacies. In the light of the moon, she was so small and feminine in his arms, even when she was bundled up. Having his hands on her heated him up, every time. But she was clearly freezing her ass off.

"You're shivering," he said.

"I was doing f-fine until the temperature drop," she chattered. "But s'okay. It's w-worth it to see this view."

And she was right. It seemed the entire town of Christmas Pass was spread out in front of them from up here. Passing headlights formed pretty patterns as cars wound their way through the streets, and the distant blinking of Christmas decorations wrapped the whole town in ribbons of light. Snow whirled over the rooftops of the sprawling neighborhoods that ringed downtown. The lights in the windows winked on and off, and puffs of smoke pumped from the chimneys. A frozen creek shimmered in the moonlight in the culvert right below them.

And for a moment, Hunter didn't care whether Christmas Pass was real or not. Because sometimes, a moment could be magical all on its own.

Kathryn shivered, but still sighed happily.

He turned her around in his arms to face him. "I think you need some warming up." He caressed her cheeks with his gloved hands, trying to take away the sting of the wind.

She leaned into him, and the warmth he found in her eyes warmed him too.

How was it that after only a handful of kisses, he felt so bound to this woman? They'd only just met, and yet he felt tied to her somehow, as if nothing would be right without her. She set his body on fire, without a doubt. But she was so much more than that. Kathryn was *necessary* to him somehow, in a way he couldn't quite articulate to himself.

Hunter knew he should be keeping his distance. But he couldn't help himself. Bending his head, he brushed his lips to hers, tasting that slow, delicious surrender that warmed and steadied him like nothing else ever could.

He breathed in deep. And there it was, that pull, that connection. *Kathryn.* Her mouth was chilly with cold against his, but they tangled together effortlessly, and things soon heated up. Lord, how he wanted her—her body, yes, but her sweetness, her understanding, and maybe even the challenge of her, too. He drank her in with lingering, hungry kisses. She leaned into him, tightening her fist in his coat as she kissed him back boldly, with no hesitation. The cold bite of the wind snapped his skin to attention and made the heat of their kiss so hot, so intoxicating that it felt like warm whiskey traveling through him. Was it the thin air up here, or was it her, making his head a bit tingly and dizzy? Pulling back, they tipped their foreheads together, breathing each other's air. Good Lord, just a few kisses, and they were both breathing hard. His heart thundered in his chest, kicking to life for the first time in so, so long.

This woman. What is it about this woman?

He wanted more—*so much more*. The air was heavy with their rapid breaths, puffing out in icy clouds. God, how he wished he could keep her here with him, even for a little while. He wished he could make time stand still...wished he could show her how he felt...

"I think I'm warm now." She grinned.

"Glad I could be of service."

She chuckled. "Is it my imagination, Mr. Holliday, or is there a *thing* between us?"

"Mmmmm. I think it's more than a thing. Maybe a lot more than a thing."

Kathryn bit down on her plump, rosy bottom lip. "I think I like the sound of that." He was about to answer her when Kathryn knotted her eyebrows up in concern. She pointed to the sky. "Didn't Miss Berry say the blizzard wasn't moving in until three in the morning?"

Hunter looked up and was stupefied by what he saw. He'd been so focused on her that he hadn't noticed the thick storm clouds rushing in all around them.

What in the— How in the world had it moved in so fast? From their vantage point, they should have seen a wall of clouds like this coming from miles away.

Unless...

Wait, hadn't he wished for more time with her? Could Christmas Pass be messing with him again? Come on, he hadn't even said it out loud! Now those roiling storm clouds were directly over their heads.

Awwww, no.

Before he could even blink, the skies opened up.

All around them, low-hanging clouds flung thick, driving sheets of snow through the air. The wind howled ominously. The cute, fluffy snowflakes were long gone, replaced by heavy, stinging slaps of sleet. They'd be stranded up here unless they started back down the mountain *right now*.

He put his hands on Kathryn's shoulders, shouting to make sure she understood over the shrieks of the wind. "We have to get back as fast as we can."

She nodded to let him know she understood.

And the winds kicked up again, gusting so ferociously it practically knocked them off their feet. They took a step away from the edge of the outlook, only to be met with rumbling and deep, groaning, cracking sounds.

The ground shook under their feet, and Hunter looked up in time to see the snow buckling on the ridge right above them. Before he could move, before he could yell, the ridge itself began thundering toward them.

Dear God, it's an avalanche. And there's no time to run.

CHAPTER 11

HUNTER SNAPPED his arms around Kathryn as the snow-pack under their feet gave way, sending them tumbling hard, head over feet. The whole world went white and cold and unforgiving. Everything slowed down, and he felt like a pinball, banking hard against every kind of obstacle as he hurtled down the mountainside. The impact of the ground jarred him as he rolled, first on a shoulder, then a hip, over and over again until he stopped.

Opening his eyes, he realized his arms weren't around Kathryn anymore. He couldn't see her, couldn't even *feel* her. Dammit, he was completely encased in snow, barely able to see anything for the snow around his face. He struggled violently but realized quickly that the snow was light and easy to move. In seconds, he'd gotten himself free. As he punched his head out of the snow bank, the sound of frantic splashing rang out.

Oh, Christ. There was a creek at the bottom of the ravine, wasn't there? His stomach seized in fear. Hunter scrabbled over to the creek's edge and saw Kathryn pop her head and shoulders out of the water. She gasped and sputtered from the icy water. Holy hell, she must have slid across the creek until the ice became thin enough for her to fall in.

"Kathryn!" he cried. "Don't struggle! I'll get you out!" He flipped onto his stomach and wiggled himself a couple of feet across the ice, straight to her. "Are you okay?"

"So co-cold," she chattered. "But my f-feet are touching the bottom. All I need is a boost out."

That simplified things. He held his hand out to her, and she grabbed it gratefully. With a few heaves, he was able to wrestle her out of the icy creek. She flopped up onto him like a near-frozen fish. They both struggled around a bit on the ice until they got to firm ground. Only then did his heart-stopping anxiety ebb a bit.

Unfortunately, they were nowhere near safe yet. The wind screamed like it had a score to settle, and the punishing heavy snowfall made for near whiteout conditions. It was so bad, he couldn't tell up from down, or north from south. Every step was filled with worry. Would their feet hit solid ground, or would they sink shoulders-deep into a snowdrift? Hand in hand, Hunter and Kathryn somehow managed to scramble out of the culvert together. It was one small victory. Now they stood near where they'd been before the snow bank had taken them down.

"Are you hurt?" he shouted over the howling winds.

She shook her head. "No. Maybe a bump or bruise or two. You?"

"The same. We got lucky. The snow cushioned our fall." He scanned the mountain ahead of them for the best path forward. "Take my hand. We have to stick together."

Kathryn closed her hand in his. Even in the near-blinding snow, Hunter could see she was a mess, soaked to the skin with muddy creek water from head to toe. Kathryn peered up at him through her long, thick eyelashes, the sodden hair around her face making her seem fragile and waiflike. Ice crystals were already forming in the water-logged strands. At this rate, her jeans would be frozen solid in no time.

His panic ramped right back up again. As cold and drenched with icy creek water as Kathryn was, she could get frostbite in a matter of minutes.

He pointed up toward the peak. "We can catch the trail up there."

She gave him a trusting little nod, as if she were prepared to follow him anywhere. It only terrified him more. How in the hell were they going to get out of this? By the time they found help, it could be too late. And how could they even do that? They had no phones, and they couldn't see up from down out here!

But then he remembered. All he had to do was...

"I wish we could see a path in the snow and find shelter," Hunter barked out. "*Now.*"

"What?" Kathryn hollered, pointing to her ear. She hadn't heard him. But Christmas Pass, apparently, had.

Before his eyes, the LED trail lights blinked to life in the snow like a runway before them.

He pointed down at the ground so Kathryn could see. "We found the trail head!" he shouted, "like Miss Berry said. The lights must have gone out for a minute!"

Relief lit up Kathryn's face. He hauled her up the path as fast as he could. And no more than a hundred yards away, just around the bend up in the distance, they came to a snow-covered sign.

Hollyberry Inn Guest Cottages.

Hunter decided right then and there that maybe he could get used to magic.

What he could see of the place was stunning. Apparently dark and unused, the cottage was more like a creek stone and timber frame house, with big windows. He'd be willing to bet that no one rented these at this time of the year. If he could make this work, he and Kathryn would have pretty swank accommodations for getting out of this storm. They hustled up the steps to the front door. Hunter pushed on the locked door but then realized it had a room card reader.

Surely my key won't work, will it? He pulled out the plastic card, still miraculously in his coat's chest pocket, and tried it. And just like that, the tumblers clicked and the door cracked open. It *worked*.

Because of course it did.

He hurried Kathryn into the cottage, desperate to get her dry and warm and safe. Peeling off her coat, he grabbed a blanket from the sofa and tucked it securely around her shoulders.

"Surely to God this place has a heater," Hunter muttered as he fumbled around in the dark.

Kathryn found the light switch and flipped it on. And they both stood there for a moment, awestruck.

This was no run-of-the-mill cottage out in the woods. Oh no, this was clearly was a getaway for the very wealthy, with a spacious living room flanked with a towering creek stone fireplace, a compact but fully equipped kitchen with marble counters, and a downright majestic bedroom. And yes, the bedroom had its own creek stone fireplace too. *Nice.* The antique wrought-iron bed faced an oversized Palladian window with a view to its own private pine forest. Tangled antler chandeliers lit every room with soft, glowing light.

Kathryn followed behind him, dripping a trail of water onto the floor. She let out a low whistle. "My God, this isn't a cottage, it's a fantasy!"

Oh, sweetheart, if you only knew.

Hunter located the thermostat and flicked it on. The

heater rumbled to life, thank God, blowing out a steady stream of toasty-warm, gently humidified air. He found a laundry room, a utility room, and hallelujah—a tankless water heater. If the pipes weren't frozen, they'd have all the hot water they needed.

"Come on. Let's run you a bath. We have to get your body temperature back up."

Apparently in no mood to argue, Kathryn followed him into the bathroom, and he tugged off her boots and socks. Kathryn shivered in front of the sink while he pulled off her sodden gloves and tested the hot water flowing from the faucet. He put her hands between his and positioned them under the water, rubbing them.

Kathryn's teeth were still chattering and she was quivering with chills. He frowned in concern, but she put on a brave face. "I'm f-fine, Hunter. I wasn't out there long enough to get f-frostbite or even h-hypothermia."

Maybe not frostbite, but she was putting too much of a brave face on it. He was chilled to the bone, and only a portion of his arms and feet were damp. She must be dangerously cold. And nothing dangerous was going to happen to her. Not on his watch.

"Keep rubbing them under the water. I'm drawing you a bath."

"Hunter, it's okay. I can handle—"

"No arguments."

Of course, this bathroom was big enough to pass for a luxury spa, with its mahogany cabinets and soft-gray marble tiles. A frosted-glass pocket door separated the tub from the toilet and sinks. Hunter set to work filling the enormous sleigh-shaped, claw-foot tub with water as hot as he thought she could stand. On a small dresser beside the tub, he found some jasmine-scented bubble bath. Opening it, he took a whiff, and shook his head with amusement. Damn if it didn't smell exactly like the light, exotic scent of her favorite perfume. He poured it in, along with some of the fancy bath oil he found beside it.

He came out to find Kathryn still huddled at the sink. "Can I take my hands out from under the water, captain?"

He turned off the taps and went back to check on her. "You able to move your fingers okay?"

She wiggled her fingers around. "See? Good as new."

"Good. I'm going to light the fireplaces and see if we can get this place warmed up faster. I want you to take off those soggy clothes and set them outside the door. I'll wash and dry them."

"Yes, sir!" She saluted as he shut the door behind him.

Lord, he had a million things to do to get Kathryn set to rights again. And he was antsy and agitated to see them all done. He moved to the enormous living room fireplace first. Luckily, it featured deep built-in alcoves stacked with perfectly seasoned firewood. With the help of the gas starter and some kindling, he soon had the fire crackling away. He went into the bedroom and repeated the process.

The bedroom. Hunter swallowed hard. It was the perfect lovers' hideaway. Had it been conjured from his deepest desires? Probably. The big king-sized, iron bed made you want to climb in and take up residence, piled high as it was with a goose down comforter, a colorful quilt, and more big, fluffy pillows than was probably necessary. Hunter tried to stop the string of images now flashing in his mind. But his brain fired with the possibilities of having Kathryn in this bed...the smooth silk of her pale skin under his hand...her breathless moans in his ear...holding her perfect ass in his hands and sliding into her hot, pulsing wetness, nice and slow. *Mmmmm.* His cock swelled in response, and the sharp stab of arousal snapped him back to reality. He muttered a string of curses and blew out a shaky breath.

No, I'll sleep on the couch tonight. I won't be some a-hole who makes assumptions.

He rubbed a hand through his hair, trying to calm himself down. Shit, he needed a distraction.

Think, Hunter, and not about what you need. What would Kathryn need?

She needed a drink—something that would chase the cold from her insides. A quick check of the tricked-out, walk-in pantry proved he had everything he could ever want to fix something, and then some. The place was so well stocked that it was overkill—really delicious overkill.

One whole section was a liquor cabinet with enough bottles of wine and whiskey to get an army drunk. And then there were baking supplies, canned foods, trail snacks, even a few assortments of Belgian chocolates, for crying out loud. Half a grocery store was in here. A quick peek in the fridge was the same. Its shelves bulged with fancy meats and cheeses, smoked salmon, bagels, and so many frozen entrees made by the inn's chef, he couldn't even keep track. And why was it surprising? Everything in Christmas Pass was over the top, and this was no exception. If they were going to be stranded up here, by God, they'd be stranded in style.

Hunter pulled out a couple of saucepans and decided he'd go for the drink his mother always made for Christmas every year—hot buttered rum. He got the water to boiling and in another pan melted some of the fancy English butter he'd found. Then he added the dark-brown sugar and cinnamon together, heating it all until they were fully mingled. Once the sugar was molten, he poured in the rum, then the boiling water. As he stirred, he felt a pang of longing for his family he hadn't felt in some time. They were probably drinking this same drink right now too. Were they opening the boxes of gifts and toys he'd sent? Were the kids playing with them? Was it snowing in Vancouver tonight?

Hunter tipped the concoction into a warming carafe he found in the cabinets. Grabbing a couple of heavy, hand-made earthenware mugs out of the cabinet, he poured himself a cup. *Oh yeah*, it was heaven—Christmas in a cup, like always. When he got out of this place, he'd call his mom and thank her for teaching him how to make this.

As he stood there propped up against the kitchen counter, Hunter couldn't help but fix his gaze on the bath-room door. He spotted Kathryn's pile of clothes making a soggy puddle on the hardwood floor. *Crap!* He set down his cup and quickly scooped up the dripping pile, taking care to dry the floor too. Hauling the mess into the laundry room, he began rustling around for detergent. It didn't take long for him to corral the necessary supplies. Then he began inspecting the pile. He was surprised to see Kathryn's filthy parka was washer safe. He popped it in, along with her jeans, a thick, long-sleeved tee with a sparkly Christmas tree on it, and heavy socks. Then, God help him, he found her *very* enticing underwear.

Damn, was there anything sexier than a woman's lingerie? He held up the pink lacy confections. They were precisely what he would've predicted an elegant, sexy woman like Kathryn would have chosen. The tiny panties were nearly see-through lace of the palest pink. He studied the springy, lacy top. What did they call this thing? A bralette? Yeah, that was right. It was made of the same deli-cate, shell pink lace, with a nice deep vee in the front. *Mmmmm, a matching set.* It was stretchy and soft and, holy hell, it sent a thrill down his spine to picture this pulled taut over the soft swell of her breasts.

As he leaned over the washer, his own filthy shirt

caught his eye. He'd gotten wet, too, but only up to the elbows. His socks were looking pretty worse for the wear. He peeled them all off and popped them into the washer. Stopping for a moment, he considered whether he should throw the rest of his clothes in while he was at it. But then he decided no. They weren't that dirty and could wait. It wasn't so bad to be barefoot and bare-chested, but it wouldn't do for him to be walking around naked. Not unless Kathryn asked him to, at least. A man could dream.

He dumped in the soap and started the washing machine, but took those intriguing lacy bits over to the laundry tub to start hand washing. He'd done enough wash in his day to know to use gentle soap and roll them out in towels when he was done. Filling the bottom of the laundry tub with a couple of inches of soapy water, he gently scrubbed and swished them around, and then turned on the faucet, rolling each piece in his hands to rinse. The water turned the lace transparent in his hands. He couldn't help but marvel at the panties. How could something so thin and insubstantial cover up the pure, primal heat of her? Turning them over in his fingertips, he could so easily imagine what it would be like to pull these panties to the side and bury his face in her—

Oh, holy hell.

Hunter groaned a little too loudly at the illicit thrill of the whisper-soft lace gliding against his hand, then winced at how pathetic that made him appear. At least no one could see him in here.

He let out a shaky breath. *Mind on task, Hunter.*

Laundry. *Right.* The linen closet was in the laundry room. So he grabbed one of the thick white towels. As he closed the closet door, a realization crept up on him. He hadn't seen a single towel in that bathroom, had he? *Dammit!*

Hunter heard Kathryn splashing around. Okay, so she was still in the tub, behind that glass door. He could sneak some towels in there, right inside the outer door, and she wouldn't see him. Grabbing two of every kind of towel he thought she'd want, he tiptoed up to the door.

And when he opened it—*aww, hell*. Kathryn was naked and dripping wet, standing not two feet in front of him.

All the breath left his body. And the world's biggest tow truck couldn't have moved him from this spot.

Kathryn didn't move, or scream, or even flinch. No, she kicked up her chin and looked him straight in the eye, a flush blooming on her cheeks and chest as he stood there and gawked at her.

Taking her all in like this was straight up going to give him a heart attack. She was so hot and real and fucking *exquisite*. Everything about her was graceful and feminine and perfectly proportioned, from the long, lean slope of her back, to her firm, creamy thighs to her high, rounded breasts. He must have been staring right at them, imagining how they'd fit so perfectly in the palms of his hands. Like magic, her peachy-pink nipples hardened up to stiff peaks under his attention. He met her gaze again. Kathryn's eyes had gone smoky and dark.

Good God.

In an instant he went hard as a tire iron, so gobsmacked with the sight of her, every thought he'd ever had fled from his mind. Another long, helpless groan escaped his throat before he had a chance to stop himself.

And still, Kathryn didn't tear her eyes away. Instead, she quirked up the corner of her mouth, ever so slightly.

To his utter shock, she stepped *forward*, took the top towel off the stack, and set the other towels aside. Getting up on tiptoe, she leaned close enough so she could murmur in his ear. "I was going for the robe on the back of the door just now, but these towels will do nicely."

He gasped, but then held his breath to keep from panting like a dog. Lightning shot through every cell in his body as she lowered herself back down, her taut nipples grazing and teasing his bare chest all the way.

"Thanks," she whispered, pulling the towel around her back.

She didn't move away. She should have.

But no, Kathryn stayed there, touching him skin to skin, and she didn't seem the least bit sorry about that. Her alabaster skin was rosy and warm from the bath. The primal allure of her pure, clean scent shocked his senses, like the heady fragrance of the first flowers of spring, pushing their way up through the cold winter ground. He breathed her in with long, shaky breaths that echoed in the quiet room.

His heartbeat raced now, the sound of each thump pounding in his ears. He watched in mute fascination as a fat drop of water beaded from her hair, snaked over the graceful curve of her collarbone, and wound its way down her breast.

And then Kathryn turned those eyes on him again— eyes that saw everything and cracked light into corners he'd been avoiding for so long. She was breathing fast too, *trembling* for him.

Good Lord—could it be she wants me as much as I want her?

As if she heard his thoughts, Kathryn pressed the pad of her finger to the dimple in his chin. "The answer to your question, Hunter, is yes."

Yes.

His whole body responded to the word. All his need, fucking *years* of it, came raging up inside him, a wild, desperate craving that demanded its due. "Ryn," he whispered.

Her mouth was *so* close to his—her lips flame-red, parted like an invitation, a full-on dare.

Hunter bent his head to hers, and he took it.

CHAPTER 12

NEVER HAD any man looked at Kathryn like that—as if he might burst into flames if he didn't touch her. Like he *craved* her, *needed* her like he needed air or sunlight. How could she resist him, resist *this*? Hunter devoured her with incendiary expertise, kiss by kiss, pushing, exploring, giving her no quarter. And she answered back, capturing his tongue with one long, languorous suck.

Hunter moaned the kind of soul-deep growl that rumbled him from his head to his toes. It tingled through her fingertips as the shiver raced up his back. And it made her shiver too.

Dear God, he was so big that he towered over her, his muscles hard and powerfully wound with tension. Hunter was so sexy, so overwhelmingly *male*—all planes and angles, muscle and woodsy, intoxicating musk. He moved his hands to her face, grasping her possessively, tipping her head back so he could deepen his kiss. Then he licked the beads of water on her neck with a shiver-inducing blend of nips and light, searching kisses.

Energy coursed between them, like a magnet and metal held too close together. She couldn't have moved from his arms if she tried. Jolts of pure, raw sensation radiated out from wherever his mouth brushed her skin. He grazed his teeth along her neck, and soothed it with a hot rasp of his tongue...*God.*

Her heart pounded in her ears. She was too mesmerized to protest as he backed her up against the cool tiles of the bathroom wall. Hunter worked his calloused hands down her body with aching slowness, trailing the rough pad of his fingertips over her neck, tracing the line of her collarbone, until he finally focused his rapt attention on her flushed, sensitive breasts. Watching his face as he explored her was a revelation, a sight she couldn't tear her eyes away from. Lord, he was so absorbed in her, his eyes riveted on his hand in amazement as he caressed and kneaded her. Reacting on pure instinct, she arched herself against him, wanting relief, wanting more of this perfect, sensual torture. His fingers finally yielded when he paused to tease and pinch the peaks just enough.

Yes.

This.

More.

She groaned with bliss, throwing her head back. Pure liquid heat poured through her veins, and she swayed on her feet.

Hunter caught her as her body sagged, and hauled her back up to him. But instead of chuckling, or muttering some overconfident quip like another man might have done, he simply stood before her, stripped of all pretention, trembling with utterly real, unfiltered need.

Kathryn searched his face again, and she saw everything —his loneliness, and pain, and desire, and the pure, raw essence of him, laid out as clearly as if she'd been reading it from a book. He needed her in a way no other man had needed her before. It caught her off guard, stealing her breath. His vulnerability made her heart beat for him. But his body, his fire, made her *burn* for him.

The time for talking was over. Kathryn caressed the side of his stubbled jaw. Humming with pleasure, she ran her thumb over his surprisingly soft bottom lip. Then she leaned forward and kissed him again, nipping his lower lip with her teeth. She took his hand and led it down her body until it came to rest on her hot, aching center.

Hunter growled, trailing his mouth over her neck as his fingers explored her, opened her. Stark hunger vibrated through his touch.

Her knees buckled again, but he caught her, pushing her higher up the wall. Wrapping an arm around her bare bottom, Hunter nudged her to wrap her legs around his waist. She wrapped her arms around his head too while he ravaged her breasts with his hot, needy mouth, sucking and teasing with every searing lash of his tongue.

He murmured hot groans of encouragement against her ear:

"so damn beautiful..."

"need you so bad..."

"wanted you from the moment I saw you..."

"there's no one like you, Ryn—*no one.*"

Ryn. She liked that. But Kathryn could barely even process what he was saying. *Sweet Jesus,* he felt so good...the earthy tang of the sweat on his skin, the scalding heat of his mouth on her body, the hardness of his muscle underneath her hands. She bit her fingernails into his meaty shoulders as she wriggled her hips against him. The hot, hard ridge of his arousal pulsed underneath her. The soft scrape of his jeans against her bare flesh sent waves of pleasure through her, radiating out to tingle her thighs, her sex.

The sound of Hunter sucking in a tortured breath echoed off the tiles. "You're making me *so friggin' crazy,*" he growled. And there were more love words pressed into her throat. But all her senses converged on the feeling of his fingers pressing inside her.

Two fingers, *yeah*, then three, invading her, pushing her. And then, he found the perfect spot, the place where everything turned to white sparks and heat. The heel of his hand beat against her with every expert stroke. She arched and writhed.

"Yes, Hunter, God *yes, like that,*" she cried, holding onto him for some kind of purchase, some kind of equilibrium in a perfect storm of pleasure that seemed to be battering her from all sides. The sensations pushed her so fast and so hard her brain couldn't keep up. Her climax cracked over her whole body, pouring over her in intense, electrifying waves, taking her out of her comfort zone—out of her mind, even.

And all the while, Hunter held her close, grounding her while the delicious tremors rocked over her body. She swallowed, barely able to catch her breath. Every part of her body tingled, enervated with pure pleasure.

Kathryn felt exhilarated, transformed, and maybe even a bit foolish. She'd never had an orgasm like that, not by herself or even with a partner. "I never knew..." She gulped against her dry throat, trying to catch her breath. "I never knew it could be like that." And it was true. She realized in this moment that, at least sexually speaking, she'd been living half of a life. She'd never experienced real, honest-to-God sexual chemistry—not like this. Dear Lord, what else would this man be teaching her tonight?

As if he'd heard her thoughts, Hunter chuckled, low and warm in her ear. "Just you wait." He scooped Kathryn up and carried her around the corner to the bedroom. When he dropped her on the springy comforter, she giggled with the pure, delicious anticipation of it. Hunter bent his head to kiss her again, then popped back up on his knees. "So many things I want to do with you. Let me take care of you." He began popping the buttons on his fly, *slowly*, one by one.

Licking her lips, she laid back and watched, transfixed, as he went about the incredibly erotic task of revealing himself, an inch at a time. She was hungry for him. *Ravenous*. Not able to take it anymore, Kathryn sprang back up on her knees, chest to chest with him again. "No, wait," she urged, stopping his hands. "Let me. I want to feel you, Hunter. I—I *need* to."

He smirked, like he might argue. But he dropped his hands like she asked, and held them up to his sides in mock surrender.

Kathryn kissed him again, deep and lingering, all the better to savor the spicy taste of alcohol on his tongue. There weren't enough minutes in this night for her to get her fill of him—the brush of her fingernails over his chest hair, the hard outlines of his muscles, the sinfully sexy turn of his lips. There was no stopping the imperative to explore him, touch him, open to him. Even now, she could see Hunter's unique brand of raw sensuality could be an addiction that would be very, very hard to kick.

Completely absorbed in her task, she tasted and touched his surprisingly lean and muscled body. He was such a sexy contradiction. His skin was fever hot under her hands, yet wherever her fingers grazed him, goose bumps followed. She'd never given a man *goose bumps* before. The power of it made her a little giddy.

She rested her hand on his heart. It thundered in his chest. *Oh yes, he's enjoying this.*

His breathing kicked up, blowing hot puffs of air along her neck. *Mmmmm, so gorgeous.* She hummed in appreciation for the masculine details of him—the instinctive flex of his biceps as her fingers traveled over them, the broad planes of his chest, the cabled band of muscle that started at his hip and disappeared under his waistband. He didn't have a six-pack exactly. No, he had the kind of powerful build that suggested an effortless, natural strength—the kind of manly power you got from hard physical work and making things with your hands. What in the hell had she been doing all her life, focusing on men with soft hands and desk jobs?

Shivering in anticipation, Kathryn cupped her hand on the straining bulge in his pants, primed and hot as a fire-place poker. *Ohhh, holy hell*—he was huge and thick and, *dear Lord*, already popping past the waistband of his pants. The possibilities *that* conjured sent a fresh wave of lust pounding through her, stuttering her control. Her fingers fumbled with the last button on his fly, and he helped her finish popping it free. He eagerly squirmed out of his jeans and clingy boxer briefs, quickly kicking them aside, and met her up on his knees again.

Kathryn gently pushed him back a bit, forcing him to balance his arms behind him. She exhaled a long, shuddering breath, and took her time appreciating Hunter's magnificent naked form. His fine, silky mat of chest hair went down-down-down to a point at all his finest assets. And damn, Hunter Holliday made every other man she'd been with seem like a bony teenager by comparison. For a moment, it was if she'd forgotten how to breathe.

Hunter caught her gaze again, and his brows furrowed in concern. "Are you all right?"

"Better than all right," she huffed out. "Hunter, you're the sexiest man I've ever seen."

Relief flashed on his face, and he reached out for her again. But she wagged her finger, pushing him back.

"*So magnificent, so mouthwatering.*" She moaned as she

traced hot, needful kisses along his belly. When she finally began kissing up the length of him, he bent back even farther. And when she took him deep in her mouth, all the way down into her throat, he fisted the sheets.

"Aww, hell yeah," he wailed.

God, he was big and beautiful and glistening now there in her hand. Pure, unbridled heat burned in his gaze as he watched her, utterly rapt, his eyes dark, and his chest flushed. Hunter threw his head back for a second, swallowing hard, and his Adam's apple bobbed along the cabled muscles in his neck.

Ohhh, yes. Kathryn wanted to laugh for joy. She was so drunk on the feel of him, the salty-sweet taste of him, the power of holding his pleasure in the palm of her hand. She took the length of him in her mouth again, caressing him in long, rhythmic strokes with her hand while she did. He cupped his hand around the back of her head to hold her close to her task.

"Yeah, you know what you're doin', don't you, babe?" he said over and over, his moans making her hot and shaky and needy too.

When she could sense him hardening even more and jolting under her touch, he suddenly pulled her away by the scruff of her neck. "No." He grimaced, clearly trying to hold himself together. "Not yet. You're way too good at that."

Before she could even protest, Hunter scooped her up and pushed her back on the bed. He spread her legs wide with his shaking palms. Exploring her folds with his thumb, he moved up to rub lazy circles around her aching nub, spreading waves of pleasure with each turn.

"Let me taste you, Ryn. I need to taste you too," he whispered.

She nodded, too turned on for words.

Hunter wasted no time wrapping his arms around the

backs of her thighs and pulling her, slicked and hot, to his mouth. "So delicious, so perfect." He groaned and dove into her like she was the world's finest delicacy. Lord, this man knew how to make her feel like a goddess, like a woman worthy of worship. She practically melted into the bed, unable to think or speak. He drove her pleasure up, just to edge her down, the sensations building and building.

She was getting close. So *close*.

But as she was approaching the point of no return, he yanked his head back and leaned over her, stroking his cock. Hunter looked pained, like he was barely holding on to his control.

He groaned again, planting more hot, needful kisses on her neck. "I want you so much, Ryn. But I don't have a condom. I can stop—"

"No," Kathryn gasped out, still breathing hard. "I have a birth control implant. Are you—"

"Healthy? Yeah, I swear, you're the first since..." His voice trailed off.

Kathryn let out a long breath as the reality of what he said sank in. *The first since Laney*. The truth, the *emotion* in his eyes reached in and touched her in a way nothing else could. She couldn't take his pain away, but she could give him this. She trusted him. And she showed it as she gently led him to her entrance. Hunter huffed out a relieved breath and pushed into her with one long, slow, sensual slide.

Hunter moaned and shook in her arms. She could tell he was restraining himself, trying not to hurt her. He pulled and stretched her with his prodigious size, but she was so insanely aroused, it only took a couple of pushes before her body eagerly accepted every inch.

She clenched around his length, and her chest got unbearably tight. "Oh God, Hunter, please! Please now!"

And he answered her with ferocious thrusts, each one

more dizzying than the last, scooting her farther and farther up the bed toward the headboard. She could only hold on as he whipped her from one shocking, incredible high to the next. Dear God, was she really raking her fingernails down his back? Grabbing his ass to wring out every inch? She *was*, like she was born to, like she was helpless to do otherwise. And the whole world shattered into shards of light. Everything inside her shook and spasmed, and Hunter hollered out, spilling his own release into her, one hard, hot pump after the next.

Hunter groaned, his breaths ragged, as his every muscle clenched and shuddered. He was taut as a bowstring, his eyes dark with pleasure as he balanced above her. Finally, he relaxed a bit and lowered himself into a tender embrace that surrounded her in every possible way. Kathryn gulped in air as her ragged breaths slowly calmed.

Oh yes, there's definitely a thing between us.

As the thick haze of lust slowly dissipated in her brain, they held each other in languid silence, still joined, their limbs tangled. There didn't seem to be any need or use for words. If she had to guess, she'd say Hunter was as surprised and overwhelmed as she was.

The silence stretched on, and doubts began to creep in. What would happen once the roads were cleared? Would he still want her then? Would this be some kind of holiday fling, or something more? The suddenness of all this suggested a fling. But the way he touched her was so open and real, it made her heart ache.

Rolling her over suddenly, Hunter positioned her so she could be on top, straddling him, yet with him still inside her. He stroked his thumb along her cheekbone with such tenderness. His eyes were bright with the start of tears, but he studiously blinked them back. "Thank you," he whispered, his voice shaky. "I'd forgotten what it felt like, until you."

"What, *sex?*"

"No. This." Hunter wrapped his big hand around the back of her head and pulled her mouth to his. His kisses were deep and lazy, and filled with an exploration and wonder that made them as passionate as the heat-soaked kisses they'd shared earlier.

This man...this man. How can he be making me feel so many things at once?

Time fell away as they kissed and explored, Hunter lingering his kisses over her, softly, sweetly, until they seemed to soak into her very bones. Kathryn was almost embarrassed to admit it, but Hunter's cherishing touch acted like some kind of balm, like an emotional antivenom for every bad thing that had ever happened to her.

Shaken, sated, they collapsed finally, spent in every possible way. Kathryn rolled off him and tucked herself underneath his arm. He absently stroked the damp curls that had tumbled over her forehead. Neither one of them seemed to have any words for what had happened.

How had she gotten here? How had she ended up in this wilderness oasis with this amazing man? This all was so different from how she'd expected her holiday to go, it was almost beyond belief. Being with Hunter was so intense that she had no frame of reference to name it. It was like some kind of waking dream, wasn't it, being stranded up here in the mountains with this virile, protective mountain man?

On the face of it, none of it made any sense. But as she laid here in Hunter's arms, she knew one thing for certain. This thing between them, whatever it was, was real. It was maybe even realer than real. And whatever crazy turn of events happened next, Kathryn was going with it.

CHAPTER 13

How LONG HAD it been since he'd felt this way?
Contented? Peaceful? Hunter had been so certain he'd
never enjoy this kind of soul-deep satisfaction again. Yet
here, with Kathryn draped all drowsy and lazy against his
side, the world stopped turning for them, just for now. With
only the firelight to brighten the room, they laid in complete
silence, watching the untamed wild of the winter landscape
outside their window. The storm had done its worst,
spending out the last of its fury. Now, soft, glittering gusts of
snow fell like a prayer over the mountain. Light, fluffy flakes
swirled and eddied, caught in gentler breezes, covering
everything with a glimmer of winter's perfect silence.

He could've fallen asleep right then. But just as
Kathryn was beginning to nod off, her eyes flew open.

"My God, Hunter. Daddy and Wilson don't know
we're up here. Do you think we can get back down there in
the morning?"

Considering how the snowdrifts had covered up half
the windows, Hunter wasn't willing to chance it. "It's too
dangerous to attempt it ourselves. There's too much
unstable snow. Someone will have to dig us out."

"What?" Kathryn propped herself up and blinked in alarm. "Tomorrow's Christmas Eve!"

His heart sank. She was right. As much as he would've loved to hole up here in this cabin with her forever, she had responsibilities. Wilson would wake up and be scared to death if he didn't know where his momma was. And who knew what kind of shape Huck would be in.

Hunter grabbed a loose blanket and wrapped it around her. "Come on. Let's see if we can find something around here we can communicate with." They searched for a walkie-talkie, a buzzer, or, hell, even a tin can and string. But there was nothing. "Boy," Hunter uttered, doing his best to sound offhandedly casual, "I sure wish they had communication system we could use to talk to the front desk."

And just like that, Kathryn's gaze fell to an intercom box by the door. "Hey! How did I not notice this thing before? It's like magic!"

Isn't it?

They both went over to inspect. There was a call button, but the small digital screen underneath it bore a message. *Front desk call system in operation between the hours of nine a.m. and seven p.m. Typed messages can be sent via the pin pad during our off hours. They will be addressed when our normal operating hours resume.*

"Shoot." Kathryn pouted. "I'd feel better if I could talk to a human, but at least we can let them know we didn't fall off the side of a cliff."

"Didn't we?" Hunter replied, drily.

She shook her head at him and, after fiddling a bit with the controls, typed in her message. *Hunter Holliday and Kathryn Winslow were caught in the snowstorm on the scenic trail and are stranded in a guest cottage. We cannot get back down. Please advise when we might get assistance getting out. Please alert Huck Wilson in room 2 1 3 of our situation and let him know we are unhurt and will be getting to them as soon as we are able.*

Hunter hung his head over hers to read what she sent. "That should do the trick. You know they're used to digging out that trail. They'll have us out of here tomorrow. I'd bet money on it."

"Lord, I hope so. After everything we've been through on this trip, it would be just plain cruel not to be with my boy on Christmas Eve." Kathryn kept staring at the intercom. "What do we do now?"

He laced his arms around her and, after fighting the blanket a bit, kissed the back of her neck. "There's nothing they can do for us in the middle of the night. But in the morning, it'll be okay. I promise. Come on. I made some hot buttered rum earlier. It's the perfect thing for waiting."

Kathryn rose up on her toes to kiss him on the cheek. "Of course you did. You're always one step ahead of knowing what I'll need, aren't you?"

Though he knew he probably shouldn't be reading too much into that statement, Hunter was ridiculously pleased by that compliment. And he realized, all at once, what these protective urges might actually mean. *Damn, could I be falling for her? So soon?*

His insides twisted up with too many emotions—excitement, fear, confusion, and especially, tenderness...

Hunter gave himself an inward shake. *Don't put too much on this too fast. Is it even possible for me to have these feelings after Laney?*

The question made him pause. If he fell asleep in bed with Kathryn, would he have another nightmare? He'd have to roll the dice, wouldn't he?

Pushing his doubts aside, Hunter poured out mugs of the amber-colored brew and took the carafe back to the bedroom while Kathryn tidied herself up. When she came back to bed, they burrowed under the covers, propping up piles of fluffy pillows so they could enjoy the view outside. But worry still niggled at him.

What allowed me to find Christmas Pass in the first place? Did I wish for a woman like Kathryn in my life? Is she the answer to those subconscious wishes?

Right here, right now, she sure felt like it.

But did that mean she was under some kind of spell?

Was he? If so, he sure as shit didn't care.

Kathryn took a long, blissful sip of her drink. "Mmmmm. This buttered rum is perfect. This must be what I was tasting on you earlier."

"Really?" He chuckled.

"Mmm-hmm. This is good. But it was tastier going down with a side of tongue."

He nearly collapsed in a fit of laughter. "A side of tongue? Oh, really? And what's the main course?"

"You have to ask?" she teased, getting up to straddle him, still holding her coffee cup.

He could feel how hot, plumped, and slicked from their wild night she still was. She was resting all too close to the danger zone, wasn't she? He caught sight of her bare, spread legs and that perfectly trimmed triangle of shimmering gold hair at her cleft, and all his worries faded away. His cock saluted and reported for duty. Kathryn clearly felt him rising up underneath her. She arched an eyebrow and wiggled herself on his lap. She still playfully sipped from her cup, though, pretending to be more interested in her drink.

Lord, this woman knows how to tease.

Grinning, he took the cup out of her hand, setting both mugs down on the nightstand. Then he wrapped his hands around her tiny waist, flipped her underneath him, and began kissing her neck. She was still giggling. So was he.

It seemed like a lifetime ago since he'd flirted like this. He hadn't forgotten how, after all. *God, it felt good.*

She felt good.

She wrapped her legs around him. Kathryn gazed at him with a lazy, satisfied expression he hoped he'd get to see again and again. Stroking the side of his face with her feather-soft fingertips, she never took those incredible eyes from his.

Giving in to the temptation, he kissed her. *Mmmmm, so soft, so perfect.* But he couldn't help chuckling.

Kathryn smirked. "What?"

"You really do taste like rum."

And she giggled again, a magical lilting sound that lifted his heart with a pure, simple joy. It warmed him, cracking away at the icy layer around his heart and sweeping away his doubts. Hunter didn't know what to make of all this. But he knew one thing for sure. Kathryn was good for him. And he would make *her* feel good too. All. Night. Long.

Hunter woke to the sounds of rustling in the kitchen. The crisp, white light of the winter morning streamed through the window. Blinking against the sun, he seriously considered pinching himself to test if he was dreaming. He and Kathryn *really had* spent the night together. Naked. In bed. He'd lost count how many times they'd made love. And when they'd finally gotten to sleep, he'd slept like a rock, all calm and sated.

It wasn't just the sex that had been so damn great. They'd stayed up for hours talking about anything and everything—from their jobs, to world affairs, to tastes in music, religion, child rearing, favorite movies, and more. They both were amazed to find how much common ground they shared.

How could it be possible that they lined up on so much when they came from such different places? They both loved Seventies hard rock and good whiskey and cheese fondue. Even their taste in movies was similar, though she was partial to political thrillers, while he was a sucker for the superhero flicks. Hell, she even liked old cars!

It had all been perfect.

Almost *too* perfect.

When they'd been together last night, it as if all his pain and worries had fallen away, and there was only the two of them, stranded up here on top of the world. There were times when she'd looked him in the eyes, and he'd felt like she could see everything in his heart without him having to say a word. A woman like Kathryn could make you feel seen, understood and, sometimes, even exposed.

Am I ready to accept the gifts she's giving me? Do I even have a heart left to give her? And why am I even thinking this way, so soon? Am I so new to modern relationships that I'll hand my heart over to the first woman who shows me a bit of attention?

No, Hunter knew there was more to this thing with Kathryn than that. And whatever it was, it was scaring him to half outta his mind.

Kathryn clattered into the room, all rumpled and freakin' adorable as she juggled a tray full of food and drinks. "I know we have a table out there, but eating in bed is more decadent, don't you think?"

"Sounds good to me, Ryn."

She set down the tray, and beamed at him. "There's that name again."

"What's the matter, no one ever give you a nickname before?"

"No, actually. Momma wouldn't allow it. Said a lady always used her full name."

He furrowed his brow. "You know, if it bothers you, I can—"

Her kiss swallowed his words. He came up grinning. "So you like the pet name."

"Ummm-hmmm," she breathed, nipping his ear. "A lot. You don't make me feel like a lady, Hunter. You make me feel like a woman. That's a first."

She went back to spreading out the food, as if what she'd said was perfectly obvious, and no big deal. But honestly, that was one of the best compliments he'd ever gotten. He rubbed at the pang in his chest, and his anxiety ebbed a bit. Maybe he did have something to offer Kathryn, after all. He helped her finish laying out the food, his stomach rumbling in anticipation.

"I brought out a selection. There's bagels, and muffins, and bacon, and this breakfast tart thing. Oh, and here's some coffee. I figure after this, we can break out the chocolate."

He arched an eyebrow.

"What? Chocolate is a good source of protein," Kathryn protested. "It should probably have its own food group."

"Hey, you won't get any argument out of me. I'm starving." He took a long drag of the coffee. She'd mixed it with a touch of cream and some sugar. It was exactly how he would've done. "This is perfect. How did you know how I take my coffee?"

"I watched how you made your coffee at the inn. You only put in cream and sugar when you can get real cream— no substitutes. Otherwise, it's black coffee."

"Your powers of observation are somethin'." He set the

food on his plate and gave her another quick, happy kiss. Kathryn watched him as he dug in. He enjoyed the food, and that seemed to make her happy.

He enjoyed her more. They'd had so many rounds in bed the night before that he was actually a trifle sore. "So, when it's time for dessert, do I get to hand-feed you the chocolate?"

Kathryn batted her eyelashes between bites of her bagel. "Knock yourself out. I figure if I've got to be stranded with a rough-and-ready mountain man, chocolate should definitely be on the menu."

He crinkled his brows at the comment. "Is that how you see me? Some kind of fantasy redneck?"

"No! Well, fantasy, yes. Redneck, no." She playfully booped his nose, clearly trying to keep the topic light.

But the suggestion still rankled. "We may have good chemistry, Kathryn, but you ought to know as well as anyone, I'm nobody's fantasy. I'm pretty fucked up, as a matter of fact. You'd probably be better off with one of your own kind, like a nice doctor, or a lawyer, or an accountant or something. Somebody uncomplicated who doesn't sling grease for a living."

"Yes, but I like *you*, Hunter Holliday. I thought you liked me too." Kathryn kicked her chin up and speared him with one of those looks—the kind that called you on your bullshit.

"I do—like you, I mean," he sputtered. "A whole lot."

"Then that's all there is to it. No need to make it more complicated than that."

Turning that over in his head for a minute, Hunter could find no argument to that. Kathryn was right. But God only knew where this was all going. Hell, he didn't even know what to hope for. If he pushed her away, it would kill him. If he pulled her close, could he even manage to be "her guy?" Did she even want him that way?

Best not to overthink things, and follow my instincts.

And right now, his instincts told him to keep her close and keep her safe, at least until he could get them all out of here. Two days from now. Hopefully. Unless this was all a big trick, and this magical place would trap them here forever.

Right now, with Kathryn here beside him, that almost didn't sound so bad. They stuffed themselves with all the breakfast treats she'd brought. She even convinced him to try his bagel with cream cheese, smoked salmon, and these little pickled green things called capers. It was damn *delicious*. Not quite as delicious, of course, as the chocolates they fed each other. Mmmmm. The way her lips closed over them and the expression of bliss on her face...she had his whole body revving for her with just a glance.

But Kathryn seemed in a chattier mood. "So," she said between bites, "what do you think of Miss Berry?"

Hunter furrowed his brows. "Is this a trick question or something?"

Kathryn pushed away the chocolate and kicked back against her pillow. "Not exactly. Normally I'm pretty good at reading people, but not her. It's like she pulls down some kind of veil over everything she says. I've never met anyone quite like her."

Uh-oh. Hunter swallowed. He did *not* want to get into all this with Kathryn—not now. Not before Christmas, and maybe never, if he could get away with it. "So, what are you trying to say?"

Kathryn paused, as if she were struggling to find the right way to describe this. "The woman somehow manages to be friendly and cagey all at the same time. Have you noticed that? Her body language is really off, and her eyes are so blank sometimes it creeps me out. I don't know what to make of it. It's like she has some kind of agenda and only she knows what it is."

Hunter swallowed hard, his mind spinning out scenarios that involved telling Kathryn what truth he knew about Christmas Pass. What would he even say? *I'm pretty sure we're trapped here. This place doesn't exist. Every time someone says "I wish," weird shit happens. All the town history is lies. I don't know whether the state roads will be cleared at the end of five days or not.*

How was she supposed to react to that? She might think he was delusional—that she'd tethered herself to a foil-hat-wearing lunatic. And that would be bad enough. But what if she believed him? She'd be terrified, and he knew it. Between her mother's death, and the crash this year, and her ongoing stress with her Dad, Kathryn's Christmas truly had been wrecked. Did he really want to add to that right now with these bizarre suspicions?

He really didn't. There'd be plenty of time to panic later. He'd tell her then. The day after Christmas—he promised himself. Until then, he'd wish up a holiday none of them would ever forget. They deserved it.

A distraction was in order. "So, what? Do you think Miss Berry's some kind of Lizzie Borden, coming in your room in the middle of the night with an axe?"

She snorted and punched him in the arm. "Stop it! I'm serious here! Something about her, and this place, seems incredibly peculiar. I mean, the service they have here is so good, so over the top. It's a little too perfect, you know?"

"You did say you wanted to have a nice holiday. Why don't you enjoy it?"

She leaned over and kissed him again. "I suppose you're right. I don't know what I have to complain about. It's just... don't you sense it too? The strangeness?"

Hunter ran his hand up the silken skin of her stomach and captured the soft globe of her breast in his hand. "The only thing I feel right now...is you."

She chuckled, and they exchanged long, lazy kisses before Kathryn pushed herself off the bed, bundled herself in a blanket, and took their trays to the kitchen.

Hunter collapsed back onto the pillows. *Man, that was close.*

Clattering noises arose from the kitchen as she put things back. He hoped maybe he could tempt her back to bed. But a squeal of delight erupted from the front of the house. She came running back into the room, and did a little happy dance. "Hunter! The plow's outside! They got our message! We're getting out!"

CHAPTER 14

WHEN HUCK LOOKED him up and down, clearly amused by the sight of him, Hunter squirmed a little. He hadn't realized he and Kathryn were still holding hands. They'd been holding hands all the way on the ride down in the back of the inn's slow plow truck, and now, they were holding hands *in front of her family*. Even Wilson seemed to catch it.

Hunter instinctively started to pull his hand back, but Kathryn only laced her fingers through his and squeezed. Then she pushed up on her toes and gave him a quick kiss on the cheek, and let his hand go. She bent down to hug Wilson, who was overjoyed she was back.

She wants them to see, doesn't she?

The whole thing should make him nervous, this soon in the game. But, somehow, it didn't.

Huck had been tucked up comfortably in bed reading the paper and sipping coffee, but he crossed the room to shake Hunter's hand. "I wanted to thank you for taking care of my girl. You seem to have a talent for that, boy."

Oh, Huck. If you only knew. Then he caught at the ornery gleam in the man's eye and realized maybe the old guy did have an inkling. *Jesus.* Now Hunter was blushing. "Miss Berry talked us into taking that scenic walk," he rushed to explain. "She said it would only take forty-five minutes. She was right about the views, but I guess she didn't count on the storm coming in so early. We were lucky to be standing with a culvert below us. If that avalanche had hit us where there was a steeper drop, I don't know what would've happened."

"So, Wilson, that means no more walks in the hills on this trip," Huck called.

"Who needs hiking? Momma, can we please stay here until I get this train figured out?" The boy kneeled at the base of the Christmas tree the inn's staff had left in Huck's room. It was lit, and decorated with fun, kid-friendly ornaments of cartoon characters and superheroes. But apparently, Wilson was confounded by the complexities the oversized train set.

"He insisted on putting on all the ornaments," Huck explained. "And he did a good job, too. But when it came to the train, I think he bit off more than he could chew. He keeps saying he can do it himself." Huck chuckled, and nodded over to his grandson. "Are you setting up that train, boy, or is it setting up you?"

Wilson set down the lead engine in frustration. "This train is so darned old! Have you ever seen train cars this big? They're, like, a foot tall! I can't figure out how any of this connects!"

"I can help you, buddy," Hunter offered, sitting down on the floor beside him. "These old O-grade train sets are easy once you know how to do it."

"You know about train sets?" Wilson asked, still scowling down at the engine in front of him.

"I build hot rods for a living, kiddo. If it's got a motor, I can work with it. Besides, my dad used to collect these. I had a whole basement full of trains exactly like this when I was a kid."

"Really?" Wilson looked up at Hunter with round-eyed amazement. "That must have been so cool!"

"It was. We had a whole city set up, with trees and stores and houses and everything. It was something." Ah yes, all the fond hours he'd spent in the basement with his dad. Hunter felt another pang of regret that he'd barricaded himself up the way he had these past three years. There was really no excuse. He'd been letting his grief eat him from the inside out. He should have gone to Vancouver this holiday. But then, if he had, who would've pulled Kathryn and her family off the mountain? Maybe some things are supposed to happen the way they did.

Hunter showed Wilson how the train connected to the track wires, and the two of them settled into companionably piecing the set together. Kathryn watched them with a wistful smile. But soon she clapped her hands together. "I see you boys have things in hand with that train. I tell you what. While you're working on that, Daddy, could you join me in my room? I think we need to have a chat."

Huck's eyes went wide and he quailed, but the man went without complaint or comment. They shut the door softly behind them.

"Uh-oh," Wilson whistled. "Granddaddy is in trouble now."

"Yeah, I don't think I'd want to be in Huck's shoes at the moment."

Wilson caught Hunter's gaze again with those wise, wise eyes of his. "He's drinkin' again, isn't he? That's why he got three of those tomato juices with the stalks of celery in them at breakfast, isn't it? They smelled like a booze bottle."

Nothing got by this kid, did it? Hunter considered

telling a white lie or two to cover for Huck but decided not to. Wilson would only figure it out, anyway. Hunter sighed. "Yeah, Wilson, I think he's been hitting the bottle pretty hard, and he's having a harder time hiding it. Huck had a bad day yesterday. If you want to know any more about it, you'll have to talk to your momma."

Wilson shook his head and pulled another couple of train cars out of their tissue paper. "That's okay. I don't need to. This will be the part where she tells him he has to go away to get off the stuff. I hate it when Granddaddy has to go away. He's fun."

Hunter ruffled Wilson's hair. "I wouldn't worry about him going away until after Christmas, anyway. We won't be able to get out on the roads for another day or two. I think your momma's worried that your granddaddy might be making himself sicker over the holidays. She doesn't want him to hurt himself. And I think she doesn't want the holidays to be ruined for you with all this grown-up problem stuff."

Wilson huffed. "I don't know why Momma worries about that kind of thing. I'm not a baby, you know."

"It's only natural for a momma to want her kid to have a magical, carefree Christmas. When you're older, she wants you to remember your childhood bein' happy. You understand that, don't you?"

Wilson canted his head as if that surprised him. "Momma wants me to be happy? *All* the time?"

"What?" Hunter shrugged. "That surprises you? It's especially true at Christmas. Every momma wants her kids to be happy at Christmas."

But Wilson scowled. "That's pretty dumb. No one can be happy *all* the time. Sometimes you worry. Sometimes you're sad. Sometimes you're just plain mad. But nobody lets you be any of those things at Christmas."

Hunter wanted to argue with him. But the kid wasn't exactly wrong, either. Still, Wilson's worldly-wise ways were concerning at his age. "Are you tryin' to tell me you're not happy, Wilson?"

"Oh, no. I'm pretty happy most days. I like school and my friends. I love Momma and Daddy and my granddaddy and even Avery. I worry about Momma, that's all. She's always trying to make sure nobody ever gets hurt or upset. But I don't think she can."

Hunter clicked the last piece of the train track in place. "You know, you're pretty smart for an eight-year-old."

Wilson puffed his chest out a little, obviously pleased with the compliment. But the boy didn't answer him. He kept at his work. Hunter did too, enjoying the comfortable silence between them. He couldn't imagine how hard it must be for Kathryn. How did she do it, all these years, being torn between her parents and their crazy problems? And then, her no-good husband bailed on her on top of it? She didn't deserve what she'd been dealt. Remembering how she'd slept tucked into the crook of his arm all night, a wave of pure emotion rolled over him. Everything about her drew him in—her sweetness, her strength, even her vulnerability.

Kathryn is a woman who needs the right man in her life. She needs the kind of man who can help her, defend her, and protect her. A man to love her.

Hunter gulped. *Let's not get carried away just yet.*

He knew he should drop this line of questioning with Wilson. But he couldn't help himself. Dying to know more, he finally screwed up his courage. "So, uh, Wilson, you say you're worried about your momma. Do you think she's not happy?"

Wilson stopped and considered that for a minute. "I guess I don't know. She smiles and seems normal, but I know she still gets upset. Sometimes I hear her cry in her room at night when I'm supposed to be sleepin'. She thinks I can't hear her. I don't think she ever really got over Grand-momma. And Granddaddy really hasn't been the same since. He had to go away once already this year, you know."

"I know. Do you think she's sad over splitting up with your daddy?"

Wilson lifted his eyebrows, as if he was shocked Hunter had asked the question. "Beats me." He shrugged. "I was only three. I don't ever really remember Daddy living with us. They're real good friends though. Avery's teaching her to cook! He's trying to, anyway."

Hunter stopped. "Wait. Who's teaching your momma? Your daddy?"

"No, silly. Avery. Avery's the French *chef,* remember?"

"Yeah, but you just said *he.*"

Wilson raised his eyebrows again. "Avery is a *he.* My daddy is gay. Didn't Momma tell you that?"

Well. You could have blown him down with a feather. Hunter gaped at the child. *Good Lord.* He was all for gay pride and all that. But Hunter couldn't even imagine what it would be like to have your spouse leave you for a person of a different gender. How would it feel to have had a child by someone and come to find out you didn't really know them at all? Like you missed something so deep down and basic that was right under your nose?

Kathryn had trembled for him, up there on that moun-taintop, and it all made perfect sense. Her fierce, primal response to him...how she said she never knew it could be this way...how she'd asked him so pointedly if he *liked* her. He could see her clearly now, and all those invisible wounds she tried so hard to hide. And his heart twisted in sympathy for her.

He approached his next question gingerly. "So, uh, your

momma, she *knew* your daddy was gay when she married him?"

Wilson seemed confused by that question. "I dunno. She never said. But I'd bet not. I don't think she would've married him if she knew he liked boys better."

"And she's not mad at him?"

"Nah. Momma's always said there's no point getting angry at Daddy over something he can't help."

"Was it Avery your daddy left your momma for?"

"Oh, no. Daddy had lots of boyfriends before he met Avery. Avery is the first one, though, who stayed around. I think Avery makes him happy. Daddy smiles all the time now."

Hunter's respect for Kathryn and this child just went up a few notches. What a remarkably levelheaded response from this kid, not to mention his momma. Not every family could have moved past a situation like that so easily.

Hunter plugged the train set into the wall and confirmed with Wilson that they had everything out of the boxes and set on the track. It was a really nice vintage train set. It was different than most sets he'd seen. It had "Christmas Pass Express" painted on the side, and the detailing on the cars was remarkable, as if it was a real honest-to-God Victorian-era train, shrunk down to size. The cars were heavy and made from solid metal, pressed with the finest workmanship he'd ever seen. There were eight big cars and enough track pieces to make a wide circle around the tree's base.

He handed the control to Wilson and motioned for him to turn it on.

Wilson flipped the switch, and they both gasped with delight. Hunter had never seen anything quite like it. The engine car chugged along with cheerful puffs of smoke belching out of its chimney. The passenger cars lit up, silhouetting a crowd of travelers sitting inside. Instead of coal cars, the train featured open cargo cars overflowing with tiny presents and toys. A miniature conductor hung off the red caboose at the end, swinging a lit lantern. Wilson pushed another button, and a medley of musical Christmas carols played.

"Oh, my Lord, would you look at that thing?" Hunter marveled. "That is a *sight*, let me tell you."

"Oh, man!" Wilson moaned. "Why does my phone have to be dead? I wish I could take a picture and send it to Caroline."

"Ooo now," Hunter hooted. "Caroline—who's *she?*"

"A friend from my school," Wilson replied, trying to act nonchalant. But Hunter wasn't buying it.

"A *friend*, huh?" Hunter nudged the boy with his elbow. "You're sure you're not crushing on her?"

Wilson reddened. "Maybe. But I still think girls are gross. And if you ask me again, I won't tell you any different!"

Hunter snickered and held up his hands. "All right! I won't ask you anymore. Your crushes are your business."

Wilson was quiet for a few long moments, watching the train. Hunter started putting the boxes away. "So," Wilson finally said. "Are you crushing on my momma?" Wilson turned and considered him with that same deep, questioning gaze he'd seen from Kathryn.

Just like Kathryn, the boy didn't give him any place to hide. "Yes," Hunter replied, surprised at how ragged his voice sounded.

A knowing grin spread over Wilson's face. "You really like her then?"

Hunter never took his eyes from the boy's. "Yes. I really do."

"What will the two of you do when the holidays are over? Will you be boyfriend and girlfriend or something?"

Hunter blew out a long breath. "I don't know. We haven't gotten that far yet."

Wilson narrowed his eyes and crossed his arms over his chest, squaring his shoulders like a real little man. "Would you *like* to be her boyfriend?"

Whoa. What am I going to say to that? Hunter had to admit that he hadn't thought that far ahead.

He couldn't fault the kid for his concern for his momma. Wilson was trying out the role of protector, and being the man of the house and all. But his question made Hunter stop in his tracks. Did he and Kathryn really have a chance, being from such different worlds? Not to mention the problems all their baggage would most likely cause in the future. They had enough grief, guilt, and pain in their pasts to last them both a lifetime. Any sane man would drop them all off at the Greenbrier two days from now and never turn back.

No, there was nothing safe or easy about Kathryn Winslow. But then again, there wasn't exactly anything safe about *him*, either.

So, Hunter looked Wilson square in the eye and answered him.

CHAPTER 15

Kathryn had finished laying down the law with her daddy, and she'd expected to go back to catch Hunter and Wilson still working on the train.

So she was more than a little surprised to find herself peeking around the crack in the door between Daddy's room and hers, holding her breath, eavesdropping on this intense conversation.

Had Wilson just asked Hunter to be her boyfriend?

Color me mortified. Dear God, what was the man going to say?

To his credit, Hunter paused, but he didn't show any signs of weaseling out of an answer. No, he looked her boy dead in the eye and said, "Yes. I like your momma, very, very much. I'd love to stay together. If she'd have me."

If I'd have him? Well now.

Wilson seemed aghast. "What makes you think she wouldn't?"

"Your momma has a PhD. She lives in a big city and runs with an educated crowd. She can do a lot better than a hillbilly mechanic."

Wilson, to his credit, shook his head. "All my momma needs is a man who looks at her the way you do."

"And how's that?" Hunter asked.

"Like you love her."

Kathryn gasped and quickly clasped a hand over her mouth to muffle the noise. She was going to have to have a sit-down with Wilson about this.

What does the boy think he's doing, grilling Hunter like this?

Poor Hunter froze like a deer in headlights, fumbling desperately for what to say next. She had to fix this, *fast.* She began stomping around, making obvious footstep noises.

They both turned toward the door, seeming relieved. She was going to pretend she didn't hear *any* of this.

"All righty." She breezed in, clapping her hands. "Your granddaddy is taking a bathroom break. So I figured this was as good as any a time to discuss how we're going to deal with his departure from sobriety for the remainder of our trip." She stopped to check out the train gliding merrily around the track. "Wow. The train is pretty cool, guys."

"Hunter showed me how to fix it." Wilson beamed like an angel. "He's a good guy and really smart about fixing things, you know."

"Yes, he is." Kathryn winked at Hunter, catching Wilson's clever nudge. "He'd have to be smart to build a car from scratch."

Wilson got up and threw his arms around her in an impetuous hug. She ruffled his hair and kissed the top of his head. "Momma, you're very buxom today. Don't you think she looks buxom, Hunter?" Wilson beamed.

"Yes...uh, yes, she does." Hunter squirmed.

Kathryn rolled her eyes. "Thanks, honey," she said to Wilson, "but you might not want to use that word. It has more than one meaning, and not everyone takes it the same way. Okay?"

"Okay, Momma, whatever you say."

Kathryn took note of Hunter's bright eyes and flushed face. The poor man was still *completely* flustered—and actually pretty cute. But she was determined to change the subject.

Wilson looked back and forth between the two of them, a little too triumphantly. Apparently, the boy had decided to take on the role of matchmaker. Wilson put on his best little face, trying to appear all innocent. "Momma, can I go lay down on your bed and watch cartoons?"

Kissing her boy on the forehead again, she excused him. "Sure, baby. Just don't get anything pay-per-view."

"Got it!" He happily skipped off, closing the door behind him.

Wilson probably imagined she and Hunter would have some kind of romantic rendezvous right now. Unfortunately, she had work to do. She wandered over to Daddy's suitcase and unzipped it. She didn't have to rustle around much in the piles of shirts and jeans to find her quarry. "I knew it," she breathed. *Three bottles of vodka, one nearly drained.*

Hunter came up behind her to see for himself. He blinked in amazement. "Man, that's pretty bad."

Considering extent of this stash, the "end stage" of Daddy's "end stage" shocked her, like the twist of a long knife that was already embedded in your chest. Fear clawed at her. With this kind of consumption, it was a wonder he could even stand upright. It was a testament to how strong of a man Daddy was. He didn't have any alcohol induced dementia or severe cirrhosis—yet. But if he failed rehab this time, would he be able to pick himself up and try again? Or would this be the downward spiral he couldn't escape?

She'd seen patients die of alcoholism, and it was horrifying. An image of her dear daddy, pinned down to a hospital bed and connected to tubes flashed in her mind.

God, I can't lose another parent. I just can't.

She stared down into the suitcase, frozen with dismay. As if he felt her distress, too, Hunter came to stand in front of her. He tipped her face up, so he could look her directly in the eyes. His expression gentled with sympathy, and he brushed her cheekbone with his thumb. It was such a small, now-familiar gesture, but it steadied her. She took a deep breath and turned away to grab one of the bottles. "Come on, Hunter, I need you to hold the funnel."

Hunter knitted his brows, but he did what she asked, holding the flask nice and steady while she filled it with the despicable hooch. "Isn't the point to get Huck *off* the alcohol?"

"Of course. But this isn't exactly my first rodeo with Daddy's drinking problem. You can't take a man like him off alcohol cold turkey without medical intervention. He needs to be in a good, licensed rehab facility where they can help him control what will surely be a week or two of pure hell in withdrawal, then maybe at least another month of in-house treatment. Since we can't arrange all that until the roads are cleared, I'm going to edge him down by controlling his intake. I'll give him enough to avoid withdrawal, but not so much that he'll be seriously impaired. That's a higher amount than you might think. Daddy has a ridiculously high tolerance."

She topped off the flask, capping it, then handed Hunter the other one. Their gaze locked as she started to tip the bottle. How in God's name was she here, filling these damn flasks *again*? It was all so upsetting, for a moment it was as if she was outside her own body, watching herself. And Kathryn didn't like what she saw.

"Wow." She winced with dismay. "One day you watch me pour out these flasks. The next day, you help me fill them. If you didn't think my family was a total hot mess before, you definitely do now. I'm sorry, Hunter. I'm sorry you had to spend your holiday getting pulled into—"

"Stop." He grabbed her free hand with his and gave it a squeeze. "Just stop. It's no crazier than the holiday I would've spent alone. Everybody's a mess, Ryn. Even the ones who think they aren't. Maybe *especially* those people."

True enough. Lord knew, she saw evidence of that parading through her office every day—the broken relationships, the crippling disappointments, the existential crises, and of course the serious mental illnesses and addictions. Though she'd never really thought of it this way, the sum total of her life, professional and personal, was dealing with other people's messes.

Is it any wonder I'm a mess too?

Right now, she'd grade her life at a D—De-flating, De-Moralizing, and De-feating, for starters. Plunking herself down on the side of the bed with him, she laid her head on Hunter's strong shoulder. He wrapped his arm around her and rubbed her back.

"Why does it never seem to get better?" she asked. "Isn't the whole point of life figuring a way out of your trials and coming out the other side happy?"

He kissed the top of her forehead. "I used to think that. It's a simple way of seeing things, after all, and not untrue, either. But then, after I lost Laney, I realized there are some messes you can't fix. There are some things you can't come out on the other side of. Sometimes a win is to survive. Sometimes things are so bad, the best you can hope for is to be like a cockroach after a nuclear bomb goes off."

It was totally inappropriate, she knew, but something about that preposterous analogy tickled her unmercifully.

She started to giggle. Arching an eyebrow at him, she smirked. "Are you saying the best thing I can hope for in life is to be a *bug?*"

He began to chuckle, and kissed her on her forehead. "Yes. But you'd be a very pretty bug."

An image of herself with antennae came to mind. "That's the most ridiculous analogy I've ever heard." She started snickering the more she thought about it. "No, really. Does that mean we're spending Christmas at the Roach Motel?" She snorted.

Then they both started giggling, a kind of punchy fit of laughter all the more incongruous for the bottles of alcohol in their hands.

"*Be* the cockroach, Ryn," He started tickling her around the ribs.

"Dear God, it's a mantra." She squealed, squirming under his fingers. "I could write a self-help book and call it *Ten Ways to Bug Everybody.*"

"Hey! Don't laugh!" Hunter cried. "You're a psychologist—you could totally sell that! Imagine the merchandise—the hats, the shirts, the charm bracelets with crystal-covered cockroaches."

To someone else, it wouldn't even be funny. Kathryn knew they were getting silly, but she didn't care. She was laughing so hard she was crying. "We'd do speaking tours. We'd get rich! They'd call us The Vermin-illionares."

They both looked in each other's eyes and collapsed into snickers again. And she squeaked as he launched into another round of tickling.

When the laughter died down, she laid there marveling at the sated calmness she felt, even if only for a moment. She'd never had someone to share a giggle with like this, had she? She rolled up on an elbow, and kissed him. "Oh Lordy, I needed that laugh. Thank you, Hunter."

"Anytime." He grabbed the flask again, and held it up, his eyes still twinkling. "Now pour."

And she did.

Other than the fact that she was letting her daddy drink every so often, everything about their afternoon in Christmas Pass was perfectly normal. The sidewalks and shops were full of people hurrying to get the last of their holiday chores done. Carolers clad in Victorian costumes roamed the streets. Last-minute sales were underway. The enticing smell of bubbling fudge and baking cookies lingered in the streets. And everywhere they went, the expectant jubilation of Christmas Eve hung in the wintry air.

She gave Hunter's arm a squeeze as they idly strolled arm-in-arm through downtown Christmas Pass. Daddy carefully tried to be on his best behavior during their outing, going along with whatever she or Hunter suggested. But Wilson grumbled that he was "bored."

And he was, poor thing. They'd been at it now for a few hours, this dropping in and out of whatever store interested them. So far, she'd purchased a stack of bestsellers at the town's bookstore, Hunter had snagged himself a new, distressed brown leather moto jacket and a pair of matching brown motorcycle boots, and she'd broken down and bought Wilson a couple of LEGO architecture sets he'd been hankering for, most of them reproductions of some of the world's great monuments.

"Why can't I do the Mountain Slide? Or at least the laser tag arcade again?" Wilson whined.

"Because we're taking it nice and easy today. That's why," Kathryn answered. "We've done stuff you wanted to do these last few days. Now you're going to do stuff *we* want to do. We're all going to play it cool and relax this afternoon. I've had enough rock'em, sock'em action to last me a while."

"But, Mooommmmaaa," he whined. "I *want* to do the Mountain Slide."

Kathryn threw the child *the look*. "People in hell are wanting ice water, too, but it doesn't mean they're gonna get it."

Hunter cracked up. "Lord, I haven't heard that expression since my grandparents were alive."

"It's an oldie but a goodie," Daddy quipped.

Wilson kicked at a skiff of snow on the sidewalk. "Man! Y'all are no fun."

"Now, don't you worry," Kathryn cooed. "We'll be getting our Christmas Eve dinner here before too long."

"Do you think they'll have a Yule log, Momma? Grand-momma used to make the best Yule logs."

It was true. Her momma had been a stellar gourmet cook—a talent that, despite Evangeline Wilson's best efforts, she'd never been able to pass down to her only child. Any time they'd tried a mother-daughter cooking session, it had usually devolved into a disaster driven by Momma's perfectionism and Kathryn's utter lack of culinary instincts. Over the years, Kathryn had tried making the chocolaty, cream-stuffed roulade that was her mother's "Bûche Noël," or "Yule Log" as Wilson put it. But she somehow could never get the thin layer of chocolate sponge cake and whipped cream to roll up into a perfect, log-like cylinder without cracking it to pieces. And then she'd never been able to get the glossy chocolate icing right. It turned out less like a tree trunk and more like a pathetic Christmas log o' poop with every attempt. This would be the first Christmas Wilson wouldn't get to enjoy his grandmomma's Bûche Noël, wasn't it? It was such a small thing, such a trivial loss, but the remembrance of it still made her gut lurch in misery.

"I wouldn't get your hopes up about that fancy dessert. You don't see Yule logs all that often in restaurants," Kathryn reminded the boy. "It doesn't matter what we eat, you know. All that matters is we're together at Christmas."

"I know," Wilson grumbled, scuffing along.

Kathryn knew their time in Christmas Pass was growing short, if the road crew reports were to be believed. And she wished she could find the right souvenirs to bring home from this trip. Maybe an ornament or two for their tree back home. Or a clever, old-fashioned Christmas decoration?

A glowing storefront caught her eye, telling her this was exactly where she needed to go.

Kathryn slowed her steps as they approached the loveliest Christmas shop she'd ever seen. It was huge, covering the footprint of at least two storefronts. "Christmas Past Emporium" the sign said, and it lived up to its name. Ingenious animated figures, trains, toys, and gingerbread houses filled the shop's display windows to bursting. She wondered how she could've gone down this street so many times before and not seen the twinkling lights of the place, glowing like a welcoming beacon.

Standing there on the sidewalk, she found herself staring with a child's open-mouthed wonder at the place, marveling at the chugging, spinning, glittering glory of it all. Sensing Hunter's gaze on her, she turned to him.

Hunter looked at her with such a fond, sad gentleness that she had to turn away. Had her sorrow and bad memories been that easy to spot? Had he seen her *longing* for the kind of bright, shiny holiday happiness this kind of place seemed to promise? The comforting way he wrapped his arm around her shoulder seemed to tell her that he had.

Hunter planted a quick, warm kiss on her temple. "You're still a believer in Christmas magic, aren't you?"

Kathryn blew out a long breath. "After everything."

"Yeah, me too. Let's go in and check it out."

She hesitated.

"Don't worry," Daddy offered, following behind. "I'll make sure Wilson doesn't get into anything that breaks."

Inside, the smell of baking gingerbread greeted them, hanging over the store like a thick, delicious cloud. Kathryn soon saw the source. The staff had pulled cookies out of the oven by the dozen for a table of kids to decorate. Without so much as a by your leave, Wilson made a beeline for the table. So did Daddy. Those two had bottomless pits for stomachs.

As she and Hunter roamed around the store, Kathryn couldn't help but gape at the place. The shelves practically bowed with the weight of its merchandise, teeming with neat rows of German nutcrackers and smokers, nativity sets, and every kind of ornament and tree and garland you could possibly imagine. The air itself seemed heavy and misty, as if seen through a soft focus lens. Like a blast from the past, this bustling shop practically glowed with the light of nostalgia for Christmases of long ago.

Kathryn couldn't help but head straight for the old-fashioned decorations. Fragile as they were, she still gravitated toward the glittering patina of mercury glass ornaments, with their silvery sheen and delicate workmanship. She bagged several, enough to anchor and theme their tree back home. It was a silly, frivolous purchase, she knew. But these decorations were so simple and uncomplicated and homey that they almost seemed like a wish. Who wouldn't want a Christmas like that? Inspired by the nostalgic tree in their room, she decided to buy some of the extra-big Christmas lights, too, which she was delighted to find half off. And then she found the *coup de grâs*—the old-timey tinsel strands. She'd probably cuss herself for the mess next year, but she couldn't resist putting them in her cart.

One of the surprising things she'd learned about Hunter today was that he was a remarkably good shopping companion. The man was patient and had a great eye for what she was looking for. Without her even saying anything, he figured out quick that she was trying to go after the aesthetic of her grandmomma's tree. As they strolled around, he always seemed to be able to put his hand on exactly the right thing for her to consider.

By the time they got to the counter with her mountains of purchases, Kathryn was full to the rim with the warm Christmas fuzzies. She checked in on Daddy and Wilson, who were happily decorating a stack of cookies, half of which went into Wilson's mouth, and the other half into a basket for the area's shut-in elderly.

The clerk behind the counter looked alarmingly like an elf. And it wasn't only the Victorian, costume-like uniform they made him wear. Thin and officious, the clerk was less than five feet tall, wearing wire-rimmed, round spectacles that made him seem like he'd stepped out of a Dickens novel. The man stuffed all her boxes with tissue, then wrapped her purchases in Christmas-stenciled brown paper and twine. He handed her a quill for signing the payment ledger—another strange Christmas Pass affectation she was getting used to. Summoning an even smaller elfin-looking man to the counter, he handed off her packages for delivery to the inn.

The clerk cocked his head at her. "Are you really sure you've gotten everything you're wishing for, miss?"

"Oh, no." Kathryn chuckled. "I couldn't possibly get anything else. I don't know how I'm going to carry it all home as it is."

Just then, the distinctive chime of a music box caught her ear. She turned toward the sound. And there on a fancy display table, she spotted something she never, ever thought she'd see again—a tower of Weisengrut snow globes. In fact, every single snow globe in the display was *the* Weisengrut snow globe.

Her chest tightened with a tangle of emotions as she walked over, and picked one up. At about ten inches across, this particular model wasn't as enormous as she remembered, but it was every bit as glorious. Weisengrut music boxes were considered some of the best, Swiss-made music boxes in the world, and *this* was a snow globe and music box in one. She wound it up, and it began playing "Home for the Holidays."

The base was different than she remembered, as it had a customized brass plaque hammered into the wood that read "Welcome to Christmas Pass." But the inside was exactly the same. The globe featured two lovers skating in a tiny, perfectly formed mountain town, kissing as they executed a showy tandem skating kick. The globe rotated when the music played, making it seem as if the tiny skaters were moving around, even when they weren't. Glittery snow fell in sparkles around the pair like pixie dust. Kathryn's gut clenched as she examined it. This globe was only a pricey Christmas collectible. Something so cute and Christmassy shouldn't dredge up such sharp, painful memories.

But it did. Suddenly a picture flashed in her mind of her momma, her face all scary and angry and twisted. Kathryn ruthlessly stuffed the memory away, cramming it into the recesses of her mind. No. *No*—she wouldn't remember her momma like that.

Tears glistened in her eyes, but she blinked them back.

Even from across the room, Daddy decoded the distress in her expression. Without hesitation, he went to her, concern etched on his face. He picked the globe up out of her hands and shook it with a rueful expression. "Exactly like the one I got for your momma, isn't it? Who knew they still made them?"

Kathryn swallowed against the tightness forming in her throat. "It's still as fascinating to look at as I remember."

Hunter watched her too. He saw her shining eyes. "You should buy that. How often do you get a chance to replay a part of your childhood?"

Kathryn swallowed the urge to groan. No, some Christmases were best left in the past. She pulled the snow globe out of Daddy's hands and set it back down securely on the display. "I've bought more than enough Christmas stuff already," she muttered.

Hunter arched an eyebrow at her but didn't argue.

They said their farewells at Christmas Past Emporium and killed off another hour or so splitting ways, each of them ducking in and out of candy stores and toy shops as they bought their last-minute gifts for each other.

Finally, they reconnected, starving and more than ready for Christmas Eve dinner. Where to go for that was a bit more of a matter of debate. Daddy wanted Chinese, Wilson tacos.

Kathryn wagged her finger. "Now, you two are being ridiculous. No one has that kind of spread for Christmas dinner."

"I don't know about you, but I'm in the mood for a nice prime rib," Hunter offered.

"Yeah, but I don't want to go back to the inn, do you? Daddy and Wilson already ate there once today," Kathryn mused.

"Yule log! I want to go to a place with a great big chocolate Yule log!" Wilson cried.

A middle-aged lady passing them on the sidewalk

tapped Kathryn's arm. "I'm sorry." The woman smiled. "I couldn't help hearing the boy saying he wanted to get some Bûche Noël. You're going to Hoot n'Annie's, aren't you?"

"I don't know, should we?" Kathryn replied, surprised to hear it was even open on Christmas Eve.

"Oh, yes! All the locals go to Hoot n'Annie's on Christmas Eve. It's tradition! They have the best buffet ever, and wait 'til you see the Yule log! It's an event in itself!" The woman gave her a friendly squeeze on the shoulder. "Really. You should go. You won't regret it!"

CHAPTER 16

THE MINUTE KATHRYN stepped over the threshold at Hoot n'Annie's again, she knew they'd come to the right place. Their new Christmas decorations were amazing, completely transforming it from the raucous honky-tonk atmosphere they'd seen before.

The expanded dance floor had been converted to a family-style restaurant with rows of long, continuous tables set with benches, not chairs. Fresh-cut pine trees covered in twinkling lights and cinnamon-scented pinecones lined the walls, making the place smell like an enchanted forest. Red plaid table runners ran down the center of all the tables, accented with a near endless line of glowing red, white, and green pillar candles of all shapes and sizes. And, like the woman had said, the whole town was here. Surely, there must have been hundreds of people queuing up to eat, both young and old. Yet, no matter how many people streamed in, there appeared to be plenty of seats left. Funny, she hadn't remembered it being so big in here before.

Kathryn blinked with amazement as she took in table after table of food. Rack of lamb, prime rib, and towers of shrimp cocktail caught her eye, but that was only a tiny fraction of the enormous spread that was offered. The variety of food was amazing—from tacos to lasagna to every kind of country-fried Christmas soul food.

But that didn't even begin to touch the Yule log. It wasn't a dessert. It was a happening. The sign out front that said, "Come see West Virginia's Biggest Yule Log" didn't even begin to cover it. It stretched halfway down the building, making it, what—fifty yards long? There were easily a thousand servings of the fancy cake there.

Wilson's eyes lit up. "Whoa. I'm so hungry, I could eat that whooole thing."

"Me too, boy!" Daddy crowed, clapping his hands.

On seeing them, Annie trotted over, her reindeer headband twinkling off and on in a coordinated pattern today. "You made it!" the woman cried.

"We had to come try the Yule log," Wilson insisted.

Kathryn returned Annie's big bear hug, drinking in the soothing gingerbread smell that always seemed to be radiating from this odd woman.

"It is amazing, isn't it?" Annie looked around with pride. "The whole town works on putting it together, so the whole town gets to eat it!"

"Is that prime rib I see over there?" Hunter pointed.

Annie pointed to the tables. "You bet, Mr. Holliday. We have more stations than I can count. Any dish you could ever wish for is here."

Kathryn chuckled. "Not *anything*. No place can have every food you've ever wanted."

"Now, Kathryn, you should give us a chance," Annie crooned. "We're very good at this Christmas-wish business here in Christmas Pass. Don't you know all you have to do is believe? The magic is real here. Don't you see it? Don't you *feel* it?"

One glance at Annie's face, and Kathryn realized the

woman was dead serious. Annie really believed in magic—like, wish-upon-a-star damn magic. *Is everyone here delusional, or just pretending to be delusional to please the tourists?*

Honestly, Kathryn was beginning to get concerned about Annie. But Hunter grabbed Kathryn's hand and pulled her out of Annie's grasp. "Right now, all I want is a plate," he said. "I'm starved."

Annie pointed them to the head of the buffet line. "Go on and fill up." She waved as she headed off. "There's plenty of Christmas magic to go around."

Kathryn rolled her eyes. "I think they take their town slogan too seriously."

"I don't know about that." Daddy cackled, rubbing his hands expectantly. "Check this out—country ham and red eye gravy. I haven't had that since I was a boy. Holy smokes! Is that cornpone?" He picked up the crumbly cornbread-like confection and stuffed a big piece in his mouth before it even reached his plate. His eyes practically rolled back in his head. "Oh, my Lord, they used bacon grease and ramps, exactly like Momma used to make back on the farm. Boy, this takes me back."

Lost in the memory, Daddy's eyes slicked with tears.

Wilson, for his part, was similarly mooning over the macaroni and cheese bar. He'd already gotten himself a taco. Now he was shoveling an enormous helping of the gooey pasta on his plate, heaping on a layer of applewood smoked bacon so thick, the pasta completely disappeared. Kathryn considered scolding the boy for his gluttony but decided she'd let it slide. It was Christmas Eve. The boy could eat the fatted pig.

Hunter piled on the prime rib, loaded baked potato, shrimp cocktail, and a big helping of collard greens, his eyes twinkling in anticipation.

It seemed that Hoot n' Annie's really did have exactly the food people were wishing for. Everyone's plate was piled high. Except for her. She should be digging in with abandon and enjoying her picture-perfect Christmas. But against all reason, her stomach shrank in misery. Nothing appealed. She had to confess that seeing that snow globe had shaken her up.

But it's more than that, isn't it?

It occurred to her all at once that this was the first Christmas in her life she'd spent away from her momma's table. She knew that of course, in her head, but her heart was still catching up to the reality of it. And now, surrounded as she was with so much so-called "Christmas magic," grief hit her with the force of a sucker punch.

Kathryn sat down with a sparse little plate and tried her best not to let her boiling pot of unresolved emotions show. She took cool sips of water to beat back the thickness in her throat and the weight of unshed tears. *Dammit, I need to get ahold of myself. It's Christmas Eve.*

It was the strangest damn thing, this case of mixed emotions. Kathryn had no reason whatsoever to be nostalgic about Wilson family Christmases. They were generally a ticking time bomb of guilt and dysfunction, camouflaged in shiny paper and bows. The fun and games would usually start around Thanksgiving with Momma lapsing into unmedicated mania. Her momma had a big personality, and she'd never done anything by half measures, especially when her illness had been doing the talking. She'd make big, impossible promises, like planning to run an entire toy drive with no help, or offering to bake all the desserts for three homeless shelters for a month. She'd spend recklessly on needless extravagances and gifts, running up the family's debts. One year, her momma had bought Daddy a Bentley he absolutely didn't want and couldn't afford, and had gone into hiding with existential mortification when Daddy had insisted on taking it back.

Then there'd be Momma's inevitable crash, of course, usually precipitated by her own body chemistry combined with the realization that all the Christmas promises she'd made would never be accomplished. This would almost always happen during or around Christmas week. Momma would do her best, trying to white-knuckle her way through it, lashing out and making everyone around her white-knuckle it too. Friends and loved ones would pull together to try to realize the impossibly perfect holiday Evangeline Wilson had conjured in her head. But no matter what they did, something would go wrong. Whether it was some trumped up infraction or a serious problem, *something* would send her momma hurtling into a downward spiral. Momma would crash hard, bottoming out into depressions so deep, she couldn't rise from her bed for weeks.

Manic depression had ravaged and ruined Momma's life in every way. Well, that and her steadfast refusal to take the medications that would've made her illness less debilitating.

Still, there were glimpses of the real woman who popped through the illness. As Kathryn pushed her food around on her plate, those images played in her mind like the stuttering frames of an old home movie:

...Momma fussing over the puff pastry on her famous beef Wellington.

...Momma glowing with pride when the kids at the shelter opened the toys from the drive she'd organized.

...Momma buying Kathryn the dress she'd secretly been coveting and taking her to the spa to get a makeover before her big Christmas dance in middle school.

Evangeline Wilson had been relentlessly critical of nearly everything in life, Kathryn included. But Kathryn had never had the sense that the criticism came from a place of spite or jealousy. No, her momma had always pushed her to be better. She'd never allowed Kathryn to wallow in self-doubt or self-pity. She'd insisted Kathryn was smart and lovely and could do anything in the world she set her mind to. In every way, Momma had demanded that Kathryn not settle for less.

And in the end, Kathryn hadn't. She'd gotten her doctorate, and a beautiful home, a wonderful son, and a great career doing what she loved to do. She was a strong, independent woman, thanks to Momma.

Then why did it all feel so terrible? Dammit, she owed her mother's memory more than these mixed emotions.

Why does Christmas have to be so complicated? Most days she got through life just fine. Until grief would sneak up on her again, stealing her peace of mind just when she didn't expect it. Kathryn's stomach churned. She finally put her fork down.

Daddy raised an eyebrow. "Aren't you gonna eat? You haven't had a bite since breakfast."

"I'm not hungry, Daddy."

Daddy's expression softened with sympathy, and he reached across the table, wrapping his hand over hers. For all his foibles, Daddy always was pretty good at reading her mind. When Kathryn met her father's eyes, he gave her look of such understanding that it took all her strength not to burst into tears at the table. "I wish you could find some peace, girl, even if it's only for a while," he whispered, giving her a one-armed hug and kissing her on the forehead. If there was one thing about the grief and guilt she shared with her daddy, at least they somehow managed take turns having their breakdowns.

Their father-daughter moment was interrupted by the perpetually cheery Hoot, bouncing down the aisle pushing a food cart. Hoot stopped at their table, his face flushed with effort and his bow tie flashing wildly with its color-coordinated lights. "Hey!" Hoot cried, pointing to Kathryn's plate. "It's Christmas! No one is allowed to have big, empty white spaces on their plate. What's the matter, honey? Nothing here whet your whistle?"

Kathryn shrugged. "Everything is delicious, I'm sure. I guess I'm not very hungry tonight."

Hoot furrowed his considerable eyebrows but was undaunted. "I'm sure we can find something you're hankering for. I was about to put this on the buffet. Why don't you try some? It's the chef's specialty!"

And with that, Hoot pulled back the metal dome and revealed the most beautiful, perfect beef Wellington she'd ever seen. She and Daddy and Wilson all gasped at the same time. It was *exactly* like her momma's yearly Christmas Eve dish, from the golden, flaky puff pastry, to the juicy beef tenderloin inside, to the silver tray garnished with fresh, gold-painted magnolia leaves.

That dish looked so delectable, they eagerly held out their plates.

Hoot chuckled as he filled them up. "In my experience, there's always room for beef Wellington. It's good for what ails ya, as my momma always used to say."

Hunter gave him a skeptical look. "What, are you saying beef Wellington has some kind of medicinal properties?"

Hoot's enigmatic smile made the back of her neck prickle. "You'll see," the man sang as he scuttled off to the next table.

Kathryn shook her head. "What was *that* about?"

Daddy took a bite, closing his eyes in bliss. "Lord be, this is exactly like..." Her father hummed in satisfaction, not even able to finish his thought. So Kathryn took a bite.

And she knew exactly what he meant.

Somehow, someway, this was Momma's recipe. There was no mistaking it. They'd even gotten her famous rosemary rub right, just between the pastry and the meat. Kathryn's appetite roared back to life. Her nausea and blue mood vanished. Suddenly, she was so hungry she felt like she couldn't get enough.

Even Wilson was feeling it. "It's like magic, Momma! Do you think Grandmomma made this for us up in heaven and sent it down?"

"No, baby." Kathryn insisted, knowing full well that was ridiculous. But it really was *perfect*. She felt instantly different, too—light, and happy, and so mellow she was certain nothing bad could ever happen to her.

Could a few bites of beef Wellington really do all that? Apparently it could when so wrapped up in love and family and memory. A hundred times more effective than any drug, wasn't it?

She looked over at her daddy. He no longer seemed haggard, and his skin glowed with satisfaction. The worry lines between his brows were gone. Hunter was completely relaxed and smiling so broadly she hardly recognized him. Even Wilson didn't seem nearly so tired as he had when they'd walked in.

It really is like magic, isn't it?

Maybe there really was something to this "Christmas wish" business. Whatever it was, Kathryn decided she'd go with it.

The good vibes lasted all evening as they piled up their plates with serving after serving. When they were done, they even decided to keep the holiday cheer going by heading off to Christmas Eve services.

They decided to go to the late ten o'clock offering at a quaint stone church. It was a lovely service, non-denominational, with pretty much everything but the ecclesiastical kitchen sink thrown in. There were vesper-like chants and incense and Christmas carol sing-alongs that went well into the night.

They'd been here for a couple of hours now. But none of them seemed to mind. Just the right amount of seasonally appropriate snow gently fell outside the windows, and inside the church, tall candles festooned with fresh pine and red ribbons were clipped in the aisle at the end of every pew. In fact, the entire church was bathed in candlelight, sheltering them against the night. The altar spilled over with fresh pine garlands and bright-red poinsettias, matching the choir's red-and-white traditional robes beautifully. The dark Tudor styling of the church's interior, with its carved mahogany beams and molded plasterwork, suited this kind of night perfectly.

"It's beautiful, isn't it? The prettiest little church I've ever seen," Kathryn whispered to Hunter. He kissed her on the cheek, and wrapped his arm around her shoulders.

She nestled up against the crook of his arm. For one moment in her life, everything seemed right in the world. All her resentments and anxiety faded into the distance. Maybe they'd have their perfect family Christmas, after all.

The pastor broke into her peaceful reverie, saying that now that the service was winding up, everyone should take an unlit candle out of the holders by the hymnbooks. Kathryn picked up a slim white candle and tipped her candle to Hunter's to light it as the congregation passed the flame around.

The organ rumbled to life, and the choir led everyone in a sing along of "Silent Night." Hunter tilted the hymnal in her direction, nudging her to see if she wanted to share. She didn't. She rested her head on him and listened to his warm, unpracticed bass gently caress the notes. Not surprisingly, Hunter had a deep, wonderful singing voice—just as mellow and masculine as his speaking voice.

It felt so blessedly good, so soothing being tucked up under Hunter's arm. Her belly was full, and her family was around her, and it was so warm and cozy right here. And there was Christmas music in the air, with its sound of spiritual peace. She found herself drifting...

"Kathryn...*Kathryn!*"

Hunter's urgent tone swung her eyes back open. Had she drifted off? Hot wax stung her hand. "Ow!"

Shit!

She'd lost her grip on the candle. The fringe on her long acrylic scarf was *on fire!*

Hunter whipped the scarf off her neck, and she grabbed it away from him. By the time she stood up and staggered out into the aisle, half the scarf was engulfed!

Thank God they were near the back. She threw the scarf on the ground and tried to stomp it out. *Frantically.* But the fire had already engulfed the whole scarf! *Dammit!*

Startled exclamations rose up from the attendees around her. Kathryn whipped off her parka and threw it down in an attempt to smother the flames.

Which was a good idea, except that her coat was so lightweight that it created a big waft of air as it hit the ground, bellowing the fire instead. The flames leaped out, lighting onto the cheap crushed velvet skirt underneath the church's oversized nativity set.

It only took two seconds for Hunter and Daddy to extricate themselves from the pew. But the entire skirt was engulfed nonetheless, hot orange streaks licking up the sides of the low table where the manger scene was propped.

"Momma!" she heard Wilson's panicked cry. "Get back!"

Half the congregation were still trying to sing Christmas

carols, while the others stared on in mute confusion. Hunter raced up to the flaming fabric and yanked it with the skill of a magician pulling out a tablecloth underneath a dinner set for eight.

A handful of the chalk nativity figures toppled over, but Hunter had the fabric on the ground now, and he and Daddy were having some success turning it in on itself and smothering the fire. An altar boy ran over, having apparently pried out the enormous silver basin out of the baptismal font.

What in the—

The kid tripped over Hunter with his heavy load but still managed to get most of the holy water on the fire. All the water that wasn't soaking Hunter, that was.

Wisps of smoke sizzled over the flames as the last of them died out.

Drenched, but relieved, Hunter was round-eyed with relief as he disentangled himself from the altar boy. The crisis appeared to have been averted.

But then a loud, ominous *beep-beep-beep* sounded from overhead. Like an ear-splitting school bell, an alarm shrieked.

And then...

The sprinklers came on.

CHAPTER 17

AFTER THAT DISASTER of a church service, Hunter was relieved to have Kathryn back in his room at the inn. But when she emerged out of his bathroom, drying her hair, the poor woman was as consternated as a wet cat.

He couldn't stifle his snickering. "Now come on. It wasn't *that* bad."

She threw down the towel on a chair. "Oh, sure it wasn't. I only plunged the whole church into darkness and made everybody scream and storm the exits."

"Hey, no one was hurt, and they turned off the sprinklers before water could cause any damage. Any *serious* damage, that is." He pulled her onto his lap.

"But the baby Jesus *melted*," Kathryn wailed, her eyes so big and round and miserable, it caught his funny bone.

Their gazes locked. And they both started giggling—first in small snickers, then in big guffaws.

"Maybe." Hunter snorted. "But how cool is it that I was literally *baptized in fire?*"

They kept laughing, their shoulders shaking, helpless to stop. Kathryn had to wipe the tears from the corners of her eyes. "Oh, we are so *totally* going to fry in hell!"

"You bring the sticks," Hunter snorted, "I'll bring the marshmallows."

They cackled until she collapsed on his shoulder and wrapped her arms around his shoulder blades. "Oh, Hunter." She squeezed him tight. "There's no one I'd rather go to hell with than you."

"Yeah," he whispered, stroking his hand softly up and down her spine. "Me too."

He loved it when she was so snuggly and curled up against him like this. Kathryn was as light as a feather straddled across his lap, and sexy as hell wearing nothing but one of his undershirts. Only a thin sheet was between them. Damn, she smelled like his fancy hipster soap. It was delicious on her.

But he could feel the warm weight of her exhaustion in her limbs.

He nuzzled her neck with a few lazy kisses.

"Hunter," she shyly whispered, "would it be okay if I just slept here tonight? I don't think after everything, I've got the energy to—"

"Sure, babe," he cut her off. "I'm tired too." He held up the covers for her, and she climbed in.

"Thanks." She yawned, and curled herself under the comforter beside him.

"I want to do what *you* want to do. You don't have to keep thanking me."

"No, silly, I'm not thanking you for that." She laid her arms over his and stroked them. "I'm thanking you for these. For letting me sleep here with your arms around me on Christmas. I'm not alone. It's the best present ever."

Hunter was grateful she had her back tucked against him, because his eyes misted up. Maybe she was his present too. His mind drifted to memories of his last Christmas Eve. He'd fallen asleep on his crappy futon, drinking cheap whiskey straight out of the bottle and staring mindlessly at a video of a fireplace on his TV.

How had this woman turned his world to sunshine in just a handful of days? It was a miracle. *She* was his miracle, a light at the end of the deep dark tunnel he'd been in.

He wanted to tell her. But when the words came up, begging to be said, he pushed them back down again, too afraid to jinx a good thing. Instead, he nuzzled his head against her and kissed the tender spot at the base of her neck. "You're welcome," he whispered.

And they both fell softly, silently to sleep.

Tangled in Kathryn's arms, Hunter felt so good, so peaceful. Sleep came easily, far more so than usual. It felt right to sleep, to fall into blackness. But soon he fell down-down-down into the place he knew dreams turned into fear.

He breathed deep and, willing or not, he was there. Tensing, he waited for the terrible visions that had chased him for years.

But all he saw was a gray, West Virginia winter sky. The air was cold and crisp and bit at his cheeks as it rushed past him, back and forth, back and forth, back and forth. The sky itself seemed to be swaying somehow.

Hunter was disoriented, but not surprised by any of this. God, these episodes always felt so real. Realer than real, even —the colors brighter, the air sharper, and his senses stronger than they would be when he was awake.

Recognizing the springy whine of the chains on a park swing, Hunter looked down, realizing his own legs were in front of him, pumping his swing higher in the air. He was wearing the black converse high-tops he'd liked to wear when he was seventeen.

Holy crap. He was young again.

A counterpointed metallic squeal let him know he wasn't on the swings alone.

Laney was there, as freckled and perfect as she was when he'd first met her, all those years ago. Her wild, curly mane of red hair tumbled over her face and shoulders in the wind. God, she was so young, just a crazy little wildflower ready to bloom, wasn't she? She was wearing his varsity jacket. He'd always thought it looked better on her than it did on him.

She was giving him the strangest Mona Lisa smile.

"What are you thinking about, Redbird?" he asked as they passed each other on the swing.

Laney tossed him a playful glance but kept pumping her legs higher. "Why are you always asking me that?"

"'Cause I wanna know. I want to figure you out."

She chuckled, and shook her head "You stupid boy. Don't you know you're never supposed to figure a girl out? That takes all the fun out of it."

That was an answer he'd heard from her a thousand times. "You still haven't answered my question," Hunter insisted. The memory warmed him. And that was what this was, a perfect replayed memory. Even in his dream state, he knew that. They were in Dorie Miller Park. They used to come here all the time in the early days.

He expected her to jump off the swing and for him to start chasing her. Then he'd pin her up against a tree and kiss her senseless. That was their thing. That was the way it had happened. That was the way it should be. His feet were almost ready to hit the ground.

But then she turned to him and spoke instead. "I'm thinking about you, Hunter."

The discordant sentence stopped him, like a needle scratching across a vinyl record.

Oh, no. This was no memory.

Laney skewered him with her gaze as she swung by, and the startling maturity he saw there nearly stopped his heart. Her eyes were different—older, wiser.

Hunter was quiet for a minute, not so sure he liked where this was going. "What are you thinking about, about me?"

"I'm thinking about how you need me," she answered, still swinging away like she didn't have a care in the world.

"I suppose I do. More than I need my motorcycle, or hamburgers, or—"

"Stop it, babe."

"Stop what?"

"Stop needing me."

"What are you talking about?" he cried, halting the swing. "How in the hell am I supposed to do that?"

"The answer isn't a how, but a who."

He blushed furiously, like the boy he was just then. But he knew the Laney he was talking to was no girl. She was his wife. And she was trying to tell him something.

Was this some kind of message? Did she know about Ryn?

"You're jealous," he finally moaned.

"No, I'm not." She said it in such a breezy, unconcerned way that it rattled him. "I'm not jealous because I'm not here. I loved you. But I'm gone, Hunter. Get it through your head."

"But how come I can't forget you?"

"Because you're not supposed to."

Hunter had a million things he wanted to say to that. He waited for the swing to come back to him. But there was nobody there.

And the swing stood still.

❄

Now there was no sky. Only ceiling.

He was awake and at the inn, in his room with Kathryn. His heart felt heavy and full. Seeing Laney, even like this, was a lot like ripping off a scab—painful, but oddly satisfying as the air met the wound.

Oh God, what a dream. It was the first one that wasn't a dream of the crash. For the first time, he'd seen Laney at her best, the way she was when he'd first fallen in love with her.

Does this mean I'm making progress?

It seemed almost wrong to think that. But he'd been so tortured for so long, even this fairly upsetting glimpse of Laney felt like some kind of get-out-of-jail-free card.

He reached over for Kathryn, wondering if he should tell her about it. But she wasn't there. The first morning light of Christmas Day cracked through the lacy curtains. Was that the sound of sniffling he heard? As he focused his eyes, he saw Kathryn silhouetted by the window. She was holding an open box, and she was...*crying?* Oh no. *No, no, no.* Not that. Not on Christmas Day.

When Kathryn saw him stir, she jumped. An apologetic frown crossed her face and she quickly wiped away her tears. "Oh! Hunter, I know I shouldn't have. But I've always been so terrible about getting into the presents early. It's like I can't stand it—I have to *know*. I think it must be something about not wanting any surprises. I got up to go to the bathroom and I saw this box for me and I just couldn't—"

"Hey, it's *fine*," he interrupted. He hurried over to her and wrapped his arms around her from behind. "But I'm a bit put out that I got you a gift that made you cry. What'd I do, Ryn?"

The minute they made eye contact, her tears started flowing earnest. Dammit! Kathryn wasn't the type of woman to bawl over every little thing. What *was* it?

She pulled out the oversized snow globe music box he'd

bought her, the one she'd admired in the store, and wound the crank. The music began to chime, and she shook it, "You're such a wonderful man, Hunter. And this was such a thoughtful gift. You deserve someone who isn't such a mess. All I've got are pro-pro-problems."

He took the snow globe, gently set it down, and wrapped his arms around her tighter. "It's only a stupid decoration. If it upsets you, I'll take it back."

"No!" she protested. "It's too nice. It's just—" Her voice broke off, and she picked the snow globe back up again and shook it, her face a strange mix of fascination and dismay.

"Tell me," he whispered, nuzzling her neck. "*Please.*"

Pressing his hand to the small of her back, Hunter gently led Kathryn back to the bed. Propping himself up against the upholstered headboard, he gathered her into his lap. She shook the globe until a frenzy of glitter fell on the heads of the tiny lovers inside.

She watched the glitter swirl for a long moment until she could collect herself enough to speak. "My daddy bought this very same snow globe for Momma when I was four years old. When Momma sat this out with the Christmas decorations, I thought it was the prettiest thing I'd ever seen. She forbade me to touch it. So I'd beg anyone who was around to crank it up and shake it for me. I'd stare at it for hours on end."

Hunter rubbed her forearms, trying to warm her chill bumps. "That sounds like a good memory to me."

Kathryn suddenly got very quiet, and Hunter waited. She finally whispered, "You had a happy childhood, didn't you, Hunter?"

He stopped to consider that. "Yeah, I suppose I did. We all got along. I had a lot of friends. Christmases were great."

She chuckled. "I wouldn't expect you to understand. When there's something seriously wrong in your family, even the good times can feel bad. For people like me, Christmas isn't unlike this snow globe—glittery and perfect when you see it from the outside. But on the inside, it's all fake and manufactured for appearances."

She wiped her eyes again, her tears finally slowing. Hunter hugged her tighter, and she continued. "One day, while Momma was busy in the kitchen with her Christmas baking, I couldn't stand it anymore. I knew I shouldn't do it, but I was tired of asking for help. I had to work the globe myself. So I picked it up, and I shook it as hard as I could. Thing was, at four, I didn't have the grip strength to hold onto this big thing. It fell out of my hands and shattered on the hardwood floor. All the water and the glitter went everywhere. I felt awful, like I'd destroyed a magical world and killed all the people inside it."

She paused and took another rattling breath. "When Momma saw the mess, she went nuts, and for the first time, the woman really scared me. She spanked me so hard she left handprints. She threw a dustpan at me and left the room, telling me I had to clean it all up. By the time I picked up all the shattered glass, my hands were cut to pieces. Momma did finally come to her senses, and rushed back. She felt terrible. She could hardly bandage me up she was crying so hard. She said Christmas was ruined. She didn't come out of her room for a week, and she said it was all my fault."

Kathryn leaned into his embrace, and was quiet for long time, trying to rein in her emotions.

"It was one of the first memories of my childhood that I can remember, and I remember it with perfect clarity," she finally managed, delicately clearing her throat. "I'll never forget the devastation of standing over those broken pieces. I felt like nothing would ever get put back together again."

Hunter turned her around and wiped some of her tears away. "What did Huck do?"

"Nothing," she said, her eyes downcast. "He was out of town that week. My Grandmomma Weiss came by, and she took care of me until Momma could again. She said I had to be careful—Momma was more fragile than most people. At four, I couldn't understand that. I came to the conclusion I was responsible for keeping Momma happy. Even today, as a grown woman, I'm still racked with guilt that I couldn't. And here I am, a trained psychologist! I *know* it isn't right. My head understands that, but my heart never will."

Hunter wrapped his arms around her tight again. "I'm so sorry. God, I'm a prize ass. Now every time you look at that damn thing, you're going to think about how stupid I was to buy it. I have to take it back."

"No, Hunter. I actually think it might be good." Kathryn grimaced. "Maybe if I can get used to this thing and set it out every Christmas without getting upset, it'll mean I'm putting my history in perspective. That's where that memory needs to stay. Maybe you're really helping me."

She wound the snow globe up again and shook it, and they watched the swirling, sparkling snow in silence. When the music stopped playing, she wrestled out of his arms and put the globe down carefully on the nightstand. Meanwhile, Hunter reached down over the side of the bed and fished out a long, flat wrapped box. When she turned around, he handed it to her.

She kissed him on the cheek. "You must have been hiding this one."

"It was in my coat pocket. Merry Christmas, babe."

It was only a small thing he'd gotten her, but her whole face lit up when she opened it.

"Oh, it's so pretty!" she cried as she pulled the silver necklace out of its package. The chain was delicate, and the pendant was a glittering silver snowflake, dusted with pink crystals. The necklace was part of a matching set that included dangly earrings, each sporting three stacked snowflakes that twirled slowly when suspended. Hunter wouldn't call it a particularly pricey set, but it was handmade and unusual.

He'd gotten it at one of the jewelry stores up the street. The set had literally materialized on the counter in front of him as soon as he'd said "I wish I could find something nice for Kathryn" aloud. *Of course.*

Pulling the necklace out of its box, Hunter fastened it around Kathryn's graceful neck while she pushed the earrings through her pierced ears.

Turning her around, he took a good look. They were perfect on her. His girl was smiling now, and happy, and that made him happy too. "I knew it. You can't get the full effect when it's up against my ratty shirt. But I think it suits you to a tee—all pink and delicate. When you wear it, I hope you'll think of Christmas Pass."

Kathryn wrapped her arms around his neck and kissed him. "When I wear this, I'll think of *you*. And as for how it works with the T-shirt, that can be fixed."

Before he even knew what had happened, she crossed her arms and lifted the shirt over her head. Kathryn was stark naked underneath it and straddling his lap now. And she leveled him with another one of those deep, penetrating looks. He could practically see the flames dancing in her eyes.

Have mercy.

His heart raced, and his throat went dry. But he still managed to choke out a chuckle. "You giving me my Christmas present early?"

"Mmm-hmmm. But only if you promise to be a very, very good boy."

He loved the sexy come-on. But part of him hesitated.

Stopping himself, Hunter pulled a finger through the bangs that had caught at the corner of her eyes and scanned her face. He ran a thumb over Kathryn's still-damp cheeks. It killed him to see her upset. He wanted to kiss away every tear.

Hunter cradled her head in his hands—hands that still bore a fine spider web of scars from the crash, and callouses from his work. The sight of hands like his running over the smooth perfection of her ivory skin gave him pause.

Hunter blew out a shaky breath. "You know you don't have to do this."

She pulled her head back, astonished. Her eyes flashed. "Do what?"

"*This*—the whole sex-kitten-trapped-with-a-mountain-man thing."

"Did you just call me a *sex kitten?*" Kathryn cracked up. "I think that may be the best compliment I've ever gotten."

He kissed her on her forehead. "Hey, I'm being totally serious. I know you've had a hard few days. And I've upset you this morning, making you dredge up things you shouldn't have to. Come on, it's Christmas. You probably need to be with your family. But how can you when I've been stuck to you like glue? I get that you're grateful, but you don't owe me a damn thing. I should...I should make myself scarce."

"Make yourself—" Kathryn gasped. She pulled her head out of his grasp. Her mouth opened, then closed, then opened again. "How are you going to do that? We're trapped here until at least tomorrow, right?"

"And that's the thing. You may be trapped, but I don't want you to *feel* trapped. I don't want you feel obligated to include me in your family's Christmas, or to sleep with me, or any of it."

Kathryn looked down at herself, as if she suddenly wished she had some clothes on. But she didn't make a move for the shirt. Instead, she sat back on her haunches, considering him. Like a psychologist, she answered his question with a question. "Do *you* feel obligated, Hunter? I mean, I *have* been kinda dragging you around—"

"What? *No!*" he sputtered. "It's not like that. I just—I just—" He couldn't answer her. There were too many emotions, too many worries tangled up in his throat.

She caressed the side of his face, lightly trailing her knuckles over his morning stubble. And his heart surged in his chest. Catching her hand in his, he turned it around and kissed her upturned palm.

How had it come to this?

Hunter was already more or less naked before this woman. But he felt strangely *revealed,* laid bare by Kathryn, in every damn way. All he wanted to do was be around her. He thought about her morning noon and night. And he craved her body more than any man had a right to. Making love to her did nothing to slake it. It only made him need her worse.

"I-I want you, Ryn," he finally sputtered.

She bit her lip and shimmied seductively on his lap. "That's good. Because I want you too, Hunter."

He groaned with frustration. "That's not what I meant! I want...I want..." He struggled to tell her. "I want *you.*"

God yes, he wanted her. He wanted all of her—the happy and the sad, the problems and the crazy messes. She believed she wasn't good enough. But the truth was, she was better than enough. She'd turned his gray world to color again. She'd made him want things. Need things.

Dammit, he couldn't get the words out. He kept

stroking the side of her face, his forehead tilted to hers. But somehow, she seemed to understand.

She brought her mouth to his and kissed him, slow and soft and so, so intoxicating. *Goddamn*, her kisses—they were like *nothing* else. Warmth uncoiled through him, traveling slowly, slowly, until he was on fire from his head to his feet.

Kathryn trailed more kisses along his jaw and neck, dragging her teeth lightly along as she went. It was a new sensation, this nibbling and nipping, and damn if it wasn't turning him to putty in her hands. She pulled the tips of her fingers against his ribs, circling, teasing him with gentle caresses that somehow had the force of electrical shocks. Shit, was he actually *shivering*? He couldn't decide whether to be exhilarated by it or scared out of his mind. He was losing control, and the steel bands he'd placed around his heart were snapping one by one by one.

Kathryn was getting to him, changing him, pushing him. And right now, he didn't give a damn. He only had to have more.

Hunter tore the sheet back and snaked his shaky hands up her bare thighs and over her smooth, rounded bottom. He cinched her in tight in his lap. *Hell yeah.* A long, gravelly groan escaped his throat. His cock throbbed as it brushed up against her plumped, slicked center. So wet. *Goddamn,* she was *so wet.*

A thousand dirty ideas raced through his mind at once. He wanted her nine ways to Sunday. But his Ryn bit her delicious, pink bottom lip and pulled the length of him into her hand. And all his plans skittered out of his mind.

A slow slide, a slow glide with her—that was what she was. Every time they touched, falling a bit deeper. Every time they kissed, getting a bit closer.

He jumped from the silky intensity of her touch, every goddamn cell in his body focused on the warm weight of her hand on him. But she chuckled and arched her back, swirling the length of him against her soft, wet heat.

Over and over.

Son of a—

"Ohhhhh, oh my *freakin'* God, Ryn..."

This took friction to a whole new level. Hunter growled and covered her breasts with his needful kisses as she unraveled his control. Kathryn pulled her hot silk across his shaft and up over her clit until she was grinding and whimpering against him. Her hard pink nipples jutted in his mouth. He sank his fingers into her perfect ass as she writhed, her muscles rippling and straining under his hands.

"Yeah, b-baby, that's it," he stuttered, helpless to do anything but let her have her way. Sweet Jesus, he'd forgotten the simple pleasure of simply rubbing himself against a woman's lush, wet heat. It was crazy good, crazy perfect.

Just when Hunter could take no more, she lowered herself onto him, pushing him inside her with one long, gorgeous, agonizing thrust. He groaned out her name, begging, pleading for more.

She chuckled in a low, silky way that ticked his ear. "If you want me, you've got me, Hunter. You know that, right?" And she nuzzled more kisses against his neck. He gulped in air, struggling to control his breathing.

Everything about his Ryn overwhelmed him and short-circuited his senses. He should be taking charge about now, right? Rolling her under him? Bustin' his moves? Being the man? But his body could only shake with wonder as she rode him, pounding hard against him then pulling up again with hot little tugs that wouldn't take no for an answer.

He watched Kathryn, awestruck. The things that normally made her so graceful—the sinuous slope of her back, the crisp definition of her collarbone—now made her the sexiest woman alive. Beads of sweat formed on her back, slicking his fingers as he held her. The alabaster skin on her chest and shoulders flushed pink with heat. And her long, lean hips pounded him with *no fucking mercy.*

He finally found the presence of mind to circle his thumb over her clit as she took him.

She sucked in a breath. "Hunter...God, you're so big, so good..." Her moans got more intense, higher pitched. Seeing her so pent up only fanned his flames. *God,* how she tightened around him, and shredded his control with every push of her hips.

Kathryn tensed, a shudder rolling up her spine as she groaned out his name. And he felt her come in the very core of him. He couldn't moan. He couldn't yell. He could only release himself to her too, breathless and holding on for dear life.

On and on it went, the shaking and the writhing and mind-numbing crush of pleasure. He felt like someone had taken him apart and reassembled him again as a new model. They unwound together, their breath slowing and their shudders calming. The minutes ticked by until they were simply quiet and joined together in each other's arms.

Until this moment, Hunter hadn't realized how badly anxiety and loneliness had strangled his life. Because right here, right now, that vise began to loosen. It was almost as if the air rushed back into his lungs, and the blood rushed back into his heart. Hunter wished he could think of the right words to explain the tidal wave of emotions Kathryn set in motion. From the look on her face, he could tell it had swept her away too.

He wrapped his hand around the nape of her neck and kissed her again, soft and slow. And when she pulled away, their gaze locked. And her eyes lit up with mischief.

Kathryn let out a low, breathless chuckle. "Well, that's the happiest Christmas morning I think I've ever had."

Hunter ran his finger down the bridge of her nose to its adorable turned-up tip. "Yeah, it's definitely right up there for me."

"I guess I must've been a very good girl."

He kissed her sweet, swollen mouth, savoring her like candy. "Oh, you've been good all right. So good, maybe Santa will put a few more gifts in your stocking."

"Hmmm. I *am* already in your lap. Wanna put the Yule log back in the fireplace?"

Hunter threw his head back and laughed. *Ah, laughter* —another one of the gifts she'd given him this morning. He kissed her again, and rolled her underneath him. This Christmas Day was off to a very good start.

CHAPTER 18

Hunter wobbled precariously on his feet. "I don't know how I let you talk me into this."

Wilson gave him another shove. "It ain't no big deal, Hunter. I've been ice skating since I was three."

"It *isn't any* big deal, Wilson," Kathryn huffed. She tried her best to skate backward and pull Hunter along by his outstretched hands. It wasn't easy. Hunter flailed so much, she wondered whether she'd actually put skates on a cantankerous octopus and expected him to be an Olympic ice dancer.

Hunter let out a miserable groan. "When you have an irrational fear of busting your butt on the ice, everything about this is a big deal."

Kathryn just grinned at the man. Regardless of what Prince Grump-a-Lot had to say about it, Christmas was the perfect day for ice skating. The temperature had topped out at a crisp thirty-four degrees. The Christkindl market they attended, like everything in Christmas Pass, looked like something straight out of a storybook. The town fathers had done an impressive job of replicating similar Christmas markets so common in Europe at this time of year. The outdoor rink was lined with adorable wooden booths selling all manner of glass and wooden Christmas ornaments, German smokers and pyramids, roasted nuts and candies, and more. The sugary scent of cinnamon hard tack traveled on the breeze as workers poured out the confection onto a marble slab, and cut it into squares. Servers circulated through the crowd, selling hot mulled cider and wassail.

And in the middle of all that, Kathryn couldn't stop giggling. Hunter really did look ridiculous, all hunched over on his skates with his knees locked with fright. "I never figured you for a coward, Mr. Holliday."

"I'm no coward!"

"Then stand up straight and loosen up your knees," she commanded.

"Yeah, so, I think that's gonna be a no right now," he huffed.

They managed to make another circle around the rink and passed Daddy on the sidelines. Daddy raised his bottle of "soda" to them in mock salute as they passed. As much as she hated doing it, Kathryn had spiked it for him on schedule, and Daddy's expansive good humor this morning showed he was feeling its effects.

"Hey, Hunter!" Daddy called. "You ready to join the Ice Capades yet?"

"Can it, old man!" Hunter hollered back. "I don't see you out here!"

"I may be old, but I ain't stupid!" Daddy waved.

Wilson grunted. "Momma, can I stop pushin' now? He's too heavy."

Kathryn nodded. "All right, honey. When you get tired, go hang out by the fire pit with your granddaddy."

Wilson saluted and skated off backward. "Sure thing, Momma!" He executed a perfect turn, kicking his leg out for effect, and was off chasing some other kids around the rink.

"Showoff," Hunter groused.

Kathryn shook her head. "Only you could be so crabby on such a perfect Christmas Day."

He scowled at her, which made her snicker more. "Crabby? No, this isn't crabby. This is terrified."

The man's sputtering indignation only made his flailing more hilarious. His outfit didn't help, either. Hunter had insisted on wearing the white cowboy hat she'd bought him for Christmas, even though in his present state, he was having a darn hard time keeping it on his head. The hat had two sides pinned up for that narrow rider style, but she still teased him about being her Lone Ranger, saving damsels in distress. He was wearing the big gunmetal belt buckle she'd bought for him, too, which was shaped like an old-fashioned muscle car. He was sheepish and flustered and entirely cute.

"I can't believe you are such a good dancer, but you never learned to skate," Kathryn chided.

"It's not the same!" Hunter wailed as he almost wiped out again. She managed to yank his arms up in time and pushed him over to the side against the wall. Grabbing onto it with both hands, Hunter finally managed to force his flailing feet to a stop. "Oh, thank God," he huffed.

Kathryn leaned on the sturdy wooden railing, put her arm around his back, and kissed him on the cheek. "Oh, Hunter, how I wish I could get you to relax and stand up straight. You could actually have fun. You could be *good* at this."

Hunter rolled his eyes heavenward. "Oh you've *got* to be kidding me."

"What?"

"Nothing," he said resignedly. "Don't mind me." He

whipped around almost like a marionette getting his strings pulled, standing up straight and unsupported for the first time. No wobbles. No bobbles. Like he'd been doing it his whole life.

"How are you suddenly..." Kathryn broke off.

Hunter gave her a courtly bow and leaned back up. "Hey. You wished it. And this town is the place where your Christmas wishes come true, right?"

She snorted again. "You've been holding out on me is more like it."

He held out his arms to her for support. "I wouldn't say that. I still haven't figured out how to move yet."

Kathryn skated close to his side and showed him how to cross hands like ice dancers do. "All right. Now treat this like a dance. We're going to lean one direction together, then the next. See how you lean in, then you push off with your opposite foot? It's like a sway."

Hunter shrugged, as if to say, "if you say so." When she pushed forward, he kept astride her, one push off, then two. Nice and easy...left, right, left, right.

Wilson whizzed by. "You're doin' it, Hunter! You're doin' it!"

"I guess I am," he breathed, and he gave her a shy smile.

Kathryn's heart turned over in her chest. Hunter's smiles—ah, they got to her, every single time. Maybe it was because he wasn't the sort of man to smile all the time, like Sterling was. Sterling wore his smile like a default setting, a mask that always hid what he was really thinking. But Hunter only smiled when you really pleased him, or when he was making a joke, or when he was deliberately trying to be friendly to someone new.

She adored all his smiles, really—the small, self-effacing ones, the ornery joking ones, and especially the wide, heart-stopping ones he'd shown her up in the cabin. But this new one might be her favorite yet. He no more wanted to be on this ice than a cat in a bathtub. But he was happy now, because he wanted to make *her* happy.

Since when have I ever had a man like that?

"I can't believe it." Hunter chuckled. "We turned a corner and I didn't fall down!"

"See, Hunter? All you have to do is believe."

"Yeah, right," he muttered.

But he kept going with her. Around and around they went, skating a bit faster with every turn. Finally, she took him out into the center of the ice and showed him a couple of tricks—how to kick out your leg and hold it around a curve, how to pop around so you can skate backward, and such. Hunter was a far quicker study than she expected him to be.

Then they moved back out into the fray again, circling the ice together hand in hand.

The other skaters smiled fondly at them as they went by. She talked him into kicking his leg out at the same time as hers, while they balanced on one foot together.

Hunter whooped. "Holy hell! It's working!"

"See? I told you! If you can get me to fly down a mountain on a piece of inflated plastic, I think I can manage to teach you this."

"We make quite the pair, don't we?"

She giggled—actually giggled—in response. Hunter pulled her back into the center of the ice, and she went willingly. He scooted around her, stopping her. That surprised her a bit, and his chest ended up being her backstop.

He wrapped his arms around her to steady her. And he dipped his head, meeting her mouth for a tender, perfect, lingering kiss.

When she opened her eyes again, the skies had opened up, and big, fat snowflakes began to swirl around their heads. Kathryn was suddenly struck with the childish urge to stick her tongue out and let the snowflakes fall on it. She did, and Hunter soon did the same.

"Huh," Hunter breathed.

"What is it?"

His eyes sparkled with merriment. "You know what, Ryn? We're like those little people in your snow globe right now, aren't we?"

"So we are." She tipped up on her toes and gave him another kiss. He kissed her back. With enthusiasm. And that simple gift filled her with more warmth, more holiday spirit than she'd ever felt before. Maybe the next time she saw that snow globe, she wouldn't remember her past. Maybe she'd remember this moment instead.

Memory was a funny thing. As a child, Kathryn had spent hours on end staring into that snow globe, wondering what it would feel like to be those tiny lovers, gliding blissfully along, hand in hand in a snowy winter's paradise.

As she looked up into Hunter's smiling face, she realized that now she knew.

Out in the streets, Christmas spirit ran high. Everywhere they went, the shops were open, music filled the air, and people mingled like they were at one big cocktail party. The Wilson-Winslow-Holliday contingent, for its part, wandered aimlessly in search of a place to have lunch. Or at this hour, it was really more like "lupper." *But who cares? It's Christmas!*

Even Daddy was in a good mood. He'd been keeping his drinking strictly in line with what she was giving him, as far as she could see, and wasn't complaining about it. Wilson had a ball opening his presents earlier, which included all the LEGO sets he'd been coveting, peanut butter cups from the chocolatier Wilson had found, some video games he'd had his eye on and, of course, the dreaded clothes. At least she'd refrained from "Santa" bringing him socks and underwear. Though she'd surely never asked him to, Hunter had gotten Wilson his favorite gift of the day—a big book of robot designs and some raw materials for them to work with.

Hunter had even bought Daddy a funny sweatshirt that said "Old Enough to Know Better, Young Enough Not to Care." Daddy adored it and refused to take it off all day.

Daddy's gift to them had been paying for this vacation. In turn, Kathryn got him some of his favorite things—a one-year Netflix subscription, six visits to his favorite massage spa, and organic chocolate ice cream delivered straight from the farm to his house, all year long. He was thrilled.

She brushed her fingers over her new necklace, enjoying the feeling of the cool, smooth silver. The gift from Hunter had been her favorite this year. Kathryn watched them all strolling along, so at ease in their companionability, and she felt an uncomfortable pang of longing in her chest.

Would it be too much for her to ask to have a man in her life again? A man who truly desired her? A man who could be her partner, her equal?

Was it wrong to want that with *Hunter?*

Yeah, probably, she winced.

It might seem like they were a couple right now. But Kathryn knew it was all too good to be true. Too much had happened too fast. What would happen once they left this mountain oasis? They lived in different cities and moved in totally different circles. How long would it be before he started ghosting her?

She wouldn't know until the time came, would she? The uncertainty formed a tight knot of misery in her stomach.

As if he could read her mind, Hunter draped his arm over her shoulders and cinched her against him as they strolled along.

And dammit, it felt *good*.

"Hey, Mom, look!" Wilson cried, pointing over to the town square park up ahead. People were gathering, and a brass band played Christmas carols from underneath and adorable white gazebo covered with glorious Victorian gingerbread woodwork. An old-fashioned cloth banner draped over the entrance said "Christmas Pass Founder's Day Celebration."

Daddy stopped and put his hands on his hips. "I s'pose that makes sense. A town named Christmas Pass would be founded on Christmas Day, wouldn't it?"

As usual, Wilson ran up ahead. "I smell food!" he hollered back.

Once they got into the park, Kathryn was amazed to see at least three or four hundred people milling about among souvenir vendors. The town's charitable society appeared to be handing out enough free food to feed an army. They got themselves a plate of chili and sandwiches, and dusted off the snow on some folding chairs in anticipation of the day's entertainment.

A bluegrass band came up and played a few rousing songs. And then the stage was ceded to a burly older man with fading red hair—Chris Carol, the current Mayor of Christmas Pass.

Kathryn turned to Hunter. "Does everyone in Christmas Pass have these ridiculous names?"

Hunter shrugged. "Seems that way, doesn't it? Somebody in the past probably started naming their kids cutesy names and it turned into a tradition."

That answer seemed too simple. But she didn't have time to discuss it. Carol was beginning his speech, and he was quite the overwhelming, gregarious fellow, rolling onto the stage like an out-of-control bowling ball ready to knock down some unsuspecting pins. He hunched over the microphone, spending several minutes welcoming everyone and dispensing a litany of thanks to all the local people and businesses that helped make the event come together today.

Finally, after numerous rounds of applause and special community service awards being handed out, he got into the meat of his speech. "Now I know y'all are impatient to get down to the real reason we're here today—to honor the many traditions that have made Christmas Pass."

The crowd went wild with anticipatory cheering. Hunter seemed to perk up with interest at that.

"So it's my honor, as your mayor, to tell the story of our brave ancestors who founded Christmas Pass. They were a tough lot—people who settled in this part of the country in the 1700s had to be. Between the elements, and the terrain, and the warring factions of Indians and colonists, it was a miracle anyone could survive. But for the twenty original families of Christmas Pass, it was even more so. The fort they'd built twenty miles from here had been burned to the ground in an Indian raid. The settlers fled to this mountain for shelter. But Mother Nature had other ideas. The skies unleashed every kind of devastation—winds, stinging sleet and, the strangest of all things, a wintertime thunderstorm with fearsome lightning. The settlers huddled in caves and under makeshift evergreen shelters. Floods poured down the mountainside, and with it, mud and snow. Lightning scorched the earth all around them."

One of the musicians rolled an ominous drum roll on the cymbals, and the crowd clapped and whooped.

"When the morning broke and they took stock, they were amazed to see they were safe and sound, even though the ground right in front of their shelters had been torn to pieces by lightning. One blast had even split up an enormous boulder. But under the boulder was a pure, mountain spring, with more than enough water welling out of the deep earth to sustain a town for generations. And the rugged mountain helped protect them from all dangers. In memory of being saved on Christmas Day, the founders named our fair city Christmas Pass—a place born on wishes and a whole lot of luck."

The crowd erupted in cheers again. Chants of "wishing *rock*, wishing *rock*, wishing *rock*" rippled through the masses.

Kathryn leaned over to Hunter. "Wishing rock. What does that mean?"

"Beats me," he shrugged.

Carol waved his hands. "Now hold your horses, everybody!"

Kathryn was surprised to see local firemen form a line behind the crowd. She hadn't noticed it before, but there was a locked fence directly behind them. The firefighters were clearly relishing their role in the ceremony, each of them wearing a red fireman's hat festooned with holly. They carefully unlocked the gate and set out a rope line.

Over the loudspeaker, Carol informed the attendees that behind the gates was the remains of that split rock, which they bring out for display every Christmas season in this park. People began lining up dutifully.

"Now remember, no pushing, no shoving," Carol warned. "Everyone will get a chance to rub the rock and have a chance at great luck in the New Year!"

Daddy whooped. "Get out of my way! I'm giving that rock a big old smooch!"

Hunter rolled his eyes. "Don't tell me you actually believe that line of bull?"

"Hey." Daddy wagged his finger. "I kissed the blarney

stone in Ireland, and I'll rub the wishing rock in Christmas Pass. Isn't half of being lucky believing you're lucky?"

"You should listen to Granddaddy. He's smart about these things," Wilson called back as he started queuing up in line.

Chuckling, Kathryn lined them all up—even a skeptical Hunter. And when their turn came, they had a marvelous time goofing around with the rock.

"What a shame my stupid phone won't work here," she mused. "I sure wish I could get a picture of us all."

And somehow, an officially sanctioned photographer appeared behind them, took a Polaroid of them posing around the rock, and handed her the print free of charge. Kathryn shook her head in wonder.

The people here at Christmas Pass sure know the meaning of the word 'service,' don't they?

"Ha! That was easy." Kathryn marveled at the photo. It was a cute little candid shot of them all posed so naturally together. They looked like a...*family*.

Hunter wrapped his arms around her shoulders as they walked off, and planted a soft kiss on her temple. "I, for one, am glad you kissed that wishing rock. You deserve something easy. You, my sweet, brave Ryn, deserve all the New Year's luck in the world."

Kathryn wrapped her arms around his waist. Maybe Hunter was really all the luck she needed.

CHAPTER 19

AHHHHH. Kathryn rolled over to her back, stretched luxuriously, and cracked her eyes open to the morning light.

Glimmers of bright white winter sun filtered through the delicate lace curtains in her room. She checked the clock on her nightstand. Eight o'clock, it read. Kathryn stretched and sighed into her pillow. God, it was such a luxury to wake up with no alarm, no calendar full of appointments. Perhaps it was the best part of being on vacation.

Then Hunter stirred against her and wrapped one muscled arm around her waist.

Scratch that. *This* was the best part about being on vacation.

Hunter cinched her naked body up against his and gave her a couple of long, languorous kisses along her shoulder blade, his stubble gently scraping as he did. "Morning, beautiful."

Kathryn chuckled softly. She'd never get enough of this man.

Even after a big Christmas Day out, they'd still had the energy to have three rounds of mind-numbingly good sex before they'd finally collapsed into sleep. It seemed to happen every time he reached for her—this explosion of pent-up need. Sometimes, he would harden up again, ready for more, even before he'd pulled out of her. If you'd told her a year ago she'd have a man with this much sexual energy in her bed, she wouldn't have believed it. But Hunter was teaching her a great many things about what she deserved and what she could do. Lord have mercy, she could practically see the smoke rise from their bodies when they touched skin to skin.

Hunter was even teaching her about the simple decadence of sleeping together nude. There was nothing like burrowing under the fluffy comforter with him and drifting off into sated sleep. Touching all his textures and angles, wrapping herself in the heady smell of his skin, sensing his warmth against her—it was a revelation.

Kathryn pulled his hand up to her mouth and kissed his palm, then lightly kissed his fingertips, one by one. The outline of his smile tickled the back of her shoulder.

If only she'd had more experience with men before she'd met her ex, she might've seen the red flags. She was always the one begging for sex. And when they had it, Sterling did a reasonably proficient job. But it was perfunctory. Rote. Passionless. Her husband closed his eyes a lot during the act. And when his eyes were open, she felt like he was a million miles away. Sterling had taught her many things about marital relations that she'd never wanted to learn. Chiefly, that it was possible to feel more alone after sex than you did before it.

Once she found out all that Sterling had been hiding, she'd stopped blaming herself. She'd even stopped blaming Sterling, for that matter. But like it or not, those years with him had colored what she expected from the opposite sex. And now Hunter Holliday had blown past those barriers.

What a precious gift Hunter had given her. And she wanted to hold on to that gift with all her heart.

Flipping herself around, Kathryn stretched out herself along Hunter's body, long and lean like a cat, and wrapped her arms around his neck. She planted kisses along his jaw.

He grinned and groaned all at the same time. "Girl, don't tempt me."

"Why not?" she breathed, running her hand over his delicious backside. "We're on vacation."

Kissing her quickly on the mouth, he sat up in bed. "Wilson will be pounding on the door any minute now. And besides, I promised myself I'd get a run in this morning."

Kathryn sat up too, watching Hunter stretch and pull his delectable nude body out of bed. It was a reasonable consolation prize, ogling his perfect posterior as he disappeared through the door of his room.

Eager for some local news, Kathryn tried to turn on the television. She pounded the remote and took the battery in and out, but it wouldn't come on. By the time she'd given up fiddling with it, Hunter had walked back in wearing a sweatshirt, colorful spandex running tights, and new running shoes.

That outfit looked ridiculous, and totally out of character on him.

"When did you get all that?" Kathryn asked, wondering why he suddenly was concerned about his exercise routine. Hadn't she heard him say that his job was so physical, he got all the exercise he needed at his shop?

Hunter shrugged, and his gesture seemed odd, like he was trying a bit too hard to be offhandedly casual. "Oh yeah, um, I bought it yesterday, when you and Wilson ducked into the candy shop. I need to catch some exercise before I get back on the road. You know, burn off some calories."

Isn't that what we were doing last night?

His circumspect body language made the back of her neck prickle.

"But the road crews are coming today," she protested. "Wouldn't you rather get your stuff packed up and come have breakfast with us?"

He bent over the bed to give her a kiss. "Now now, don't pout. My stuff's already packed up in a couple of shopping bags. I'm ready to get out of here, aren't you?"

Yes—yes, of course I am, but...

Kathryn looked in his eyes and got the distinct impression something was off here. Was he hiding something from her? For the life of her, she wasn't sure what that could be. But there was no doubt he was acting itchy and strange this morning. Was he pulling away from her, distancing himself now that their Christmas fling was winding up? Was it *her* he wanted to get away from?

"I'll be back in a bit. And...I have some important things I need to tell you, okay?"

"Okay," she answered, wondering what that was all about as the door snicked shut behind him.

The silence in the room suddenly seemed deafening.

She told herself he was only going on a run, for God's sakes. But he hadn't been able to look her in the eye just now. *Why?*

Against her will, Kathryn's stomach knotted up with dread. She didn't want to let Hunter go, not after everything they'd shared. But would she have to? Is that what he wanted to tell her—that this had been fun but vacation time was over? He'd told Wilson he wanted to keep things going after the holidays, but had he only said that to placate the boy? Had he really meant it? They hadn't bothered to discuss it, had they?

Oh God. Kathryn could just kick herself for not being

more open with him by now. She'd been so afraid to break the spell of this place. But whether she liked it or not, she'd have to pull him aside at some point and broach the subject of their relationship like a grownup. When though? When she felt like she was strong enough to hear the answer, whether it was yes or no?

Kathryn shook herself. No, she would *not* cling. She would *not* act desperate. Hunter had to come to her of his own free will, or not at all.

Reluctantly she rolled out of the bed and padded across the room to grab one of the fluffy, Turkish terry robes out of the bathroom. Hmm. Odd. They'd always had a change of towels and a fresh robe each morning. But today the bathroom hadn't been touched, even though she'd put a housekeeping hanger on the doorknob before they'd gone out. Oh well. It didn't matter. They'd be leaving today, anyway. She started laying her clothes out for the day and making sure all her items were pulled together and folded neatly in her suitcase.

She paused for a moment by the window, surveying the street. The road outside was deserted, save a few cars. Usually the streets were noisy with the sights and sounds of downtown Christmas Pass. But this morning, an eerie hush seemed to fall over the town. Day-after-Christmas blues, she supposed.

Like Hunter predicted, Wilson knocked on her door. He was dressed and bouncing around in the hallway. "I'm starvin', Momma!" he declared. "I want my Belgian waffles! Why aren't you dressed?"

"I slept in, child. Why don't you go down with your granddaddy and get started without me? I'll catch up in a minute. I need to grab a quick shower."

Wilson hugged her and bounded back down the hall.

Kathryn turned the spigot on in the bathroom sink to

brush her teeth. Nothing. No water pressure. She tried the shower, desperately turning the knobs this way and that. Nothing. Then she went around flicking the light switches. *Nothing.*

Well, damn.

Muttering, she brushed her teeth with no water, tried to refresh her makeup, and pulled on a clean sweater and jeans.

She'd no sooner gotten her feet in her shoes when a loud, insistent knock sounded on her door. When she opened it, she wasn't too surprised to see Daddy and Wilson there, all round-eyed and indignant.

"I think we're out of luck for breakfast," Daddy announced. "There ain't a soul downstairs. The restaurant's dark as pitch. We rang the bell at the front desk and even called down there, but nobody came."

"It's like everyone's just *gone*, Momma!" Wilson cried. "We went out on the street, and everything out there's shut down too!"

"Don't be silly." Kathryn frowned. "Surely we'll find something open."

Daddy shook his head. "I don't know about that, Katie-belle. It's like we're all alone in this building. I've not seen hide nor hair of another guest, or anyone on the street, either. It's damn strange."

Walking over to her window again, Kathryn peered out through the curtains. On closer inspection, she saw that they were right. The town really did seem deserted. How could that be? The day after Christmas was one of the biggest shopping days of the year!

Kathryn scratched her head. Lucky for them, the road crews were scheduled for today. There was no doubt about it, they needed to get out of this strange, strange place, sooner rather than later.

She turned back around, trying not to let her worries show. "Hunter stopped by to say he was going for a run. I tell you what. I'm going to go out and try to find him. Better safe than sorry. Maybe while I'm doing that, I'll find some-place open where we can get some food for the road. Daddy, why don't you and Wilson get the Suburban loaded with all our things? Hunter said his stuff was packed, too, in his room. Go on and take it all. That way, we'll be ready to go as fast as the roads get cleared."

They agreed on that plan and disappeared down the hallway. Kathryn tugged on her coat and headed out into the bitter winter's wind. The weather, it appeared, was taking a turn for the worse. The sky was a leaden gray—a noticeable contrast to the picture-perfect weather the day before. Scraps of litter tumbled down the street, pushed by howling, threatening gusts. The town was *entirely* different now. Only yesterday, the whole population of the town seemed to be out on the streets. But today? It was like they'd never been here in the first place. Not a single tourist could be found. Storefronts were locked and dark, some even boarded up. No music played. Decorations drooped, and tinsel collected by the sewer grates. Honestly, it seemed like they were *completely* alone.

She really needed to find Hunter. She knew he'd be smart enough to find his way back to the inn, but some-thing was wrong—definitely, seriously wrong. Surely he ought to be able to see that. Why hadn't he turned back by now?

Everywhere she looked, creepy shadows loomed. Why were all the people gone? Had they evacuated? Was there about to be some kind of natural disaster coming, like a tornado, and she didn't know?

Considering the worsening weather, that didn't seem so farfetched. Black clouds formed quickly, angrily blotting out the sun, roiling and cracking with menace. With clouds like that, anything could happen.

We have to get out before we're trapped here even longer. Dammit, where in the world is Hunter?

Trembling now, Kathryn ran from corner to corner, desperately searching the streets to find some semblance of life. But there was nothing. Streets that seemed familiar and easy to navigate only yesterday now seemed to tangle hopelessly away from her in every direction.

Thunder boomed directly overhead.

Fear prickled along her spine as she stood there, gawking. Kathryn ran a panicked hand through her hair and rubbed her eyes. But when she opened them up again, she saw the strangest thing. The buildings around her seemed to flicker, as if they might disappear entirely. For a moment —just a fleeting second—she could almost see the outlines of an entirely different, deserted, dilapidated mining town underneath the charming Christmas Pass facade. *Oh God.* It looked like Christmas Pass *itself* was some kind of projection that was actually faltering.

She screamed in shock, the sound echoing down the lonely street. Her heart thundered in her chest. Terror wrapped its icy fingers around her, squeezing her from her head to her toes.

Okay, Kathryn, get a grip. Your eyes must be playing tricks on you.

She scrunched her eyes shut, and then opened them again. All the breath left her body. It was the same with the flickering. Except this time she could very clearly see the ghost of the reality underneath. *I'm not seeing this! I'm not seeing this!*

Christmas Pass wasn't just strange. It *wasn't real.* It was some kind of fantasy place—some kind of Christmas oasis that was about to disappear.

Holy Mother of God. All those people, all those experiences we had—were they fake too? A projection? Some kind of manifestation of what we all desired?

Kathryn took off at a dead run, not even registering what direction she was going in. She had to find Hunter, hold him, and reassure herself that he was real too. Hunter was real, right? *Right?*

She had to find him. Now.

CHAPTER 20

KATHRYN'S LUNGS burned with exertion as she ran. But she didn't care. She pounded down every street, crashed around every corner. *Where is he? Oh Jesus, where is he?*

Every street seemed longer and lonelier than the last, until she wasn't quite sure where she even was anymore. Her heart ached and her mind spun with every dire scenario she could conjure.

She wiped her frantic tears away as her legs pumped underneath her. What about Daddy and Wilson? Were they okay back at the inn? Was the inn even still there?

It *had* to be. They *had* to still be there. And she *had* to find Hunter. And—

She collided with something as she rounded a turn.

Not a something. A someone. *Hunter.*

"Ryn!" he cried as he pulled her back to him and wrapped her in his arms. "What are you doing out here?"

"I was trying to find you! All this weird stuff started happening and I got scared and—" She buried her head in his broad, broad chest, too relieved, too overwhelmed to even speak. No, the tears did her talking now. Gulping in big, heaving breaths, she sobbed like a child in his arms.

"Hey, hey, hey now. Shh," Hunter crooned, holding her tight in his arms. "None of that. I'm right here."

"You're real!" Kathryn wailed, hugging him as tight as her arms would squeeze him.

He petted her hair and chuckled. But then he stopped and pulled her away. "Wait. You thought I wasn't *real?*" But then his face lit with recognition. "You—you saw it too, then. The flickering."

"Yes." She wiped her tears away with her coat sleeve.

"And you thought I was some kind of figment too?" Hunter continued. "Something conjured up by your subconscious to fulfill your wishes?"

Cheeks flaming with embarrassment, Kathryn nodded.

He grinned, scooping her up and hugging her until her feet dangled off the ground. "If I wasn't so scared right now, I'd say that was the sweetest thing anyone's ever said to me."

They stood there for a moment, happy to have found each other. He tipped her head and kissed her. But they didn't linger long. The skies still churned overhead, and a single peal of lightning cracked ominously in the distance.

"We have to get out of here, but, Kathryn—I—I think we may be trapped in here."

"*Trapped?* Trapped how? Aren't the snow crews supposed to—"

"Can they even find this place?" he interrupted. "Can anyone? I ran all the way to the edges of town. I finally got to this giant wall of swirling snow that surrounds the place. It was thick, like some kind of barrier. I couldn't walk into it. The snow was so heavy, you couldn't see your hand in front of your face."

"This is what you wanted to talk to me about this morning, wasn't it?"

He grimaced. "Yeah. I've actually known something

wasn't right about Christmas Pass from the beginning. I wanted to have some proof before I told you."

She narrowed her eyes at him. "And you didn't want to scare me either, did you?"

He winced. "That too."

"If we ever get out of this place, we're going to have a long talk about keeping things from me, Hunter Holliday. But right now, I'll give you a pass. I'm not ready to accept that we're trapped here. Are you? We got in here, didn't we? There's got to be a way out. Maybe we could punch a hole in it somehow."

Hunter rubbed his chin, thinking about that. "With the truck, you mean. I'm willing to try it if you are."

"But first we've got to get to Daddy and Wilson, back at the inn. They're getting us packed up to go. I'm so turned around, I can't tell you where I am."

Hunter pulled a paper out of his pocket. "Lucky for you, I have a map. I've been charting it every time a new street or path materialized."

She grinned appreciatively at him. "Of course you did."

They both hung their heads over it until they'd figured out they weren't all that far away from the inn. Only a few blocks and a few twists and turns.

And that was when they heard it.

A blaring beep-beep-beep-beep that echoed over the hills. It was loud and accompanied by the roar of an engine —the distinctive clatter that could only be a snowplow.

They shouted and clapped as they realized what was happening. The state road crew—they were here! *Could it really be?*

Hunter snatched her up in his arms and twirled her as they both whooped for joy. He sat her back down and laid a pure, jubilant kiss on her. It was hard, and brash, and turning up at the corners with a smile. And for a moment, the world stood still—until lightning lit up the sky.

The wind howled. Sudden, stinging snow pelted them, as if it'd been hurled down from above.

He looked at her, and she looked at him.

And they ran back to the inn as fast as their legs would take them.

CHAPTER 21

"Why are you drivin' so fast, Hunter?" Wilson asked, still squirming to get his seat belt hooked. They'd loaded themselves in the tow truck, the Suburban still strapped to the back.

Hunter tried his best to be breezy and calm. "We've got to get ahead of the storm, buddy."

Huck squirmed to help Wilson get clicked in and dried off. "Dammit, I'm soaked to the skin!" he declared. "Wouldn't it be safer to wait out the storm?"

"No!" Hunter and Kathryn cried at the exact same time.

"I still don't see what the all-fired hurry is," Huck grumbled.

Kathryn turned around, and smiled reassuringly. "We have reservations. I want to get the most out of them. I have all kinds of things planned for us at the Greenbrier—excursions, hiking, and zip lining for starters. Everything should be super fun."

Boom! Lightning sizzled down from the sky, scorching the earth.

"One second between the flash and the sound!" Wilson

cried. "That's only one mile away, isn't it, Granddaddy?"

Then another unholy flash rent the sky, coming down in a deafening roar off to their right.

They screamed as the car rocked. A tree split in half straight down the middle and started to smoke not more than ten feet away from them.

Hunter swerved reflexively and hit the gas. They flew down the road, straight toward the barrier. If the snow trucks got through, they would too. Hunter pushed the pedal down, their speed climbing. The sleety snow thickened to a total whiteout, and winds swirled around them, creating a kind of white, wintry tunnel.

"Hold on!" he yelled. Hunter braced for an impact that didn't come. They punched through the barrier, only to be met with sudden blue skies on the other side.

Hunter craned his neck to look behind them. The ground shook, and the snow swirled, and the outlines of the buildings and structures of Christmas Pass just simply melted away. That was the only way to explain it. Only a few decrepit buildings were left, the crumbling ruins of a long-abandoned mining town. It was as if that perfect tourist town had never been there in the first place.

Christmas Pass was *gone*.

As he turned around, Hunter exchanged a long, disbelieving look with Kathryn. He could tell from the dazed expression on her face that she'd seen the same thing. Neither of them said a word.

Catching that something was wrong, Huck and Wilson turned to see. But by then, everything was obscured by the eerie snowstorm that was now fully behind them.

"Helluva strange storm," Huck muttered.

"You can say that again," Hunter answered. "I'm glad to be through it."

All at once, Hunter's phone started vibrating in his

jacket pocket. All four of their phones pinged with messages and alerts, filling the cab with insistent noise. Miraculously, their communication devices came back to life with their full charges as soon as they left the Christmas Pass city limits.

"Yay!" Wilson cheered holding up his phone. "It works!"

Kathryn groaned as she scrolled through her messages. "Wilson, you got a lot of messages from your daddy, didn't you?"

"Yeah," he answered.

"Yeah, me too," Kathryn muttered. "I wonder what Sterling wants. He's supposed to be in France until the fifth of January. He warned me not to expect to hear from him over the holidays." She scowled. "It would be just like him to make things complicated. The man will have to wait his turn. I'll check in with him this evening, when we have some downtime."

They traveled to White Sulphur Springs, the home of the Greenbrier, in mostly companionable silence. Kathryn scrolled through her phone, grumbling at the backlog of her messages. She told him she was sending messages of reassurance to her patients who were melting down over the holiday, and setting appointments for when her office would be open again. Hunter smiled to see her humming along to the contemporary bluegrass channel he'd punched into his satellite radio, tapping her foot in time to the beat. Another thing they had in common, evidently.

Hunter watched the road carefully, going nice and slow to give other drivers plenty of warning as his hulking truck inevitably crowded the oncoming lane. He kept watch for more freak snowstorms, but none came. The roads were crisp and recently scraped, and what snow remained was melting away. Clearly, the *real* Greenbrier Valley hadn't had a snowstorm for days. The weather was actually unseasonably warm, almost fifty degrees, with a winter-crisp, steel-blue sky.

Sunshine flickered through the trees and poured through the windows as they barreled down the road, mottling Kathryn with warm sunbeams. Her hair and eyes shimmered with the magic of the morning's rays, and she had no idea.

Damn, she's perfect, isn't she?

Unable to stop himself, Hunter smiled over at her like some kind of smitten fool. Kathryn caught his gaze, and smiled back, before bending her head to her phone again. Hunter suppressed the urge to sigh and put his attention resolutely back on the road.

What will happen now, with us?

Was she serious about this thing between him? Part of him wanted to ask. The other part was too terrified to open his mouth. He ground his teeth as he gripped the steering wheel. He'd never been through this before, had he? Laney had always been there—his constant, his compass. He didn't have the first clue about how to navigate the adult dating scene.

They made a pit stop at a convenience store on the way. Kathryn finally got her coffee and browsed the aisles with Wilson, negotiating what kind of junk food they were going to end up choking down for their breakfast. They'd probably get some kind of fancy lunch once they got to the Greenbrier, but right now, they were all starving. Meanwhile, Huck seemed especially strapped by phone calls, pacing around outside the truck as he talked.

For his part, Hunter considered the razors and men's toiletries, wondering if he should pick up some in case he ended up spending time with Kathryn in her room at the Greenbrier. But he abandoned the idea, not wanting to seem presumptuous. He could always buy something at the resort if she decided to invite him up. Now that their strange trip to Christmas Pass was over, an ongoing relationship was hardly a done deal, was it? Should he go home and allow them to have their vacation in peace? Anxiety pinched his stomach a bit, and he swallowed hard.

Turning to meet Kathryn at the counter, Hunter startled when the door to the convenience store opened with a jangle of bells and clatter. Two wizened old people walked in—a thin, rangy fella in overalls, a red plaid coat, and a tattered "Wild, Wonderful West Virginia" hat, accompanied by a little bitty with frizzy, red-dyed hair that he could only assume was his wife. For some reason, both their heads swiveled right to Hunter, and the couple gave him a long, hard once-over. Hunter immediately got the same creepy premonition he'd gotten when Miss Holly Berry had introduced herself at the inn, and his jaw clenched.

"Hoo!" The man cried. "Look at you! You've been running from something—and right quick too!"

Hunter glanced down at his outfit and groaned. He was still wearing those ridiculous turquoise-and-orange running tights. How he'd ever thought they'd make him *blend*, he didn't know. Hunter shrugged sheepishly. "I'm trying to get some exercise."

The man's wife cackled, setting loose a riot of laugh lines on her face. "Oh boy, you're a terrible liar. You were trying to run your way out of Christmas Pass is more like it."

Hunter's jaw dropped open. "Christmas— But— *Wait*, how did you know that?" he sputtered. "What do you know about that place? Who *are* you?"

The frizzy-headed woman cast her critical eye on Hunter, then grinned enough to expose her gold tooth. She stuck out her bony hand. "I'm Candy Caine, and this here is my husband Earl Caine. We run Stuckey's Christmas

Outpost down the way. And if you're wondering how I know where you been, it's your hat. Only an elf could make a cowboy hat with stitching that small. We sell 'em in our store too."

Hunter raised his eyebrows at all the elf talk but pumped Candy's hand up and down nonetheless. He pulled the couple away from prying eyes and lowered his voice to nearly a whisper. "I don't know what you two are about, but obviously you have information I don't. So I'm asking you now to be straight with me. How come I'd never heard about Christmas Pass before I ended up stuck there? And if it's just up the road, how have I never heard of Stuckey's Christmas Outpost, either? I've lived here all my life. What the hell is going on?"

Earl clucked his tongue. "Boy, it ain't no secret! Ain't you heard of the legend of Christmas Pass?"

Hunter scowled. "Legend? But it was *real*. I was *actually* there!"

Candy stuffed her hands into the pockets on her loud-as-hell Christmas cardigan and rocked back on her heels. "I'm not gonna say whether you were there or not, see. But I can tell you this. You hadn't hearda Christmas Pass because you hadn't been chosen. Up until now, of course."

"Chosen?" Hunter exclaimed. "What do you mean, *chosen?*"

"See, that's the legend part," Earl chimed in. "Legend has it that Christmas Pass doesn't really exist on the same plane with the rest of us. Legend has it that on certain days, and for certain people, it'll, I dunno, *appear*. Kinda like that old musical from the sixties... Awww, what was it called, honey-cakes? You know that show where them people, they find that Scottish village in the mist that only appears every hundred years..."

"*Brigadoon,*" Candy offered.

"That's right." Earl snapped his fingers. "*Brigadoon!* Yeah anyway, it's kinda like that—but only for people who are lost and need to find their way."

Hunter scowled at the two of them, more confused than he was before. "But I wasn't *lost*. I knew exactly which road we were on and everything..."

Candy cackled again and patted Hunter patronizingly on his arm. "Not *that* kind of lost, child."

Hunter frowned, wondering whether he should be offended by Candy's implication. Who the hell were these people, anyway? And where did they get off acting like they *knew* him? Outside, an industrial truck painted with the Stuckey's Christmas Outpost logo was parked out by the gas pump. It was loaded up with piles of dirt and pine tree saplings, bound up in burlap.

"All right, then." Hunter huffed. "Assuming that your crazy story is true, then what about your place? Is it like *Brigadoon,* too? How come I've never seen your place or your truck before?"

Earl and Candy chuckled like Hunter was the biggest dumbass they'd ever met. Candy sighed. "Boy, you ain't seen our store 'cause you ain't ever needed anything we have to sell. Let's leave it at that."

Just then, the bespectacled clerk behind the counter spotted them all standing there. "Oh hey, Earl; hey, Candy. Gettin' some gas?"

"Yep," Earl called. "Pump three. Put it on the Make-peace account, like usual."

The man waved, pulled a ledger out from under his counter, and made a notation in it.

Earl turned back to Hunter and clapped him on the back. "Time for us to go." Earl motioned over to Kathryn, who was counting out her cash and gathering up her bags of food at the checkout. "You'd better go tend to your lady friend. You've got a bit of road still ahead of you with her, doncha?"

The sight of her warmed him. Kathryn looked particularly adorable this morning, all bedraggled but happy to be sipping cheap coffee and tearing open a big bag of little powdered donuts.

And when Hunter turned back to Earl and Candy to wish them well, all he saw was the door jangling shut. He looked out to the gas pump, and the couple was...*gone*. Gone—as in, they'd *totally disappeared*. Truck too.

All righty. That was weird.

I should probably be flipping out over that, shouldn't I?

Honestly, he couldn't even summon the energy. Having stirred up enough freaky shit for one day, Hunter plastered on a smile as Kathryn walked up.

"Who were you talking to, babe?" she asked.

"Only a couple of locals," he answered, kissing her on the cheek. "I'll tell you about it later."

They got back in the car, and while Kathryn passed around the food, Hunter took some time to check his messages. His heart sank. His parents, brother, and even his tiny niece and nephew had tried to call him. Even when he hadn't visited at Christmas, he'd always managed to at least call to wish them a happy holiday.

He sent his brother a quick text.

Sorry. Cell service has been out. Hope you had a very Merry Christmas. Quiet holiday here. Hope the kids liked their gifts. Had a lot of calls to tow people from snowstorm. Everything is okay. I'll call in a day or so.

Hunter pushed his phone back into his jacket pocket, and before long, they were all back on the road again. It was a short drive to the Greenbrier now. But Kathryn kept her eyes trained out the window the whole way. "God, it's beautiful here," she breathed.

Hunter was a little surprised to hear her say that. "You really think so? I figured it would all be too countrified for someone used to living in a place like Roanoke."

She snorted. "Roanoke is hardly New York City."

"Might as well be by comparison."

"Yes, but we don't have this small, close-knit community, or this kind of scenery. It's like I hardly know where to look first."

Being a local, he'd gotten too used to the stunning view. She chattered away, noticing every historic detail and scenic vista. But when they turned up the road that revealed the entirety of the resort, she fell silent with wonder.

"Whoa, Momma!" Wilson cried. "It's like a castle, but so much bigger!"

"Sure is," Huck agreed. "It's got, what—eight hundred rooms? It's one of the fanciest resorts in the whole world."

And that was no overstatement. Greenbrier Resort had been built shortly after the American Revolution, and it featured the kind of grand, Georgian architecture made famous in this period. The enormous, gleaming white buildings with their endless colonnades never failed to impress.

"My God, look at that Christmas tree!" Huck exclaimed.

The colonnade leading up to the main entrance was always a sight to behold, but no time more than Christmas. Neat hedging and lush, manicured gardens gave way to a Christmas tree several stories tall, twinkling with the remnants of the snow, and a shining star on the top made of brilliant white lights.

Kathryn turned to him, her eyes glazed over with amazement as a footman in a red riding coat, black top hat, and white breeches came to greet them. Though Hunter almost hated to muddy up their entryway, he rumbled his enormous tow truck up underneath the columned, red-carpeted entrance.

"Maybe our perfect holiday isn't over, Hunter." She beamed.

And he couldn't help but smile right back at her.

CHAPTER 22

KATHRYN STOOD in the lobby with her mouth hanging open. She couldn't help it.

Hunter chuckled. "Cat got your tongue?"

"You could say that," she answered. "I saw the photos online, but I mean—"

"Happens to everyone the first time. Most people never get a chance to go to someplace this big, this old, and this grand. They don't know what to think."

The Greenbrier was, in a word, glorious. Kathryn suddenly felt silly and underdressed in her jeans as elegant people milled past her. The place was like something out of a Regency-era romance. The lobby gleamed with an endless checkerboard of black-and-white marble flooring. A grand staircase swept gracefully through the center of the space, decorated with the most intricate, white-painted ironwork railings she'd ever seen. A live pianist played "Carol of the Bells" up on the landing, and the scents of fresh Christmas trees, pine garland, and poinsettias filled the air. The footmen busied about the tow truck, not batting an eye at having to haul all her junk out of the back of the truck bed.

Daddy marched straight up to the counter and began

working with the hotel staff to secure their rooms again. He turned around and gave her a thumbs-up sign, and she sighed in relief. They still would be able to get a room, even though they'd bailed on the first few days.

Hunter stayed busy making sure the footmen got all their bags and gifts out of the truck, while Wilson killed time jumping from marble square to marble square like it was hopscotch. Not exactly the best behavior in a place like this. Kathryn was about to correct the boy when Wilson's focus snapped to the doorway.

"Daddy!" he shouted and went tearing off across the lobby.

Oh, no. It couldn't be. She turned. *Sterling. And Avery. What in the hell?*

"Heeeyyy! How's my boy!" Sterling crooned, as Wilson gave him a full body, flying leap hug.

Avery sauntered up behind and kissed the top of Wilson's head. *"Allo, mon petit chou. Joyeux Noël!"*

Kathryn squelched the urge to roll her eyes. Her son was not Avery's "little cabbage." It was a common French term of endearment for a child, like *sweetheart*, but sometimes Avery's Continental routine really grated her nerves. Sterling and Avery were impeccable, of course. Sterling's model-perfect looks were on full display. He'd slicked his wavy sable locks back with the right amount of expensive pomade. Even his casual, weekend clothes were cultured and precise. His houndstooth polo coordinated perfectly with his hiking boots, his slim-cut khakis, and his camel mohair pea coat. Avery's sense of fashion was diametrically opposed to his partner's, with slim-cut jeans, a tight Ramones T-shirt, an army-style jacket, and a choppy yet studiously mussed close-cropped haircut. Apparently Avery had gotten himself a colorful new tattoo of a flaming phoenix on his neck. Tattoos weren't so unusual anymore, especially for the chef crowd. But seeing her strait-laced ex with a guy with so much obvious ink made her smirk. Sterling would've never tolerated her getting one. Kathryn guessed opposites attracted, after all.

She wondered how much she really knew Sterling as she got on tiptoe to kiss his aftershave-soaked cheek. "So, this is a surprise," Kathryn muttered drily.

"You'll find you tend to get surprised when you *don't answer your phone.*"

Hunter walked in with some of their bags, interrupting them. Apparently, Hunter had walked up in time to see her kissing Sterling. Even at a distance, she could see the possessive flash in Hunter's eyes, but his face soon relaxed when he figured out who was who. Kathryn silently thanked Wilson for being the one to tell Hunter her ex was gay. The look on Hunter's face seemed to say he was taking this turn of events in stride.

"You were supposed to be in France!" Wilson cried. "How come you're back?"

"I wanted to see you, short stuff. And I couldn't wait any longer." Sterling twirled Wilson around while the boy whooped.

Kathryn raised her eyebrow. "You said you weren't coming back until January fifth. What happened?"

"You're not going to believe this, *mon cher.*" Avery beamed, grabbing her hand. "But Sterling has been offered a job. He took it! Such marvelous luck! He found a job, and we found a big, beautiful flat right in the city center of Montpellier. The family can start its European adventure early!"

Kathryn's stomach dropped. She'd known this was coming, but the suddenness of it reminded her of how much time Wilson would have to spend away from his father. "Oh, no. You're leaving? *Already?* But you weren't moving until the summer." She pulled her hand away from Avery.

Judging the look on her face, Sterling reached out and rubbed her upper arm, trying his best to be contrite. "Sweetie, I know, it's sudden. But it's a great post—a supervisory one. Even taking into account the cost of living differences, I'll be making more than I ever did here. Starting on February fifteenth seemed like a small sacrifice to make."

"A small sacrifice..." Kathryn pinched the bridge of her nose, not even knowing what to say.

Sterling patted her back, like she was some kind of goddamned child. "That's why I'm here," he soothed. "I figured we'd come back as fast as we could so I could spend as much of the Christmas break as possible with Wilson before I had to leave."

Kathryn stiffened. "So you came here to horn in on my Christmas vacation with my son?"

"Now, now, don't get testy. I came here to ask you, since you *won't answer your phone*, if I could take Wilson to Snowshoe Resort for the rest of his break. Avery and I already have a room reserved and everything."

Kathryn blinked. She was too blown away to even speak.

"Snowshoe!" Wilson started jumping up and down. "Skiing! You mean we could ski for days? Woo-hoo!"

Kathryn continued to stare coolly at Sterling. "Stop your celebrating, child. I haven't said yes yet."

Hunter had been standing off to the side, trying not to get in the middle of things. But now she felt his arm snake around her waist as he came up behind her. "Everything okay here, Ryn?"

Sterling's eyebrows went in the air as he took Hunter in. Hunter had a good four inches of height and about fifty pounds on Sterling—one of the few men out there who could tower over her ex. Kathryn bit back a smile, thinking how ridiculous Sterling must think Hunter looked. Poor Hunter was still wearing those awful clingy pants from his aborted morning run and the cowboy hat she'd gotten him for Christmas.

"Who's the spandex cowboy?" Sterling smirked.

"That's Hunter!" Wilson cried. "He's cool. He's Mom's new guy friend. He builds hot rods for a living. And he pulled us out with his tow truck when we were wrecked!"

Sterling fixed her with a droll stare.

Hunter gamely stuck his hand out. "It's a long story. The name's Hunter Holliday. Nice to meet you."

Sterling returned the shake with obvious interest, and cocked an eyebrow at Kathryn. "Nice to meet you too. Under normal circumstances, I'd invite you to sit you down with a fifth of bourbon and get that story out of you. But we don't have much time for pleasantries if we're going to get to Snowshoe by nightfall."

Oh. My. God. Is he even serious right now? "Sterling. We need to talk in private. *Now.*" Kathryn glowered. "Wilson, hang out here with Hunter and Granddaddy for a minute."

"Aww, Momma, don't yell at Daddy. I want to go. Pleeeaaaassse?"

"I said *stay here*, Wilson."

Wilson nodded with glum resignation. She hauled Sterling off to one of the anterooms off the lobby, one that was uninhabited at the moment. When they were out of earshot of the rest of them, she rounded on her ex. "What in the *hell* were you thinking?"

"What?" he replied, seeming genuinely confused by her reaction. "All I'm trying to do is spend some time with my son over the holidays. Isn't that what you wanted? You know, I don't get it. First you're pissed because I went to

France for Christmas. Now you're all upset because I came back early to spend time with my son!"

Kathryn had always tried to keep her temper with Sterling, in the name of being a good parent to Wilson. Even after everything that had happened between them, she considered Sterling a friend. But now, she looked at her ex like she'd never really seen him before.

Was Sterling really that self-absorbed that he didn't understand he was wrecking their vacation? Anger rolled up her body, starting in her chest and working its way up. She balled her hands into fists. "You selfish prick! You *goddamn selfish prick!*"

"*Kathryn!*" Shock and hurt stole over his face, and somehow that only made her madder. Kathryn had always tried to be calm and rational with him. She'd never called him an ugly name in her entire life. But today, she sure as shit didn't care.

"I mean it!" She glowered. "First, you announce you're going overseas and leaving your son alone over the holidays. Then, you tell us you're planning on moving for good. So I roll with those punches. Daddy and I went to considerable effort to create the perfect Christmas for Wilson this year. *For once.* We just wanted to have a happy Christmas *for once.* And what do you do? You come crashing in here, turning his head with all this Snowshoe talk."

"Snowshoe talk? I only want to spend some—"

Kathryn pounded him on his shoulder, knocking him back a step. "Oh, stop it! I don't want to hear your story about how you're such a selfless martyr, giving up your European vacation. No one asked you to do this. It's another example of how you shove your way in and expect everyone to fall in line with whatever you want."

All the charm drained out of Sterling's expression, leaving his eyes hard and his mouth compressed into a thin line. "I *am* the selfless one, Kathryn. I've been selfless about every damn thing. You know that more than anyone."

She sneered. "Oh, yeah, I see where this is headed. This is the card you're playing today? You're selfless. Selfless enough to marry poor little helpless me when you knocked me up."

"Yeah, that's right," he spat, crossing his arms over his chest. "And I've been here for you ever since!"

Tension hung thick in the air. The room practically crackled with her frustration.

Being here for me. Is that what Sterling calls it? Is that really what he thinks?

Terrible memories of Sterling's big admission came to mind. They'd been married for four years and Wilson was so little still. She'd caught Sterling texting a lover. In a strange way, it had almost been a relief. Suddenly, she could see the whole confusing, unsatisfying pattern of their marriage in terrible clarity, like finding the missing piece to an ugly jigsaw puzzle you'd been working on far too long. Somehow, she couldn't summon any anger, even then. Sterling had been so upset, so remorseful, Kathryn had actually felt sorry for him at the time.

But to hear him talking like this *now*?

An image of Sterling standing at the altar in his Armani tux flashed in her memory, unbidden.

She'd thought her husband had truly wanted her for his bride. Oh, she'd known it wasn't the love match of the century, but she'd thought Sterling had cared about her, at the very least.

Had she been wrong?

Kathryn didn't think it was still possible, but her stomach roiled with disappointment. And embarrassment. And anger. She was *seething*. "Your *sacrifice*. Is that what our family was to you?"

Sterling's expression gentled as he realized how badly he'd stepped in it. "Oh, Katie-belle, that came out wrong. I—"

Kathryn held up her hand. "Stop it. Just *stop*." She took a deep, rattling breath. "For once I'd like you to consider what *I* sacrificed. Let's review the past from where I'm sitting, shall we? I got pregnant all those years ago because you were too drunk to be bothered to put your condom on right. Then when I told you about the pregnancy, you insisted I marry you, because you wanted our child. When we got married, you cheated on me with every man who crossed your path. And when you got caught, you said you had to, because you had to experiment, to know for sure you preferred men. Every step of the way, you made the decisions, and I paid the consequences. Today is another example of how I don't get a say. And I'm *fucking sick of it!*"

His jaw dropped. "A say. You wanted *a say?* So you're saying you would've preferred me to walk away back then and abandon responsibility? To let Wilson be *illegitimate?* Good Lord, woman! I made the supreme sacrifice for you!"

Kathryn actually stepped back a step at that one. "You said it wasn't a sacrifice back then. You said you *loved* me."

But Sterling stared mutely at her, as if he couldn't fathom how to answer her.

As she stood there gaping at him, understanding dawned on her, slow and creeping like a bad stink. "Oh my God. You *knew*. You knew you were gay back when you slept with me. You weren't experimenting with other men. You'd already *had* men. You were experimenting with *me*."

The worst part was, Sterling didn't deny it. He didn't deny how he'd lied to her all those years ago, making her believe his sexual awakening had been gradual and unintended. But the more she turned it over in her mind, the more everything made sense. She supposed it shouldn't make her angry. But it did, rising up until she felt like she could spit nails. All the hurt and heartbreak of her marriage boiled down to this—Sterling's grand selfishness.

"Lord, it's so easy to see what you were thinking!" she growled. "Why not fool around with me? I was a friend of the family, and safe, and I could keep your Bible-thumping parents off your back. You never expected me to get pregnant, but hey. You hit the bonus round! How many gay men get to have children the old-fashioned way? You could marry me and be the noble family man, at least for a while."

"Was that really so bad?" he wailed. "I was being a man, a father!"

"*Yes*, Sterling! It was goddamn awful! You could have been a dad and paid me support and spent time with your son. But instead, you *cost* me. How long has it been since we met? Nine years? Ten? Let me tell you what all the years of your lies and illusions meant to me. Until a few days ago, I've never known what it's like to be with a man who really, *really* wants me—for myself, and for my body too. Someone who looks at me with true, honest desire. You took that from me, Sterling. You took my perspective, and my confidence and, on some level, my hope. Every time I had another bad date, it drove the knife in deeper, and made me wonder if there was something wrong with me deep inside, something that would cause these men to turn away from me, every single time. Jesus, it's sickening to think about it."

Sympathy flickered in Sterling's eyes. He reached out to touch Kathryn's arm again, but she shrugged him away.

"Don't," she whispered.

His features fell. "I'm sorry, Katie-belle. God, you *know* I am."

Kathryn's throat was tight and thick with unshed tears. She let out a long, shaky breath. "I think on some level, I knew you were into men long before I would admit it to myself. If I'd been smart, I would have seen it from day one." She gave her head a rueful shake. "Do you have any idea what it was like being your wife? You'd try to hide it, but your gaze raked over every attractive gay man that crossed our path. When you left me, you got to go off and be true to yourself. But who was true to me, Sterling? *Nobody.* Do you have any idea what that does to a person?" Kathryn's chest heaved from the strain of that terrible confession.

Sterling jammed his hands in his pockets and looked miserably at the floor. "What do you want from me, Kathryn? I've apologized a thousand times. What's done is done."

"Yes, it is," Kathryn moaned, the fight slowly draining out of her. She'd often chastised herself for not seeing the signs with Sterling. But now that she really understood the depth of his deception, she simply felt nauseated.

Kathryn realized, with queasy hindsight, that in the years post-Sterling she'd never been able to connect with any man, probably because she couldn't bring herself to trust one. She entered every date practically wincing, waiting for whatever man it was to pull away, to want another. And it became a self-fulfilling prophecy. Deep down, she had no confidence that she'd ever be enough.

"Look. I—I overstepped," Sterling stammered. "We'll go. Avery and I can have a good time at Snowshoe without Wilson. I'll catch up with him later." He wrapped his arm around her shaking shoulders and kissed her temple.

Kathryn let out a pent-up breath. "No," she answered, pulling away. "Take him. I'll never hear the end of it unless you do. He loves you, Sterling."

"He loves you too, Kathryn."

She patted his shoulder. "I guess we did at least one

thing right. Wilson has one suitcase. And a bag of toys he'll probably want to take. He'll show you."

"Are you sure? Really?"

"Yes. Go. Before I change my mind."

"Thank you, Kathryn." He tucked her in for a hug and kissed her on the top of the head this time. "Thank you for *everything*."

"You're welcome," she whispered, her throat still thick with emotion. It was enough that she had said her piece. Finally.

They both walked out together to find Hunter pacing around near the door. How much of that had he heard? It was probably enough to make the man run for the hills. She groaned under her breath. Avery was there too, his expression full of sympathy.

But Hunter was at her side in a handful of ground-eating strides, grabbing her hand and kissing it. He shot her one of his reassuring half smiles, and it steadied her a bit. Together, they walked over to where Wilson was standing. When the boy heard he really was going skiing, he whooped and hollered.

Daddy finally walked up, having finished his marathon session with the concierge. When she told him about the turn of events with Wilson, he winced.

"Don't worry, Daddy," Kathryn reassured him. "We can still have a good time. I have lots of activities planned. We could go falconing, or bowling, or—"

"Ah, yeah, that's the thing." Daddy squirmed and swallowed hard. "I'm not stayin', Katie-belle." He took a moment to assess what must have been her stricken expression. "I'm sorry, baby. But my ride is outside. They're taking me to the Greenbrier airport so I can catch a connector. I've got myself checked in to the Ocala Institute in Arizona this time. No more foolin' around. I hear it's the fanciest rehab place out there. I'm gonna have a view of the Red Rocks from my room, they say."

Kathryn made a concerted effort to swallow her dismay. *Of course.* Of course Daddy would want to start rehab right away. He needed it.

She walked with him to the portico at the main entrance while he filled her in on the details. The stay was open-ended for as long as he needed it, and she could check in on him whenever she wished. He expected to be there about two months, "getting his head on straight," he said. He didn't need to tell her how many fancy celebrities were alumni of the place. She'd heard of it before. Its reputation was beyond reproach.

Realizing she was standing there wringing her hands, she balled her fists up in her coat pockets. Part of her wanted to argue for him to stay, but she knew better than that. His treatment was more important. Sterling and Avery set about loading Wilson's things into their rental. Kathryn began to tear up, but blinked them back.

Finally, Daddy turned to face her, grabbed her hand, and squeezed it. "I have to go, baby. You know I do. That mess I got into a couple of days ago showed me it'd better be sooner rather than later. I'm sorry I had to bail out on you like this, darlin', but you know, it's time you stop thinkin' you have to take care of me. I can do this one on my own. I promise."

This was the first time her daddy had ever stepped up and taken responsibility for his recovery. Kathryn had always been the one to schedule his rehab, talk to his doctors, and set his limits. But now her heart swelled with pride for him. He'd not only taken charge of this fight, but he'd pulled out the big guns, going to arguably the finest rehab facility in the nation. Impetuously, Kathryn threw her arms around his neck, smelling his ever-present, reassuring scent of mint and leather. "I understand, Daddy, and I'm glad."

"Really?" he whispered.

"Yes, really. I'll miss you, but you're doing the right thing," she whispered back.

Sterling walked up the steps, seeming guiltier than ever. "You know, Kathryn, you could come with us to ski. You could even bring Hunter along."

She glanced at Hunter, who shrugged. But she shook her head. "Go. Have a good time. I'll manage."

"You sure?" he asked, giving her a peck on the cheek.

"Yeah," she answered.

Wilson came bounding back up and gave her a big hug. "Thank you for letting me go. I promise I'll be good, Momma."

"You'd better. Or you'll have to answer to Avery." She patted her boy on the head. "You know he's tougher than me."

Wilson scampered back over to her ex. The sound of his giggle and childish chatter melted away as the three of them walked to their car. They left at the same time Daddy loaded himself into the Greenbrier shuttle.

Kathryn watched them all drive away, trying her best to look cheerful and wave as they went. She supposed she should be glad to have some "me" time at one of the nation's finest resorts. But her heart ached to see them disappear down the road. Christmas wasn't the same without them, even though she knew Wilson and Daddy were in good hands.

Hunter came up behind her and wrapped his arm around her shoulder. "So, do you think Wilson will tell them all about Christmas Pass?"

"Probably." Kathryn shrugged. "But I don't think it'll matter. Sterling doesn't know a thing about this area. He'll probably assume it's all real. What are you going to tell people about where you were these last few days?"

"I'm going to tell them I was at the Greenbrier with a beautiful woman. And it won't be a lie."

Kathryn turned to him. "You know, my family may have left me here, but you don't have to stay. You don't have to keep me company if you don't want to. You've been trapped with us for days now. Go on. You can get back to your normal life now. You must have a million things to do."

Hunter frowned, and his eyes flashed with—with what? Warning? Possessiveness? "Do you really think I'd collect my fee for the tow and be on my way? After everything we've been through?"

"You said before that you didn't want to be an obligation. I don't either."

Hunter wrapped his arms around her waist and pulled her to him—hard. His mouth was on her before she could even form another word. His kiss was hot, thorough, and insistent, deepening as his hand curled around the base of her neck, massaging away the tension with the hard tips of his fingers. A small, helpless groan escaped her when he ended the kiss. He smirked. "Does that feel like an obligation to you?"

She smiled. No, she didn't suppose that it did.

CHAPTER 23

"I've never gone cruisin' in a tow truck before."
Kathryn tapped her finger on her armrest. "If it wasn't so
cold out, I'd stick my head out like a dog."

Hunter smiled. "No matter how much you stick your
head out, I doubt anyone would mistake you for a dog."

"What can I say? It's tempting to get all this mountain
air. This place is beautiful. We don't get this kind of rugged
beauty in Roanoke. We're far too civilized."

As they left Lewisburg's small downtown, they drove
farther out into the country, dotted with one small farm
after another, set on the rolling hills. Holliday Hot Rods was
out this way. They'd stop there long enough for her to drop
off her car, and he'd switch them out to one of his finer rides.
Maybe she'd enjoy a ride around the countryside before he
took her back to the Greenbrier and they spent the night
testing out the quality of their luxury resort mattresses.

Hunter watched her as they wound down through the
hills and toward town. Kathryn was smiling a little wist-
fully, but her face was still wound with tension—tension he
desperately wanted to erase, preferably horizontally. She'd
been through the wringer. It seemed to him that Kathryn

somehow got the bad end of all her family's problems. She was the fixer. The confidant. The strong one.

And yet, he'd seen her soft and vulnerable, quivering with the need to be held. It was like they were taking turns holding each other together, weren't they?

They pulled into downtown Lewisburg, and Kathryn's face lit up. "Oh, how sweet! This downtown is absolutely adorable!"

Hunter had never really considered his hometown "adorable." But from Kathryn's perspective, he supposed it was. While Lewisburg was the seat of Greenbrier County, it was still a very small town of under 4,000 people—tiny compared to what Kathryn was used to, and populated with a mix of locals and people who owned luxurious second homes there. Nestled against the backdrop of soaring hills, the embellished brick storefronts gave the town its own unique artsy, mountain-Americana vibe. Lush, tree-lined neighborhoods fanned out from downtown, a drive down any street revealing a mixed patchwork of architectural styles, from 1930s Tudor to cute bungalows to story-and-a-half colonials, and even the occasional log cabin. Every street was "established," every house neatly maintained despite its age. Yeah, Lewisburg had earned its historic patina. It stubbornly held on to its allure—through floods, and wars, and everything history could throw at it.

Hunter stopped to consider that. Maybe the town's quiet endurance had rubbed off on him. Maybe it had given him enough roots to keep him from simply floating away these last few terrible years.

"So, these few blocks here, this is downtown?" Kathryn's words snapped him out of his thoughts.

"Oh—yeah, it is. This town was founded in 1782. Most of this was built in the 1800s. You can tell, can't you?"

She nodded. "Yeah, it reminds me of the historic bits of

Roanoke. There's nothing like an old building to make you feel grounded."

Yet another example of how she'd guessed what he was thinking.

Hunter filled her in with historical facts and town lore while they drove out past the edge of town, and wound their way to Holliday Hot Rods. It was a big place—an abandoned old factory that Dad had bought for a song twenty years ago, and remade to his purposes. Surprisingly, the lights blared inside, and cars belonging to his employees littered the parking lot.

What were they doing? Didn't he give them strict orders not to work over their Christmas break?

As soon as he pulled into the driveway, the metal bay door rolled up automatically, allowing him to pull inside. A cheer went up, and Hunter was surprised to see three of his employees clapping and hollering. Heavy metal music blared over the company sound system.

Hunter jumped out of the truck, came around, and helped Kathryn down.

Hopper, his right hand man, was the first to make it to his truck. "Where the hell have you been?" the man called out, slapping his big hand on the side of his truck as he sauntered up.

But when Hopper spotted Hunter, he stopped, and fixed him with an incredulous stare. "Spandex? This is a new look. Now I'm really afraid to ask what you were doing on your Christmas vacation."

Hunter took Hop's outstretched hand and clasped it, closing the distance with a slap on his back. He grinned. "What? I was just doing some running, that's all."

Hopper snickered. "Whatever you were running from, I'm sure your ass looked great."

Ross, his ace metalworker and resident smart aleck also

stopped in his tracks when he saw him. "Aww now, don't pick on the boss," the boy said, crossing his arms over his chest. "I mean, if the man wants to show the world his junk, who are we to—"

"Would you stop it?" Hunter yelped, self-consciously pulling his sweatshirt down over his crotch.

"Sorry, man," Hopper clapped him on the back. "We're just glad to see you. We were worried. You dropped off the grid, and the tow truck was missing, and nobody knew where you were at."

Hunter grinned at him. "You missed me? You were supposed to be on break, *not* missing me."

"You know we can't stay away," Leta called, striding up in her ever-present ripped-up jeans and paint-splattered T-shirt. "We have too many family members to hide from, you know. My house is packed with distant relatives, God help me." She paused and canted her pink-haired head at Kathryn. "Who's this?"

Hunter swallowed hard as he introduced her to his ragtag crew. He hoped she liked them. They were a bunch of crazy sonsabitches, that was for sure. There was Hop—his shop manager. A big rugged guy with salt-and-pepper hair and his share of scars and tats, Hopper looked a little dangerous. But even though he'd spent almost fifteen years in jail, Hopper had turned out to be a brilliant business manager and fabricator, and the best employee he'd ever had. Then there was Ross, with his shaggy black hair and a slim hoop earring in his eyebrow. Ross was a study in contrasts, a well-mannered, soft-spoken goth with a genius for shaping metal and an uncanny ability to fix about anything. And of course, there was Leta, their resident rock-n-roll fairy princess, and the kind of girl who liked to change her pastel hair color with her mood. Leta was his ace painter and wizard with upholstery—capable of doing intricate artwork on cars. He often considered her his unfair competitive advantage, making his cars more distinctive than anything out there. They had a couple of part-time mechanics who worked for them, too, and two more full time employees who'd taken a big chunk of vacation time and weren't coming back until mid-month.

Hunter held his breath as he introduced Kathryn around to everyone, expecting some kind of off-color remark or relentless ribbing. But his team surprised him by being on their best behavior. Even though he hadn't introduced her as his girl, they must've put two and two together. They couldn't have been more respectful if they were inter-viewing the queen.

When Hunter slid his hand around Kathryn's waist, more than a few eyebrows went up, and sly nods were exchanged. But Kathryn didn't shrug out from under him, as he'd half expected her to. Instead, she wrapped her arm around his waist too, neatly short-cutting their need to explain that they were "together."

She looked up at him with such happiness in her eyes. Almost against his will, his chest bowed out. How could he help himself when Kathryn gazed up at him, all adoring like that? Maybe they *were* together. Maybe he could trust this thing that was growing between them.

The gang all seemed pretty eager to pump Kathryn for information, so he decided to cut them off. "So seriously, would y'all mind telling me why everyone is here? This shop is supposed to be closed. No exceptions."

Hop shifted from foot to foot. "We know. And for the record, we're not workin.' This is a party, pure and simple. We got Guns n' Roses on the sound system, beer in the cooler, and the pizza has been delivered."

Kathryn's eyebrows shot up. "Did someone say beer?"

"Yeah," Leta called over, holding up a dripping bottle of dark lager. "You want one?"

"Oh yeah, honey, I could use one," Kathryn called over. She caught the bottle in mid-air as Leta tossed it.

Ross raised his eyebrows when she cantilevered off the cap using the edge of the table. "That's a pretty intense brew. Wouldn't a pretty little thing like you rather have a chardonnay?"

"Real women drink real beer," Kathryn called back, wiping down her mouth after a long swig. "I got a taste for the dark beer when I was working on my doctorate. I did an exchange program in England for a while, and it was every-where. Before long, no other beer sufficed."

"So you're a doctor then?" Ross asked. "A doctor of what?"

"Psychology," Kathryn replied. "I have my own clinical psychology practice in Roanoke."

Hop let out a long, impressed whistle. "Good God, Hunter. Where'd you find *her*?"

"He saved my life," Kathryn answered without a hint of drama. "I was wrecked off the side of a mountain on 220. He pulled my car out before I went over the ravine for good. Ever since then, he's been stuck with me."

Hop clapped her on the back. "Honey, there ain't nobody better to be stuck to than our Hunter here. Come on. Let me show you around. He's too modest to brag about this place, but I'm not."

Hopper and Hunter walked Kathryn around the place and, to his surprise, she seemed totally into every detail of their operation. She must not have been lying about liking cars. Lingering over their inventory of parts, Kathryn asked questions about every pile of scrap and stuck her head into all the personal car projects the staff had brought in to work on over the break. Holliday Hot Rods must've been quite the sight to her. Leta was in the midst of painting a wizard on the side of a 1970s van. Covered in grease, Ross bent over the parts he had stretched out on the ground for the rebuild of his '67 Chevy.

The Holiday Hot Rods building had been a small shirt factory years ago, and its size made it perfectly suited to the needs of a big fabrication and repair business, with lift bays, and big plate-glass windows to let in the light, and high-beamed ceilings to keep the air flowing. With twenty thousand square feet to work with, Hunter had turned the front of the building into his showroom and consultation center, lining the place with some of his best, competition-grade hot rod projects.

"Dear Lord." Kathryn whistled when she saw the lineup. "Did you really design all these?"

"Yes, he did," Hop replied before Hunter could answer, "and don't let him tell you different. Hunter gets on the computer and draws out the designs and specs for every hot rod that comes out of here. We help him execute it, but Holliday Hot Rods are sought after by car collectors all over the world because Hunter knows what it takes to make a damn showy car."

"You can say that again." She ran her hand along the 1939 Oldsmobile Convertible sitting in their display window. "How much does this beauty go for?"

"It's not for sale," Hunter answered.

"Of course it ain't!" Hop chuckled. "It won the US Street Rod Con a few years ago. This baby has been about ninety percent reshaped. Took us two years to work with it until we got the lines right. The body is entirely eighteen-gauge steel now. See the starburst pattern on the upholstery? That Leta's work. And see the burled wood on the dash? Ross did that. But, really, this car is mostly Hunter's doing. Just like all of them."

The long, lean lines of this opalescent gray street rod were the perfect match for Kathryn. He should have her pose with it for an ad for the shop or something.

Kathryn caressed the car with her lithe little hand, clearly dazed with car envy. "Can I take a ride in it?"

Hop raised his eyebrows and smirked. "This car hasn't been out in a year..."

"Sure, we can go out." Hunter waved his hand to cut off the ribbing he knew would come from Hopper any minute. "You can gas it up for me, right?"

"Sure thing, boss." Hopper chuckled as he walked to the gas can.

Yeah, so Hunter was trying to impress a girl. So what?

While they waited for the gas, Kathryn lingered over all the finished hot rods, from the 1964 Mustang to the silver 1939 Chevy Truck with the exposed engine to the 1970 Camaro that Leta had painted with giant bat wings.

Question after question tumbled from her mouth. Hunter got a kick out of seeing her eyes shiny and excited, as if she were experiencing a visual feast. "You weren't just saying that when you said you liked cars." He chuckled.

"I didn't even realize cars existed on this level, Hunter. You're an artist! It's incredible!"

Hunter kissed her cheek. The admiration on her face was darned cute, and not what he would've expected. After all, a greasy garage wasn't exactly her kind of world. But maybe this was a world she could embrace.

As he was constantly discovering, there was a lot more to Kathryn Winslow than met the eye. He left her briefly to go stow his clothes back in his loft, and change back into his nicer clothes from Christmas Pass. When he came back down, the team offered them some pizza, and they sat down gratefully to eat. The day had been so crazy. He realized that neither of them had eaten since their paltry breakfast this morning. He handed her a piece and made her sit down with him to eat, while Hop wandered off to get to work on the GTO the man was restoring.

Kathryn rolled her eyes with pleasure as she bit into the slice of Sicilian-style pizza. "It tastes like heaven. I've been so out of the habit of eating this stuff."

"Why?"

"You know, I've been trying to do the clean-eating thing."

"Sometimes dirty can be delicious."

"Mmmmm, yes. As you've been teaching me." She reddened up like a schoolgirl.

He leaned over until his mouth was right beside her ear. "I've got about a thousand lessons to teach you, Ryn," he growled. "And I won't stop until you've moaned out the answers to each and every one." Then he nipped her earlobe in his teeth and nuzzled her under the ear, enough that his hot breath caressed her skin.

She pushed him away playfully, seeming guilty, and excited, and flushed, all at once. Clearly, Kathryn was enjoying his attention. But she was shy about flirting and teasing in public places, wasn't she? He supposed that was charming and cute and...somehow *sad*. He could strangle that Sterling about now. For as self-assured as Kathryn was, and as naturally responsive as she was in bed, she should be able to look him in the eye and tease him until he practically came in his pants. He'd have to work on helping her build up her confidence. Kathryn had no idea how incredibly sexy she really was, and he couldn't wait to prove that to her.

He was about to suggest going back to the Greenbrier so he could get right on that. But his cell phone began ringing.

Hmmm. It was Mike, a buddy of his currently renting his old house. Mike was the kind of renter who almost never

bothered him with anything. But as soon as he hit the
button to take the call, Hunter realized with a groan why
the man had reached out. Mike and his wife were moving,
heading to Virginia to take a job Mike had gotten with a
large factory. Hunter had forgotten he had to do the walk-
through and take back their keys this evening. And now he
was fifteen minutes late.

He apologized all over himself, embarrassed and guilty
now that he'd forgotten his promise to his friend. But it
wasn't so surprising it had slipped his mind. After all, he'd
done everything he could to avoid that house. This was one
more way his brain refused to deal with the mess his grief
had left behind. He promised Mike faithfully that he'd be
there in less than an hour, and hung up.

"Kathryn, I have to take you back." He explained the
situation. "It's late afternoon. Why don't you go sample the
fun stuff at the Greenbrier, maybe get in a massage or something before the night is up, and I can catch with you later
tonight or in the morning for brunch."

"Can't I come with you?" she begged. "I'd like to see the
farm. It's getting pretty close to sunset. I'll bet it's
beautiful."

Hunter swallowed hard. He wasn't so sure about this
idea. The last time he'd been inside that house had been
more than two years ago, the day he'd moved everything out.
That day, he'd fallen to his knees and sobbed like a little boy
for a half hour in his entryway. But today Kathryn's warm,
supportive presence steadied him. Could he do it now?
Could he really handle being at the family farmhouse
again? Or would the ghosts of the happiness he once knew
be too much for him?

Kathryn reached out and grabbed his hand. Though she
didn't say it, she must understand the significance of what
she was asking—of what it might cost him. But hadn't he

been braver than he expected, these last few days? Hell, they'd had three life-threatening situations, at least, and several really upsetting episodes. And they always seemed to come out okay, as long as they were together.

He could do this. He smiled and opened the car door for her. "Get in the Oldsmobile, Kathryn. Let's go."

CHAPTER 24

Hunter's chest felt tight as he drove up that country lane and unhooked the gate. The gravel road was more familiar to him than the back of his hand. This was home—and heartbreak. A swell of bittersweet memories flowed over him, and he swallowed hard as he got back into the car, pulling his racing thoughts back under tight rein.

Come on, Hunter. You can do this.

Though he knew better than to drive the low-slung Olds on this gravel road, Hunter pushed his favorite hot rod back into gear, gravel flying as they revved up the steep hill. Kathryn had taken such a shine to the car that it was well worth any buffing out of pings and dents later.

Kathryn swiveled her head around to scan the hills that rolled out in every direction. "Wow, it's so peaceful out here."

"It's a slice of paradise my ancestors earned for their part in the Revolutionary War. Back then, this part of the country was still frontier, and they needed tough people to settle it."

"Wow, I can't even imagine. What a tremendous

connection that must give you. Like a thread that binds you through the generations."

"Yeah," Hunter mused. "I guess that's exactly right. When you grow up on family land, genealogy isn't something you spend much time thinking about. It's more like something you in your bones, like history is somehow in the dirt under your feet, and the very air you breathe,"

"Hmm, that's pretty deep."

"Deep thoughts from a simple man."

Kathryn patted his leg. "Oh, Hunter, there's nothing simple about you."

The thought amused him. He supposed that was true.

They drove through a few more twists and turns, rumbling over the deep tire tracks rutting the road now. He'd have to put more gravel on that before the spring rains rolled in. And once it warmed up, he'd have to find someone to cut and bale the grass. And—

"Hunter! Oh! It's so beautiful!" Kathryn cried.

Looking up over the ridge, Hunter felt a familiar surge of pride. The house. He'd forgotten how majestic it was, sitting up over that steep, grassy rise. From this vantage point, the setting sun silhouetted his childhood home in nature's perfect frame, setting it in stunning relief against glowing rays of purple and pink and orange.

In many ways, the Holliday homestead was like so many that ringed the outskirts of Lewisburg, which had more than its share of idyllic farms, most of them graced with lush, green rolling hills, and cows and horses placidly grazing their acres. But Hunter's ancestors had built the house to be a cut above the rest, gracing this Victorian mansion with a wrap-around porch ringed with crisp white spindles, and two peaked turrets roofed with copper. Flush with cash from a booming family timber and sawmill business, his three-times great-grandfather had spared no construction expense, investing in an abundance of fire-places, arched doorways, and windows topped with stained glass transoms.

Even in the height of winter, Hunter still sensed the leashed energy of the land, lying in wait for spring. In weeks, the garden around the house would burst to life again. Vines heavy with fragrant honeysuckle would soon creep along the south wall, and the daylily garden his mother had started when he was little would be thick with yellow and orange blooms. He'd missed three springs here now, hadn't he? And now it was about to be four...

"Wow, how amazing," Kathryn exclaimed, snapping him out of his brood. "This is an estate! I didn't expect to see this. You made it sound like it was only a small farm."

Hunter took another turn on the long road to the house. "It's pretty modest by farm standards these days. The house is the second one built in that spot. When my family got a little more money, they knocked down the old clapboard farmhouse and built this."

"What a legacy. I would think living in a house like that, you'd feel like you could step around the corner and talk to your ancestors."

Hunter almost groaned at that. If there were any ghosts, they were the ghosts of his shattered life. The place had felt so empty after Laney's death that he would've surely welcomed a visit from a ghost or two of Great-Grandpap's past. But the house had been quiet as a tomb—so quiet, it had damned him with every tick-tick-tick of the clock.

"Oh, look at the barn and the fences! Do you still have horses here?"

"No," Hunter sighed. "Not anymore."

The moldering whitewashed barn up ahead had been empty for years now. When he was a boy, it had been filled with horses and cows. When he and Laney had lived here, they'd sold all the animals except for two horses, which they'd ridden practically every day. There had been nothing like it, riding over these hills with her and watching the wind whip through her long red hair. The horses had adored Laney, and after his wife had passed, they'd whined and nickered for her whenever he'd come near. It was too much. Eventually he couldn't even glance at those beautiful brown quarter horses. He'd had to hire someone to come feed and care for them. Finally, Hunter had simply given them away.

"Do you ride?" he asked, his voice sounding a bit wobblier than he'd like.

Kathryn stared longingly at the barn. "I haven't had much time for it these days, but I spent a great part of my childhood on the back of a horse. Momma made sure I got lots of riding lessons. I loved it. It was my refuge—my escape, really. There's nothing like the freedom of riding. I even did some jumping and competing for a while. Can you believe that?"

Hunter gave her a long, considering look. "Yes, I can."

"I was good, but not good enough to really make something of myself in the sport. Eventually it became a childhood activity that fell by the wayside. God, it's been forever since I've thought about riding." Kathryn chuckled and shook her head. "I wonder what would've happened if I'd kept going, whether I was winning ribbons or not. Funny how you can let things that were once so important to you drift away like that."

Yeah, funny.

Wasn't that what the last three years had become? Letting go of what made him happy and whole? Letting it all drift away? Did he even have a choice?

He'd been so distracted, he barely registered that he'd

stopped in the circular drive at the front of the house and clicked off the ignition.

Mike bounded up to his door, grinning. Still a young man at twenty-six, Mike was a big, strappin' ex-Marine who hadn't turned loose of his military buzz cut. He shook Hunter's hand up and down as soon as Hunter got out of the car. "Hey, man! Good to see you! Sorry I had to break up your holiday and all, but we had to stay on schedule."

Hunter shrugged. "No big deal. I'm always happy to help out a friend. So, is Josie still keeping you in line?"

"You could say that. My wife missed her calling. She's tougher than any drill sergeant I ever had. She's got this move plotted on a spreadsheet broken out in one-hour increments. But, hey, it's running perfectly, so who am I to complain?"

Kathryn popped out of the car before Hunter had a chance to open her door for her. She moseyed around, and Mike's eyebrows went up at the sight of her. "Aw now, who's *this?*" He clucked.

Hunter casually draped his arms around Kathryn's shoulders. "This is Kathryn Winslow. She's my girlfriend."

Surprise flared for a second on Kathryn's face, as if she couldn't believe he'd said it out loud. But she smiled as she recovered herself, and a pretty flush colored her cheeks. "Uh, hi," she stammered, flustered but still shaking Mike's hand. "Nice to meet you."

"I see now why I couldn't get you on the phone for a week." Mike winked. "I wouldn't be answering my phone, either."

She laughed, and they spent a few minutes talking good-naturedly about the house and the move. Mike Smith and his wife had rented the house for the last two and a half years, ever since Mike had left the service. Their families had known each other for years and years. In a small town like this, everybody knew everybody, and everybody helped everybody. After all, the Smiths were good people. These days, Mike worked in cyber security, with some private eye work on the side, and his wife was a nurse. They'd been the perfect people to take over the house and the grounds for him. They were more than renters, really. They were caretakers. And he couldn't have turned those keys over to a nicer couple.

As they walked up the steps, Hunter saw his trust in Mike and Josie had been well placed. The porch spindles and window jambs had a fresh coat of white paint, and the couple had painted the ceiling of the wrap-around porch that particular shade of light robin's egg blue most people in these parts referred to as "haint blue."

Hunter pointed to the light blue porch ceiling. "I love what you did with the porch paint."

"Oh, glad to see you like it! Josie insisted on it. She said we had to make sure we didn't let any of the ghosts in."

Hunter chuckled about that old Southern superstition. People in the South often painted their porch ceilings this particular shade. Spirits couldn't cross over water, so the legend went, so if you painted your porch this shade of blue, they'd get confused and wouldn't enter your space.

Oh, Mike, if only it were that easy. He doubted his ghosts would ever leave him.

Mike opened the door for them. "Now, if you'll recall, I called you once or twice to say we were making improvements. You always said to do whatever I wanted, so don't be too shocked, okay?"

They stepped inside, and Hunter had to admit, he *was* shocked—in a good way. The place looked a whole helluva lot better than it ever had. Laney had been a big believer in what she'd called "shabby chic" and had painted all the walls stark white to set off her collection of bright, chalk-painted antiques.

But Mike and Josie had outdone themselves, truly transforming the house into a showplace. Every room was painted now in beautiful warm tones, such as sage green or pale beige, with accent walls in soft reds and browns and greens. Mike must've refinished a lot of the thick chestnut woodwork, because it was *gleaming*. There were new stained glass fixtures hanging throughout the house, new sconces by the fireplace, and a new Craftsman-style chandelier in the dining room.

Hunter pulled on the pocket door to the expansive dining space and, sure enough, it rolled right out. "I don't believe it," Hunter breathed. "You fixed it."

"It only needed a new pulley and a piece of rope." Mike shrugged.

Hunter's gaze fell to two brand-new built-ins—glass-fronted china cabinets that folded out into servers flanking either side of the dining room fireplace. "You built these too?"

"It wasn't any big deal, Hunter. You know my dad owns the hardware store down the road. I got all my supplies for free or at cost. Besides, I love to mess around doing projects. I taught myself a lot while I was doing it."

Kathryn walked over to the built-in, pulled out a drawer, and studied it. "Seems like a big deal to me. Check this out—that's a dovetail joint. And the drawers are lined with anti-tarnish felt so the silver won't turn. That's workmanship if I ever saw it."

"If you like that, let me show you the rest." Mike motioned for them to follow him.

He quickly led them around, showing off the new built-in bookcases he'd made alongside the family room fireplace. In the bathroom, Mike had added a fresh new glazed finish in the antique claw-foot tub, installed new bead board and new lights, and had tiled the bathroom in historically appropriate black and white marble.

"Wait until you see the kitchen." Mike beamed.

As Hunter turned the corner, his mouth fell open in amazement. Mike had given the kitchen a total facelift. The cabinets and his grandmother's commercial-sized, old-timey appliances were still there. But Mike and Josie had painted the cabinets white, added bead board accents and new hardware, taken up the old black-and-white checkered linoleum, and rehabbed the hardwood plank underneath. More of the haint blue accented the walls.

"Wow! Look at those subway tiles! Very trendy!" Kathryn pointed out the horizontal white tiles that formed a backsplash all around the room. "Yet, it's perfect for this vintage space. You've got talent, Mike. Maybe you should be a contractor."

"Nah." Mike chuckled. "It's more fun as a hobby. Hey, did you see the island? Can you believe I made this from the leftovers of one of my dad's kitchen rehabs? I nailed these cabinets together to make the base. This leftover piece of marble makes the perfect counter. All I had to do was grind off the edges."

The island *was* amazing, giving the room a sleek, expansive, and much-needed workspace. Hunter was so overcome, he had no words to thank the man.

Mike furrowed his brows. "You're not saying anything. Do you not like it?"

"No," Hunter sputtered. "Just the opposite. I mean —*damn*, Mike. I lived here for seven years and hardly did anything with it. But, you—I mean, I can't believe how hard you've worked on the place, and it isn't even yours. It's totally amazing. But I feel bad. You didn't have to do all this, you know."

Mike clapped a hand on Hunter's shoulder. "Hey, you did me a solid, letting us rent this place for two hundred dollars a month. With all the wealthy retirees and tourists in this area, you could've easily gotten a couple thousand a month."

"I couldn't stand the idea of strangers living here. And I knew you deserved it. I knew you'd take care of it," Hunter protested.

"And you got that," Mike countered. "You were going through a bad time. Truly, it was the least we could do. It would've taken me another five years to save up for a house down payment if we'd had to rent somewhere else. It was fun doing all these projects. We got to enjoy it, you know, while we lived here. It was a labor of love."

Hunter shuffled his feet a little and stared at the ground, suddenly too choked up to answer his friend. Kathryn took the moment to come up beside him, and wrap her arm around his waist. He draped his arm around her shoulder, and kissed her gratefully on the temple.

Mike checked his watch and fished in his pocket for the house keys. "I gotta go. If I don't, Josie's gonna kick my ass."

Hunter clapped his friend on the back. "In a good way, I'm sure."

Mike laughed.

"I'll walk you out," Hunter offered.

Kathryn must have sensed that Hunter needed some space. She excused herself, saying she wanted to explore a bit more.

The two men trotted back out to the driveway, and Mike plunked the keys in Hunter's hand.

Hunter tucked the keys in his pocket. "I'm really grateful, you know. You did a lot for this place, and for me."

Mike shrugged, and scuffed his feet in the gravel. "Yeah, I know. This place is a treasure. It's special. Promise me you'll move back and enjoy it. I'd hate to think of another renter coming in and messing up my work."

"I—I don't know, Mike."

"Why not? The place is teed up perfect for you. And now that you've got a new girl, maybe it's time."

"I tried staying here after Laney died. But the ghost of what we had...loss was around every corner I turned. It almost killed me. I don't know how else to put it."

Mike stuffed his hands in his pockets, and looked out over the horizon. "You know that's pretty much the exact opposite of what Laney would have wanted. She loved this place as much as you did. She'd want you here. Maybe it's time you started thinking about the good memories, and what you had here, instead of everything you lost."

Hunter groaned. "When I figure out how to do that, man, I'll let you know."

Studying Hunter for a long moment, Mike seemed like he was about to argue with him, but thought better of it. Instead, he gave Hunter's shoulder a friendly pat. "Promise me you'll think about it, okay?"

"Okay," Hunter agreed, trying to leave it at that. He didn't have the headspace for figuring out the future of the farm. Not yet, anyway. He needed some time.

They shook hands again, and Hunter pulled Mike in to a manly, back-slappin' hug. Honestly, he didn't know what he'd ever done to get such a great friend. But Lewisburg was like that. Sometimes your friends and neighbors knew what you needed before you did. They said their goodbyes, and Hunter watched Mike's truck disappear down the drive.

Hunter let out a long, pent-up breath. As he walked back up the steps and into the house, he silently regarded his family home, the place where nearly his entire life had played out. Everything was the same, and different, all at the same time. With the house now empty of furniture, his footsteps echoed a bit on the hard, polished wood. Hunter had the strange, jarring feeling that he wasn't seeing the Holliday family farmhouse. He was seeing a blank slate. Maybe that should make him uncomfortable. But somehow, it didn't.

He walked past his old master bedroom, expecting to hear the echoes of his wife's distinctive, playful giggle. But he couldn't summon it. He ran his hand over the wooden finial at the top of the stairs. It used to be all wobbly and loose, but Laney would never let him fix it. She liked it that way, saying it reminded her of George Bailey's broken stair in her favorite movie, *It's a Wonderful Life*. But—surprise, surprise—Mike had fixed that too.

Hunter huffed out a surprised chuckle when the rock-solid finial wouldn't budge. Somehow, the explosion of pain he'd expected from being here didn't happen. Was it the passage of time? Or was it the paint? The last time he'd been here, he'd felt like his anguish had practically lived and breathed in these walls. But now, as the last scraps of evening sun streamed through the windows, he realized the house wasn't any more haunted than any other place. The house was harmless. Comforting. Home.

This was only a house, after all. It was *his* house, full of more meaning and history than Hunter could ever put into words. No matter how much he tried to put this place out of his mind, it stubbornly refused to be dismissed. After all, wasn't it time he tended to the family legacy?

Maybe he was ready to move back. Maybe he was...

Hunter rounded the corner to see Kathryn propped against the kitchen window frame as she gazed outside, appreciating the last purple tinge of dusk.

Kathryn turned at his approach, and his heart somersaulted in his chest. Ryn. *His Ryn.* Could this woman help him heal? Love him through his pain? Did he even deserve that?

Right now, Hunter desperately hoped he did. He crossed over to her, wrapped his arms around her waist, and pulled her to him.

"This place is incredible, Hunter," she whispered.

"It is, isn't it? I made myself forget."

"Maybe it's time to remember. Maybe it's time for you to move back. It's ready and waiting."

"Maybe," he muttered, reaching out to stroke the side of her jaw with his thumb. "But I'd still be all alone."

She wrapped her hand over his. "You might be living here on your own. But you're not alone, Hunter. Not anymore."

"No," Hunter answered. "I suppose I'm not."

He bent his head to kiss her, and the warmth—the pure reassurance of her—seemed to hit him right in the middle of his chest. The undeniable heat of her kiss flowed through him, and Kathryn folded herself against him, as if she were always meant to fit there. He'd just kissed another woman in the house he and Laney had made home. And it didn't hurt. No, Hunter felt lighter, like a heaviness that had been weighing on him had lifted.

Hunter pulled himself back, holding her head in his hands, his forehead inclined to hers. "Ryn," he whispered, "how can I need you this much?"

She traced her hand over his cheek. "Does it scare you, to need someone?"

"Something like that," he answered, rubbing his thumb languidly over her lip. "All I know is, I haven't been able to step foot over this threshold for years. I'd fall apart. But today, here with you, it's like I'm home again. How could you have done that for me in only a few days? How is that even possible?"

"Oh, it's possible. Because I feel it too."

Kathryn looked into this big, strong man's face and was not at all surprised to see his eyes shining bright. Hunter shook his head to try to pull back the sudden swell of tears. But a single drop escaped anyway. She raised her hand to his face and wiped it away.

"Don't name it. Don't question it. Let it happen, baby," she urged, knowing that survivor's guilt was the source of his conflicted emotions. She kissed away the salty track the tear left on his cheek. A long, ragged exhale left his body. Grasping her head in his hands, he kissed her again.

Hunter took her mouth with an intensity she'd never felt before—desperately, like he'd die if he couldn't have her.

"Ryn," he breathed. There was that nickname again, and somehow it pulled at her heart. It was such a small endearment, really, but there was a thread of intimacy in it, a kind of plea wrapped in passion-soaked kisses that she couldn't ignore. The touch of his mouth to hers was so over-whelming, so insistent, her knees went weak again, buckled by the pure electrical charge that could only be Hunter Holliday.

Scooping her up, Hunter turned and hauled her back-ward until the jut of the counter's edge met the small of her back. Before she even realized what he was doing, he had boosted her up to sitting on the counter.

Kathryn sat eye to eye with him now. In shadow of dusk, his face was dark. Heat and desperate longing were written plainly on his face.

She slipped her hand up under his clingy Henley shirt, and Hunter's breath hitched. *Mmmmm*...his skin was fever-hot under her touch, the muscles in his lower back coiled to spring. He loosened his grip on her long enough to rip the shirt over his head.

Her hands moved over his overheated skin. "Ryn," he groaned "*My Ryn...*"

He blinked back his tears again and gathered her hands up in his. He kissed her fingers, and her open palm, and the hammering pulse points at her wrists. She knew how hard being back in this house must be for him, knew he was reaching for her in his deep emotional need. But she was certain he wasn't using her. No, she felt needed, and essential, as if he were reaching for something more than sexual. He kissed her like she was a second chance, a redemption, maybe even a benediction.

Hunter trembled as he moved his lips over her mouth, her neck, closing his eyes in reverent concentration. In this moment, here, in his home, his pain and history and heartbreak were laid bare before her. She could see him, all the way down to his soul.

He was broken, yes.

But he was beautiful too. They were beautiful *together*.

All the breath left her body for a moment.

And there it was. Heaven help her, there it was—the whole world in the space of a moment.

Dear God, I love him, don't I?

This feeling was almost like a physical lurch, like that moment at the top of a rollercoaster, before it plunged into a tangle of rolls and dips. Now she was the one trembling. But she was too exhilarated to be afraid.

Hunter's hands were everywhere now, roaming over her back, rasping over the tender skin of her ribcage, making her jump and squirm.

He ripped her tunic over her head and let out a low whistle at the sight of her lacy bralette. He showered her neck with hot, needful kisses, setting off a riot of flutters in her stomach. God, the hardness of his naked chest against her was like nothing else. There was no inch his mouth didn't explore—the tender skin behind her earlobe, the sensitive ridge underneath her jaw, and the hollow of her collarbone. And all the while, the scrape of his stubble and the heat of his mouth sent her senses soaring.

Finally his hands came to rest on her tender, aching breasts. Grazing his fingertips lightly over the sheer pink lace, he tortured her touch by touch until her nipples stood at stiff peaks. His groan reverberated down his back, tingling Kathryn's fingers. Tipping her backward, he locked his mouth on her nipple through the fabric. She gasped. No man she'd ever been with had done that before. *Mmmmm...* the unfamiliar damp rasp of lace and the heat of his mouth...God, *yes*. Soon she was arching her back against him, her hips scrambling to find the jut of his erection underneath his jeans.

"Hunter, please..." She didn't even know what she was pleading for. But he knew. He dragged her hips flush against him and pulsed the hard ridge of his arousal against her in slow, confident slides.

"Is that what you wanted, babe?" He moaned.

She nodded. *Jesus,* he felt incredible against the thin fabric of her leggings, hot as a blast furnace and hard as iron. She could only moan in response. They swayed together, making a perfect rhythm of anticipation. The beat picked up as they both grew more and more frantic, more needful.

Pushing back the cups of her bra, he landed his mouth on her nipple and sucked the aching tip right between his teeth.

It was too much, too good. "Hunter!" she cried out, holding taut, right on the edge with him.

Hunter's desire turned frenzied now, a long groan rattling from his throat. He hooked his fists at her waistband

and yanked off her leggings in one long pull. With one hand, he pushed her back against the countertop.

His hands found her wet, aching center, circling her nub before he dipped in his fingers. She was hot, and waiting for him. Their eyes locked. He saw her, and how raw her need really was. And he nodded, breathing hard as he pulled his fingers out and unzipped his jeans.

Yes...in seconds, he was inside her, every exquisite inch seated up to the hilt. Dimly she was aware of being lifted off the island and held upright while he drove up into her, over and over, pushing deeper...deeper.

It all came down to this. The two of them together, searching and finding, falling and catching each other, again and again. He pushed past her barriers, hot flesh sliding, pounding her harder and harder until she shattered with it.

"Ryn...*God*," he wailed, and joined her at the summit. His whole body clenched and he wrapped his arms around her like steel bands, locking her to him. Nothing could ever be as good as this—as good as they felt together. They held on to each other to keep from falling apart. Maybe someday they'd put each other's broken parts back together again.

Their heavy breaths echoed in the stillness of the house.

And outside their window, the sun slipped below the horizon. Tomorrow, everything would be new.

CHAPTER 25

THE DOORBELL RANG as Kathryn fastened the last clasp on her party dress. She slid her feet into her strappy, high-heeled silver sandals as she opened the door.

My, my, my. There he is.

It had only been a couple of weeks since she and Hunter had first rolled into Christmas Pass. But now here, in the real world, the two of them had fallen into a marvelous groove together. She'd had three days left on their reservations, and she and Hunter had made use of every minute, going on ATV rides, falconing, horseback riding, couple's massages, long hikes, bowling, and dancing until dawn. She'd come back home to Roanoke a few days ago when their reservation had ended, so happy she almost felt like a different person. And Hunter, to her enormous relief, never let their relationship skip a beat, in spite of the distance. He called and talked to her until late in the night. He texted her throughout the day while he worked on the Suburban's repairs. And now that it was New Year's Eve, he'd come here to her home turf for a big night out.

Even after a couple of nights apart, the sight of Hunter Holliday nearly knocked her off her shoes.

She threw her arms around Hunter's neck and gave him a thorough, if short, kiss. Yum. He was all warm from the car and smelling better than a man had a right to. "Hey, baby," she breathed.

"Hey." He smiled back. "Nice dress."

Yeah, the dress was pretty awesome and a bit out of her comfort zone, to be honest. It had a deep, plunging neckline in the front and was cut tight to her body, even though its swingy silver fringe obscured it, covering the dress from top to bottom. Her assets were on a bit more of a display than she was used to, but Hunter eyed her up and down hungrily, seeming to appreciate the view.

He was about to go for another kiss, but Wilson crowded in the doorway and threw his arms around Hunter's waist.

"Hunter!" he cried. "Did you bring my robot down?"

"Sorry, kiddo. You know you don't have the time anyway with your daddy comin'. Give it a week or two, and we'll get goin' on it, I promise. Besides, I brought something better than the robot."

"What is it, what is it?" Wilson shouted, jumping up and down like a much-younger child would.

"Over there." Hunter pointed, directing their eyes to the lot in the back of their condo. And there, sitting on top of the tow truck, was her trusty old Suburban. It was so perfect, she didn't even recognize it.

Now it was her turn to squeal and jump up and down. Kathryn couldn't have been happier if the Publisher's Clear-inghouse had showed up in her driveway. She hoisted herself up on the platform to see her beautiful old SUV and ran her hand over the supple, perfect new paint job. Holliday Hot Rods had given it a cheerful combination cherry-red and cream paint, shiny and executed in perfect detail. But that wasn't the best part. Kathryn scrambled inside the car and couldn't believe what she saw. Hunter had redone the *entire* interior—new upholstery, new seats, and new carpet. And it was *so cool*. The flooring was beige, but the seats were a combination of the same cream as on the outside, with precisely matched red piping and red starbursts on the headrests. God bless him, the man had even replaced the decaying dash with a totally new one, tricked out with burled walnut accents.

Wilson had climbed into the backseat and was currently trying his luck climbing over and under the seats. "Can you believe this, Momma?"

No, she couldn't. Kathryn was so excited that she was really, truly speechless. Sure, this was her second car, but it was her baby. And never in a million years did she think she'd get to drive something that was this crazy cool.

By this time, Hunter had lowered the bed so her truck was level with the ground. Hunter furrowed his brows and stuck his head in the open window. "Now I know this was way more than you asked for, but it needed so much. Y'all had bled on everything. I felt like you'd be better off starting over. Once I got started, I couldn't get stopped. I hope you're not upset—"

"*Upset?*" She grabbed both of his cheeks and kissed the stuffing out of him. "Oh, you wonderful man!"

Hunter chuckled as he finally came up for air. "I want you to know, all this work is free of charge. It's the vehicle that rolled you into my life, you know. Maybe I'm sentimental about it too."

She grabbed his face and kissed him again. And again.

"I think that means she likes it, Hunter," an amused voice rang out behind him.

"Daddy!" Wilson cried. The boy scrambled out of the truck and gave Sterling a big hug.

Avery ambled up behind them, and Wilson hugged him too. *"Bonsoir, Wilson. Comment allez-vous?"*

"Ugh," Wilson groaned. "This must be the part where I tell you how I am in French, right?"

Avery tapped his watch, and grinned.

Cocking his head to think, Wilson finally replied, *"Je vais tres bien, merci. Et toi?"*

"I'm very well, thank you." Sterling smirked. "Nicely done, son! Now if only you could be so polite in English."

"Ah! The tutor is paying off," Avery said. "But I will quiz you without mercy all weekend. You'll be speaking like a Parisian *toute suite*."

Kathryn had said her piece, and made her peace, with Sterling over the last few days. They'd fallen back into their regular, friendly pattern. But there was a reserve there and an awareness on Sterling's part that hadn't been present before—like he'd touched an electrical fence and now knew where his boundaries were. Maybe that was a good thing.

Sterling walked around the truck and let out a low, appreciative whistle. "I cannot believe this is the same truck you drove in grad school."

"It's a hot rod now! I have my own hot rod!" Kathryn exclaimed.

"Not exactly," Hunter interjected. "It's still the same engine. We put in new belts, oiled it up, and gave you new filters. It was in surprisingly good shape. This is mainly a little bodywork. You know, cosmetic stuff."

Kathryn popped out of the car, and Sterling gaped. "Why so dressed up?"

"Momma has a hot date." Wilson grinned.

"With the rugged Mr. Holliday, no doubt," Sterling answered, rolling his eyes.

"Yeah, and Hunter has to get dressed still," Kathryn

chirped. "Your suit is inside, babe. Why don't you go on in and get dressed?"

Avery clapped his hands. "Ooh. I want to stay to see how you look when you're done! It'll be like the prom. We can take pictures!"

"Oh, it's not all that exciting. It's the Mental Health United Charity Ball," Kathryn answered. "I'm surprised you don't remember, Sterling. It's always on New Year's Eve."

Her ex rolled his eyes again. "How soon I forget."

She punched Sterling in the arm but understood his retort. Sterling might have loved to play dress-up, but he detested dancing and loathed small talk even more. She'd had to drag him along kicking and screaming every year of their marriage, though, because she was a board member and had been for ages.

Kathryn wagged her finger at Sterling. "You're welcome to stay, but only until we're finished getting ready. We've got places to be."

Everyone trooped good-naturedly up the stairs to her condo. Sterling kicked off his shoes and flopped down on her modern, white leather sofa with a familiar ease, propping up his feet on her glass table and flipping on the TV. Avery helped himself to a bottled water from her fridge, while Wilson dove into another one of his video games.

Kathryn snuck back into her bathroom and dumped out her new bag of makeup onto the long, white marble counter. She'd always kept her style natural and minimal. She swallowed hard and decided it was time to step it up a notch. She flat ironed her hair, turning in her natural waves for an evening of choppy, sophisticated bangs. Drawing on thick points of new black eyeliner, she was pleasantly surprised at the results a little makeup could give her. By the time she added in smoky grey eye shadow and false eyelashes, her whole face was transformed.

Kathryn put on her new, bright-red lipstick and paused, transfixed by her reflection. She'd never worn a shade this bold before. She seemed...self-assured. Savvy. *Sexy*. Maybe she was, after all. This wasn't like every other charity ball she'd forced herself to attend to over the years. Hunter made it different. He made *her* different. She popped on her new dangly silver earrings with the rhinestone teardrop at the end, and called herself ready.

When she stepped out of the bathroom, Sterling whistled. "Look at you!" he cried. He reached out and gave the tops of her arms a friendly squeeze. "I can't believe how beautiful you look in this outfit. I don't have a single suggestion. You'll turn the head of every man in the room."

She shrugged. "There's only one man's attention I want."

Sterling chuckled. "Oh, darling—you've got his attention. That boy is like a dog with a new bone."

"Bad analogy," Avery quipped as he walked up.

They cracked up laughing.

But then the door to the spare bedroom eased open, and Hunter stepped out. Everyone went quiet. She, Sterling, and Avery stood there for a moment with their mouths hanging open.

To say he cleaned up well wouldn't even begin to cover it. When Hunter had given her his credit card and asked her to pick out his suit, she'd known this jet-black number would be exactly what he needed. But she was unprepared for how good it made him look. Hunter had buttoned the top button of the jacket, a move that made his shoulders seem impossibly broad and his waist toned and tapered. His ruddy skin glowed against the crisp white shirt and the necktie she'd chosen—an unconventional black, gray, and dark purple stripe. He seemed powerful, even worldly—like some kind of backwoods, international spy, as ready to play cards in Monaco as he would be to scale a mountain.

Kathryn whistled and ran her fingers over Hunter's jacket seams as she circled him. "Am I good or what?"

Sterling cracked a bemused smile. "Let me guess, she picked out the suit for you and somehow worked out all your measurements by eye."

"You bet I did!" Kathryn crowed. "I knew he'd look incredible in a designer suit. See how the cut catches the curve of his back and cinches in so elegantly at the waist. And the slim line of those pants. Mmm-mmm-mmm! Perfect!"

"Yeah, well, you're not so bad yourself." Hunter beamed at her, giving her a peck on the cheek for good measure. "I won't be able to keep my eyes off you all night!"

Sterling stood back and rubbed his chin while he considered the two of them together. "You both look smashing tonight. But something's missing. What is it?"

Avery snapped his fingers. "Hunter needs a pocket square."

Sterling clucked meaningfully. "I've got it handled. Hunter, come with me," he tutted, shoving Hunter in the direction of the master bedroom. Sterling left them all standing in the living room. Avery and Wilson scampered off to play video games. But Kathryn watched them walk down the hall, wondering what in the heck was happening here.

A pocket square? What was *that* about? *Since when has Sterling ever cared about how my dates are dressed?*

No, something was definitely up, and there was no telling what Sterling was going to say to Hunter. Even Avery seemed to be in on it somehow. On a hunch, Kathryn muttered some excuse about leaving her purse in the bathroom, kicked off her heels, and tiptoed after them in the hall. She flattened her back to the shadowy alcove by her bedroom door, which was cracked, and listened to Sterling grumble.

"Damn. She must've rearranged her drawers. I used to know exactly where everything— Ah! Here they are!" Sterling cried, pulling out one of her silk scarves. Kathryn wondered what in the world her fashion-obsessed ex was doing. That scarf was covered with teeny tiny violets, worked into the pattern.

Hunter raised his eyebrows. "What in the world? I'm not wearing that girly thing!"

"Oh, ye of little faith." Sterling snapped the scarf with a flourish. "Watch. I can origami this into something manly enough even for you. Don't think of it as a woman's scarf. Think of it as a piece of fabric I'm repurposing. Dear Lord, I've never understood straight men and their phobia about wearing color." Kathryn found herself smiling as she watched Sterling lay the scarf out on the bed and fold the slippery fabric into submission. "And now, voila! Come over to the mirror."

Hunter stood obediently in front of Sterling as he stuffed the scarf down just so into Hunter's front chest pocket. Sterling turned Hunter to face the mirror. "See? When it's barely peeking out of the pocket like this, it's a great counterpoint to the stripes in your tie. The pattern's so small you can't even see the flowers."

A few sounds of adjusting and rustling, and Hunter seemed gratified. "That is better—more finished, and refined. Thanks, Sterling."

Kathryn lined herself up against the cracked door to get a better view. She grinned. Hunter had passed muster, apparently.

Sterling turned Hunter around to face him. "You're

welcome, but the truth is, I don't give a rat's ass about your pocket square. I need to talk to you about Kathryn."

Oh God, here we go. Kathryn held her breath and pulled back, afraid to move, her eyes riveted to the mortifying tableau playing out in front of her.

Hunter crossed his arms over his chest and narrowed his eyes warily. "Okay, shoot."

"What are your intentions with her?" Sterling blurted out, drawing himself up to his fullest, most intimidating height.

"My *intentions?* For Christ sakes, she's a grown woman. What, are you her *dad* now?"

"Answer the damn question, Hunter. It shouldn't be hard."

Hunter huffed. "I don't see why I owe you any... Oh. All right." Hunter shuffled around and stared at the floor before he finally managed to say, "Kathryn is really...*well*. She's really special to me. Maybe even *important* to me."

A long silence hung in the air while Sterling processed Hunter's answer. Sterling slowly nodded. "I wouldn't have expected that chicken-shit answer from you, Hunter, straight-shooter that you seem to be. But okay, I'll take it. You're serious about her in your own way. *Good.*"

"I promise I'll take care—"

"Oh, you'd damn well better take care of her," Sterling interrupted. "Or I'll drive up to Lewis-wherever-the-hell-it-is and kick your ass!"

That stupid threat was so strange, so utterly out of character for Sterling, Kathryn had to cover her mouth to keep from crying out in shock. But still, she couldn't get her feet to move and go into the room to break it up.

There was a brief silence as Hunter apparently refused to rise to the bait.

"Don't you smirk at me," Sterling finally fumed. "I'm

sure I could land a good punch or two before you put me on the floor!"

"Hey, nobody's smirking. Or questioning your masculinity, for that matter," Hunter answered, holding up his hands. "I'm only surprised to see an *ex*-husband get this worked up over his *ex*-wife's dating choices."

"She's the mother of my child! And probably the best friend I've ever had!"

"And yet, *you* left *her*." Hunter glowered. "Remember?"

The comment seemed to take the wind out of Sterling's sails. All his bravado faded and, shoulders slumped, Sterling sank down to sit on the edge of her big white iron bed. Her ex patted Kathryn's favorite handmade quilt, and the oddest expression crossed his face, a mingling of regret and pain. "See this quilt right here?" Sterling pointed, sounding strangely wistful. "Kathryn made this. Did she ever tell you she's a quilter?"

"No," Hunter answered. "I guess she hadn't gotten around to mentioning it."

"I'm not surprised. She hasn't had time to do much of anything since our divorce, let alone indulge her artistic passions. But it wasn't always like that. She used to quilt like crazy all through her childhood, and while we were married too. She poured her heart into these pieces and always said it was her stress reliever, her therapy. See those pieces of fiber art hanging on the walls—the modern abstracts, the more traditional landscapes? They're perfect, aren't they? She didn't buy them at a gallery. Kathryn made every one of them, and the old-fashioned quilts she's got on every bed in the house too. There are more in the antique trunks. This one here, she made when she was pregnant with Wilson. These interlocking rings are called the wedding ring design—"

Sterling's voice broke, and he shook his head brusquely.

"This *damn* blanket. How I hated it. Every night, I'd pull it up under my chin as we'd go to sleep. It was as if Kathryn had stitched all her hopes and dreams into it, like a girl from long ago filling up a hope chest with her wedding trousseau. And here I was, a total and complete fraud. I wasn't fit to lay underneath it."

Tears stung her eyes at the memory, and Kathryn's heart sank. She'd always assumed Sterling hadn't felt the pain that she had. But she was beginning to suspect that he felt it more. Her ex just seemed so weary and sad just now. How could she have missed that?

Sterling picked at the comforter, not quite able to look at Hunter. "I really believed I could love her the way she needed, once. Do you believe me?"

Hunter paused to consider him, but finally answered, "Yes."

"You have to admit Kathryn is lovely, more beautiful inside even than she is on the outside, and that's saying something. And Wilson? I couldn't have a better son. He's the light of my life. God, you have no idea how badly I wanted to love Kathryn like a man should love his wife. How I wanted to be the family man she deserved. But I couldn't. I'm not wired—"

"Hey," Hunter broke in. "Don't. I get it."

"Do you?" Sterling's voice cracked with misery. "I don't think anyone can. I disappointed her, Hunter, in every way possible. I didn't understand how badly until recently. I disappointed everyone—Kathryn, the men I cheated with, and especially myself. I cheated everyone, denied them a shot at real happiness, all because I was too fucking scared to be honest about who I was."

Hunter crossed his arms over his chest again, apparently unsatisfied with that answer. "Why didn't you tell her before she married you? She deserved to know the truth, and you damn well know it."

Sterling closed his eyes and pinched the bridge of his nose. "I'm ashamed to admit this, but I was a coward. I had reason to be. I knew my family would never accept it if I came out, and boy was I right. Hoo! You should have seen the fireworks when I, their heir, their only son, told them about why we were getting divorced. The fallout for them was huge. They lost friends, had to change churches, even. And because of me, they've cut off Wilson. *Wilson, the only grandson they'll ever have!* I'll never, *ever* forgive them for that. Oh no, the entire judgmental, hypocritical lot of them are out of our lives, and good damn riddance."

Hunter's expression softened, and he walked over to clap Sterling on the shoulder. "Hey, man. I'm sorry that happened to you. It wasn't right."

Kathryn shook her head. No, it really wasn't. She was outraged over that, to this day. And watching Hunter comfort Sterling made her like him all the more.

Sterling drew a ragged breath. "Yes, well. At the end of the day, it wasn't even about them. Every bit of this was my fault because it was my choice. I let other people's opinions of who I should be guide my life. And it cost me. It cost Kathryn, too." He shook his head. "Hiding from your own heart. It's the most terrible thing you can do. I don't recommend it." There was another long silence. Sterling waved his hand, as if to erase his thoughts. "But enough about me."

He stood up again and faced Hunter. "I suppose the reason I'm spilling my guts like this is I want you to understand how special Kathryn is, how...*different*. Even after everything that happened between us, she never once turned her back on me. She's a friend, a confidante, and the best damn mother to our son. She even opened her arms to Avery. And she's done all that while she's been going through hell. When she wasn't wading through all the bouts of drama with her parents, I've had to stand here and watch her dip her toe in the waters of dating with one regrettable, lackluster creep after another. *I* did that to her, ultimately. She'd probably be happily married with a white picket fence by now if I hadn't slowed her down, and the reality of that kills me every damn day.

"But now it's different." Sterling poked his finger meaningfully in the center of Hunter's chest. "*Finally*, here standing before me, is a man who could go the distance. Someone capable of loving her body, mind, and soul."

Good God. Kathryn winced with embarrassment. What in the hell was Sterling thinking, needling Hunter like this?

"You know, it's only been a couple of weeks and we're still figuring out—"

"Shut it," Sterling commanded, holding up a finger.

Hunter gaped at him like a deer in headlights.

"I'm only going to ask you for *one thing*. And it's simpler than it sounds. Don't disappoint her. Don't be like me. Don't promise what you can't deliver. She deserves more than that. She deserves a man who's either all in or out. No games. Got it?"

Hunter swallowed. "Got it."

Kathryn's eyes welled up, listening to this. Maybe Sterling understood her, better than she realized. Wiping her eyes, she tiptoed back up the hall a few steps, pulled her shoes back on, and then stomped around as if she were just coming down the hall. "Come on, fellas! What is this, an episode of *Queer Eye?*"

Hunter practically collapsed in relief when he saw her in the doorway.

She hooked her arm through his. "Come on, baby. I think it's time we got the party started."

CHAPTER 26

HUNTER TUGGED on his itchy starched collar and wished real life was as simple as the mysterious Christmas Pass. He would've taken Hoot n' Annie's any day over this parade of stiffs.

A stab of guilt went through him for being so negative about it. But if this was the professional world Kathryn had to navigate every day, he felt kinda sorry for her. It was hard to fault the mission of Mental Health United, which raised money for counseling and treatment for those who couldn't afford it. But he hated that they needed this big dog-and-pony show to do it. At least five hundred people were crowded into this standard hotel ballroom, making his head swim trying to keep track of all the names and faces. But Kathryn navigated the crowd like a champ, stopping to talk every few feet to another one of her colleagues.

She introduced him around, and Hunter did his best to make small talk. But this wasn't exactly his scene. They chatted about whose practices were merging with whose, and who was retiring. For his part, he sipped his watered-down bourbon while he watched the crowd form and reform into cliquey clumps. Funny how all these hotel ballrooms were exactly alike—with the same flowery carpeting and blocky crystal chandeliers and waiters circulating around in black uniforms. Even the people themselves seemed to blend into each other, one no more distinct or interesting than the next.

It seemed to him, anyway, that all the good for the organization had been done before the event even started. After all, the charity made its money from the donations and the ticket sales. Too bad they couldn't stop there. Once the party began, this ball was nothing more than a lot of self-important, uppity medical types, all trying to outdo each other with their expensive outfits.

Thankfully, the company at the Winslow, Peters, and Dodd table was decent. Kathryn's coworkers and fellow doctors were more than a little interested in him, in fact, peppering him with questions and exchanging knowing nudges, as if Kathryn hardly ever had a date for one of these things.

Dear God, is that true? Hunter gulped. No wonder he'd gotten the inquisition. He was glad when dinner was over, and he and Kathryn began circulating through the more impersonal crowd again.

"Hunter," Kathryn interrupted, grabbing his arm. "I'd like you to meet Dr. Aldon Hogan. He's a psychiatrist here in Roanoke. And he's going to become one of our contributing clinicians, now aren't you, Aldon?"

A distinguished man with a red bow tie that matched his red, horned-rim glasses, Hogan chuckled. "That's our Kathryn. You never let up, do you? I didn't even get a *hi* or a *how have you been* in this time."

"What can I say? I'm committed." Kathryn grinned. "Now if only we could get your practice to send us more volunteers. Twenty percent of my patients are reduced pay or pro-bono. How many of your partners can say the same?

Come on. Don't you think the hospital could donate a bit of space and resources for group counseling at least? If we could get your psychologists to get out from behind their desks a bit, think of what we could do."

Aldon shot Hunter a bemused smile. Hunter saw this would take her a while. He excused himself to get them more drinks so Kathryn could cajole the man in peace.

The line for the cash bar seemed to go on for miles. Hunter dug his hands in his pockets and settled in for the long haul. Though the noise was deafening, the band was pretty good at least, churning out danceable oldies. But soon the players set down their instruments, telling the crowd they'd be back in fifteen minutes. Thank God. Hunter could finally hear himself think.

Unfortunately, Hunter could also hear the two jack-asses in line behind him now, gossiping like a couple of old hens. To hear them tell it, they were real playas, bedding a new woman every couple of days.

Hunter glanced behind him to fix eyes on these idiots. Both of them were in their early forties, Hunter guessed. And the two men were remarkably average—not too tall, or too thin, or too fat, or too hot. But they both had that refined air that came with the highly educated, a sort of *I've-figured-out-the-world* attitude that made Hunter's skin prickle. One of them appeared to be Indian-American, the other, blond-haired and blue-eyed. But they might have well been interchangeable.

"Pickings are pretty slim tonight," one of them said as he surveyed the room.

The other one tut-tutted. "Oh you've got to be kidding. You actually come to these things to pick up women? How prosaic!"

"Said the man who gets all his women from speed dating. At least we're running with the right crowd here."

His friend snorted. "At a charity ball? Maybe if you're into married women."

"That's not true!"

"Okay, name one attractive single lady that's here."

The man scanned the crowd. "Kathryn Winslow's here."

"She brought a date."

"But my *point* is, she's not attached. Not yet. Just because she brought some arm candy to this event doesn't mean she's off the market."

Arm candy? Hunter didn't know whether to bust out laughing or punch that asshole in the face. But he didn't do either, for Kathryn's sake. It wouldn't do for him to start a brawl. And besides, he wanted to hear what the turd had to say.

The tall blond man leaned in and lowered his voice. But Hunter was close enough that he could still hear the man plain as day. "Why would you even want her? She's kind of a mess."

"Mmmmm, I dunno about that," the other joked. "Have you seen her legs?"

"Don't be an idiot. That's not what I mean," his companion hissed, trying to whisper, none too successfully. "You heard about the way her mother died. Now I hear her ex-husband is getting remarried—to a *man*. How in the world could a woman, and a trained clinician at that, miss the signs that her mother is suicidal and her husband is gay? She's either terrible in the sack, or a terrible doctor, or both."

Hunter ground his teeth. *What freaking assholes!* He spun around and glowered at the men, who instinctively took a step back. "I don't know who raised y'all, but where I come from, if you don't have something nice to say, you don't say anything at all."

They actually had the gall to stand there and look put

out. "And where I come from," the big one quipped, "eaves-droppers often hear things they don't wish to know. We were having a private conversation. I don't recall asking you to join it."

Hunter took another step closer, looming over them to make sure they got his point. "Yeah, but when you're telling tales out of school about *me*, and *my* date, I tend to take it personally. Kathryn is a woman who has had a lot of hard knocks, but she's still got light in her. See her over there?" He pointed in her direction. "She looks like a million bucks tonight, and she's working the room like a trooper to try to help out needy patients. Which is a helluva lot more than I see you two sonsabitches doing."

The smaller one took offense to that. "You don't even know who you're talking to! I'm on the board! And I'm a donor!"

"The same board Kathryn's on?" Hunter spat. "Do you talk this unkindly about everyone on the committee? Or just her?"

Comprehension and, Hunter hoped, a little shame, lit their expressions. The taller one held up his hand. "Okay, um, I'm sorry. You're right. We were speculating when we shouldn't have. I hope you won't tell her about what you overheard. It could be, you know, awkward."

"I won't," Hunter growled. "But for her sake, not yours. And for the record, in case anyone's askin', Kathryn *is* attached. To *me*."

Hunter stalked off, still fuming. Only moments ago, he'd finally reached the front of the line. But he didn't want a drink right now. He wanted to get back to Kathryn. *So help me God, if one more person says a bad thing about her...*

Kathryn had finished up with Aldon when Hunter made his way to her. Smiling at her with interest he hoped the whole room could see, Hunter slid his hand around her waist and squeezed.

"I sweet-talked Aldon into doing some free group therapy sessions." Kathryn beamed.

"I don't doubt it. I can't say no to you either, especially when you're sweet-talkin'."

Kathryn giggled a little, and trained one of her dazzling, broad smiles on him.

He put that smile there. Him. The thought made his chest expand a little. Oh yeah, he loved lighting up that pretty face of hers. Hunter laid as much of a kiss on her as he felt he could in this environment—and she responded eagerly, her plush, delicious lips leaning into his *just enough.*

When she pulled back, he saw that flash of appreciation in her eyes. Oh no, there was no way in hell he'd let these people think he was some kind of cardboard boyfriend to be trotted out for one night.

The band started up again, kicking up a fast beat.

Kathryn winced and leaned over to talk to directly in Hunter's ear. "I know this isn't exactly your cup of tea. I've done everything I need to do here tonight. We can go."

Hunter's mind flashed to the little shits he'd been talking to. They'd expect her to slink out of here, wouldn't they?

Not on my watch.

He held his hand out to her instead and shook his head. "No, Kathryn, I think it's time to dance."

She furrowed her brows. "But wouldn't you rather—"

"No arguments, woman. We're dancin'."

The music thudded loudly in the crowded space, practically shaking the parquet dance floor when he drew her out. Even though the dance floor was full, there was still room to move among all the sweaty patrons, who were, at this point, getting drunker by the minute. And as he led her out to the floor, Kathryn's confusion gave way to a bemused, questioning gaze. When they finally made it to the center of the floor, he put his hands up for her to clasp.

What are you doing? she mouthed.

He understood her confusion. The band was playing a medley of disco tunes, and everyone was shuffling around, parading their best, middle-aged *I-haven't-done-this-since-my twenties-but why-don't-we-relive-the-past* solo moves. But not them.

Oh no, sweetheart, we're gonna to show them how it's done. Grabbing Kathryn's hands and holding them up between them, Hunter pantomimed a simple step-ball-step move. He put his mouth right up to her ear. "Do this step and go where I push you, okay?"

She nodded.

Before she had a chance to protest, he led her into the couple's version of the hustle. He couldn't hear her, but he could see her throw her head back and laugh. Kathryn stumbled for the first couple of steps as he pushed her out, then pulled her back in close to his chest. But soon she was keeping up like a champ, her dainty feet not missing a beat even in what had to be four-inch heels.

Other dancers started to notice him pushing her around the floor in lazy circles as he went.

Let them look.

He let go of Kathryn's left hand, spinning her out and back to him again. God, he loved this—the tension in her arm, the willowy softness of her as her body met his again. The fringe on her dress spun with her every time he completed a turn, the multi-colored lights illuminating the silvery strands with fire.

Damn, Kathryn was dazzling—the most beautiful woman in the room by far. And she had her eyes trained just on him, watching him breathlessly for any clue about his next step, his next move. *Aw yeah. This* was why this country boy had learned to dance.

You ready? he mouthed to her, cocking up one eyebrow.

She nodded and bit her delicious little bottom lip in concentration.

He spun her out and back in, grabbing both hands and pulling her so they were spinning side by side with hands joined over the backs of their shoulders. It was a relentlessly showy move, straight out of *Saturday Night Fever*, and when they did it, the crowd parted around them and started to clap.

"Oh my God!" Kathryn cried, wide-eyed at the attention. "Hunter, what—"

"Follow my lead, girl. Don't stop," he growled.

He spun her out, and when she came back he grabbed her around the waist with one arm, cinching her in tight against his hips. He raised her other hand above their heads, linking fingers. "Lock your knees," he commanded, and he spun them both together in tight circles, over and over, while the crowd went wild.

The whole room was a jumble of spinning lights with Kathryn at the center, staring up at him as if she were too mesmerized to look away. Lord knew he couldn't look away, either. The exhilaration in her eyes, the rhythmic sway of her bare back under his palm, the fine mist of her sweat— they were doing him in, right here in the middle of the dance floor.

Hunter spun her back out and let go of her hands this time. In a fit of showmanship, he pointed to her, shimmying like a bad disco playboy, and reeled her back in. She was truly giggling at his tricks now, but her feet never stumbled as he moved her through one more turn, two, three...and then he tucked her to him chest to knee, his arm snaked around her back, and dipped her, right on the last beat of the song. Cameras flashed as the crowd whooped and hollered. He kissed her, and they both made a quick bow to the crowd.

She tumbled into his arms and twined her arms around his neck as the next song started. It was a slow one. "Hunter Holliday." She chuckled with disbelief. "You are so full of surprises. Who knew you could turn me into a dancing queen?"

"Yeah, I was cribbing from John Travolta. And you, my Ryn, have all the instincts you need for dancing. All you need is the right partner to teach you a thing or two."

"Yes." Kathryn's eyes lit with a naughty gleam. "I'm beginning to see that."

She kissed him again, soft and slow. And he sighed with contentment as she laid her sweet head on his chest. He folded her tight against him as they moved to the music, suspended for a moment as if they were the only ones in the room. He had one hand on the small of her back, the other covering the hand she held over his heart. It was beating wildly, more from her than his dance moves.

This woman, dear Lord, this woman.

Truth was, he *was* attached to her. He didn't know how it had happened exactly. He hadn't been searching for it. He wasn't even sure it was possible for him again. But it had only taken a couple of short weeks for him to see how incredibly special she was. Every moment of every day, he craved her touch on his skin and the sound of her throaty, feminine voice in his ear. He needed her, maybe too much.

Kathryn's long, luscious curves pressed against him. Lean and willowy, she bent to him like a reed. Dear Lord, the gentle jut of her breasts brushing his chest and the swish of her narrow hips turned him on beyond all reason. He

344

went hard as a rock and moved away from her self-consciously.

Kathryn looked back up at him, the hottie, and pushed his hips back to her, rubbing herself up against him like a cat. Then she bit her bottom lip to let him know she knew exactly what she'd done.

Jesus Christ, the things he wanted to do to her.

"Ryn," he choked out, too turned on to even finish the sentence.

"I'll get my coat." She smiled, reaching down to make sure the button on his jacket was fastened and rubbing her knuckles over his straining hard-on as she did. She bit her lower lip again. *Vixen.*

"Right," he huffed out, chuckling and watching her wave across the room to her coworkers. The line for the coat check seemed to take forever. But she finally emerged wearing her mother's old fur stole. God, he didn't know how he was going to make it home. His cock throbbed with need, straining in his pants. He wanted her so badly that every step to the top floor of the parking garage was torture.

"You're awfully quiet. Didn't you have a good time?"

"Anywhere I go with you, I have a good time."

"Funny." She chuckled. "I think the good time has really only gotten started."

He stole a glance at her. Exactly what did that girl have planned for him?

They'd finally made it to the largely deserted upper floor of the parking garage, and she clicked her key fob to open the locks to her Suburban. She'd insisted on driving this snowy night. He walked around to the driver's side to open her door. But she opened the back door instead.

She pointed to the back seat with a sexy smirk. "Get in."

"Babe, what are you—" Then realization dawned on him, one tantalizing erotic vision at a time. *Have mercy.*

She backed him up against the car, cupped her hand around the back of his neck and bent his head down so she could put her mouth right next to his ear. "You know, I can't have my man driving with one of these," she hummed, hot and sexy and low, running her palm up and down over his straining cock. "It wouldn't be safe, now would it?"

Well now. She didn't have to ask him twice.

Hunter gulped, tore off his coat, and practically leaped into the backseat, dragging her with him. Kathryn landed on his lap, and she hiked up her dress so she could straddle him, pushing herself up and over his bulging hard-on.

"*Jesus,* girl." He groaned, already so in her thrall he could hardly think straight, the heat of her in his lap sending waves of pleasure up his spine. Then, holy hell, she began to move, teasing him, pushing him to barely leashed insanity as her slicked heat passed over him, again and again. God, she was so hot, it was almost like the material of her panties and his pants weren't even there. He pulled her head back in his hands for a deep, hungry kiss, marveling at her heat, her taste.

Sterling's right. She's so lovely...so...perfect.

Even in the dim fluorescent light of this garage, she wrecked him. Streaks of light and shadow played on her skin, making her pale skin seem even more ethereal, more mysterious. Sure, he'd had some time to get used to the idea of them being together. But it didn't matter. Every time she reached for him, Kathryn caught him up short and unraveled his control.

His hands shook as he drew them up her strong, long legs. He breathed in the familiar scent of jasmine on her neck. Softer than the finest satin, her cheek brushed against his.

He winced, regretting he hadn't shaved off his rough stubble before they'd left. But she just shivered and moaned, low in her throat. His breath left him in a long exhale.

Ryn.

His Ryn.

Yes, dammit—*his.*

He didn't need Sterling or anybody else on God's green earth to push him in her direction. He was staking his claim. A primal kind of need wound its way around his arousal, a need to possess, a need to hold her to him and never let her go.

His Ryn. His light in the dark.

Damn, her skin was hot to the touch, burning up for him, even on this chilly night. Kathryn grabbed the sides of his face in her hands now and held his gaze. Desire danced in her eyes, passion mingled with...something more?

She bent her head and kissed him deeply, desperately, tilting his head up to meet her.

Yes. There it is. She feels it, too, doesn't she? The need. The desperation.

Kathryn didn't kiss so much as devour him, the sparks between them rising up like a living thing. He wanted her so badly, he almost didn't know what to do next. Fumbling his fingers through deep open vee of her dress, he finally cupped his hands over her perfect upturned breasts. She felt like heaven in his hands.

Goddamn, it was too much.

He yanked down her straps until she was naked to the waist and trained his mouth on every sexy, shimmery square inch of skin he saw. He feasted on her shoulders and the gentle rise of her shoulder blades. And he ran his tongue over the frantic pulse point in her neck, sinking his teeth into her impossibly soft skin. She arched to him. "Hunter..."

He traveled his greedy mouth over her flushed skin, teasing her nipples until they were rosy and stiff. She fumbled with his tie, finally unraveling it and unbuttoning the top couple of buttons. Hissing with frustration when she saw his undershirt in her way, she wormed her fingers down and yanked his shirt out at the waist. When she found his hot, sweaty abdomen, she hummed with satisfaction.

Such a small thing, but it made his head spin. She wanted him, hard and fast and needy, just like he wanted her. Another low groan escaped his throat, and his cock pulsed in his pants, straining already for some kind of release.

"I *need* you, Hunter." She whipped open the buckle on his belt. "I need you right now."

Hunter watched, spellbound, as she unzipped his pants and pulled his cock out of his snug boxer briefs. She pushed the tiny patch of fabric from her thong over to the side and, good, merciful God, slid her wet, pulsing heat down onto him—all the way to the hilt.

Together. Bound.

Already her slicked walls shuddered around him like a hot velvet fist, snapping tight with tension.

"Ah, God! You feel so good..." She wrapped her arms around his neck and began riding him. And there was no slow start, no working up to it. No, Kathryn rode him like a true force of nature, a perfect storm of desire playing out right in his lap.

Harder, faster, they both raced to take in more, feel more.

He drove up into her, meeting her thrust for thrust until his fingers dug into the sweet flesh of her ass. He gave her a ringing slap on her hot, sweaty cheeks, and her eyes flashed.

"More, Hunter!" she cried. "More like that!"

And he obliged her, giving her tart little smacks to sting her backside with every thrust.

Fun, yes, but he had to have more—more of her taste,

her heat. He flipped her underneath him on the seat, clasped his hands in hers, and shoved them above her head, holding them down.

The surprise in her eyes revved into flaming desire, like he'd stepped his foot onto some unseen gas pedal and sent her into overdrive.

He pushed his way into in her again, pounding so hard, so fast, two bodies joined and racing toward the finish line. For a moment, he couldn't tell where she stopped and he began. Their eyes locked and he watched the pleasure overtake her. She screamed and writhed as the tremors rocked her core, and she fell apart in his arms. And he tumbled after her, shattering, his body coming apart with explosions of pleasure that wracked him from head to toe. Wrapping himself around her, he held her tight, tight enough to take him in, tight enough to keep him from simply floating away. He buried himself in her in every way possible. And when he finally came back down from one of the most explosive orgasms he'd ever had, she was there, stroking his sweaty hair, planting kisses along his neck. Gentling him. Holding him. Taming him.

He was breathless, dazed.

Finally, he felt like his heart could start beating again and he gulped in more air. Their panting had come out in icy puffs when they'd gotten in the SUV. But now? Their heat hung heavy in the air, warming everything around them.

"C'mere." He sat up and urged Kathryn back into his lap again. Kathryn complied, leaning into his sweaty kiss. Her lips were swollen from kissing him, her porcelain skin flushed and fragrant under his hands. Lord, this woman was something else. How could he have ever considered her delicate?

As his heartbeat gentled and his frantic breaths slowed,

Hunter couldn't stop basking in the beauty of this amazing woman in his arms. He let his gaze roam over her. If you'd told him a year ago that he'd be prancing around like a disco king at a charity ball and having mind-numbing, earth-shattering sex in a freaking *parking garage*, in *January*, he would've laughed his ass off. At every step along the way, this girl had challenged him and surprised him, nudging him out of the dark corners he'd been hiding in. In every possible way, she forced him, blinking, out into the light.

His Ryn.

His.

His heart overflowed with passion and joy and...*her*. She made him feel again and it almost physically *hurt*. Damn, it was practically spilling from him in waves, these feelings he was too afraid to name and definitely not prepared to handle. He didn't trust himself. Was he being foolish, hard up and desperate for affection? Or was he nothing more than a grasping, needy idiot? Was it even possible for one man to have two great loves in his life?

Kathryn didn't talk, either. She peered at him with those sexy, smoky eyes—eyes that always seemed to cut right to the heart of him. One side of her mouth curled up into a smile, and she reached out to pet his cheek with soft, tender strokes.

He wiped a sweaty tendril of hair off her forehead, and their eyes caught. "Babe," he breathed. "You're incredible. You're..." He trailed off and couldn't say more. Emotions overwhelmed his ability to speak. He stroked his hand through her hair and grabbed her by the nape.

Hunter had so many things he wanted to say to her.

You're the sexiest woman in the world to me...

I want to be your one, your only...

You're everything to me...

"I think I might be falling in love with you, Kathryn, and I don't know what to do."

Wait—did he say that last bit out loud?

Kathryn's round eyes glittering back at him told him that yes, he had.

Oh, damn. Kathryn needed to get that message over wine and candles, not in the back of some ancient SUV. He felt foolish, and exposed, and naïve for blurting that out. Hunter couldn't breathe, couldn't blink while he waited for her to respond. For a moment, silence hung in the air as she ran a tender hand over his jaw.

"I love you too, Hunter Holliday, and I don't know what to do either." A corner of her mouth turned up. "Can you promise me that whatever it is, we'll do it together?"

He chuckled softly. They didn't talk anymore after that. Sometimes there was no need for words between them. Sometimes she understood him better than he understood himself.

He pulled the straps of her dress back up and wrapped his arms around her.

And they held on, like they'd never let each other go.

CHAPTER 27

KATHRYN WOKE to the tingle of Hunter's fingers tracing lazy circles on her lower back. She pushed herself up from her stomach, blinking at her pillow. She hadn't slept that deeply in an age. But then again, Hunter had kept her up most of the night in *all* the most delicious ways.

"Wake up, sleepyhead," He nuzzled her neck. "It's eleven in the morning already."

"What? Are you serious? I—I don't sleep in. I haven't woke up this late since, since—oh my God, since college!"

Hunter chuckled. "I'd say you earned it then, sugar. Here, try this." He handed her a steaming cup of coffee—hazelnut, with a splash of cream and a teaspoon of sugar, just the way she liked it.

She rubbed her eyes and blinked at him in amazement, taking the cup. "I'm so embarrassed. Here I invite you to stay over at my house, and *you're* making *me* coffee."

"I made some pancakes too." He pulled out two breakfast trays, fully outfitted with juice, a stack of pancakes, and fresh-cut fruit. "They're chocolate chip. Now move on over."

"Good Lord, I didn't even hear you get up. How did you do all this?"

He shrugged as if making breakfast in bed was the kind of thing he did all the time. "I saw all the mix and stuff sitting on the counter. It didn't take a genius to see what you had planned. I was awake and hungry, so I thought, why not? Besides, after the night we had, I should be fixing you a ten-course meal."

She kissed him on the cheek. "So how did you know how I take my coffee?"

He smirked. "You weren't the only one paying attention at the Hollyberry Inn."

She poured on the syrup, sank in her fork, and cut off a slice of the pancakes. They were perfect—fluffy and light and browned to perfection. When she took her first bite, she groaned in bliss.

Satisfaction lit his face. "They are pretty good, aren't they? They aren't quite as good as the recipe I make from scratch, but they'll do in a pinch."

"You cook too?"

"Yeah, I used to do all the cooking at my house. But now that it's only me left, I don't bother much anymore. But this felt good. I enjoyed rockin' the frying pan again, actually. It's been a while."

Kathryn shook her head. "So let me get this straight. You're a man's man—strong, capable, fishin', campin', and building cars for a living. You're kind, considerate, built like a brick shithouse, *and* you cook?"

The comment clearly tickled him. "Not just a brick house, but a brick *shit*house, huh? All this—" He motioned, up and down over his chest. "—and I'm good in the sack too."

Kathryn cracked up. Maybe nearly falling over a cliff

was almost worth it, if it meant being rescued by this wonderful man. What a beautiful day this was. The sun was shining bright and crisp and the room was toasty warm, thanks to Hunter turning on the tiny gas fireplace in her cozy Victorian-era bedroom. The two of them were tucked up tight in her big iron bed, propped amongst all her extra goose-down pillows, a fluffy comforter, and her favorite quilt. Her heart swelled with a feeling a lot like...contentment.

Normally by this time, she would've been up with three loads of laundry done, the grocery list made, and probably be off delivering Wilson to some kind of lesson or party or sports event. Had she ever allowed herself to have this kind of a decadent, lay-about morning? Maybe she could, now that she had someone to lay about with—someone who *loved* her. Things would be different.

New day, new Kathryn.

"I'm kinda mad at myself for sleeping in, actually," Kathryn finally said. "By now we should probably be out and about. You know, doing date-like things like going to the movies or something."

Hunter forked up another bite of pancakes, and play-fully fed it to her. "We could go to the library and see if we could find out any more information about Christmas Pass. I haven't tried the archives here yet."

"What for? You've already checked all the land trans-fers and census documents for the whole southern part of West Virginia. If you didn't find anything there, you're not going to find anything here."

"Yeah, but if Christmas Pass really was founded before West Virginia was a state, shouldn't there be a record in the Virginia archives?"

Kathryn let out an exasperated huff. "Yes, but—"

"Then you're proving my point."

Kathryn narrowed her eyes playfully at Hunter while she chewed another bite of pancakes. The man was making a hobby out of researching the elusive Christmas Pass, but he'd been utterly unable to find a single shred of evidence that Christmas Pass had ever existed. She'd done extensive searches here in Virginia herself, all to no avail. In fact, librarians and archivists looked at her as if she had lost touch with reality when she asked them questions about it. Maybe they both had. But they were back in the real world now.

"It's time to let sleeping mysteries lie, Hunter. You know we're not going to find anything. I've already scrubbed the archives here with a fine-tooth comb."

He gave her his best puppy dog eyes. "Just one more scan of the newspaper archives and old state maps. Pleeease?"

She chuckled and shook her head. "How about this. We stay at the library until three, then go over to the Grandin Theatre for a free matinee. I think they're showing Hitchcock films this week.

Hunter considered that. "All right. I'm always down for a little classic suspense."

She was about to reserve their spot, when they heard the distinctive ring of her cell phone. Picking it up off the nightstand, her heart sank when she saw the name on the screen.

It was Daddy. She'd checked in with his doctor at the rehab center, and the man had said Huck Wilson was a model patient. And she'd talked to Daddy herself only two days ago. He'd sounded great. So why was he calling her now? Instinct told her something was up.

She swallowed hard and picked up her phone. "Hey, Daddy."

"Hey there, Katie-belle. How've you been?"

Katie-belle. Now that sealed it.

Kathryn clucked her tongue and paused for a long moment. "What's wrong?"

"Come on, girl, what makes you think something is wrong? I can't call to hear your voice?"

She chuckled. "You only call me Katie-belle when you're being contrite. What'd you do this time?"

Daddy huffed. "Not a damn thing! I've been the perfect angel up here. You wouldn't even recognize me."

"Mmmm-hmmm. Then why do I suspect you're holding out on me? Come on. Spill it."

"I never could charm you, could I? You know all my tricks. Fine. I'll tell you." There was a long pause. "I've been keeping a secret from you for a few months," he finally blurted out. "And it's kind of a big one. I sold off my company and every last gas station."

"What?" Kathryn yelped. "*Why?* And why didn't you tell me?"

"I didn't want to disappoint you, that's why!" Daddy grumbled. "You kept saying how it was good that I had my company, that I had something to distract me from my grief. But darlin', the truth is, I'd built that company for your momma. I did it all so she could have the kind of life she wanted. When she died like that, I—I couldn't keep it up. It didn't have any meaning to me, anyhow. Do you understand what I'm sayin' to you?"

Kathryn paused for a long time before she finally answered. "I do. But I still don't understand why you didn't tell me. Why did you let me think you were going off on trips and talking to your employees all the time? That was a lot of lying for one man to do."

"I know, baby, I know. But I was afraid you'd think I was a basket case. I was afraid you'd think I was drinking too much again."

Kathryn huffed out a breath. "You were."

"I ain't gonna argue with ya. I was."

Kathryn took a minute to mull that over, deciding that maybe she understood. Though she couldn't condone his lying, the man had every right to make his own business decisions. She sighed resignedly. "I suppose now that you've owned up to it all and you're getting the right help, it's not such a big thing. You've worked hard all your life. You deserve to be happy and do what you want to do. But that raises a whole new set of questions. What *are* you going to do now, Daddy? I can't stand the idea of you rattling around the house all day. You need some kind of outlet."

"See, that's the thing I wanted to call you about."

Kathryn could practically hear him squirming in his seat. This must be big. Somehow sensing her unease, Hunter rubbed her tensed neck muscles in soothing circles.

"I'm selling my house, baby girl, and I think I'm going to move out here to Arizona."

"*Move?*" Kathryn's breath caught in her throat. "You're serious?" she garbled out. "But you were born and raised in Roanoke! All your friends! And family! You'd really do that?"

"Abso-freakin-lutely!"

"But, Daddy, why?"

"Too many ghosts, girl," he ground out. "Everywhere my eye lands in that Godforsaken house, I see your momma. You cleaned her stuff out, and somehow, that made it worse. I need it gone—all of it. There's not a single thing in it I want. I want a fresh start out here. I want to look out my window and see a clean, clear horizon. I need a new beginning."

Daddy spent the next few minutes explaining it to her how he'd worked it all out. He'd already contacted an old family friend who was a real estate agent. He'd arranged for an estate sale expert to come in and handle cataloging and selling all the contents. And, leaving no stone unturned, he'd hired a crew that would manage all the painting, repairs, and buffing the hardwood floors.

She wouldn't need to do a thing, he'd explained, except go through the house and pick out anything she might want for herself.

"Anything I might want." Kathryn groaned. She put her hand to her head, thinking about how difficult it had been to gather up her mother's things and dispose of them. Though her family home was filled with fine art, lovely collectibles, and valuable antiques, she found she didn't have the heart to take them, either. "I don't think there's anything I'd want either, Daddy."

"Sure there is," he answered. "And whatever the heck it is, get it figured out in the next forty-eight hours. The estate crew will be coming in and tagging everything for sale on Tuesday."

"Gee, Daddy. Thanks for the lengthy head's up." Kathryn sighed, rolling her eyes.

"Oh, and I've emailed you a list of things of mine that I need in there," Daddy continued on, unfazed by her irritation. "Don't worry, it's a short list. They're a few personal things, like photos and papers. I don't even really want my clothes. Everything I need would probably fit into a couple boxes. Would you mind boxing it up and sending it to me? I don't want that stuff to get mixed up with the items at the sale."

"Aren't you coming back?" Kathryn asked.

"No. Well, maybe not until later in the year. I've got a lot to do up here to get my new house set up. It's perfect—a big one-story stucco house with a terra cotta roof and a pool out back. It's close to everything. And the good thing is, I can stay close to my doctors. I think I need that."

Kathryn pinched the bridge of her nose. "You bought a house. Already. And you're going to be out there all alone?"

"Not exactly alone," Daddy answered. "I've met someone."

CHAPTER 28

CHRISTMAS PASS WASN'T REAL. After the exhaustive research she and Hunter had done on *the not-town*, they'd been forced to accept that conclusion, even if they couldn't explain it.

And right now, she would have given anything if she could run back to that freaky, magical time warp of a place. Anything would be better than facing the task in front of her.

Parked in the driveway of her childhood home, Kathryn realized she was gripping her steering wheel until her knuckles were white. Feeling foolish, she put her hands in her lap, but she still couldn't quite bring herself to go inside. This was too much change too fast.

Daddy was selling the house and moving in with a woman she'd never even met. By all accounts, Alice was a lovely woman and about his age. Widowed for five years, she served as the head nurse on Daddy's wing at the rehab center. The lady had surely seen her father at his worst. If this Alice still wanted him after all that, shouldn't she have him? In the photo Daddy had sent her, Alice seemed lovely and blonde and kind. And Daddy was smiling so wide in their little candid shot that Kathryn almost didn't recognize him. There was no talk of marriage—at least not yet, thankfully.

Kathryn had let herself worry about this match, though she'd been unable to turn up any red flags. The woman checked out. Alice was the head of nursing at that hospital, and the widow of a successful lawyer. Clearly, Alice had plenty of money of her own. Kathryn probably didn't have to worry about her being a gold digger. Kathryn had talked to her on the phone twice now, and she really seemed very sweet. Though it made Kathryn feel small to admit it, she was probably all wound up about the idea of another woman taking her daddy so far away.

Kathryn winced at the thought. She sounded just like a petulant little child, didn't she? She shouldn't begrudge the man his happiness. The good Lord knew that Daddy deserved some.

But she still hadn't quite wrapped her mind around what the future was surely going to bring: people circling around Daddy's things at the estate sale like vultures... another family living in the house she grew up in...

Kathryn shook her head, as if it would somehow clear out her mind. She didn't know why she was being senti-mental now. Who was she kidding? *You hate this place.*

But she wished she didn't. Kathryn's stomach churned as she sat in the car, all alone.

She hadn't *always* hated the house. But *she* was the one who'd found Momma, dead on a blood-soaked bed. Anything good, or happy, or comforting that had ever happened in that house had been erased for her that day.

She'd tried to hide the wild, traumatic revulsion the house brought on for her Daddy's sake. But truth was, the house had become intolerable to her—a place visited only as rarely as she could get away with. Now it was an in-between place where she could mentally pin all her troubles, her disappointments, and her grief. The house was like a giant box where everything bad in her life had come to be stored. At long last, Daddy had come to see the place in the same way too. How could she blame the man for wanting to start over?

Kathryn laid her head down on the steering wheel for a moment. An icy bath of guilt and regret washed over her, and memories of the worst day of her life played out in her head.

Daddy had been on one of his near-constant business trips at the time, and Momma had made specific plans for Kathryn to meet at the house that morning so they could go hit some after- Christmas sales together.

Momma had suffered from a particularly bad cycle of depression in the months prior. But in the week before she'd taken her life, she'd appeared to have a good period. She'd been clearer and calmer than she'd been in a long time, actually seeming to enjoy the holidays a little for once. No one had suspected for a minute that her calm had masked suicidal intentions.

Clearly, Momma had wanted Kathryn to find her, probably because she was the one person in their small family who could stay steady enough in a crisis to manage things.

Kathryn groaned. She felt shaky and nauseated now that she'd allowed these thoughts to creep in. Daddy was right. There were too many ghosts—ghosts of things all of them should have said, or done, or been. No amount of paint or disinfectant could ever make it feel like a home again to her.

Kathryn willed herself to raise her head, but she could only stare bleakly at the grand old house. Such a pity they had to let it go. The house truly was lovely—magnificent even. Located in Roanoke's prestigious Old Southwest section, the Winslow family home was a white-painted, Georgian-style manse with grand two-story columns. Concrete lions and huge pedestaled pots filled with spiral-trimmed topiary graced the front porch. Built in the early 1800s, the grand old dame was 4,000 square feet of pure Southern charm, from its sweeping curved staircase to its crystal chandeliers to its chestnut paneling in every room. Momma had seen to it that it was professionally decorated and meticulously maintained. It was the envy of every society belle in town and a frequent stop on many a charitable historic home tour, especially the Christmas ones.

One thing was for certain. Kathryn's childhood home was proof that *nothing* was ever as it seemed.

Kathryn finally hiked up her metaphorical "big-girl panties" and got out of the car. Gritting her teeth, she forced herself to slide her key in the lock and turn. When the door swung open, Kathryn was a bit taken aback by the general disarray in the house. Had Daddy fired the house-keeper? Or had he neglected to send in his payments to the cleaning service? By the looks of it, the housekeeper hadn't been here since at least Thanksgiving. Was *this* why Daddy had insisted recently on always meeting at her place these past few weeks?

A thick layer of dust covered everything. Piles of books and magazines and photo albums lay about. Clothes were strewn carelessly over the delicate French provincial chairs in the dining room, as if he couldn't be bothered to hang anything up. She walked into the kitchen and found a recycle bin that was stuffed, not surprisingly, with vodka bottles—Daddy's drug of choice.

Her poor momma must be turning over in her grave.

Kathryn opened her phone and sent a text to Daddy's housekeeper that he'd need a spring-cleaning early this year, to prepare for the sale, offering to pay double and in advance.

She found some empty boxes in the garage and began walking methodically from room to room picking up the items her daddy had asked her to retrieve for him.

In spite of the mess, going through Daddy's things made her wistful. Somehow it was endearing to gather his favorite items, a bit like helping a small child put together a shoebox full of their treasures to keep under their bed. The first order of business was pulling out the five or six thick photo albums they had, stuffed as they were with the one-hour prints of her childhood.

Kathryn sat down on Momma's favorite Victorian settee and began paging through and removing photos she wanted to keep for her own album. A sad sense of nostalgia overtook her as she turned past page after page of old school pictures, annual family Christmas card photos, and silly outtakes of the three of them on family vacations. They appeared so remarkably normal—aspirational, even—like an upscale family in a stock photo. Momma seemed for all the world like a preppy fantasy in her hot-pink polo dress, perfectly styled platinum-blonde hair, and crisp white espadrilles. In a tight-fitting polo shirt and shorts, Daddy seemed so rakish at this age, with his dark-brown hair and a brooding sexuality she'd never noticed before. Just a toddler, Kathryn had been perched proudly on her momma's knee in a matching pink polo dress and a lime-green and pink striped grosgrain bow almost as big as her head. There was no reason why any of them shouldn't have had the world at their feet. But life wasn't that simple, was it?

Her heart heavy now, Kathryn laid the album box aside and set about gathering the rest of the items Daddy had asked for—his financial files, his favorite snakeskin boots, a few hand-tooled belts, and a signet ring with the family crest on it, which he wanted Wilson to have when he was older.

She went into the family room to retrieve his favorite books from the shelves when she noticed a pile of journals by the hearth. Apparently, half of them had been burned in the fireplace, and half were still here, presumably waiting to be burned.

Picking one up, she immediately recognized her mother's broad, looping script.

Oh God. The journals Daddy found in the attic.

She stood to go throw them away immediately. But then, she...didn't.

Before she even realized what she was doing, Kathryn sat down cross-legged in front of the fireplace and began reading every word. Kathryn hadn't known this about her at the time, but evidently Momma had kept meticulous journals, with a page devoted for each week. They held her memories, and her rants and were, from what Kathryn could see, a kind of self-administered therapy for her.

Daddy had burned up the ones from the years when she'd been a smaller child. But the last four or five years were here still. She cracked one open, afraid of what she'd see. And it was every bit as bad as she'd feared. Worse, even.

This journal was dated the year Momma had died. In between some lovely poetry and sketches, Momma had used this book to vent all the spite she'd felt but couldn't quite express in the real world. And it was bad—really bad. Kathryn's heart sank as she toured through the pages. Momma had clearly been spiraling deeper and deeper into despair and searching for somewhere to affix blame for her afflictions.

She railed against Daddy in particular for dumping all the household responsibilities on her and never being at home. Momma imagined Daddy out gallivanting over the countryside, having affairs. While Daddy's absences had been a legitimate beef, Kathryn didn't quite believe her father had cheated. Huck Wilson had worshipped her momma. The man had, most likely, been out drinking himself into a stupor. Which, of course, was almost as bad. The two of them had been caught in some kind of terrible feedback loop, each one of them somehow making the other worse.

Kathryn rubbed at the throbbing pain building behind her eyes. Momma never seemed to be too good at understanding how her behavior had had consequences—how other people hadn't wanted to be dragged along with her rages, and obsessions, and reclusiveness. She'd always seemed to teeter between ruthlessly hiding her symptoms or simply letting them run free, and damn the barricades. When the people around her had reacted negatively to her symptoms, she'd rarely apologized. That was the way she was, she'd reasoned. She couldn't help it. Other people had to understand and make exceptions for her.

Of course, the world rarely worked that way. Everything about her life had become a recipe for disappointment for everyone involved.

If only Kathryn had read these journals before Momma had died, she would've clearly seen the suicide coming like an oncoming train. But her momma had chosen to hide all this bitterness well. The journal was a sickening read. With every passing entry, Momma had flung some kind of blame on everyone in her life—her sisters for their estrangement, her long-dead parents for not understanding her, her friends for being fickle, and especially her husband for not being more attentive and supportive.

On the whole, Momma seemed to think everyone had left her to the wolves—alone and desperate in her bedroom during her depressions, and conveniently out of reach during her manias.

Except for Kathryn. No, Momma had accused *her* of seeing too much.

Kathryn's peering at me again with those icy gray eyes. She looks exactly like my momma, and me. And yet I wonder how I ever birthed this child. Even as a baby, Kathryn stared and stared at me like if she looked long enough, she might somehow figure me out. Doesn't that girl know it's impossible? I haven't figured myself out yet, either.

And yet she tries, the ink still fresh on her PhD in psychology. I'm proud of her, of course, but a part of me wonders if she did all that studying so she could find the answers to me. She fervently believes she has them. Pills. Talk sessions with some dried-up prune of a doctor. Making lists. Meditation. Chopping up my credit cards. Cutting out caffeine and wine. And of course, just being a better person.

But doesn't she know? None of that will make me better. None of that will make me a "good person." And what is "good" or "better," after all, except for fitting into the world's unreasonable expectations?

Kathryn loves to tell me stories. She tells me stories all the time about other people's mothers who suffered from my ills. They followed her advice. They got "better." And everyone around them was so wonderfully happy.

But what about the patients? Did anyone ask if they were happy?

When I was young, I chased happiness like a child with a butterfly net, running hard with hope but sinking into despair when, once caught, the very thing I wanted so badly died in my trap. No, I realized many years ago I'd never be happy. Not really. Not in the sustained kind of happiness people talk about in romance novels or toothpaste commercials. I'm simply not made for it.

And I'll be damned if I become something I'm not, hopped up on pills, just to make everyone else happy. Even if it means my daughter cannot love me the way that I am.

Kathryn set down the journal softly in her lap. So that was it. Momma believed that no one loved her, or accepted her, or understood her.

Damn her! Hot, angry tears poured down Kathryn's cheeks. *How could she? Didn't she know how hard I worked to help her? To cover for her? To help her maintain that image of the perfect, happy family she loved to cling to so much?*

Every day for years, Kathryn had watched her mother's illness tear her apart. Momma's case was severe—too severe to be managed any other way but with real medical treatment. And there Kathryn had stood with the tools that would've eased her suffering. And yet, every time she'd offered those, Momma had thought she hadn't *loved* her?

That's it.

Kathryn had finally had enough. She turned up the gas flame in the fireplace to full blast and chucked the cursed journal into the flames. Kathryn sat there for untold minutes, watching it burn. Then she threw on another. And another. It felt good, watching the flames lick up and burn every last hurtful word to ash.

Damned if she did, and damned if she didn't. Wasn't that always the way it'd been between her and Momma? If Kathryn had distanced herself, Momma would've blamed her. If she'd involved herself in all her family's dramas, Momma would've blamed her then too.

As it was, Kathryn had tried to take the kinder, healthier

route, being supportive and encouraging Momma to get the help she needed. Her momma, had she been serious about it, might've gotten some control over her illness and been able to lead a life mostly free of rages, free of soul-crushing depressions, free of dangerous attacks of mania. All she'd wanted for Momma was what she'd been able to do for other patients. And *still* Momma had blamed her.

Kathryn had spent the last year choking on guilt, wondering what she could've done to help, outside of having her momma involuntarily committed. It was a question that tormented Kathryn every damn day. Today, the answer was right there on those pages. The answer was nothing. Only Momma could've made the decision to help herself. As it was, Momma had been too wrapped up in her illness to see any way out. Momma had wanted to die on her own terms—quick and absolute, without the uncertainty of pills or doorknob nooses.

It was time for Kathryn to let her. There was nothing else that she, as her daughter, could've done. Kathryn needed to forgive herself before the guilt ate her alive. Wasn't this the very thing Kathryn had been telling Daddy to do all this time? Maybe it was time for Kathryn to follow her own advice.

The journals burned so damn slow, it seemed like forever before she could put the last one on that fire. But finally the embers of the others had burned away, and there was room. Kathryn tossed it in and tsked with surprise as a letter landed at her feet. It must've fallen out of that last journal. She was about to throw it in too when she noticed it was written in handwriting different from Momma's. Postmarked a week before she'd died, the return address said Miles McLaughlin. It was from "Uncle Miles," the man Daddy had suspected was the object of Momma's true love.

Kathryn still doubted that. A big, impeccably groomed,

garrulous man with white-blond hair, Miles had been Momma's best friend, and Kathryn truly believed that was all it had ever been. Everyone knew Uncle Miles was gay, after all. Kathryn was pretty sure the man had a boyfriend, even. Daddy had known about Momma's little excursions and dates out with Miles and had never seemed to mind one whit at the time.

In many ways, Uncle Miles was the only person who'd seemed to understand her momma, possibly because, Kathryn suspected, he was a little depressive himself. Regardless, Miles was the one friend who'd stuck with Momma no matter what. How strange it was, then, that Momma had never opened this letter from him. Miles never had been one to send much by way of mail. He was far more likely to call or stop by if he had something to say.

Still, there must've been a reason Momma had kept this letter. And there must've been a very good reason Momma had never opened it.

Kathryn knew she should throw it on the fire. It wasn't any of her business. It would be the right thing to do. But somehow, Kathryn's hands had a mind of their own, tearing through the seal anyway. She couldn't stop herself from reading it.

My dear Evie,

Imagine how alarmed I was when Hector said you'd declined our wedding invitation. Gay weddings are quite the rage now. You'd be ever so fashionable if you joined us.

But I know I'm wasting my breath. You'll never come, will you?

Ever since he met me a few years ago, Hector said there was something not right about the friendship between you and me. I'd never thought it so odd, of course. It was only us —Evie and Miles against the world.

I hope you know, Evie-heart, that you've always been my

soul mate. We were two spirits joined in understanding from as early as I can remember. Oh, the adventures we had—our bare feet in the summer grass and our knees skinned from one flight of fancy or another. The long summer days we spent swimming in the lake, and catching fireflies in a jar with you...they are some of the purest, happiest memories I have, my dear, darling Evie.

I've always loved you, you know, in my way. But as time went on, I began to think you loved me more, or differently, or both. You were so lovely, fresh on the brim of womanhood, that I believed maybe I could love you that way too. You let me try. I believe it doomed us both. It doomed me to knowing I can never be a physical partner for a woman. It left you believing that you could never fully love anyone else.

I should've pushed you away when we were young, before it was too late. But I suppose I'll never know if Kathryn is really my daughter, will I? I was always too chicken-hearted to ask, and your hasty marriage to Huck made it a muddled point, anyway.

We settled into a friendship, you and me—one where we could love each other to the extent that we could. But I realized too late that you'd become the firefly in my metaphorical jar, my dear. Though I surely never meant to, I captured you and fixed you under glass. You were trapped eternally in one moment in time, never free again to fly through the world as the bright, shining thing that you are.

You couldn't have made that clearer by declining our invitation. This is your way of saying goodbye and turning your back, isn't it? I can hardly believe it, actually. You still hold it against me that I couldn't love you back in the way you needed. You couldn't fly out of that jar, even though the lid was open.

You surprise me, Evie. Perhaps you always have.

Yours friend always,

Kathryn's hand shook as she neatly folded the letter and put it back in the envelope. *Well.* There was one bit of snooping she wished to hell she'd never done. Kathryn felt like all the blood had left her body, and she was living through every kind of terrible emotion all at once. Her skin ran hot and cold. Her stomach pitched and rolled. Could it be possible she was another man's daughter?

Running on shaky legs to the toilet, Kathryn quickly vomited up the remains of her breakfast. Then she carefully cleaned herself up and wobbled back over to the fireplace.

Kathryn turned the letter over in her hands, over and over. Such a little slip of paper, yet it held the answers to so many of her questions. *Solving a mystery has its price, doesn't it?*

Everything made sense now. The subtle but always present tension between Momma and Daddy. Whenever Kathryn had picked up one of Daddy's country expressions or in any way had tried to act like him, Momma had ruthlessly corrected her until the behavior had stopped. Momma had been so insistent that her only daughter be educated, and cultured, and artistic. Just like Miles. The day she'd told Momma she was giving Wilson her maiden name as his first name, they'd had a terrible fight about it. Kathryn had been mystified by it at the time. But it was crystal clear now. Momma hadn't been a hundred percent sure her daughter actually *was* a Wilson, had she?

And damn, Momma had fallen for a gay man. Talk about history repeating itself. Momma had always adored Sterling and had never really forgiven Kathryn for "allowing" him to divorce her. Momma had always maintained there must be something Kathryn could do to get him to stay. Which was patently ridiculous, of course. Kathryn had thought her mother was too naïve to understand the true nature of their marital problems. But no, perhaps Momma had understood better than most.

Kathryn took the letter and threw it into the fireplace with conviction, watching in relief as the edges turned black and eventually turned to fine, powdery ash. No one could ever know about any of this. Her mother had taken her secrets to the grave. Kathryn would make damn sure they stayed buried. Kathryn had been born and raised as Huck Wilson's daughter. By God, that was the way it would stay.

But as painful as this all was, Kathryn realized her time here hadn't been wasted. Her momma had managed to give her one last gift—understanding.

Kathryn finally understood her momma for who she truly was, once and for all. And maybe that was enough.

CHAPTER 29

"I'M NOT HERE."

It was only a whisper, but Hunter felt the cold breath on his ear and the echo of the words in his mind. The voice was familiar, and yet not. "What? Who are you? What do you want?" he shouted into the void.

There was no answer. Only silence.

This was a dream, right? He had to be dreaming...

Not knowing what else to do, Hunter walked forward into the blackness. As he kept moving, he realized that he was passing through a long, dark corridor, his footsteps sounding all the way on some kind of hard floor. There was a light at the end. When he reached it, he was in the kitchen at his farmhouse. Kathryn stood with her back to him, looking out the kitchen window. She wore nothing but one of his white T-shirts, and the light silhouetted every single one of her curves. Yessss. Maybe this would be a sexy dream, for once. His heart raced. He crept up behind her, and turned her for a kiss. But it was Laney, instead.

He gasped, but Laney only giggled. "I'm not here," she simply said. And she snapped her fingers and was gone.

"Laney!" he hollered after her. But the wild wind only howled in response.

He wasn't at the farmhouse anymore. The skies above him darkened with an oncoming storm. Everything seemed blurry around the edges, and not quite right. Finally he figured out where he was standing. The cemetery. Laney's cemetery.

She was trying to tell him something. She was trying to reach out to him.

Her grave—there, up ahead, on the hill. Hunter ran to it, panting with exertion. He spun around frantically to see where his wife had gone. When he came back to where he'd started, there Laney stood.

"Redbird, it's you," he whispered, falling to his knees before her. He reached out to embrace her, to pull her against him one more time. But his arms went straight through her.

"I'm not here, either, you nutball. I'm gone."

He blinked, and he saw she was right. She was gone, and he was left, staring at a black granite tombstone: "Lane Holliday, Beloved Wife, Gone but Never Forgotten," it said.

But he had been forgetting her. He had! Goddammit!

"No!" he screamed, pounding the stone with his fists until his hands bled, until the pain and confusion took him over...

A sharp crack broke through, and he woke.

His wooden headboard was in his hands and his hands were stinging and raw. Good God. He'd been dreaming again—and pounding on his headboard, evidently. That was new.

He dropped the headboard and collapsed back on the bed, staring at his battered hands in shock.

He truly believed he had conquered the worst of his

nightmares—maybe turned the corner to living a happier life. But he hadn't, had he?

Would these damn dreams never leave him alone? Would he ever be able to move on?

Hunter knew he had real feelings for Kathryn. That much was certain. Was this his brain's way of working that all out somehow? What did it mean when Laney kept telling him she wasn't there? Was she giving him her blessing? Or was she asking him to chase her, come after her?

The dreams seemed so real that it felt like Laney had been there with him. But if that were true, why was she doing this, and why now?

Oh God, I have to pull myself together. It was only a dream. It has to be just a dream.

This must be his brain's way of putting the past behind him, working it out, bit by bit. Why, then, had it seem like some kind of warning?

Feeling agitated and strangely empty, Hunter resolved to get ready for work. He looked like hell after a night like that, but damn. He had to get into the shop. He had a meeting with a new custom build client in a half hour.

He was buttoning up his jeans when he got a text.

It was from Mike.

Sorry to bother you again, but we realized once we moved that you have some of our stuff in your storage unit. There's an old Victorian trunk, two boxes of books, a rocking chair, and some other stuff. I'm coming back into town today and I'll have my truck. Can you meet me around noon at the unit?

Yeah. I'll see you at noon sharp.

Thanks, man. Sorry about the short notice. You're the best!

No prob.

Hunter scrubbed his hands over his face. Of all the days he didn't want to be reminded of Laney. But dammit, he knew it was important if Mike was asking for it. And besides, he owed the guy big time.

Hunter went into work and spent most of the morning trying his damnedest to pour all his concentration into it. And he'd thought he'd been doing a decent enough job of it.

But as he was getting into his Mustang to go meet Mike, Hop trotted up to him, concern creasing his normally gruff exterior. "Where you goin'?"

"I gotta go meet Mike out at the storage unit. I've still got some of his stuff, and he needs it. Don't worry. I'll be back in about an hour."

"No worries. We've got it handled. Say...um, are you feelin' okay?"

"Yeah I'm fine." Hunter huffed. "Why do you ask?"

Hop crossed his arms and eyed him suspiciously. "For one thing, I want to know whose face you punched in, with your knuckles all banged up like that. And second, you're lookin' as bad as I've ever seen you since Laney passed. And that's awful sudden. Did something go wrong with you and Kathryn?"

"No," Hunter bit out. "Kathryn's fine. She's great, actually. I had an...accident at the house. I'll be good in a day or two."

Hop stared him down for several long, long moments. It was clear the man didn't believe a word he'd said. He threw up his hands. "Okay, boss. So you know, if you ever need anything or someone to talk to even, I'm right here." His gravelly voice got even lower. "Don't forget it."

"I don't need anybody, Hop. I'm fine," he muttered as he closed his door and sped off.

I don't need anybody. But Hunter knew that wasn't true.

377

Images of Kathryn's sweet face played through his mind. Could he even subject her to somebody like him? Somebody who was, quite literally, *haunted?* Hadn't the poor woman been through enough?

His thoughts churned in his head all the way over to the Sunshine Storage Park. Was it guilt that was producing these dreams? Hunter wondered if it was possible to love a ghost and love a new woman at the same time. That appeared to be his problem. And Kathryn deserved better than that.

Could he work his way through all this? Could he be the man she needed? He wanted to be. Badly. But he didn't know the answer to the question, did he?

When he crunched over the gravel in the parking lot at the storage unit, Hunter found Mike standing by his beat-up Ford F-150, beaming with happiness. Seeing his friend's expansive smile helped Hunter's foul mood.

Hunter walked over and pointed to Mike's truck. "When are you going to let me fix up that old thing? You know I wouldn't charge you."

"Nah, I got other things on my mind, man. I'm going to be a dad! Josie's having a baby!"

So that explained Mike's excitement. "That's the best damn news I've heard all day," He gave his buddy a quick congratulatory hug. "Now I know why you moved out of the farmhouse."

"Yeah, we wanted to have some property of our own before we had kids. It's going to be a boy. We're pretty stoked."

Hunter snorted. "And I bet Josie's been planning this all like a foreign land invasion."

"A real slave driver, let me tell you," Mike replied. He pointed to the unit. "I have to get these items now if I'm going to paint and stencil them in time."

"Nice idea," Hunter answered as he unlocked the key on the padlock and pulled the rolling metal door up. His unit was actually three units that interconnected. It took all that space, because his entire life with Laney was stuffed in here, right up to the rafters.

Hunter swallowed hard as he scanned the space. Pure emotion welled up in his chest. Funny. Even after three years, he could still smell the faint hint of Laney's favorite perfume. Their whole marriage was stored in this place, scooped up and thrown into a dark, climate-controlled hole when he'd been at his lowest ebb after the wreck. He'd been completely incapable of sorting through or throwing out a thing. There was her vinyl album collection. All the Victorian and wrought iron antiques Laney had ferreted out of every antique shop in the tri-state area. The china pattern with the delicate pink roses she'd saved up so long to buy. Their high school yearbooks. Their blankets. Their pillows. Their pots and pans. *Everything.*

"Hey." Mike put a hand on his shoulder. "You okay?"

"Yeah," Hunter answered, his voice sounding far more gravelly than he would've liked. "Come on. Let's get this over with."

The job was harder than it appeared. Unfortunately, Hunter hadn't taken much care where he'd laid their stuff, and it was a haphazard mess. They climbed over and under piles of things until, thankfully, they dug out the items Mike had left with him. Hunter helped his buddy get everything fastened securely onto the bed of the truck with some rope.

Mike thanked him for his help, and Hunter gave him a brisk handshake to send him on his way. "Take care of yourself, okay?" he told Mike. "And when the time comes, bring the baby by. It wouldn't do for y'all to become strangers."

"I'll promise you that. As long as you promise me you'll

call if ever you need anything." He glanced quickly at Hunter's hands. "You have friends, you know."

Hunter cleared his throat. "Yeah. I know."

Mike got back in his truck and gave Hunter a quick salute as he drove away.

Hunter waved back, too choked up still to speak normally. He was a mess. Was it that obvious?

Hunter took a ragged breath, checking the place one last time before he shut it up for good. He should probably clean all this out at some point, but the idea of that made his chest hurt. Still, he felt bad about how everything had been tossed around in here. Maybe he could come back another day and organize it all, at least. An old, turned-over night-stand from their master bedroom caught his attention. Lying on its side, the piece had fallen from the top of the pile, and the drawer had spilled. He must've kicked it over when he'd climbed on top of that pile of stuff earlier.

Setting it up straight again, Hunter gathered up the mess that had tumbled out of the drawer. To his surprise, he found a small, oblong package, all wrapped in fancy red-and-green Christmas paper. *What the heck?*

With shaking fingers, Hunter read the tag: "To My Wonderful Husband. Finally the gift you've always wanted."

He wondered what in the hell *that* could be. The box didn't offer any clues. It was long, and skinny, and it rattled, like maybe it had a fancy pen in it or something. Laney must have been hiding it in the nightstand drawer.

Then the memory flashed back to him—Laney, the night of the crash. She'd mentioned she had a present for him and was planning on giving it to him when they got back from dinner. He'd assumed she'd been referring to her lingerie, but had she really had an *actual* present for him that night?

Holy shit. She had. And he was holding it in his hand.

If ever there was a time when he felt like he was right there, right on the ragged edge, this was it. His heart throbbed painfully in his chest. He couldn't leave it here, could he? He *had* to open it.

Trembling from head to toe, he untied the thick, silky ribbon and lifted the lid off the box.

And suddenly, his whole world was spinning—flying off its axis forever.

He crumpled to the ground, unable to breathe.

In his hand was a pregnancy test that was too aged and pock marked to read. But that wasn't necessary. Because on the inside of the box lid, Laney had written, "You're going to be a daddy!" in permanent ink.

And in that moment, Hunter realized he hadn't just killed his wife that night. He'd killed his family.

CHAPTER 30

JANUARY FIFTH WAS her first day back at work after their extended Christmas break. And Kathryn was beginning to get worried about Hunter.

Whenever they couldn't be together, they always had a long talk right before they both went to bed. And he usually texted her throughout the day too. So it was definitely concerning that he'd gone radio silent like this. It'd been three whole days now!

She'd texted him and left messages on his cell. Hell, she'd even tried to reach him at the shop, and still, nothing. Could it be she was getting ghosted? *Again?*

Kathryn stood at the front desk, reviewing files for upcoming appointments. But she wasn't concentrating on them much. No, she couldn't help scrolling obsessively through her phone.

Cookie, her buddy and long-time receptionist, tapped her acrylic nail tips on the desk and gave her a sly look. "Still worried about Hunter?"

Kathryn chucked her phone on the counter, disgusted with herself now. "Yeah," she admitted. "But I'm afraid if I send another text or make another call, I'm going to turn into a stalker. Would it be weird and clingy to panic if a guy doesn't contact you for three days? Oh God, it is, isn't it? It's official. I'm turning into a needy girlfriend."

Cookie swiveled around in her chair to consider her. "Come on, you're not being needy. Sometimes guys need some space, and time to pump the brakes a little. But you know, Hunter doesn't seem like the type."

"How so?"

"I saw how he was with you at the charity ball. That man is besotted. He's probably been kidnapped or is lying in a ditch somewhere."

Kathryn gave her an ironic stare. "Is this you trying to help, Cook?"

Cookie batted her fake eyelashes at her. "I do my best."

Kathryn shook her head at her friend. Cookie was a couple of years older than her and the sort of woman who, through the artful application of makeup and good taste in clothes, always seemed to have herself pulled together. Her clothes fit immaculately over her trim figure, her dyed raven hair was perfectly curled, and her nails never had a chip. She was a single divorcée with no kids. And after some of her love life's notorious ups and downs, Cookie had developed a healthy suspicion of men. But even so, after the charity ball, her pal was firmly on #teamHunter.

The practice phone rang, and Cookie answered it. After conferring with the patient, she said, "Your four o'clock called to say they have a sick child and need to reschedule. Shall I?"

Kathryn nodded, still distractedly scrolling, hoping she'd hear something, anything from Hunter.

Almost like a miracle, a text popped onto her screen from him.

Kathryn, I have something I need to say.

Cold dread washed over her, and she watched those

terrible texting dots dance as he typed. She didn't like the sound of this.

I think it's time you and I parted ways. It's taken me some reflection to finally come to this, but I don't think I can be with you when I'm not really over Laney's death. I need more time— maybe a lot more time. And a woman like you shouldn't have to wait for me. It could be years. It could be never.

Kathryn actually felt the color drain from her face. Maybe her heart stopped beating entirely.

She was paralyzed for a moment, but soon she started typing.

So that's it then. You're being noble. You're breaking up with me. BY TEXT?

It wouldn't go any better if I called you by phone.

Anger pooled deep in Kathryn's gut and radiated out until it burned the top of her scalp and tingled the ends of her fingers. *How dare he?* After everything they'd shared? He walked away, saying he wasn't ready? Shouldn't he have told her this *before* she'd slept with him a zillion times? Before he'd said they'd have a relationship? Before he'd made Wilson adore him? *The bastard!*

Her hand itched to type a thousand things. She wanted to rail, to scream, to pound on his chest. Had he ever really felt anything for her? She'd believed so. Hell, he'd said he loved her. *Loved. Her.* How stupid she'd been to believe those words, uttered so soon. What was she expecting with the whirlwind nature of this thing? That she'd meet Prince Charming and go off into the sunset together after *not even a month?*

One thing was for sure—Kathryn didn't need this. She'd

had enough of men who didn't know their own mind, who seemed caring and kind one minute and the next were throwing you out like yesterday's trash. This was her life's story, getting dumped. And she wasn't going to spend another minute beating herself up, wondering why. It was *his* problem. *His loss.*

If Hunter Holliday wasn't "ready" for her, he could go to hell. She'd never stand by, soggy with tears, begging a man to love her again.

Never again!

Kathryn's fingers shook, but she finally typed out her reply.

You said you loved me. But if you don't want me, I won't ask you to stay. Goodbye, Hunter.

She practically stared a hole into her phone, waiting for him to respond, waiting for him to say *but I do want you.* But he never did. There was...*silence.*

Cookie furrowed her brows. "Girlfriend, are you all right? You look like you're gonna toss your lunch. What did you see on that phone?"

The devastation must have been branded on her face. When Cookie looked up from her desk, her eyes widened. "Oh my Lord. Sweetie...did you hear from Hunter?"

Kathryn's mouth felt like it was full of sand, but she finally managed to answer. "He broke up with me. By text." She turned the phone around so Cookie could see.

Honestly, Kathryn thought she was smarter than this. What a stupid, stupid child she'd been, to fall for man so fast. Hunter was complicated, and so was she. What did she think was going to happen? As Cookie snatched the phone and began reading, heat burned in her cheeks as the humiliation began to spread through her.

"That rat bastard," Cookie spat, her mouth set in a thin, angry line. "I sure never saw that comin'." She grabbed

Kathryn's hand and squeezed it. "Oh, honey, I'm so sorry. You didn't deserve this. Would it help if I told you all men are pigs?"

"No." Kathryn chuckled ruefully. "Even if it's true."

Cookie sat up in her chair, her eyes suddenly twinkling with mischief. "You know what? There's only one cure for a broken heart—a girls' night out. I'll find you a sitter for Wilson. And after the office closes, you and me, we'll go out and get us a pitcher of margaritas and a big, cheesy plate of nachos, and we'll hash all this out. Then we'll go to the ice cream shop and split one of those ice cream sundaes that are as big as your head. When we've stuffed ourselves, you can waddle over to my place, and I'll help you make a Hunter-shaped voodoo doll. I'll even make screaming noises when you stick in the pins. Come on! It will be fun!"

Maybe it would be. But Kathryn's heart felt like it weighed a thousand pounds. "That's really nice of you to offer, Cook, but I think, right now, I want to go home. Clear my schedule, maybe until noon tomorrow?"

"All right, girlfriend. But you call me if you need anything, okay? I do home deliveries."

Kathryn reached down and gave Cookie a hug. "Thanks. I'll see you tomorrow."

Absently she gathered up her things and trudged up the steps to her condo. She'd never been so glad to work above her office. She felt drained, mind, body, and soul. Kicking off her boots, she padded over to the pantry. Thank God there was still a half bottle of Zinfandel left.

With shaking hands, she poured nearly all of it into a tall tumbler until it was about a quarter inch from the top. She tipped her head back and sucked about half of it down before she finally stopped. Despite her dubious genetic heritage, she'd never felt the need to drink excessively. But damn, that wine sure tasted good right now.

Willing herself not to cry, she laid her head down on the cool surface of her kitchen table. She curled her arms over her head, shutting out the light.

This whole mess had been inevitable, wasn't it? Thrown together by the wreck, Kathryn and Hunter had no choice but to come together. Their relationship had flourished in a hothouse of forced proximity, and in a weird magical place, at that.

Had it all been a dream? How had they even ended up there, in Christmas Pass? Was the weight of their wishing for something better in their lives what had made it appear?

She almost wished she could've been trapped there forever. Because when the rubber met the road, and real life intruded, Hunter apparently didn't have what it took to keep things going. Apparently, their relationship couldn't survive when the pixie dust wore off. *Apparently,* there hadn't been anything else between them but mutual need and attraction. He'd only mouthed the L-word because he'd felt like he should. He'd never cared about her.

Except, why did it feel like he did?

And why did it seem like her insides had been removed with a grappling hook? If she were really honest with herself, she'd have to admit that she cared about Hunter Holliday more than she'd ever cared about any man. She'd loved him with everything she had. But it wasn't meant to be. She'd opened herself up to him entirely, without reservation. And he'd handed her back her heart, as if she'd given him a gift that was the wrong size, or something.

Just when she was about to pour herself a hot bath and mope, Wilson burst through the door, breaking up her pity party. "Momma!" he cried, "what are you doin' here?"

"Oh." She groaned, raising her head up and straightening her clothes. "I had a patient cancel. I decided to take it easy for a bit."

"Does taking it easy usually include wine?"

She huffed out a bitter chuckle. "Often, child."

Wilson raced over and gave her a quick hug. "Guess what, Momma? I got a package! The delivery guy came right as I was walking up. It's out on the porch!"

Kathryn stood up as her boy raced to drag it in. The box was so big the boy could barely get it through the door. "What in the devil? I didn't order you anything."

Wilson was nearly beside himself with glee. "It's not from you. It's from Hunter! Same-day delivery, too, so you know it's important. Aw man, aw man! This is going to be *so cool!*"

Kathryn cut the box open with box cutters and held her breath while Wilson rid the box of all its protective stuffing. When he lifted the last of it out, his little face fell.

"Look, Momma!" He pointed. "It's my robot. And it's all...*done.*"

Wilson pulled the robot out. It *was* done, and done beautifully. Hunter had painted it up with a Black Lightning logo and blue flames, and had added an extra arm for flipping over opposing bots.

"We were supposed to do this *together*, Momma..." Wilson frowned, his voice trailing off.

"I know, honey. You know what? There's a letter inside. Why don't you read it out loud to me."

Wilson tore at the envelope clumsily but finally got it out.

He held it up with both hands as he read. *"Buddy—I know you weren't expecting this, but it turns out that I'm not going to be able to work with you in the shop like I thought I was. It's been a real treat being your friend, Wilson. But I don't think things are going to work out between your momma and me, and I don't want to lead you on. I'm sorry things happened this way. Someday, I*

know you'll get a great stepdaddy. You deserve it.
—Hunter."

Wilson threw down the letter, and the devastation in his eyes tore her heart to pieces. His eyes blurred with tears. "Did you know?"

Kathryn's throat was so tight she could barely speak. "He texted me and told me he wanted to break up, right before you came home."

Her dear, dear boy stood there, quivering on his feet as a tear escaped down his cheek. He quickly wiped it with his sleeve. "I really liked him. Why doesn't he love us no more?"

"Anymore, baby. It's *any*more." Her knees started to shake, and her chest heaved with her misery. Too weak to stand, she slid back into her chair again. Wilson crawled into her lap and laid his head on her shoulder—something he hadn't done in an age. She wrapped her arms around him, and took a long shaky breath. "He lost his wife three years ago in a car crash, and he said he hasn't gotten over her death. But honestly, I don't know why he left. Not really. He's just...gone."

She ruffled the hair out of his eyes with her fingertip. His precious face was so filled with hurt and disappointment. His chin wobbled, and he blinked, trying to hold back more tears that were threatening to well there. Wilson quickly tucked his chin down, so she wouldn't see. He didn't want to upset her.

And wasn't that precisely like something she would do?

Her heart hurt, actually hurt and throbbed, like it might break. Oh God, it was all just too much.

Years ago, she'd sworn she'd never let another man make her cry again. But against her will, against every instinct she'd ever had, she started to sob. And she wasn't sure when she'd ever stop.

CHAPTER 31

IT HAD BEEN two weeks since she'd gotten unceremoniously dumped, and Kathryn was still miserable beyond words. But she had, at least, become functional again. She could paste on a fake smile and power through her day. Her devastation was like a low-grade, atmospheric hum—something that was profoundly disorienting but could be isolated and ignored, nonetheless.

So she was shocked when Cookie popped into her office to tell her that there was someone on the line from Holliday Hot Rods.

"It's not Hunter, is it?" she asked.

Thinking it over, Cookie clucked her tongue. "No, I'd know that boy's drawl anywhere. It's someone else. Whoever it is has an odd, gruff kind of voice. Should I tell him to shove off?"

That must be Hopper. Why would *he* be calling her? Kathryn paused for a moment—not seeing what good could come out of this. But she told Cookie to forward the call, anyway.

Hopper was apologetic as he reintroduced himself. But the man didn't take very long getting to the point.

"Kathryn, you've gotta get up here. Hunter is really losin' it."

She massaged the knot at the base of her neck. "I don't see how this is my problem. Hunter made it very clear that he doesn't want me in his life anymore. And I'm loathe to go against his wishes."

"Did he really—" Hopper growled and muttered a couple of curses. "I swear to God, I'm going to smack that boy upside the head."

"Didn't he tell you? He sent me a text two weeks ago saying he wasn't ready to go any further in our relationship."

"Ignorant ass," Hop muttered. "Doesn't he know you're the best thing that ever happened to him? We were all so happy to see him with you. It was like he started to come back to life again. He was turning back into the old Hunter we all knew. You've gotta make him take you back. You *have* to."

Kathryn snorted. "Oh, yeah. That's what I want to do —*make* a man take me back. No, I don't, Hop. I don't have to do a damn thing. He doesn't want me, end of story."

"I'm tellin you—nothing about this adds up," Hopper pleaded. "It was all too sudden, too weird. Hunter was great and whistlin' a happy tune one day. Then the next day, he comes down to work with bloody knuckles, looking like shit, like he'd barely gotten an hour's sleep. Then, he goes out to meet Mike at the storage shed. And after that, we've seen neither hide nor hair of the man. Hunter's been missing client appointments. He's hardly working. His deadlines are slippin' left and right. I finally cornered him at his apartment. He's not talkin', and he's rattling around here like the walking dead. I'm telling you, something happened. Something big."

"Look, Hunter made it very clear he wanted to be on his own—"

"And that's the last damn thing he needs! You know it! His family is in another country, for God's sake. And we can't do a thing with him. You're the only one who can help him, and that's a damn fact."

Kathryn didn't answer for a long time. Her heart hurt too much.

"He saved you," Hopper uttered. "Now it's time for you to save him."

Kathryn strode into Holliday Hot Rods on jittery, trembling legs. Which was ridiculous, of course. Things were over with Hunter. D-O-N-E done. He'd made that more than clear. She was only here on a mission of mercy, more in her capacity as a psychologist than an ex. She owed it to Hunter to help, since he'd saved her life. But that was all she owed the man.

Even though he'd been missing a lot of work, Kathryn had been sure she'd find Hunter somewhere nearby. But Hopper trotted up to her instead. The rest of staff dropped their tools and came right up behind him.

"Is he here?" she asked.

"Nope," Leta replied. "He left about an hour ago. Said he had things to do."

"So he's not upstairs?"

"No," Hopper answered. "I saw him drive off. Anyone know where he went?"

They exchanged glances and shook their heads.

"You know, you should check out Greenbrier Memorial Gardens," Ross piped up.

All their heads swiveled in Ross's direction, their faces lined with varying but consistently worried expressions.

"It's where Laney is buried," Ross explained. "I have to

go out that way to get to my house. And I've seen his car parked up there three times this week."

"I'll bet you're right," Hopper mused. He motioned for Kathryn to follow him to the reception desk, where he wrote down the address and handed it to her.

Kathryn took the paper, trying to keep a stiff upper lip about this whole mess. The idea of seeing his face again might just be more than she could take. And in these circumstances, there truly was no telling how *he* would react to *her*. *Am I really strong enough to do this?*

Hop gave her arm a sympathetic pat. "I'm sorry. I'd go with you. But I really think he'll do better if it's just you. Too many people will make him antsy."

Though she wished she had backup, she knew Hopper was right. They made arrangements for her to come back to the shop if Hunter wasn't there, and they'd all fan out to find him, if necessary.

The team wished her luck, and she turned her Suburban down the road with grim determination. All the way to the cemetery, she debated about what she'd say to Hunter. She'd only known the man for such a short time. Yet, she'd connected with him, maybe more than she'd connected with anyone. That's why she couldn't get past the hurt. Honestly, every time her mind turned to their breakup, her anger grew. Where did the man get off, running away like a damn coward?

Nothing about Hunter's behavior made sense, on the face of it. The man she'd known in Christmas Pass was grieving and traumatized. But his wife's death was nearly four years past, and he seemed ready to move on. Yes, he still had guilt and anger to address, but Hunter seemed happy about the new path his life had taken. He seemed genuinely excited about their relationship, and they'd never said an unkind word to one another. So why the sudden backslide? What was she missing here?

Kathryn cursed herself under her breath. She was doing it again—making excuses for him. It was the same tired old train of thought she'd been riding on for the last two weeks, and it got her nowhere. Hunter didn't want her. He didn't want to fight for her. *The end.*

Except that wasn't the end, was it? No, she had to relive all this, every time she looked at Wilson's face. The poor boy was every bit as heartbroken as her. He'd been moping around, barely showing interest in anything since Hunter had called things off. It wasn't too hard to understand why the boy was so upset. Even though they'd only been together a short time, they'd packed a lot of quality time into those days. Wilson had gotten close to Hunter, and thought of him as a friend, and a mentor. Maybe he even thought Hunter was a man who could make his momma happy. Maybe he thought Hunter was the sort of man who would stay.

As it turned out, they'd all been wrong about that.

Kathryn tensed her fingers around the steering wheel, and gritted her teeth. Today was *not* about their breakup, and she was dead set and determined not to let her devastation show. No, she'd swoop in, and maybe help convince Hunter he needed therapy. She'd find him a counselor or some kind of therapy group, and that would be it. That was all she could manage. And, frankly, it was all he deserved.

Before she knew it, she had reached the lush, well-tended cemetery gates.

Winding through the manicured drive, she quickly spotted Hunter's black Mustang, parked at the bottom of the hill. In the distance, she could just make out Hunter, crouched in front of a large black granite tombstone. He seemed so alone, so desolate. Against her will, the sight pulled painfully at her heart. She swallowed, steeling herself.

Kathryn parked her car and quietly walked up behind him. He was completely oblivious to her approach, as if he were in some kind of trance. Hunter wasn't crying. He wasn't praying. No, he sat stock still, staring dully at the tombstone.

The tombstone was finely crafted, with two interlocking hearts carved from black granite. Kathryn's breath caught as she realized the stone was two-sided and Hunter's name was already carved on it, with his year of birth and an empty space for the year of his inevitable death. But it was what she saw sitting just below that inscription that told her everything she needed to know.

There, sitting among the piles of roses he'd brought, was the unmistakable silhouette of a pregnancy test stick. It was too yellowed to be new, or readable. But she could read the lid of the box it sat in just fine. *You're going to be a Daddy!* And there was a date. A due date, three years old.

Dear God. It's Laney's.

As the news took root in her brain, the anger she'd so carefully bottled up began to drain away. *Oh Jesus, poor Hunter!*

Laney had been pregnant the night of the crash, hadn't she?

Had he known?

If the way he was acting right now was any indication, she'd bet not. His grief was too new, too fresh. Somehow, he'd just found that box. And he couldn't handle it.

Dear God in heaven. Could anything be more horrible?

Her heart broke for him. She couldn't move, couldn't breathe. The weight of his despair hung like a shroud over them both. And all her carefully prepared speeches drained out of her head.

But now she understood. She truly understood everything.

Hunter still didn't notice her standing on the hill behind him. She took the moment to collect herself and set her spinning thoughts aside. Kathryn grabbed a small, smooth pebble from the ground, walked up to the tombstone, and placed the rock gently on its cool, polished top.

Hunter startled. "What are you doing?" he muttered, as if it cost him even to form a syllable.

She got down on her knees in front of him. "Placing a rock on the top of a tombstone. It's an ancient way of paying respect to the dead."

He flinched and turned his head away. His jaw tensed with irritation. "Why are you here, Kathryn?"

"Your friends are worried about you."

That brought a quick reaction. He turned to her again, his eyes weary and somehow piercing all at once.

She met his gaze. "Okay, *I'm* worried about you."

"It's not your job to be worried about me," he ground out. "I'm not your boyfriend, remember?"

"Yes, you've made that clear enough." She tried her best to swallow down the zing of hurt. "But I care about you anyway."

He huffed out a surprised breath and stared bleakly at the tombstone. "You shouldn't."

"I know."

That seemed to piss him off. Hunter jumped up to his feet and wheeled around to face her. "I don't need your worry, or your pity. What I need is for you to get in your car, drive all the way to Roanoke, and never contact me again. Do you understand? It's over! You need to leave!"

"Why, Hunter? Why should I leave?" she shouted right back, snatching the test stick off the grave. "Because of *this?*"

Stony and white-faced, Hunter appeared totally at a loss for words.

Kathryn got up, set her feet, and stood her ground. "You didn't know, did you? Somehow, you just found out. That's what all this is about, isn't it?"

He shuddered, and Kathryn watched as the last drops of emotional strength seemed to visibly leave his body. Another man might've started to cry. But Hunter's eyes were hollow and red-ringed, like he didn't have another tear left in him.

She waited for a long, long moment, the air charged with his unspoken answer.

Hunter. Ah, my poor, dear Hunter.

"I'm right, aren't I?" she finally whispered.

Hunter's face brimmed with as much anguish as any man could bear. "I found it by chance at the storage unit the other day, in a drawer in our old bedroom nightstand. She'd wrapped it up in pretty wrap. She'd told me she had a present for me the night of the crash. We were on our way out to have this big romantic dinner she'd arranged. Did you know that? I thought it was just another nice night out. But it was important, and...she never made it home. Never made it so she could..."

He didn't have to say more. Kathryn leaped forward, and wrapped her arms around his shaking frame.

Hunter's heart felt leaden, sinking like a stone in his chest. Kathryn, *dammit, why did you come?*

Dammit to hell! He didn't want her to see him like this —battered and so, so broken. He couldn't speak to finish his sentence. Frankly, he could hardly stand up right now.

Hunter thought he knew what it was to be truly beside himself. But no, he'd never felt more wrecked with grief and remorse than he did at this very moment. It was almost like he was looking down at himself from above and seeing what a total loss he'd become.

No, he hadn't even begun to hit bottom. *Until now.* Kathryn had held that pregnancy test up in front of her, and he couldn't look away from it. He couldn't hide from the biggest failure a man could experience—the failure to protect his spouse and child.

"Why couldn't I keep them safe?" he whispered before he even realized it was coming out of his mouth.

Fierce determination lit Kathryn's face. She put down the stick and wrapped both her hands around his. He stared at their joined hands, wondering how this sensation could be so foreign and yet so familiar at the same time. "You're blaming yourself for the wreck as if you *intended* to spin out the car, as if you *wanted* to. It's not the same."

"Isn't it?" Hunter spat, wrenching his hands away. "It might as well be! I killed them as surely as if I'd whipped out a gun and pulled the trigger! I shouldn't have driven on roads that icy without snow chains. I should've taken a different car. I should've—"

"Hunter, stop it! You can't—"

"The hell I can't!" Hunter boomed. "Do you know what the difference between life and death is, Kathryn? A half turn of a steering wheel!"

She canted her pretty head at him, clearly not understanding what he was saying.

He sighed. "When you're driving in a car and you start sliding on the ice, there's only one thing you can do to fix it —turn your steering wheel in the direction of the skid. Nobody knows that better than me. I fix banged-up cars for a goddamned living. But the day of the crash, I—I panicked. I turned the wheel the wrong way and we spun out, bad."

"Yes," Kathryn insisted, "but even then—"

"No." Hunter put his finger over her lips to hush her. "No." He was shaking all over, the agony of it squeezing his chest like a boa constrictor. "If we hadn't been spinning, the truck would have hit *me*—on the *driver's side*. But I made us turn and turn like some awful game of spin the bottle. When we stopped, Laney was directly in the line of that coal truck. Do you have any idea what that was like? My beautiful, wonderful wife was sitting in the middle of a target, the truck getting closer and closer, and I couldn't even open my mouth to warn her..."

He bent down and snatched up the box that held the test stick of the gravestone. He pointed to the date on the inside with shaking fingers. "See this date?"

Kathryn nodded, mutely, tears welling up in her eyes.

"This was six months after she died. And that's a big thing, cause she'd had those miscarriages..." He drew a ragged breath, misery swamping him. "You see, the doctor said if she could get through the first trimester, the baby would be likely to live. She must have known for a while she was pregnant. Lord, she would have been so excited. But we'd been disappointed before, you know, and she didn't want to tell me until..."

Despair clogged his throat, and the world started to spin a little. "That's why she'd made such a big deal about our night out. This baby, it would have made it. She wanted to tell me..."

It was too much, too much. The tears tore through him, deep, wrenching sobs that seemed to resonate in every cell of his body. The memory of it howled through his soul all over again, as bright and hot and horrible as it had been the day Laney had died.

"I couldn't save her!" he wailed. "I couldn't save our baby!"

He swayed on his feet, the world seeming to go black

around the edges. Dimly, he was aware of Kathryn catching him and lowering him slowly to the ground again. She slid her slim arms around him, holding him as if she could somehow put the pieces of him back together.

He held on to her for dear life.

Finally, he managed to bring himself under control, his tears replaced by an aching hollowness again. The shaking began to subside. And Kathryn placed her hands on his cheeks, forcing his head up to look at her. But she didn't say a word. She brushed away the tears instead, and kissed the tracks they made, slowly, reverently.

"Kathryn, don't."

But her stormy eyes stripped his heart bare. She shook her head with a decisive *no*.

Suddenly her mouth was on him, soft and sure, kissing him with a tenderness that was all comfort and no demands. And Hunter met that kiss, falling into the deep of it, grasping for it, as if she was the one thing that would make his life roadworthy again. But how could she be?

Ryn.

Brave Ryn. The woman I'll never deserve.

Remembering himself, he pushed her back, and she tottered back on her haunches and onto the ground.

She kicked up her chin with indignation. "You can't push me away that easily."

"I have to," he wailed. "Look at me! I'll never be right! I'll never get over this! Is this what you want?"

"Yes!" she shouted, as if he was stupid for even asking the question. "Yes, goddammit, I want you! I *love* you, Hunter Holliday. Don't you get it? When I said it, I *meant* it. Didn't you?"

And with that, he felt like he was freefalling, tumbling, unable to catch himself.

His world tilted onto a different spin. Did he really just

hear that? How could she love him? After the way he'd treated her? After seeing what a total loss of a human being he was? Did she think he was some kind of fixer-upper, a man who could be rehabbed with a few spare parts?

But Kathryn didn't waver. "Tell me you don't feel the same way," she demanded. "Tell me you have no feelings for me, that what we had didn't mean anything, and I'll drive down that road and never bother you again."

But he couldn't answer her. His vocal cords were frozen in shock.

"Tell me you don't love me!" she yelled. She may have been flat on her ass on the cold, hard ground, but she was a woman undeterred. Chin quivering, she stared him down, right in the eye, her fists balled up by her sides.

"I can't," he finally managed to whisper. "I could never —" He pulled her up to him and held on to her, stroking her hair, smelling the hint of jasmine and musk that clung to her like...like home. She was his *home*, wasn't she?

The idea rocked him to his foundations.

Maybe it really was that simple. Maybe he could hope. Maybe Kathryn was the light in the dark that would lead him back to himself, to life. He had to move toward that light, toward her.

And God, how he wanted her. There was no denying it. He'd forgotten how much he missed Kathryn's touch. The warm weight of her arms around him was unbearably perfect. "You *know* I love you," he whispered. The words had tumbled out of his mouth, all on their own. But he found he couldn't bring himself to regret them. "You've known it all along, even when I wasn't strong enough to admit it, even when I don't deserve it. I do...*love* you. Damn, I love you so, so much, Ryn."

"Oh! Thank God!" she cried, in exhilaration as much as relief. Tears splashed down her cheeks. And he held her while she shook in his arms, soothing her, rubbing circles along her spine.

"God, I'm so sorry for everything—for what I said, for pushing you and Wilson away. I'm so sorry..." His voice cracked. "I'm such an idiot. Can you ever forgive me?"

Kathryn stroked his hair, and smiled. "Yes. And hopefully someday, you'll learn how to forgive yourself."

He looked away, considering that. "And how am I supposed to do that?"

"By holding onto the people who love you, that's how. Your life isn't defined by your mistakes. It's defined by the future. You have to keep on living and keep on loving. You owe that to Laney. You can't close yourself off to other people because you lost her. You can't close yourself off to life. Otherwise, all the love she gave you and all the ways she worked to make your life better? All that will have been for nothing."

He couldn't argue with that. Reaching his hand out, he stroked her satiny cheek. Just as he was about to kiss her again, a red-tinged cardinal, a female of a brood pair, landed lightly on the top of the tombstone.

A redbird, of all the things. Of all the days.

Neither Kathryn nor Hunter made a sound. They stared in fascination as the bird hopped along the ridge of the stone, looking intelligently at them, back and forth, back and forth. It seemed to be considering them, measuring them. Then it scooted over until it was perched over the pebble Kathryn had placed on tombstone. For one long, breathless moment, the little thing cocked its head at Hunter one last time. With the pebble still in its grasp, it flew off to the heavens, off and away, until they couldn't see it anymore.

"Goodbye, Redbird," Hunter whispered.

ONE CHRISTMAS LATER

"It's your laaaast chance before I put the tray away," Alice sang. She held up one of the homemade chocolate chip cookies she'd made earlier in the day and waved it enticingly in Daddy's direction.

Daddy skittered over like a moth to a flame and bit off a piece while it was still in her hand. "How can I resist so much sugar in one place?" Daddy pinched her on the bottom as he snatched it from her hand.

Alice blushed and laughed.

The woman had turned out to be the perfect partner for her daddy. Alice Rosegard was lovely, kind and full of fun—just as Daddy had described her. The lovebirds exchanged another heated look. Kathryn rolled her eyes, smiling all the while. Those two were so sweet—they could give you cavities. And Kathryn couldn't be happier about it.

Happiness seemed to be catching at the Holliday family farmhouse. It was the first Christmas after she and Hunter had gotten married, and with the house completely decorated with live pine garlands and a towering Christmas tree, it truly felt like home. Now with her family all around her, maybe she'd have her perfect Christmas, after all.

Everyone pitched in with the Christmas Eve dinner dishes, Wilson included, until they'd cleared every last crumb, and the expansive country kitchen was sparkling. They toddled around the corner to the great room and put their feet up in front of the fire.

Kathryn surveyed the room with the satisfaction of a woman who had things decorated exactly the way she wanted it. The Holliday family farmhouse had truly become a place where Hunter and Kathryn could blend their lives, and start a new chapter. They both had sold off most of their things, opting to create a new space all their own. They'd chosen handmade furniture from the Amish country, all of which blended beautifully with all the stained glass accents Mike and Josie had left behind. She and Hunter did keep some things though—Laney's vinyl album collection and favorite stenciled armoire for instance, as well as Kathryn's quilts and fiber art, and the big white iron bed from her old condo. As it turned out, Hunter was *very* fond of it.

Wilson picked up the snow globe Hunter had bought for her in Christmas Pass. The boy cranked it, and shook it hard enough to whip the glittery snowflakes into a proper blizzard. He grinned with satisfaction as the music box chimed out "Home for the Holidays." Kathryn waited for the childhood memories of Momma's broken snow globe to crowd her mind. But they didn't. Somehow, displaying it smack in the middle of her coffee table had taken the sting out of the object. Now, it had become her son's favorite Christmas decoration. And he could play with it as much as he liked.

Wilson cocked his head. "Momma, how come the plaque on the side of this is different? It used to say *Welcome to Christmas Pass*. But now it says *Wild, Wonderful West Virginia*."

Daddy chuckled. "You know enchantment like that can't live in the real world. When Christmas Pass disappeared, its magic did, too."

Alice rolled her eyes. "That crazy story again? Boy, I've heard of family legends, but you all really take this whole Christmas magic thing seriously."

"It's true! Christmas Pass is real! We were there!" Wilson cried.

Daddy had broken down and told Alice about Christmas Pass. But the poor woman only took it for another one of Daddy's heavily embroidered tales. Kathryn could hardly blame her for not believing Daddy. Daddy told so many exaggerated stories, he had become a bit like the *Boy who Cried Wolf*. No matter how much they backed him up, poor Alice would never realize the man was telling the truth.

Daddy bent down to Wilson's level, tapped the side of his nose, and winked at the boy. "Remember what we agreed to say, whenever the topic of Christmas Pass came up?"

Wilson saluted like a soldier. "What goes in Christmas Pass, stays in Christmas Pass!"

Daddy guffawed, and slapped his grandson on the back. "That's right, kiddo!"

Eager to change the subject, Kathryn took note of the time. "It's ten o'clock," she declared, giving Wilson a pointed glance. "Time for you to go to bed, mister."

"But we haven't done the gift thing!" Wilson whined. "You always say we all can pick out one gift to open before bed on Christmas Eve."

Kathryn looked over at her husband. "We haven't really discussed it, but do you want to keep that tradition?"

Hunter shrugged. "I don't see why not." He sat down on their favorite leather sofa and beckoned to Kathryn to come snuggle up under his arm. She readily agreed, propping her head up on his strong chest and tucking her feet underneath her. Her cheek landed on the "on" button on his tacky Christmas sweater though, and she groaned. A full-on light show erupted on the front of that cheap acrylic thing, illuminating the branches of a Christmas tree design that covered his whole chest. At least this time, the sweater's music feature didn't come on. He'd been having far too much fun, chasing her around the house all day, torturing her with its barking dog rendition of "Jingle Bells."

Hunter chuckled sheepishly, and switched it off.

Wilson scuttled to the back of the tree, lugging out an enormous and very heavy box wrapped in striped green foil paper. The package was about as tall as he was. "I want this one!" he cried. "It's from Hunter."

"Okay, child, open it up!" Kathryn answered.

Wilson eagerly tore into the wrap, throwing it over his head as he went. The plain brown box perplexed the boy momentarily. But Daddy leaned over and opened up the taped seals with his pocketknife. Wilson practically dove into the box and squealed with delight.

"I don't believe it! My own toolbox!" He whooped and danced all around, making everybody smile.

Daddy helped him cut the rest of the box away. It wasn't hard to see why the boy was so excited. The toolbox was quite the outfit—about four feet tall—made from red painted steel, with several drawer trays to hold every kind of item. Each tray was filled with tools that went far beyond the standard wrench and hammer sets. Wilson was mesmerized, more awestruck than he'd been with any other toy or video game she'd bought him before. Of course, it was the perfect gift. Hunter had spent weeks scouting for the right tools to include.

"That toolbox is going to live at Holliday Hot Rods," Hunter told him. "This is a full set of mechanic's tools. It'll be your own set, and nobody else will be able to use them. And now that you've got the right tools, you'll be able to help me with anything in the shop that doesn't involve a press or a blowtorch. Does that sound okay to you?"

Wilson didn't answer, but ran over to him instead, and jumped in his lap. He gave Hunter a long hug. "Thank you, thank you! Thank you soooo much! Are you going to let me build a car?"

Hunter chuckled. "I'll let you *help me* build cars, as your schedule allows. Maybe by the time you're a teenager, you'll have the skills you need to actually build one of your own. You should start saving up now so you can afford the parts."

"I'm going to do it! I'm going to have a Mustang some-day!" Wilson cried, leaping back off Hunter's lap again to go inspect each and every tool in the box. The boy's wide-eyed wonder was infectious.

"All right, Daddy, it's your turn," Kathryn urged.

Daddy walked around the tree, mulling over his choices, finally settling on a gift from Alice. He peeled off the ribbon on top of a flat, rectangular box. Surely she hadn't gotten him a tie, had she?

When Daddy lifted off the lid, he guffawed, pulling out an apron that said *Kiss the Cook*. Then he found a piece of paper under it. "Now, this is perfect. A one-year subscrip-tion to Apron Ties! Thank you, baby!"

Alice beamed as he gave her an appreciative kiss on the cheek. "Apron Ties is local to our area," she explained to the rest of them. "They send you those boxes with food and recipes to make the most wonderful healthy dishes. Every-thing is organic and locally grown. Since I'm at work all day, your father has developed a real interest in cooking, and cooking healthy these days."

"'Cause of you," Daddy added. "I got a reason to eat healthy. Gotta be slim and trim."

She shoved his shoulder playfully. "Now, you know I don't care what you look like, Huck. But you can't deny you feel better, right?"

"Like a new man." Daddy flexed his muscles and struck a pose, for effect. "But you're never going to convince me to like avocadoes. A fella has to draw the line somewhere. Now it's time for you to pick out a gift. How about the one with the big gold bow over there?"

Alice tentatively tiptoed over to the tree. "This one?" She pointed. Daddy nodded. She tore through the paper and opened the box, her brows knit in confusion. "A Hawaiian shirt?"

"The real gift is under the shirt," Daddy instructed.

Alice did as he said, lifting the shirt onto her lap. Then she whooped in joy. "Airplane tickets! To Jamaica! Oh, honey! It's too much!"

"No, it ain't." Daddy kissed her on the cheek. "I figured we could take a quick trip down there, you know, scout it out and all. Might be the perfect place to have our wedding later. We could get everything set up while we're there."

Alice hugged the stuffing out of Daddy. And the man enjoyed every minute. Everyone clapped and hollered at the idea of having a wedding in Jamaica. Huck and Alice had been engaged for a month, so Kathryn was delighted to see them making some strides toward getting the wedding planned.

When everyone settled down, Kathryn chose a gift, going for an envelope that was peeking from the top of her stocking that hung over the fireplace. Hunter had hidden this behind a box of her favorite truffles a day or two ago, and the curiosity was eating her alive. But she'd been good. This year, she'd managed not to peel back the wrap on any of the presents, even once.

Hunter raised an eyebrow at her choice. "It would figure you'd go right for that. That's probably the biggest gift for you under the tree."

"This little thing?" Kathryn held the envelope up to the light, but couldn't get any clues. "How could it be a big gift?"

Mischief twinkled in Hunter's eyes. "You'll see."

She tore open the envelope to find a picture of the most beautiful saddle she'd ever seen—a black, hand-tooled woman's saddle designed to be comfortable and durable. Underneath, he'd written, *"I hid it out in the barn."* Sneaky boy! It was *perfect.* "Oh, Hunter," she breathed, and her heart swelled with gratitude. How could it not?

They'd rehabbed the barn and bought three horses—one for each of them. She couldn't even describe how wonderful it'd been to ride again over the rugged hills of this lush green farm. Most days, they managed to get in a sunrise ride before Hunter left for work and she went in to her new position as head counselor at the Veteran's Hospital nearby. She could always count on Hunter to drop Wilson off at his new private school on his way in to the shop.

She ran back to the couch and gave her darling husband a quick kiss. "It's the prettiest saddle I've ever seen, Hunter. I can't wait to try it out tomorrow. Now, it's time for you to open yours. Which one do you want to open?"

"I've been wondering what that card is about in my stocking." He made a beeline over to the fireplace.

Kathryn crossed her arms over her chest. "Ah-hah! You *were* snooping! And here you said you didn't care about your presents."

"I don't," Hunter replied. "I've got you."

"Awwwww," the whole family chimed in.

Wilson rolled his eyes. "Are you gonna start kissin' again?"

"I make no promises, boy." Hunter wagged his finger. "But I am curious about this." He cracked open the card and found the gift she'd really bought for them both—couples massages at the Greenbrier Spa.

"Now *that* looks fun!" Hunter hooted, rubbing his hands together.

Kathryn gave him a little peck as he sat back down. "They gave me a good deal since we had our wedding reception there. I've been holding on to that for months."

They had, in actuality, had the wedding at Holliday Hot Rods with all their friends, family, and half the town of Lewisburg in attendance. Then they'd led a parade of all the cars in the shop's showroom from there to the Greenbrier. Their food bill hadn't been small, but it'd been worth every penny. They'd ordered one of practically everything on their catering menu, including a giant cake covered with real flowers. Then they'd danced the night away.

"Smart negotiating." Hunter draped his arm around her, and gave it a squeeze. "I'm ready to go when you are. Wanna go after we come back from our visit to Vancouver?"

"Sounds like a plan," she agreed. It'd be the perfect end to the holiday season this year, one she'd looked forward to with all her heart. This first Christmas in their new home was everything she'd ever hoped for, and after becoming fast friends with Hunter's family, she couldn't wait to spend some quality time enjoying the snow in Canada too. Sterling and Avery even planned to fly in from France to meet them there. After their visit with Hunter's family, her ex planned on spiriting the boy off for more wintry Canadian delights, which no doubt would include skiing.

Watching her family so easy in each other's company, Kathryn realized that they were, at least for now, at peace. The fire crackled and popped in the fireplace, and Daddy and Alice were making eyes at each other, finishing off the last of their non-alcoholic eggnog. Wilson was drowsy with his stomach full of beef Wellington and Yule log. Working together, Alice and Hunter had finally been able to help Kathryn get Momma's recipes right.

Yes, this perfect holiday had been hard won, for all of them.

Kathryn clapped her hands. "Okay, Wilson, you can mess with the tools tomorrow. It's time for bed."

"Aw, I haven't even got through all the drawers yet! Can't I stay up?" he whined.

"Not if you want to get up at zero dark thirty to get into the gifts like you always do," Kathryn answered, brooking no argument.

Wilson grumbled, but he finally acquiesced and shuffled off to his room. Eager to make an early night of it, Daddy and Alice followed.

That left Kathryn and Hunter all alone in front of the fire. Big, fluffy flakes spun and eddied outside their window, dressing the dark velvet night in glittering wonder.

Now it was Kathryn's turn to enjoy the sparkle and shine of their Christmas tree, laden down as it was with the tinsel strands and reproduction ornaments she'd gotten in Christmas Pass. How strange it was that these ornaments would still exist, even though the city they'd come from had collapsed into the magical mists of time. They had all their things from there—her glasses, Hunter's clothes, Daddy's sweatshirt—yet the Christmas Pass tags and branding were all gone, replaced by tags for other well-known national brands. And somehow, their picture from the Founder's

Day celebration changed too. Instead a photo of the family standing in front of the wishing rock, the portrait now showed them in front of the Greenbrier. Kathryn glanced at the photo, sitting in a frame on her end table. Whether it was creepy or cute, she couldn't decide. But she wouldn't change that magical, life-changing holiday for the world.

They never did get a charge to their credit cards for anything from Christmas Pass. Had it all been truly been magic, or some sort of beautiful dream? Kathryn wished she knew. Hunter had told her about meeting that strange couple at the gas station and all their "Brigadoon" conspiracy theories. Hunter seemed to buy into it. But her scientific mind had a bit of a hard time wrapping her head around that crazy story. So, she'd decided to simply file Christmas Pass under "can't be explained."

Kathryn sighed with satisfaction as she looked out at the swirling snow, dotting the moonlit night. "It's so peaceful, so gorgeous out there, isn't it?"

Hunter nuzzled her hair and planted a soft kiss on her temple. "Yeah, but it's still not as gorgeous as the view from the cabin we were in last year."

"Nothing could be as beautiful as that. It wasn't real."

"It sure felt real at the time," Hunter answered, squeezing her tighter. "Truth is, I can't tell you how or why we ended up in Christmas Pass. I'm just damn glad we did. But I think for the record, I'm going to avoid driving on that stretch of road when it's storming. I've had about all the adventure I can take."

Kathryn chuckled. "Yeah, me too."

They were quiet for a long time, enjoying the sensation of being together and soaking up the Christmas peace that had descended on the house.

But then she spotted a shopping bag, over by the couch. "Oh, I almost forgot!" She jumped up and rustled

around in the bag, realizing she had one last thing left
to do.

Hunter grumbled when she disentangled herself from
his languid embrace. She stood with the bag in front of the
tree, and motioned for him to join her.

"I got something new for the tree. I couldn't resist. I
want you to hang it." When he stood in front of the tree, she
pulled out a tissue wrapped item and handed it to him. "I
spotted this in a store downtown when I was out running
errands this morning. A local artisan made it. I couldn't
believe my luck. Go ahead—open it."

Hunter gave her a quizzical look as he tore the paper
back. And there in his hand was a beautiful, wooden, hand-
carved ornament—a cardinal, stained in a muted shade of
red. Hunter's eyes misted over as he hung it in a prime spot,
right in the middle, in the front. The little bird was so life-
like, it almost seemed like it was cocking its head at them.

Kathryn wrapped her arm around his waist as they both
admired it. "You know that old country saying—when a
cardinal appears, loved ones are near. Seemed appropriate. I
think it's just what our tree was missing, don't you?"

"A redbird," he breathed. "Every tree needs a redbird,
doesn't it?" Hunter leaned over and kissed her on the forehead. "This is a beautiful tribute, babe. Thank you."

"I figured before we leave for our trip, we should take
some of our live pine and holly berries over to decorate
Laney's grave, and Momma's too, don't you think? Maybe
we could make it an annual tradition."

"Yes," he answered, smiling softly as he considered the
ornament hanging there. "I'd like that."

She wrapped her arms around her husband and buried
her head in his chest. She breathed deep. Funny how even
now, the smell of his skin reminded her of the mountains.
Of home.

It didn't matter what was under the Christmas tree. This was her real gift—the warmth and comfort of this man. So much good had come to her this year, and every last bit of it had been because of Hunter. Well, perhaps it would be too simple to say it quite like that. Hunter had set in motion a series of events that helped her to make sense of her losses, and make peace with her regrets. Here in this quaint mountain valley, she'd found a new sense of place and purpose—a shared path.

She'd like to think she'd helped Hunter to do the same. Oh, there'd never be a day that went by that they wouldn't wish they could have done things differently. That maybe she'd been able to stop her mother before it was too late, or he'd turned the wheel a different way. Regrets like that never truly *leave* you. But while they couldn't wish away the past, they could face the future knowing they were doing their best with the time they'd been given.

Yeah, when Hunter had found her on that mountainside, he'd saved her, in more ways than one. And now, they were saving each other, one day at a time.

Hunter kissed her on the top of her head. "We've made quite a family here, you, me and Wilson."

Had he been reading her mind?

Hunter's expression was all warmth, and contentment. She couldn't help but smile back at him. "You like that, having a little nuclear family, don't you?"

"I do. More than I can say."

She stroked her fingertips over the stubble on his jaw. "Yeah. Me too."

Hunter searched her face for a couple long moments, as if he was making some kind of decision. "What do you say we make that family a little bigger?"

Her breath caught for a moment from the surprise of it.

414

But it was hardly a shocking question. She'd been thinking about it too. Her implant was set to expire soon and she had wondered ...

Hunter's face brimmed with hope. Clearly he was serious about this. She let out a long breath. "A little brother or sister for Wilson. Our own child. That's what you're asking for?"

He nodded.

A picture of a toddler with Hunter's warm brown eyes flashed in her mind. And the idea took root, deep in her heart. Yes, she'd very much like to have another child, and have it *with him*.

"Are you sure? After what happened with Laney, I'd never want to replace—"

He placed a finger over her lips, to stop her. "That's an opportunity I'll never get back, having a child with Laney. But that doesn't mean we shouldn't have a child together. I love you, Ryn, and you love me. Together, we can put more of that goodness out into the world. What do you say?"

Kathryn couldn't stop a sly smile from spreading across her face. She trailed her finger down his sweater, and poked the tree topper star on his chest. The stupid thing erupted into another one of its crap-tacular light shows. "Well, I say we should get right on that, sparkle pants. Practice makes perfect. You got a dance to go with this floor show?"

"Just this one," he smirked, and threw her over his shoulder before she even realized what had happened.

Kathryn whooped and kicked her feet in mock protest. Her giggles echoed down the hall as he carried her off to their bedroom.

At the Holliday homestead, flames dimmed in the fireplace grate, and a timer turned the Christmas tree lights off with a soft snick. Outside the clouds had cleared, revealing a brilliant full moon. The new-fallen snow carried the moonbeams, turning the rugged landscape into a glitter-frosted dream.

It was going to be another magical night.

The End

DON'T WANT IT TO END?

IT DOESN'T HAVE TO!

Want to know what Kathryn and Hunter's wedding might have been like? Sign up for my email newsletter, and find out ! The wedding planners at the Greenbrier have provided a rundown of all the exciting deets. Best of all, as a VIP reader, you'll get all the exclusive bonus material for all my books as they are released. And you'll be the first to learn of giveaways and deals and new releases. What's not to love?

https://lizajonathan.com/wrecking-christmas-bonus

Turn the page to read an excerpt from the next book in the series, *The Christmas We Knew*, coming October, 2020. You'll fall in love with the hot, magical, second-chance romance between Hopper and Cookie!

CHAPTER ONE

Christmas Eve, mid-afternoon

"You're a good man, Hopper Vance."

Hopper looked into the watery eyes of Mrs. Honeycutt, the sweet little old lady who'd paid him that compliment, and bit back a bitter laugh. *A good man? Yeah, it's way too late for that.*

Swallowing down a twinge of embarrassment, Hopper inclined his head as if he were tipping an imaginary hat. "It's no trouble."

Hopper tightened the last screw on the small boy's bike he'd just finished assembling, one of the Christmas presents he'd talked his employer, Holliday Hot Rods & Collision Repair, into donating for the Honeycutt family. The whole team at the garage had pitched in. It was the least they could do.

In a small town like Lewisburg, West Virginia, everybody knew everybody. So it was common knowledge that old Mrs. Honeycutt was scraping by on social security and Meals on Wheels after her husband had died. The woman was barely keeping the lights on in her decaying metal trailer, perched on the slope of a hill. And then her junkie granddaughter had dropped two little great-grandkids on the woman's doorstep last summer and disappeared.

Hopper had spent his childhood on the receiving end of that kind of parenting. So he was damn glad he could do something to lighten Mrs. Honeycutt's load this holiday. It made him feel, well, almost Christmas-y.

Hopper sighed with satisfaction as he took in the bitchin' little flames he'd painted on the bike himself. No, he'd never be a good man. But a *better* man? Yeah, he could manage that.

The flimsy trailer door opened with a clatter, and Hopper's boss, Hunter Holliday, hulked his broad, athletic frame through the narrow doorway, pulling a big black bag full of Christmas presents. He looked back over his shoulder. "For God's sake, Ross, would you stop pushing? I worked hard on those bows."

Ross quickly dropped the bag at the base of the wobbly wooden stairs and pulled out a present. "Sorry, man." Ross grinned, his bright eyes smiling past his shaggy, jet-black, goth hair. "The bag's too big for the doorway. Here, I'll just take them out and pass them through to you."

Hopper gingerly moved the bike in front of Mrs. Honeycutt's sagging pullout sofa so it'd be out of the way. Adjusting the sheet and blankets, he rolled the bed back up to make room for all the presents. He winced as the rickety frame creaked ominously, then snapped shut way too hard. The kids apparently had been using this rusty, dangerous claptrap for their bed. Somebody could lose a finger. Hopper made a mental note—*next year's charity project: find the kids some beds. And a new couch.*

While their other team member, Leta, worked on painting cheerful snowscapes on the inside of the windows,

Hopper, Ross, and Hunter worked together until one by one, they'd made quite the mountain of fancy wrapped toys, books, clothes, and candy in Mrs. Honeycutt's living area.

Ross pulled out a bigger, unwrapped box. "A Barbie Townhouse? Wow! This thing is huge!"

"Oh, yeah!" Leta exclaimed. "I bought that one. Didn't wrap it, because it needed to be put together. You can do that while I finish this up, right?"

Hopper was already on it, pulling out big plastic rods and floor pieces.

Still in her mid twenties, Leta was a brash, loud, punk chick. But she eyed the box with a sense of childhood wonder still. "It's still got an elevator in it, just like the one I had."

"*You* played with Barbie dolls?" Ross snorted.

"What did you expect?" Leta huffed. "Barbed wire and poison darts?"

The boy grinned. "*Yeah*, actually."

Leta squawked and threw a spare pillow in his direction. "Duhhh, everybody played with Barbie dolls. Barbie had all the cool stuff. The hot tub, the pink sports car—"

"The not-so-anatomically correct Ken," Ross offered.

Leta laughed. "I may or may not have gotten in trouble for throwing away Ken's stupid fedora and painting tattoos all over him. Teeny-tiny stencils may have been involved." She sighed, holding her hand over her heart.

Hopper worked on snapping the last of the townhouse together, smiling with satisfaction as he got the tiny elevator to go up and down, and set it up in the corner with a big pink bow on it. He propped up the dolls they'd gotten beside it—Doctor Barbie, and a Barbie with blue hair and thicker hips. And Ken. *With a man bun.* Hopper just shook his head.

Looking over their presents, Hopper took stock. These

toys, they weren't just trinkets, were they? They represented something. Hope, maybe. Possibilities. Dreams for a bright, shining future where you could make the world whatever you wanted. Proof that the adults around you cared. Shouldn't every kid have that, especially at Christmas time?

Maybe this holiday intervention would be the thing that would really help these kids. Maybe being dropped off with their granny...well, maybe they could help turn a tragedy into a blessing. Save those kids from going down a dark path. How he wished someone had done that for him.

Shaking away those thoughts, Hopper pushed himself up to his feet. Dammit, Christmas really did a number on him sometimes. Most days, he didn't *feel* like an ex-con. But times like this reminded him he had a lot to atone for still.

He wandered into the tiny kitchen area, where Hunter and Ross were busying themselves, pulling all the fully cooked food out of the cooler and getting it set to warm up in the oven. When the kids came back, all Mrs. Honeycutt would have to do is pull out the serving dishes to have one kick-ass holiday feast.

Hopper made himself useful setting out dishes, trying to remember which side of the plate the forks and knives were supposed to go on. They were so busy puttering around that they hadn't noticed that old Mrs. Honeycutt had gotten awfully quiet. When they paused to finally look at the lady, they found the little sweetheart simply standing in the corner of the room, leaning on her walker, bawling her eyes out.

Leta had been the first to turn around and notice the crying first. She threw down her snowflake stencils and put her tattooed arms around Mrs. Honeycutt's thin, trembling shoulders. "Oh now, now," Leta cooed. "Don't cry. It's Christmas!"

"It's just—it's just that y'all are so *good* to me," Mrs. Honeycutt sobbed, "and you didn't have to do any a'this, but you *did*." The old woman dabbed her eyes with a crumbled-up tissue while Leta rubbed her back. "The kids, they won't be able to believe it. Their mama, you know, she never did anything like this for them neither. So when I said I couldn't afford a Christmas tree, they just said that Santa had never stopped for them anyhow, so it didn't matter. Can you imagine two kids in grade school saying such a thing? And now...and now...it all just makes me so *happy*. And it's going to make them *so happy*. Thank you!" Mrs. Honeycutt toddled over and gave each of them a surprisingly bone-crushing hug.

"We're happy to do it," Hunter insisted. "Neighbors helping neighbors—isn't that what the season is all about?"

They nodded in agreement and smiled at Mrs. Honeycutt. And she beamed right back.

But Leta twirled her long pink hair uncertainly as she surveyed the room. "Hey, she still doesn't have a tree. Don't you think we should get her one, guys?"

Hunter pulled out his smart phone and checked the time. "Well, I suppose we could. We still have, what, two hours left before their friend's mom drops them back off? Right?"

Mrs. Honeycutt nodded, then loudly protested that they didn't need to go to any trouble. But none of them listened. Before long, the whole Holliday Hot Rod team was bickering about who was going to take on the huge freakin' task of finding a live tree, dragging it back here, and decorating it good and proper.

But it seemed like everybody else had somewhere to be. Hunter was hosting a big holiday dinner at his house. Ross was expected at his parents. Leta needed to get on the road within the hour to drive to her sister's house in Virginia.

"It's gotta be you, Hop," Leta declared, putting an end to all their arguments. "You're the only one without plans."

Hopper sighed resignedly. It made his chest ache a little to hear it out loud like that, but it was true. What little family Hopper had was gone with the wind, and disappeared for good. At forty-one, he had no woman and no family of his own. Oh sure, he could've taken Hunter's offer to come celebrate at his house, but Hopper didn't want to horn in on the man's Christmas with his wife and newborn baby. Better to celebrate alone, with a couple of beers, old Christmas movies, a nice, long winter's nap—and this charity project, of course. Helping Mrs. Honeycutt *really was* his Christmas, when it came right down to it.

Resigned to his fate, Hopper scrubbed his hands through his hair. "Fine. I can do it. But where am I going to get a Christmas tree at this hour? It's four o'clock on Christmas Eve, for Christ sakes!"

"I'll bet if you just keep driving around on the outskirts of town, you'll find one of those little pop-up places selling trees and ornaments," Hunter offered. "You know how they are. They'll stand out there until the bloody end if they have a tree left on the lot."

And just like that, Hopper agreed to this last-minute scheme. Luckily, he'd driven his banged-up work truck to this gathering, so it wouldn't be any trouble to haul everything in one trip.

So he said his goodbyes to his team and began his methodical drive through town, looking for a tree—any tree. And it was taking *for-freakin-ever,* his carefully mapped route yielding him approximately squat. But that didn't mean there wasn't anything to see. Everywhere he went, the hush of Christmas had fallen. Few cars were on the road. The quaint Victorian-era shops downtown were shut up tight, in honor of the blessed holiday. The houses he passed had extra cars in their driveways and warm lights glowing from the windows as friends and families gathered.

There'd be no lights in the window, glowing in the dark for him. No, his house was cold and empty tonight.

And whose fault is that?

Hopper curled his hands tighter around his steering wheel, willing the sadness back into its familiar, dark corners. Yeah, he'd turned his back on the love of his life once. He'd had his reasons, but it didn't make it any easier, even all these years later. He felt a familiar deep pang in his chest. Disgusted with his lapse into self-pity, Hopper set his jaw, concentrating instead on the open road in front of him.

On and on he drove, up into the Allegheny Mountains that surrounded this valley town. The trees glittered from the remnants of a recent ice storm, their branches twinkling almost magically in the sunset, reaching out like arms embraced in the sky overhead as he wound his way along this long, black ribbon of road.

But he didn't exactly have time to enjoy driving through this little perfect little Christmas card. The snow was starting to blow around hard now, making it hard to see. Looking down at the clock on his dashboard, Hopper let out a string of curses. He was running out of time. Weaving carefully down the mountain roads, he craned his neck and squinted his eyes to find a sign, any sign, that some rando had Christmas trees for sale.

And that was when he saw it: plain, hand-painted cardboard hanging haphazardly from a stake in the road's shoulder, pointing down a little one-lane side road. *Stuck without a Christmas tree? We're Open,* it said.

Hot damn!

Hopper whooped to no one in particular, hardly able to

believe his luck. Even though he'd never seen that side road before, had never realized it even existed along this familiar stretch of highway, Hopper yanked his wheel into the turn.

He was going to buy that tree, by God. Maybe he'd get this Christmas back on track, after all.

CHAPTER TWO

As Hopper continued to rumble down this uneven, unpaved trail leading to God knew what, his niggling doubts turned into worry. How far up into a holler was he going to have to drive? Shouldn't this tree place be right off the road?

But soon he saw another sign, red paint scrawled on cardboard again. *Don't wimp out now. You're almost there,* it said.

Cute. Real Cute.

Turning in the direction the sign indicated, Hopper continued to mutter as he bounced over one rut and ditch after another, rumbling ever deeper into friggin' no-man's land. Jesus, who'd have a place of business so far out? Was he being lured out to some kind of psycho compound or something?

But then there was another sign, written in the same red paint. *We're not psychos. Honest,* it said.

Seriously, what the fuck?

Hopper slammed on the brakes. And for a brief moment, he considered just turning the truck around and going back. This was getting *way* too weird.

But he could see the store off in the distance. And he was probably being ridiculous. It was just a stupid sign. So Hopper put his foot to the gas pedal and motored off to the place, parking in the gravel lot out front of a countrified shop called Stuckey's Christmas Outpost.

And sure enough, fresh beautiful Christmas trees surrounded the place, all propped up and ready to sell. To Hopper's shock, Stuckey's wasn't just some little pop-up stand. The place was really a big, welcoming country store —an old log cabin that several expansions had turned into a mismatched, timber frame house. The place was covered in blinking, multicolored lights and fresh-cut wreaths with big red bows. Christmas lights twinkled from the old-fashioned merchandise displays in the windows, and the whole place seemed all warm and glowy, with little puffs of smoke rising out of the chimney.

Hopper couldn't help but stop and stare through his windshield at the place. It was like some kind of twinkling, Christmas mirage out in the middle of a snowy, unspoiled wilderness.

But then he was startled by the sound of his truck door opening—from the *outside*. Alarmed at first, Hopper sighed with relief to see the thin, rangy-looking old man with a straggly white beard standing outside his truck.

Bouncing up and down on his toes with excitement, the little fella was obviously friendly. He was the type of old coot that was instantly endearing, with his shit-eating grin, beat-up insulated overalls, and a fraying "Almost Heaven, West Virginia" hat. "I knew it! I knew you'd come!" the man cried, his sharp blue eyes dancing with glee.

Hopper carefully slid out of the truck, closing and locking the door behind him. "You were *expecting* me? I didn't tell anyone I was on my way."

"But we *always* get someone on Christmas Eve. The

later, the better," the man crowed. "And look at you! Just look at you! You need us, don't you?"

Hopper wasn't quite sure what he meant by that, but he cut the guy off before he got on a roll. "What I need is one of your trees and some lights and stuff to put on it, sooner rather than later. What do I need to do?"

The old man, who introduced himself as Earl, showed him around the tree lot and dickered with him a bit until they settled on a five-foot Christmas tree. The tree was perfect, all crisp and fresh and just the right size for Mrs. Honeycutt's cramped trailer. Earl even threw in a free stand and started binding it up with rope so Hopper could load it in the bed of his truck.

"You'll have to go inside to pay and get you some finery for this here tree. The boss will get you fixed up."

Hopper couldn't help but grin back at the old coot. "The boss?"

"My wife. Believe me when I tell you she's the boss."

Hopper laughed and gave Earl a little salute as he went in. The bell on the door clattered behind him, and Hopper was immediately hit with a wave of warmth and the smell of baking cookies and apple-scented candles.

Before he could even really get a look around the place, an old woman was right up in his grill, holding out a plate full of cookies. "Snickerdoodle?" she asked, grinning enough to expose a gold tooth.

"Uh, sure," Hopper murmured, stepping back a bit to get a little more personal space. He felt a little sheepish about it. The old lady was obviously sweet and welcoming, but there was something about her that poked at his instincts.

"You look like you need some nog too, boy. You'll like it. It's homemade." she insisted, shoving a mug of the stuff in his hand. "I'm Candy Caine, by the way. And don't you go laughin' about my name. I can tell you're about to. I got the name when I married old Earl out there a way long time ago. There ain't a joke you can make that I haven't heard. 'Course, now that my husband's gotten to be a dried-up old fart, I've started calling him Raisin, just for payback."

Hopper stopped, cocked his head a minute, and then started to laugh. "Raisin Caine? Oh, that's a good one." Candy may be a little odd, but she was a funny old buzzard. Hopper extended his hand and shook hers. "Nice to meet you Candy. I'm Hopper Vance."

The woman sat down the plate and shook his hand. Then she put her hands on her hips, looking him up and down like a drill sergeant eyeing a new recruit.

Hopper wasn't quite sure what to make of her. This Candy was a skinny, wizened old biddy, her face tanned and wrinkled as an old saddlebag. But the woman was dressed for the holidays in spades, what with her battered red leggings, flashing Christmas light earrings, and an over-sized neon green Christmas tree sweater. Her frizzy, coppery hair was pulled back in a braid and showing more white roots than red. An honest woman, he'd bet, who obviously put in a lot of work to make this outpost so super nice. She and Earl probably dedicated their whole lives to it, to make it this nice.

So why had he never heard of this place?

Candy looked Hopper over and smiled really big again, like she knew him somehow. Honestly, the woman looked more like a carney than the proprietor of a Christmas shop. Hopper wondered if he was being sized up for a mark or something. But that was bein' a little paranoid, wasn't it? For Christ's sake, he was just here buyin' a tree, not checking into the Hotel California.

Since he really was pretty hungry, Hopper grabbed another cinnamony, crispy cookie and swigged down the nog. He'd never had eggnog made from scratch before, and the thick, creamy drink was just about the most delicious thing he'd ever tasted.

"Mmmmm..." he found himself groaning before he could stop himself.

The old woman cackled. "Good, iddn't it?"

Hopper smacked his lips as he guzzled the last of it down. "It must be the rum."

"Naw, it's the Christmas magic!" Candy grinned.

Hopper rolled his eyes.

"Now, don't you roll your eyes at me, young man. Wassa matter? You don't believe?"

"Christmas magic is better left to Hallmark movies and Christmas cards," Hopper huffed. "I gave up believing in fairy tales long ago."

Candy moved behind the counter and rested her head on her fist. "And yet, here you are, late on a snowy Christmas Eve, risking life and limb to buy old Mrs. Honey-cutt a tree."

Hunter wrinkled his brow. "How did you—I don't remember saying—"

"Christmas magic network," Candy drawled, wiggling her fingers in the air. "Must have been the elves, or maybe a little snowflake sprite who told me."

Hopper barked out a laugh. He realized with a little start that he was wearing his work shirt with the Holliday Hot Rods patch on it. She and Earl must've gotten wind of their charity project. Lewisburg is a pretty small town, after all.

He excused himself and began shopping in earnest. He didn't have much time, and the shelves practically groaned with the weight of all the Christmas decorations. The store really was something to see, with all the spinners and snow globes and little train sets around. In the end, Hopper went for what was easy to hang and compact to store: some tinsel garlands, multicolored lights, and ornaments that looked like glass, but were really just painted plastic. Then he grabbed a matching tree skirt and a star that lit up and blinked different colors for the top of the tree. And best of all, he found what he needed in five minutes flat.

Hopper looked down at his watch. He had a little over an hour before the kids got home. By his calculations, he'd make it back and have the tree up by the skin of his teeth.

Rushing up to the counter, he plunked his finds down and swiped his card for the lady.

Candy handed him his receipt and his bags. "I see Earl's got your tree all loaded. So the only thing you've got to do is pick out an ornament."

"But I just—"

"Not those ornaments, boy. These." She nodded over to an enormous Christmas tree in the middle of the store, one that was practically tipped over with the weight of all the stuff on its branches. "Nobody leaves here without a free ornament. It's Christmas tradition. Go on. Pick. Get something just for you. Something meaningful. You'll know it when you see it."

Reluctantly, Hopper walked over to the tree in question and began looking it over. Jesus, there must've been hundreds of little ornaments on this tree, each one of them with a different little figure, or photo frame, or landscape on it. How was he supposed to choose from this?

"Look." Hopper sighed. "Just keep it. I don't have a tree at my place, and I don't have the time—"

"Now, don't give me any lip, son! I'm not letting you out of here until you pick!" Candy raised her eyebrows and put her spindly fists on her hips again. "If anyone needs a big, fat dose of Christmas magic, it's you."

Hopper wanted to argue with the woman, but he huffed

and gritted his teeth instead. *Fine.* He scanned over the tree until something practically jumped out at him: an ornament that was a perfect replica of a 1976 BMW R90S motorcycle with a big red bow draped along the front. He knew the model, because he'd bought and restored one just like it years ago. How weirdly specific—and good Lord, it even had black paint. Just like the one...

Hopper curled his fingers around the ornament and plucked it off the tree. It was so beautifully made and perfectly articulated, it looked like it'd been shrunk down from full size or something. What were the odds he'd find this here? His throat tightened up a little bit as bittersweet memories flooded him, more memories than were good for his heart. But yet, it felt good, maybe even *right*, to hold this silly little thing in his hand.

"I'll take it," Hopper blurted out, tucking the little motorcycle in his pocket.

Candy shot him a knowing smile and handed him his bags again. "Isn't it just like a man to pick *that* one? Well now, you make the most of it. Don't forget, Christmas is only as good as your memories."

Hopper gave her a sideways glance. What in the hell was *that* supposed to mean? But Candy just shot him a weird, wizened grin, like she knew something he didn't.

Whatever. I've got a deadline to meet.

Hopper turned for the door and caught sight of Earl outside, strapping the last of the bungee cords around the tree in his truck bed. The doorbells made a racket as Hopper whipped open the door and stepped outside.

Into....

Nothing.

Everything was black. Hopper couldn't see his hand in front of his face.

Holy hell!

What in the world is—

I'm flat on my back. Why am I flat on my back?

Wherever he was, it was warm and cozy. And it was dark.

But not too dark. Now that his eyes were beginning to adjust, he could make out shards of light peeking through the blinds on the window, just over there.

Dear God, where am I? And how did I get here? Wait, am I in the hospital?

No, the place was too raggedy to be a hospital, and there were no machines or monitors. And there was definitely something *familiar* about that window. Hopper looked down, his eyes finally adjusted to the low light. He was in a bed, and on the nightstand was a backlit alarm clock.

I'll be damned. Is that my old alarm clock?

He ran his hand over the fake plastic chrome on the tacky old thing, a backlit retro 1950s clock he'd bought in a thrift store on a whim because it had an antique car on it. Man, he hadn't seen that old thing since he'd rented his first little house just outside Douglasville, Georgia. What was that, more than *sixteen years ago?*

Is that where I am?

How in hell—

Hopper shot up in bed, rubbing his eyes. He was naked under the covers, like he always used to sleep.

Even in the low light, he could see it was all still here— the same ratty black comforter, the same rock posters on the wall, even the same piles of battered jeans and boxer briefs and hoodies on the floor. This wasn't a dream. It *couldn't* be. He hadn't gone to sleep! Anyway, he could actually *feel* everything, touch everything...

A dark shadow moved in front of the window. There was a rustle, and then the blinds flew open, the room flooding with the hazy white rays of late morning.

And the most beautiful woman in the world, the only woman he'd ever wanted, was standing there in nothing more than his favorite gray flannel shirt.

Delilah Jones.

His *Delilah.*

And she looked for all the world like the young, beautiful woman she'd been when he'd loved her and lost her, so many years ago. No way could she have aged a day. Her pale, supple legs gleamed in the morning light, and her mane of rich, jet-black air tumbled in rowdy waves down her back.

Oh my freakin' God.

Am I really seeing this?

I'm not dead am I? I can't be...

His mind spun to the outpost, which had been kinda creepy, now that he thought about it. Shit—was there something in that nog?

He didn't have the brain cells to process any of the questions swirling in his head. Honestly, Hopper couldn't give two shits about how he got here. No, he was simply too paralyzed with awe, unable to speak, or move, or even breathe.

"Mornin', sleepyhead!" Delilah cried and sashayed her sexy ass over to his bed.

Without thinking twice about it, he slid his arms around her—arms that were leaner, less scarred, and held fewer tattoos than they did now.

Am I younger now too?

Gliding under the covers, she straddled his lap and gave him a long, slow, good morning kiss. She curled her hand in the back of his hair—hair that was hanging to his shoulders now, just like it used to. And she twisted it in her fist, and yanked, just a little, just like he liked it.

He moaned, helplessly.

God her hot little mouth was just as perfect, just as delicious as he remembered. *Better* even.

When Delilah pulled back with a smile, Hopper simply gaped at her, dazed and bewildered and relentlessly turned on. He was naked under this sheet, he realized with a gulp.

Taking notice of his sudden raging hard-on, Delilah glanced down at his lap and wiggled her hips triumphantly. She idly traced her fingers in his chest hair. "Since it's the Christmas season and all, I thought I'd come sit in your lap this morning, Santa. Figured you deserved a reward for being such a good boy." She laughed a sultry, musical laugh and bit her lip. "I still can't believe you got me a motorcycle for Christmas. And a BMW bike, no less! If I hadn't already known it, I'd say you're the perfect man, Hopper Vance."

God, it *really was her.*

Delilah, with her witchy gray eyes and skin that felt like liquid silk under his hand. Delilah—the only woman who'd ever mattered.

God in heaven, it really was her.

He didn't know how, he didn't know why, but...

Choking back tears, he kissed her again, grabbing both sides of her face, tangling his fingers in her hair, plundering her mouth as if she'd disappear. As if all this would end and she'd be snatched away from him again, just like before.

Holy hell, it was *impossible...*

"Delilah," he breathed. "My God. You're really here."

This book is dedicated to Stacey King Smith, my number one fan. No, really, she's my first fan. Thanks for making me feel like a rock star when I needed it most.

ACKNOWLEDGMENTS

The immortal Louisa May Alcott once observed that "it takes two flints to make a fire." In the case of making a book, it takes a great many more flints than that.

I'd like to take a moment to acknowledge the many, many people whose patient advice and mentorship were the flint that gave spark to my imagination. First, I'd like to thank my beta readers, who not only read all the many versions of my books but gave me the up-or-down, yes-or-no feedback that kept me creatively on track. Stacey King Smith, Ava Cuvay, Carey Moore and Kirstie Marie, y'all are the best—even when you tell me to start over.

I'd also like to thank the Indiana Chapter of the Romance Writers of America, without whose support I could never call myself an author. This group of crazy fun, crazy generous romance authors have held my hand every step of the way, answered my every boneheaded question and shown me that making money off my books was an achievable ambition. I'd especially like to thank the fabulous Jeanna Mann, Gina Drayer, Ava Cuvay, Melanie Jayne, Aleatha Romig, Anna Hague and Donya Lynne for their mentorship. I couldn't have done any of this without them.

(And check out their books, available on all major platforms. They'll burn up your nightstand, I promise!)

I'd also like to thank my buds at the Carmel, Indiana Barnes & Noble, whose encouragement kept me going when it would've been easy to give up. I'd especially like to thank Carol Carr, whose sage advice showed me I had a series-worthy idea, and Jonathan Smith, whose advice on men's fashions and pocket squares was invaluable to this book.

Of course, a big shout-out is owed to the team of consummate professionals who helped me polish this book to a sheen, including my ace editor, Rhonda Merwarth, cover designer extraordinaire Elizabeth Turner-Stoakes, and photographer Sunni Wigginton, one of the few people on earth who can snap a picture when I'm *not* blinking. Thanks for making my dreams come true.

ABOUT THE AUTHOR

Liza Jonathan is a writer of big, sexy paranormal romances filled with legends, lore and locations from the thirteen Appalachian states. She's a West Virginia native, but has spent most of her adult life in Tennessee, Kentucky, and in more recent days, the flatlands of Indiana. For the record, she's still not used to it. When she's not dreaming up a book, you can find her working as a freelance writer and corporate PR consultant, or kicking back with her husband Paul and her two very nearly adult-aged sons. (Or making noise with her rowdy girlfriends. But that goes without saying!)

Never one to miss an opportunity to talk to fans, you can find her on most social media platforms, linked here. And if you'd like to get VIP exclusive reader bonuses, give-aways and promotions delivered to your inbox, don't forget to sign up for her email newsletter at:

https://lizajonathan.com/wrecking-christmas-bonus

Stay tuned y'all. There's so much more to come!

❄

If you enjoyed this book, do the author a solid and post a review. Your honest review will help other readers find this book more easily online. Want to help out? You can do that by posting reviews to the platform where you purchased this book, or by posting your reader comments and recommendations on Goodreads:

https://www.goodreads.com/book/show/47575850-wrecking-christmas

or BookBub:

https://www.bookbub.com/books/wrecking-christmas-by-liza-jonathan

Thanks again for being a Liza Jonathan reader!

facebook.com/Liza-Jonathan-Romances-114911106536480

twitter.com/lizajonbooks

instagram.com/lizajonathan

CPSIA information can be obtained
at www.ICGtesting.com
Printed in the USA
LVHW041453051119
636418LV00001B/36/P